ALICE BLISS

Alice Bliss is fifteen. She's smart, funny, and clever. Not afraid to stand up for the things she believes in. She also idolizes her father, and when he leaves home to fight a war she doesn't believe in, Alice is distraught. She and her mother negotiate his absence as best they can — waiting impatiently for his letters, throwing themselves into school and work respectively, bickering intermittently and, in Alice's case, falling for the boy next door. But then they're told that he's missing in action and have to face up to the fact that he may never return.

LAURA HARRINGTON

ALICE BLISS

Complete and Unabridged

CHARNWOOD
Leicester

First published in Great Britain in 2011 by
Picador
an imprint of Pan Macmillan
London

First Charnwood Edition
published 2012
by arrangement with Pan Macmillan
a division of Macmillan Publishers Limited
London

British Library CIP Data

Harrington, Laura, *1953* –
   Alice Bliss.
   1. Teenage girls- -Fiction. 2. Fathers and
   daughters- -Fiction. 3. Families of military
   personnel- -Fiction. 4. Bildungsromans.
   5. Large type books.
   I. Title
   813.6–dc23

   ISBN 978–1–4448–1049–3

Published by
F. A. Thorpe (Publishing)
Anstey, Leicestershire

Set by Words & Graphics Ltd.
Anstey, Leicestershire
Printed and bound in Great Britain by
T. J. International Ltd., Padstow, Cornwall

This book is printed on acid-free paper

For Patrick

Prologue: August 20th

This is the first time Alice has been allowed to walk back to their campsite from the Kelp Shed alone. She is fourteen, barefoot, her sneakers tied together by the laces and slung across her shoulder so she can feel the soft, sandy dust of the single-track road between her toes. Her sister fell asleep halfway through the square dance, dropping from hyperexcited to unconscious in a flash. Her father carries Ellie draped over his shoulder, and casually, or so it seems, her mother says, 'Come home when the dance is done.'

She can hardly believe it. The dance is still in her feet, still in her bones, the steps like an intricate game. She danced with everyone and anyone at all, old and young, men and women, just to stay on the floor and moving. The caller was a blind man with two fingers missing from his left hand. His face was wrinkled and brown from the sun, his body heavy and the voice that called the steps strangely high and sweet. A boy's voice in a man's body. A boy's wildness, as though he had no awareness of himself in his body.

She gave in, finally, and danced with her father — embarrassed to be asked by him, worried that everyone would be watching and judging and

1

thinking her still a child. But he surprises her. He is a good dancer. Precise. His hands firm on her back or her hand or her arm. She is suddenly dancing better than she has ever danced before, suddenly experiencing the freedom inside the squares. She can let go because he is so confident. She is tasting something adult, grown-up, or almost tasting it. It is just beyond her reach, this feeling, what it is, how to name it and understand it. Now it is pure sensation, unadulterated fun. Years later she will remember his touch on her back, pulling her in, letting her go, her own helpless laughter, the way he guided her, his touch steady and strong, and how he held her close and let her go, over and over again.

The dust beneath her feet now is cool, the day's heat long gone. It is mid-August and already you can feel fall coming with the way night rushes in. She pulls on her sweater and as she crests the first hill she can see almost all of Small Point, the shape of the island dark against the water. She can hear the waves on the beach below her. There are fires still burning at a few campsites, but mostly it is true dark. Alone on the road, she stops. What is she feeling? Intensely awake. Aware. A bit scared. She senses everything, her body open to the sky and the night, the smell of salt and pine and wood smoke, the wind, the scratchy wool of her old sweater, her hips loose in her jeans, her feet cool and tough and sure on the road.

In the distance she sees what look like stars on the water. Following the dip in the road, she

2

loses sight of them, but cresting the next hill she sees them again. She breaks into a jog and takes the turn down to the ocean, away from her campsite. There it is again. Another curve and she can see where it is: the Devil's Bathtub. She is on the beach now, walking toward the outlying rock formation, a wide cleft in the rocks that becomes an eight foot pool at high tide and empties to sand at low tide.

There are fires on the water. How can that be? And now she sees them: a group of boys lighting small wooden rafts on fire and setting them afloat in this natural pool. They are quiet, intent. Why are they doing this? It's so beautiful, the small rafts floating, in flames, and then gone.

The boys have run out of boats; the last fire winks out. Now they strip off their clothes, daring one another to dive in. She crouches where she is, watching them, their pale bodies against the dark rock. She has never seen a naked boy before. She is not close enough to see much, but their nakedness is loud in the dark. Her eyes pass over each boy as though she could run a hand across a face or a chest, along a thigh.

She turns and lies in the sand, listening to their shouts as they dive and splash, listening as the cold and the search for their clothes quiets them. And the sky overhead is raining stars. These are the Perseids her father has told her about. She wants to get up and go and find him, she wants to tell the boys, Look up! Look up! But she can't move; there is magic occurring in front of her eyes. The heavens are throwing

3

jewels at her feet. It is impossible, as impossible as fire on the water, as impossible as her hand on the chest of a naked boy, and yet here she is, seeing it with her own eyes.

January 29th

Matt Bliss is somebody who knows how to be happy. A former engineer, he's now a carpenter, doing what he loves, a craftsman, meticulous. He likes to say he escaped from his career and got himself a job. He coaches Little League even though neither of his daughters shows any aptitude for baseball. He was a pitcher on the local farm team right out of college, until his father told him to get serious and he went to grad school for his engineering degree. He still pitches for a local team.

Matt grows vegetables. Alice helps. They grow the best corn and the best tomatoes in town, not like there's much competition anymore. Ever since Mr. Hendrickson down the road died, the old time guys who put in vegetables every year have really dwindled. Matt says, 'You just wait, the hippie kids will bring it all back again; all that poison in our food now, people are waking up. You can do it yourself. Good food. Cheap.' And they've got this black dirt he loves to go on and on about. Topsoil eighteen inches deep. 'Beautiful stuff!' He keeps trying to get Angie interested in canning or preserving or freezing their bounty, but this is not Angie's bailiwick.

So Alice and Ellie and Matt are the ones to

snap beans, make tomato sauce and tomato juice and salsa, grape jelly and grape juice. Matt wants to plant three more apple trees in the side yard where Angie would like to have a nice patio. Two more cherry trees, too, right next to his grape arbor. Apple butter, he tells her, apple pies, cherry pies. Angie rolls her eyes and says: 'Matt Bliss, you did not marry a farm girl.' He laughs and picks her up and kisses her. Times like this the two of them head off for a 'nap' hand in hand. Eventually figuring out just what this euphemism means makes Alice a little queasy. Here it is, right in front of her face, the power of opposites to attract.

Angie would love to stay in a nice hotel; Matt likes to camp. Angie is upwardly mobile, a striver if ever there was one; Matt likes things just the way they are. Angie thinks they're living in a starter house; Matt thinks they're home. Angie likes French perfume; Matt likes to get his hands dirty. The fact that Angie might like those workman's hands on her perfumed skin is a thought Alice vigorously chases from her mind.

The army reserve was a bone of contention, too. Angie all hung up on what's fair, why should Matt have to do it, what about his own family. Matt talking about doing what's right, not letting somebody else do what he should do: serving his country, an example to his girls. Finally they agree to disagree and Angie seems reconciled to it, even seems to enjoy the additional income, the occasional dinner in a nice restaurant, all dolled up in a new dress and high heels. And, oh, there's that perfume again, Matt's laughter,

Angie's surrender, and another closed door.

But now, with the war dragging on and on, Matt's unit has been called up. He's heading to Fort Dix. Until recently reservists got six months of specialized instruction. Now they are fast-tracking volunteers through six weeks of supposedly high-quality, hurry up, move 'em out training.

The weeks prior to his leaving are an insane rush. Angie and Matt talk late into the night, every night, sitting at the kitchen table. They argue, Angie tries not to cry again, they pore over health insurance, Matt's will and living will, the power of attorney forms. They try to anticipate what Angie will be facing in the coming months.

★   ★   ★

They are running out of time. They all know it. It's in the air they breathe.

★   ★   ★

Alice is so tired her eyes are burning but she can't sleep. As long as her father is still awake and still in the house and still talking or drinking coffee, Alice wants to be near him. So she sits in the dark at the foot of the stairs and listens.

'Why are you insisting — ?' Angie's voice pops up a register when she's upset.

'You know why.'

'Tell me why the United States Army is more important than your own family.'

'It's not an either or equation, Angie.'

'You like this. You're actually excited.'

'I like the work, I like my crew, I like the challenge, the chance to — '

'But leaving us, Matt — '

'You know I don't want to leave you.'

'They'll throw you right in the middle of — '

'I'm going where I'm needed.'

'I need you. Doesn't that count anymore?'

'Of course it does.'

'I never imagined — never — that you would do something like this. You were going to play baseball for god's sake. *Baseball!* How did we get from baseball to — '

'Angie, it's not just about you and me.'

'Okay, so you're the selfless hero and I'm the selfish wife. You think I want this role? I didn't sign up for this. This was not part of the plan.'

'I know.'

'I hate this, I really hate this.'

'Sweetheart . . . ' Alice can hear the ache in his voice.

'I want . . . ' Angie's voice breaks.

'I don't want to be one of those guys who gets old and says, I wish I had done this, I wish I had done that.'

'Oh, Matt . . . '

'I want to contribute, and I don't think we should just send our kids to this war.'

'But what if — ?'

'Don't you have any faith in me?'

'Of course I do.'

'I'm coming home, Angie.'

7

'Promise me.'

'I promise.'

It's quiet for a moment.

'I want letters, you know,' Matt says. 'Real letters. With perfume. You can't carry an e-mail around in your pocket.'

'You're not so deluded you actually think this is romantic?'

'I do. A little.'

'It won't be romantic if — '

'Oh, yeah,' he teases her, laughing. 'The fallen hero, blah, blah, blah.'

'Matt!'

Alice hears the kitchen chairs scrape across the floor and knows it is time to beat a retreat up the stairs to bed. But she waits another moment, and another. She wants to see her dad one more time tonight.

They walk through the kitchen door. The dining room light is nothing more than a warm glow, illuminating them. Matt pulls Angie to him and kisses her, and kisses her some more.

Alice backs slowly up the stairs, carefully stepping over the creakiest step, third from the top. She puts her freezing cold hands under her armpits to try to warm them as she walks down the hall to her room. She waits to duck inside her door until she hears them on the stairs. Matt has his arm around Angie's waist and he has even managed to make her laugh. That soft, musical, surrendering laugh Angie saves just for Matt and his beautiful blue eyes.

Alice closes her door as softly as possible and leans against it, hoping they have not heard her.

8

She hears them pass by whispering and giggling like little kids.

Ellie has kicked her covers off as usual. Alice pulls the quilt over Ellie and then climbs into her own bed. She listens to Ellie breathing; she closes her eyes, tight, tight, and tries to breathe through the knot in her chest. She wishes she could call Henry but that would mean waking up Mr. and Mrs. Grover and getting into trouble for calling so late. She wishes they still had their walkie-talkies hooked up. She could ask Henry to leave his on so she could listen to the static and hear him sleeping and breathing the way she did that whole terrible month in fourth grade when her grandfather was dying. What happened to those walkie-talkies she wonders, and what's Henry doing right now? She'll ask him tomorrow. If it doesn't sound too crazy in the cold light of day.

January 31st

Matt is in his workshop puttering around with a cup of forgotten coffee sitting on the windowsill. It's a cold day with flurries and a gusting wind, so he's got the woodstove going full blast and he's wearing his tan work jacket with the ripped pocket. Alice slips in and sits on a wooden crate near the stove. What is she doing here, exactly? Her English homework lies forgotten in her lap. She is, what? Hanging out? Breathing the air? Daydreaming? Making a nuisance of herself? All

9

of the above? She brought her dad a toasted muffin as a way of interrupting him and then stuck. Like a burr. She is uninvited, she feels awkward; but this is where she has to be even if Matt would rather be alone.

But Matt would not rather be alone. There are things he wants to say to his daughter before he leaves but they all sound so portentous and ominous that he can't bring himself to begin. There are things she needs to know, things she needs to prepare for, and it's really not fair to leave all the talking and informing and awkwardness to Angie. So he talks about the garden instead. He pulls out last year's plan and asks Alice to come over and take a look. She throws another log in the woodstove and joins him at the workbench.

'So I was thinking less corn because there will only be three of you.'

'What about Gram? She can always take the extra.'

'Because that way we could squeeze in another row of yellow beans.'

'Okay.'

'And beets.'

'You're the only one who likes beets, Dad.'

'Okra?'

'Blech.'

'Broccoli?'

'Two plants at most.'

He notates the changes as they talk.

'You can do peas spring and fall like we did last year.'

'Can we do basil?'

10

'Sure. And Mom likes arugula.'

'Yeah.'

Suddenly Alice's hands are clammy and she can't lift her eyes from the plan.

'You don't like it,' he says.

'I liked it just fine last year. I thought last year was perfect.'

'No changes? No building on our successes and learning from our failures?'

'We didn't have any failures.'

'Just way too much yellow squash.'

'Okay. Let's take out half the yellow squash.'

'But keep the corn?'

'Yes.'

'And everything else.'

'Just like last year,' Alice says, slowly and carefully.

'Because . . . ?'

'Because I want it to be the same.'

Alice manages to look him in the eye, which is when he can see how hard she is working to stay in control.

'Okay.' He smiles at her. 'We'll go with last year's design.'

'Good.'

'You want gourds even if I'm not here?'

'Yes!'

In the far corner of the garden Matt grows decorative gourds. They are strange things: bumpy and lumpy and misshapen. But they are colorful and surprising and they serve no purpose other than to amaze. Alice has every intention of growing gourds this year and every year for the rest of her life.

11

Matt labels the plan with the date and tacks it up on the wall.

'You can rototill mid-April if the ground isn't too wet and heavy. You can call Jimmy Rose to do it; or ask Uncle Eddie to help you.'

'Got it.'

'You might have to pester Jimmy. He gets busy.'

Matt looks out the window at the snow covering the garden.

'And I want you to help your mom.'

'I know.'

'No, Alice. Really help her. Like you're her partner. I want you to help her take care of Ellie and the house and . . . She's gonna need you.'

'Okay. But tell her to remember to ask me.'

'What?'

'She acts like I'm supposed to know everything she wants and when I don't she gets mad. If she'd just tell me. Or ask me — '

'You tell her.'

'She doesn't listen to me.'

'Keep trying.'

Alice looks at her feet.

'Honey? Keep trying.'

'Okay.'

'You know where all my papers are.'

'Dad! We've been over this!'

She doesn't want to hear about his will and his life insurance again. She doesn't even want those papers to exist.

'I opened up an account for you.' He reaches into his back pocket and holds out a bankbook from the local bank. 'It's just a basic savings

12

account. But I put five hundred dollars in there for you. In case you need something.'

'Dad, it's okay.'

'Or there's an emergency.'

She's backing away from him. She doesn't want to touch the bankbook.

'Or your mom can't handle things for a few days.'

'Dad!'

'Alice, there are things you need to know.'

She trips backing away from him and sits down, hard, on her butt. Which is funny. In an awful sort of stupid, annoying way.

He reaches out to help her up and pulls her into a hug. It's a real hug, the kind of hug he used to give her before she started turning into a teenager and growing breasts and getting sweaty and unsure. He holds her for a long time. She breathes him in. Sawdust. Wood smoke. Cold coffee. Aftershave. Linseed oil. *Dad*.

Matt is trying to stay right here with Alice; he is trying not to let his mind run off with all the *what ifs* that have been keeping him awake at night. He's wishing his parents were still alive. His mom would know how to pick up the slack, or how to step in if Angie and Alice really can't get along. And his dad . . . his dad would plant the garden with Alice, and take her to baseball games and . . .

'I need to show you something.'

'Not your will again.'

'Come over here.'

He leads her to the big wooden tool chest. He pulls out the first three levels of tools, then opens a drawer and slides that out completely. Underneath the socket wrenches there's a plain white envelope with her name on it. He opens the envelope and fans five one hundred dollar bills.

'What's *that* for?'

'It's there if you need it. And in the envelope there are some important numbers. The VA so you can get benefits, my lawyer, my life insurance . . . '

'Dad! You're talking like you're not coming back.'

'No, no, no.' He grins at her, and his whole face lights up. 'This is like carrying an umbrella in case it rains, and then it doesn't rain, so . . . '

'What?'

'It's just insurance. It's just an umbrella. You can't take it too seriously.'

She wants to believe him.

'And together, right now, I want the two of us to make a list of who you can call if you need help.'

She's looking at the floor and she's thinking, no list, no cash, no strategies. Can he just back out, refuse to go, change his mind? Could they move to Canada? Or Mexico? Could they just get into the car and go? Or could she get violently sick right this minute or have some awful but minor accident that would keep him from leaving?

'C'mon. A list.'

'Define help.'

'Shoveling the driveway, jumpstarting the car, advice on a repair, moral support, somebody to

14

take you to the movies or the library or out for ice cream.'

So they agree on Gram and Uncle Eddie and Henry and his parents and her favorite teacher, Mrs. Cole, and Mrs. Minty, who lives down the road, in a pinch, and her parents' friends the Hoyts, from the old neighborhood, and her dad's baseball buddy Bobby Lester. She adds Mrs. Piantowski, the lady who bakes bread for Gram's restaurant, at the last minute.

Her dad writes all these names down in his perfect block printing and adds the phone numbers from memory or the phone book. And then he adds the family doctor, dentist, banker, and insurance man.

He writes up a second copy to put in the house and tacks the original to the inside lid of his toolbox. He pulls the only chair over to the woodstove next to Alice's crate and opens the door to the stove so they can watch the fire burn. He picks up the muffin and hands a piece to Alice before sitting down and stretching his feet out to the fire. They sit like that, not talking, for what seems like a long time.

Outside the back window Alice can see the outlines of the garden, some of the furrows visible under the snow, stretching away in long thin rows. She can't imagine doing the garden without her dad. It's his thing; she's always thought of herself as his assistant at best. She can't imagine doing anything without her dad and she starts to feel like she can't breathe. And then she looks at him. Just looks at him as he watches the fire with muffin crumbs on his lap.

'I'll write to you.'
'I'm counting on it.'
'Every day.'
'Good.'
She takes a breath.
'Dad . . . '
He closes up the woodstove.
'We need to go in, I think.'
Not yet, Alice thinks, not yet.
'I wish . . . '
'Me, too, sweetheart. Me, too.'

February 1st

Matt is getting on a bus headed to Fort Dix, New Jersey. That's not so bad. Nothing to worry about, really. It's just a bus. It's just New Jersey. And if anybody actually gets to know Matt Bliss on base it's absolutely a foregone conclusion that they will find him so useful, so essential to the running of, well, everything, that his superior officers will choose to keep him stateside. And safe. And alive. Until they send him home. On his own two feet. Much sooner than expected. This is what keeps running through Alice's mind as they go through the motions of saying good-bye.

Henry wanted to come with them, but that idea got nixed. So he and his parents stood out on their front steps to wave at them as they drove along East Oak Street. Henry was waving his baseball mitt over his head, which got a laugh out of Matt. Matt slowed the car way down and

16

cranked his window to wave back before he blasted the horn and sped away.

Now they're standing with the other reservists and their wives and families at the Rochester Greyhound station. The men are in fatigues, the wives are in jeans or stretchy pants, the kids are wearing dirty parkas and have pink cheeks and runny noses from the cold. It's not romantic like all those classic movie scenes of parting at train stations; it's more like being stuck at the mall with a lot of strangers. There's no brass band, no sound track at all, just the tinny annoying bus terminal Muzak and the muffled announcements. There are also no wonderful hats, or handkerchiefs, or stockings with seams. No one is dressed up at all, except Angie, who is wearing high heels, a skirt and a blouse, her dress coat and her favorite silk scarf, the one that Matt gave her. She is not, Alice notices, wearing her glasses. She never wears her glasses when she gets dressed up, which Alice thinks is just plain stupid, because then she can't see anything much past the middle distance. But once Angie gets started with the silk and the perfume and the high heels, the glasses get left behind.

Alice is watching her mom and her dad and holding on to her dad's other hand until Ellie worms her way in and pushes her out of the way. Then she hangs back feeling forgotten.

She wishes she knew what to say, but every phrase that pops into her head sounds stupid or childish. And Matt's not one for big gestures or big speeches, and he's definitely not one for spilling his guts at the Greyhound station

17

surrounded by strangers.

Last night Matt gave Alice a map of the Middle East. They put it up on her wall together and put pins in where he's supposed to be going. Not that anybody knows for sure. Alice wonders how anybody can get things done when nobody knows anything for sure.

And then he's walking away from them, his duffel slung over his shoulder, his too-short hair bristling out the back of his cap. The backs of their necks, she thinks — the skinny, tense ones and the ones with rolls of fat — they look like kids, like boys, really.

She sprints out of the waiting group and catches up with her dad.

'Dad . . . Dad — '

He stops and lifts her off the ground in a hug. When he sets her down, he slips his watch off his wrist and puts it into her hand. She's working as hard as she can not to cry. It suddenly seems so important to see him, really see him. He turns away and the wind picks up and the grit of the parking lot blows into their eyes, and Alice thinks desert and Alice thinks land mines and Alice thinks will she ever see her dad, this dad, the way he is right now, full of this life, again?

She stands there watching until every last one of them is on board and the bus begins to back out of its bay.

She turns around to see that some of the families are waving little flags, like the ones you get for the Memorial Day parade. It begins to snow, the heavy, quiet snow that blankets the world in stillness and makes the road surfaces treacherous within minutes.

Angie waves her scarf as the bus drives away. She stands there too long, long after the bus is out of sight, long after the other families have piled into their cars and left. She blows her nose and finally crosses the parking lot to join Ellie and Alice at the car.

'Could you unlock the car please?' Alice asks, shivering.

Angie gives Alice a long, unreadable look.

'It's *cold*, Mom.'

For once Alice and Ellie do not fight about who gets to sit in the front. The three of them get into the car and it's way too quiet. Angie pulls the seat forward so she can reach the pedals and reaches up to adjust the rearview mirror. Ellie has brought her recorder along and thinks that now might be a good moment to practice.

'Not now, Ellie.'

'But Mom — '

'Not now!'

Angie backs up and turns and when she reaches the street she doesn't seem to know which way to go. These hesitations are so unlike her mother, Alice thinks.

Driving down Monroe Avenue, Angie pulls her silk scarf off, rolls down her window, and holds the scarf outside, billowing and snapping in the wind.

'Mom — ?'

When Angie lets the scarf go, Alice turns in her seat to watch it float away before it drifts to the snow-covered ground. The car behind them runs over it.

'What did you do that for?'

'I love that scarf! You could have given it to me,' Ellie chimes in.

Angie just keeps driving.

'Mom! It's cold back here! Close the window!'

'I think . . . ' Angie begins and then trails off.

'Mom!' Alice says. 'The window!'

'Who wants frozen custard?' Angie asks.

'In this weather? Are you crazy?'

'I do! I do!' Ellie shouts.

Angie makes a sudden U turn, throwing Alice against the door. Alice feels a jolt in the pit of her stomach. The car fishtails in the snow as she tries to grab the door handle.

'Mom! What are you doing?!'

'Can I get jimmies?' Ellie wants to know. 'Extra jimmies? A cup full of jimmies?'

Alice is looking at Angie. She is driving way too fast. Angie never drives too fast. And, Alice registers again, she is not wearing her glasses.

'Mom, do you want me to drive?'

'You don't know how to drive.'

'I think you need to pull over.'

'Why?'

'You need your glasses.'

'I'm *fine*.'

'You're driving really fast and you're scaring me.'

'And it's freezing in here!' Ellie adds. 'Close the window!'

Angie turns to look at Alice.

'We're going to Don and Bob's. We're getting frozen custard. Then we're going home.'

'Okay. Okay. Would you just keep your eyes on the road?'

'I sure could use a scarf back here where it's as cold as the arctic tundra!' Ellie says.

Alice wishes she could laugh.

'Is anybody listening to me? I'm probably catching a terrible cold right this minute. Mom! Earth to Mom! Come in, Mom!'

Angie manages a smile.

'Your window!?'

Angie rolls up her window and turns the heat up high.

'Can I have hot chocolate with my ice cream?' Ellie wants to know.

'You can have whatever you want,' Angie answers.

'Onion rings?'

'At the same time?' Alice makes a face.

'No. Onion rings and a vanilla shake. Then hot chocolate. Then ice cream.'

'You're gonna be sick.'

'Mom said whatever I want.'

'You're crazy.'

'I don't care. That's what I want.'

They pull into Don and Bob's, and Angie nearly clips the SUV at the entrance as their car slides a bit on the snow. She gives the fat guy in the front seat a jaunty wave, like we're all in this crazy weather thing together, aren't we?

Crossing the parking lot, Angie is tiptoeing through the snow trying not to ruin her new heels. She slips and grabs on to Alice to steady herself.

'Wrong shoes,' she shrugs.

'Yeah,' Alice concedes.

'I was trying to look pretty.'

'Yeah.'

'For Dad.'

'Yeah.'

'He likes heels. He likes a woman in heels.'

'That's about all I want to know about that, Mom.'

Ellie has run ahead and grabbed a booth. She's already chatting up the waitress as she shakes the snow from her shoulders and takes off her coat. Alice slides in beside her and picks up the menu.

'I'm ready!' Ellie announces to no one in particular.

'Give me a minute.'

'You know what you're going to have. It's what you always, always have.'

'I like to look. Just in case.'

'Just in case what? You turn into another person?'

'Just in case it's a grilled Reuben kind of day.'

'Yeah, yeah, yeah. Stick to the tried and true.'

'That could be boring.'

'You're already boring, Alice.'

'Thanks a lot!'

Alice looks up to see that Angie has her head resting against the back of the booth and her eyes closed. Her long, fine fingers are crossed over her stomach. She looks pale and tired in the fluorescent light. She's sitting in the middle of the booth as if she can cover up Dad's absence. Alice checks to see if Ellie has noticed any of this.

22

'Can we order, already?' Ellie asks.

'Yup.'

Ellie waves to the waitress, who comes right over. Her name tag says 'Marge.' Her glasses are incredibly thick and her hair looks like it's been teased and shellacked with hair spray. Who wears their hair like that anymore?

'Hi, Marge!' Ellie says. 'Can I get started with onion rings and a vanilla shake?'

'You bet.'

'I'll have the classic burger and a root beer, please. Mom? What do you want?'

Angie opens her eyes and sits up. Alice holds out a menu, Angie ignores it.

'Do you have soup?'

'Beef barley or chicken vegetable.'

'Chicken, please. A cup.'

Marge heads off to shout their order to the cooks behind the counter.

'We could play hangman,' Ellie says.

'Okay.'

'Mom, you got a pen?' Ellie asks.

Angie finds a pen in her purse, and Alice fishes her carefully folded geometry homework out of her back pocket. Ellie, Little Miss Genius, instantly takes the pen and thinks up a nine-letter word, drawing the short lines carefully

'Nine letters?'

'You're never gonna get this one.'

'E.'

Ellie fills in two blanks.

'A.'

Two more blanks.

'Where did you get that?' Angie's voice is

23

maybe a little sharper than she intended. To Alice it's coming at her with enough force to induce whiplash.

'My homework?'

'No. Daddy's watch.'

'What? Do you think I took it?'

'I'm just asking.'

'No, Mom, you're accusing.'

'I am not!'

'Or insinuating.'

'Oh, for heaven's sake.'

'He gave it to me.'

'Why didn't he give it to me?' Ellie wants to know.

'He gave it to you,' Angie says, her voice flat and disbelieving.

'Why don't you believe me?'

'He didn't say anything to me about it.'

'Why would he? It's not your watch.'

'Let's just drop it.'

'Do you want the watch, Mom?'

'No.'

'Why does Alice always get the good stuff?' Ellie asks.

'Shut up, Ellie.'

Which is when, thank you Marge in the Coke-bottle glasses and the Elvis Presley updo, the food arrives.

February 5th

Gram, a.k.a. Penelope Pearl Bird, or Penny to her many friends, owns the last remaining café in

24

Belknap. When Grampa died six years ago, Gram sold her house out on Plank Road, bought one of the old Victorians at the Four Corners, moved into the apartment upstairs, and resurrected Belknap's one and only coffee shop. She roped her sister Charlotte, who was also recently widowed, into helping her. They call it The Bird Sisters and are open for breakfast and lunch, six a.m. to two p.m. Wednesday through Sunday.

Angie was predicting the worst from Day One, thought it would be too much for Gram, thought Gram was throwing her money away. According to Angie, all kinds of dire emergencies were going to crop up, from a leaky roof to poisoning patrons. But Gram would retort that she's got her son Eddie and her son-in-law Matt for the roof and anything else that involves carpentry, plumbing, or electrical, and as for the food poisoning, Gram says nobody ever died from eggs, toast, and coffee.

And what do you know? Gram has the touch: she's a savvy businesswoman, and she's having fun with The Bird Sisters. There is no one in Belknap she hasn't met. Most people come in at some point or another needing a cup of coffee and someone to listen, which is Gram all over. Some people have taken to calling her the mayor of Belknap.

It was more fun, of course, before Aunt Char died last year. The Bird Sisters closed its doors for a month while Gram worked out whether she could go on without Char. Gram needed time to reassess and recover from that long string of losses: her husband, James; her kid brother,

George; her brother-in-law Bobby; and her beloved sister, Char.

Ask Gram about Char and she'll say, 'Oh, Char was the pretty one,' or 'Char was the smart one,' like Gram isn't pretty and smart? But Gram has this open-hearted way with the people she loves. Some people focus on your flaws, but Gram focuses on your best feature, or tells you that she actually, honestly *likes* your supposed flaw. Gram's highest forms of praise are 'He's a real gentleman,' or 'She's true blue.'

As an example of the loving your flaws thing, Aunt Char was a whistler. She'd even whistle classical music. Drove her husband, Bobby, completely bats, but Gram loved it. She'd brag to customers: 'My sister, Charlotte, can whistle Schubert's 'Trout Quintet.''

'Just try it,' she'd challenge anybody who laughed.

When Gram reopened she tried to do it all herself, relying on her two short-order cooks, Ginny and Dave, to carry plates now and then. Luckily, Sally Perkins walked in the door one day, ate the best breakfast of her life, so she says, tied on an apron, and never left. Sally's a divorcée from down by the lake. Her kids are grown but still going through their troubles right in Sally's neighborhood, sometimes right outside Sally's backdoor. Her husband's still in the neighborhood, too. Some people say he's trying to make amends. Sally says, what that man broke cannot be fixed.

Sally's a little short and a little stocky, but curvy, too, and she likes to accentuate the positive. She's also got that bottle blonde, tough broad thing going on. And it's like she does backward flirting, giving guys such a hard time they can't believe it, but they keep coming back for more. People from out of town assume Sally and Gram are sisters. Gram always says, 'We're like sisters, but we're not the *original* sisters.'

Playing on the Bird theme, Gram has birdbaths and bird feeders galore. There's suet hanging in the oldest apple tree next to the house, hummingbird feeders stuck to all the windows, and supposedly squirrel-proof feeders hanging from most branches. All the bird activity, especially the hummingbirds, keeps little kids occupied while their parents get to talk. It's fair to say it's the most popular place in town, but then again, it's the only place in town.

Mrs. Piantowski makes all the bread for the restaurant, right out of her own kitchen. Mrs. Piantowski is forty-something years old, has eight kids, and wanted to make a little money on the side. She didn't really know anything about bread when she sold Gram on this idea, so she started small, just white, wheat, and rye. But Mrs. Piantowski fell in love with bread: Portuguese sweetbread, Finnish Nisu, Swedish limpa rye with caraway and fennel seed and orange rind, anadama, sticky buns, biscuits and scones and on and on. She got her husband to move the fridge into the pantry and install a second double oven. It is a bread adventure with Mrs. Piantowski, and Gram says she's happy to go along for the ride.

Of course people started asking to buy Mrs.

Piantowski's bread. But Gram and Mrs. Piantowski were already pushing it given that a home kitchen was supplying a restaurant. Strictly against board of health rules, and nobody wants to get the board of health involved, with regulations and testing and surprise inspections. Until it turns out the board of health inspector is one of their best customers. In fact, Charlie Prophett eats breakfast at The Bird Sisters five days a week and is often seen knocking on the door and begging them to open up on Monday and Tuesday, too. So far he has managed to control himself and not walk up on Mrs. Piantowski's porch on the days the restaurant is closed. But there are bets on how long it will be before he's knocking on her door to say, 'Just a piece of toast, Mrs. Piantowski. Or two or three, if you don't mind.'

There are people in Belknap who dream about Mrs. Piantowski's bread. Maybe some people even dream about Mrs. Piantowski. She has dark brown eyes and long reddish hair that she wears pulled back or piled on top of her head, and she has lots of freckles on her nose, chest, and arms. She always wears colors, wonderful rich colors, and skirts and sweaters and sometimes a scarf twisted in her hair. She's not exactly pretty, but she has this bearing; it's almost regal. Maybe it's her height, maybe it's her very straight spine and her very straight nose and her no nonsense way of speaking. Maybe it's that nobody knows her first name.

Gram knows but she's not telling. Some men have tried to flirt with Mrs. Piantowski, and

28

women try to get friendly, but she just sails on by. Maybe she's got everything she needs with eight kids and twenty-two different kinds of bread up her sleeve.

Alice's job is to pick up the bread every Saturday and Sunday morning at quarter of six and then help Gram with whatever prep work still needs to be done at the restaurant. Even though every other teenager in America is still asleep. Even though Alice sometimes wonders how she gets roped into this stuff. On the other hand, Alice has never met anyone who can say no to Gram.

She used to use Ellie's red Radio Flyer wagon until neighbors complained about the noise as she squeaked and bumped her way along the sidewalks in the predawn. Then Gram got her a rubber wheeled grocery basket like the ones old ladies use in metropolitan areas. Alice feels ridiculous, but at least now she's quiet.

It's exactly quarter of six Sunday morning when Alice arrives at the backdoor to Mrs. Piantowski's. She leaves the cart on the porch and knocks softly before turning the knob and walking in. The youngest baby is sitting in a bouncy chair on the kitchen table looking around with her big, dark green, and very grave eyes. There are two dozen loaves wrapped and ready to go and Mrs. Piantowski is pulling twelve more out of the double oven.

'Hi, Alice.'

'Hi, Mrs. Piantowski.'

'Snowing?'

'Not yet.'

29

Mrs. Piantowski works at the stove. She is brushing the loaves with a blend of sugar and cardamom.

'I'm running a little late. You're going to need to take these right in the pans. Can you bring me the pans on your way home later today?'

'Sure.'

Usually all the loaves are stacked and ready to go, and then she and Mrs. Piantowski pack the cart together: coolest loaves on the bottom, warmest ones on top. Alice understands that this is probably about allowing the loaves to cool without getting soggy, but it also creates this heady perfume as she walks down the street. She imagines the fresh bread smells wafting like a banner over her head — the best advertising imaginable.

'What's that spice?'

'Cardamom.'

'Smells good.'

There's never much chat with Mrs. Piantowski. She's not exactly unfriendly; she just doesn't talk much. Maybe she doesn't know how difficult it is for a fifteen-year-old to initiate a conversation. Maybe with eight kids of her own she cherishes the quiet of these early-morning hours and is not willing to sacrifice the silence to talk to one more child.

But Mrs. Piantowski's quiet today has more to do with the fact that her husband has taken to leaving their bed to wander through the house like a refugee from his own life. Isaac will not say they have too many children, he would never say that. Instead he turns away from her, leaves their bed in the darkest hours, only to return when her alarm sounds at three a.m. It is a new dance they do each night, a dance of sleep and wakefulness and loneliness, instead of the old dance of love.

But these aches recede as she steps into her kitchen, lights the stove, puts an apron and the kettle on, and sets the first batch of dough to rising.

Alice doesn't mind the quiet. It gives her a chance to experience Mrs. Piantowski's kitchen. There's eight of everything: eight hooks on the wall for coats, eight hooks above for hats, eight stools around the table, which is set for eight for breakfast. Everything is spotless; nothing is out of place. Alice thinks Mrs. Piantowski must either be a drill sergeant or the most persuasive person on the planet.

The baby starts to fuss.

'Can I pick up the baby?'

'She's fine.'

Alice crosses to the baby.

'I never met anyone named Inga before,' she says, extending a finger, which the baby grabs.

'My grandmother's name.'

'Hi, Inga,' Alice whispers, and lays her hand against Inga's cheek.

Eyes closed, Alice inhales the baby smells and the baking smells; the yeast and the sugar and . . .

'Go ahead.'

'What?'

'You've held a baby before?'

'Sure.'

31

She releases the Velcro holding Inga in place and scoops her up in her hands, remembering to support her head as she pulls her close against her body. Alice and Inga engage in a long staring contest until Inga's nose wrinkles and she sneezes. Laughing, Alice is rewarded with one of Inga's smiles. Alice sways with the baby, her weight transferring from foot to foot, and then she starts to dance with the baby, right there in the kitchen. Not too fast, not too jittery; just a slow swirl and glide, anything to keep Inga smiling.

Mrs. Piantowski starts to sing. In a foreign language. What is that, Polish? The song is halfway between a lullaby and a lament. Why would you sing this song to a baby? It's so sad, Alice thinks, it could make you cry. And then Mrs. Piantowski starts to clap and before you know it she is dancing; hitching up her apron and her skirt and doing something fancy with her feet as she continues to sing. The song changes from a whisper to a shout and Inga loves it; with each change in tone, each surprise, Inga turns her head to watch her mother and smiles her toothless smile.

Alice looks back and forth between the two of them, baby Inga laughing, Mrs. Piantowski's face shining in the warm kitchen, and wonders, did this ever happen in her life, with her mother?

She must be looking famished because Mrs. Piantowski pours her a big glass of milk and sets a cinnamon bun on a plate. Then she hands her a cloth napkin and invites her to sit down. She waves away Alice's worry about being late and takes baby Inga from her. This is too much. Mrs. Piantowski is a completely different species from Alice's own mother.

Alice doesn't realize how fast she's eating until she looks up and catches Mrs. Piantowski grinning.

'Good?' she asks.

'The best ever,' Alice replies, before she gulps down her milk and slides off the stool to head out the door into the predawn darkness on her way to deliver bread to The Bird Sisters.

March 13th

'Mom? Mom! Are you up? Get a move on!'

The Monday following Angie's surprise birthday party, which Matt and the girls had carefully pre-planned and executed with help from Gram and Uncle Eddie, Angie does not feel like getting up or going to work. When Alice calls up to her, she's still in bed, still feeling devastated and idiotic that the promised phone call with Matt never came through, even though she waited up almost all night, just in case. And it's ridiculous, really. How many times does she have to be reminded that his time is not his own anymore?

The girls, with Gram's help, gave her a silk scarf to replace the one she tossed out the window. They made her favorite cake, angel food stuffed with strawberries and whipped cream, Gram cooked Angie's favorite dinner, even Uncle Eddie came through with a basket of

33

spring bulbs. Matt had wrapped up the far too expensive French perfume she loves and left it with Alice for safekeeping. Why did it all make her feel so sad and so incredibly angry and so stupidly childish all at the same time? Angie feels like a yo-yo; the simplest things set her off. It's exhausting. And she doesn't even like birthdays.

'Five more minutes!'

Downstairs Ellie is half asleep in her cereal, her braids dragging in the milk. Alice is trying to find her sneakers, air out the armpits of her dad's button-down blue shirt, which she has worn for three solid weeks now and refuses to wash, and scavenging for enough change so Ellie can buy milk at lunch. Oh yes, and packing the sandwiches: sliced bananas on graham crackers.

'Mom, we're out of bread!' Alice shouts up the stairs. 'And peanut butter. And jam! Again,' she mutters under her breath as she returns to the kitchen.

'Get creative,' Angie shouts from the bed-room.

The bananas keep sliding off the graham crackers when Alice tries to fit them into the sandwich bags.

'Don't put that crap in my lunch box.'

'You can't say crap.'

'It's like big tall letters flashing over my head when I open my lunch box: fucked up family!'

'Ellie!'

'What? You say it!'

'Not when I was in second grade!'

34

'I want lunch money. Not this stupid excuse for a sandwich!'

'I'll ask Gram.'

'Yeah. She could set up a lunch fund. And a clothing fund and she could drive us to the supermarket to stock up on food and — '

'Okay, you ready?' Alice asks, handing Ellie her lunch box.

'You can't go to school in that,' Ellie says.

'Let's get a move on.'

'Dad's shirt? Again? Does Mom know?'

'What do you care?'

'It doesn't fit.'

'So?'

'Aside from the fact you're not cool, I think you're starting to smell, Alice. You could at least wash that stupid shirt.'

'I aired it out last night.'

'That's not enough.'

'It'll be fine.'

'You need to burn it.'

'Henry's gonna be here any minute.'

'Maybe Gram would take you shopping. New jeans, new . . . '

'I'm all set. C'mon.'

'Okay, but I'm not walking next to you and I'm definitely not holding hands with you. Not even at the crosswalk.'

'Whatever.'

'I'm reaching my limit with you, Alice. Just so you know.'

God, she sounds just like Angie, Alice thinks.

★ ★ ★

35

Matt's been gone almost six weeks. He's in the last days of training at the mobilization center with his army reserve unit. The reservists have been kept pretty much in lockdown conditions at Fort Dix: no time off, no time off the base, and very little contact with home. Supposedly this is all preparation for being deployed. It's very strange for Angie and Alice and Ellie. He's gone but not gone; and there's no coming home at this point, not until his one-year tour of duty is done.

Everything is different with Matt gone. Same house, different air, different space inside the rooms. Angie is impatient and irritable; she's working at the insurance company more than ever, and on top of that, she brings work home. It's like she doesn't really want to be at home at all so she piles on the work and makes the kitchen table a second office. That way she has a good excuse to be distracted and tense all the time. She's pretty much dropped the ball on domestic duties and says she's 'not interested in eating right now.' So Alice does her best with spaghetti most nights and occasionally macaroni and cheese and lots of tomato soup and grilled cheese sandwiches. Ellie is spending inordinate amounts of time with her friend Janna and even manages to get herself invited for dinner several nights a week. Alice is spending too much time alone in the house every afternoon. She wants to be there in case the phone rings but it never does.

Angie was starting to let herself go for a bit but yanked herself right back from the edge with an iron hand. She got a new haircut and renewed her fitness commitment, swimming half an hour three days a week after work. The housework and the cooking are not so high on her list of priorities, but the personal appearance thing has become very important. Alice thinks her mom secretly likes the fact that stress and worry have finally made it possible for her to drop those last pesky ten pounds. She is slipping back into some pre-Ellie clothes. Okay, so it's natural to think your mother is a total idiot at this age, but when your dad's out of the picture it's hard to have your mother quite so strange and foreign. It's a little disconcerting, the sudden lack of parents. Or, to be honest, when nobody prefers you. When you are not anybody's special somebody. This is when it would be nice to have a dog.

★ ★ ★

Alice doesn't know, can't know, what Angie is going through. Angie, who can't sleep at night or if she does fall asleep, wakes with a start to the unfamiliar silence that is Matt's absence. They have been together since their sophomore year in college; in eighteen years they have slept apart on very rare occasions. Angie wonders whether it is even possible to sleep without him.

In the middle of the night she haunts the house and the closets, running her hands over his jackets and shirts, feeling inside the pockets of his coats for coins, or keys, or penny nails, or anything at all that he has touched.

She's having trouble concentrating at the

office, and she's terrified of losing her job. With Matt gone she's suddenly aware of every bill, every little possible repair. It feels like the Camry might need new brakes, and she knows they're due for two new tires. All the things that Matt would take care of or that they would discuss and decide together now tick through Angie's mind like an endless scroll.

Yesterday Angie drove out to the Holschers' farm and sat at Edna Holscher's kitchen table to go over this year's policy and then broke down crying for long minutes when Edna asked how she's holding up. This is not professional, she thinks, this is not what old man Beeman had in mind when he gave her these accounts.

Angie keeps a pair of tall rubber boots and a slicker in her car for her visits to her farms. Once she's appraised them for insurance purposes, everything from buildings to outbuildings to barns to vehicles and tractors and tools and animals, she feels like she belongs to them or they belong to her.

She knows the cost per head and replacement value of every last animal on every farm that she covers. This is another side of Angie, the flip side of the high heels and silk blouses. It was a surprise when old man Beeman took Angie under his wing and taught her the farm side of the business. Pretty Angie, the least likely adjustor in the office to be chosen by Beeman for farm work. Give her commercial real estate, give her residential, give her life insurance, who could say no to Angie? But farms? Try making sense out of that.

It's the big animals, she'll tell you; she fell in love with cows and horses and fields and farms and the way Route 20 curves through mile after mile of fertile, rolling land. Like stepping into another century.

The farmers and their wives were leery of Angie at first, even with old man Beeman vouching for her. But Angie sits in their linoleum-floored kitchens drinking coffee from percolators, adding sugar and cream until they laugh at her. The year she left her own Thanksgiving dinner to follow the fire trucks out to the Holschers' farm for the worst kind of fire, a barn fire, and stayed until every horse and cow was accounted for — the dead animals named and mourned, the living safely housed in temporary quarters — and sat, again, in the kitchen, her coat scorched, ash in her pretty hair; that was the year they took her in. Edna Holscher held her hand at the kitchen table, whispering in her ear so that Hank, pouring whiskey, couldn't hear: *Don't let this be what ruins us, Angie; don't let this be the last straw.*

And here she is, driving nearly an hour to sit in Edna's kitchen and cry because Edna will understand and because really, where else does she have to go?

★   ★   ★

Alice found her dad's blue shirt in the hamper the day she decided to do laundry because no one had any clean underpants left in their drawers. She set the shirt aside instead of

39

tossing it into the washer. She laid it out on her bed for an afternoon, then put it under her pillow for a few nights. Now she's wearing it. Every night she airs it out and every day she rolls the cuffs up half a turn. She had to spot clean the left front when she inadvertently got into the middle of a ketchup fight in the cafeteria. She hates the fact that the Dad-ness of the shirt is evaporating. She still likes wearing it, though, no matter what Ellie says. Her mom just rolls her eyes. Alice thinks the two of them are planning an intervention so she's started to get very smart about where she airs it out each night.

Henry slams through the backdoor with a blast of clean, cold air, shouting, 'Good morning, Mrs. Bliss!' just like he does every morning, whether she's in the kitchen or not. Henry's energy is just the catalyst they need to grab jackets and backpacks and get out the door.

On the way to the elementary school, Henry teaches Ellie and Alice a new round he has written especially for Ellie. It features about four hundred mentions of the word *fart*. He gets Ellie giggling so hard Alice thinks she's going to wet her pants. Henry grabs Ellie's recorder out of her backpack so he can play the tune and make big, fat *splat* sounds every time they sing the word *fart!* Tears are streaming down Ellie's face and she has to stop walking and cross her legs to keep from peeing.

Henry is the only person Alice knows who would sing, play music, and dance around like a maniac to make a second grader laugh. In

40

public. Henry is also capable of walking to school carrying his clarinet case in front of him — sideways, which is so awkward, you think who carries *anything* like that? — while *at the same time* banging his knees against the case to work out some complicated rhythm for jazz band. This sort of thing used to mortify Alice; now it makes her laugh.

When they reach the grammar school bus circle, Ellie grabs her recorder from Henry and sprints to catch up to Janna. Alice and Henry head off across the playground and up the hill and through the playing fields that separate the schools. Henry pulls out his iPod and offers Alice one earbud.

'Listen to this, Alice.'

They listen for a bit, walking shoulder to shoulder.

'Who is it?'

'Art Tatum. You ever hear of him?'

She shakes her head.

'He makes the piano *rock*. Listen to the way he rolls those bass notes.'

She listens.

Henry reaches out his left hand, imitating what he hears with his fingers, as though he's playing air piano. It's amazing the way he can do that. He's got his eyes half closed, he's making funny faces, he's lucky he doesn't trip and break a leg. He opens his eyes and glances over at her, a grin on his face.

'Good, huh?'

'Yeah,' she says, grinning back at him. 'Really good.'

March 15th

Two days later Alice is sitting in the kitchen, in the chair closest to the phone hanging on the wall, her homework scattered across the table, untouched. Matt ships out tonight and he will have a chance to call between five and nine. Alice staked out her spot by the phone at three, the minute she got home from school. Angie is coming home from work early, to be here by five, just in case.

Ellie and Janna are in Ellie's room playing dress up. Last week Gram gave Ellie a whole bagful of scarves and belts and hats and purses she's been collecting at yard sales. This is their first chance at the stuff.

For two hours as she tries to read chapters six through nine of *A Separate Peace*, Alice can hear Ellie and Janna laughing and talking. She can tell they've moved on to Angie's closet and are searching for high heels. They creep downstairs barefoot, slide into the heels and clomp their way to the kitchen for a TA DA! moment: two eight-year-olds in polyester old lady dresses, elaborately and multiply belted at the waist, fake fox furs, pillbox hats, high heels, and too much lipstick.

Alice tells them they look lovely.

'We're going on the *Queen Elizabeth!*' Ellie says.

'Around the world! The whole entire world,' Janna adds.

'Really!'

'The most marvelous boat in the world, darling!'

'Just the two of you?'

'And Luke Piacci!!!!!'

Ellie sweeps out like an elegant matron, trailing fur and too much perfume. Janna wobbles and then trips making her turn, but tosses a brave smile over her shoulder anyway.

Watching Ellie and Janna reminds Alice of her friend Stephie Larson or, more accurately, her former friend Stephie Larson. They were inseparable all through ninth grade after they both got stuck in crazy Mr. Bartolotto's French class. But over the summer Stephie stopped eating and stopped being a pudgy kid and when tenth grade began she started hanging out with a different crowd at school. Last month, when Alice's dad left for Fort Dix, Stephie was being kind of friendly, actually speaking to her in the girl's room or between classes. Not a lot. Not anything like the way it used to be, not laughing, not making plans, just the occasional word or two, when nobody else was around. Today Alice must have lost her mind because she approached Stephie while she was talking to Jennifer White and Stephie actually pretended she didn't hear her or see her.

She looks up to see Ellie in the front hall daring Janna to kiss the newel post.

'Pretend it's Luke Piacci,' she giggles.

Alice wishes the phone would ring right now, with Mom gone and Ellie otherwise engaged. She wants five minutes to talk to her dad without an audience, without anyone telling her to hurry up, without Ellie shouting, 'My turn! My turn!' She stares at the phone, willing it to ring, and when it does she nearly jumps out of her seat.

'Dad?'

'No, it's me, Alice. Henry.'

'I can't talk right now. We're waiting for my dad.'

'I thought that was after five.'

'It could be anytime.'

'Have you done your math homework?'

'Henry!'

'I can't get number six. Or number five either.'

'I haven't looked at it.'

'Oh.'

'I have to go.'

'Alice — '

'What!?'

'Did you — '

'Henry, hurry up!'

'Are you avoiding me?'

'No. But I have to go.'

'Really?'

'Really.'

'Okay.'

She hangs up and sits with her hand on the phone, thinking call now, Dad, right now. She glances at the clock: ten to five. You and I could talk, then Mom gets home and you guys have your time, then Ellie. Just five minutes. Just one minute. Just . . .

She closes her eyes and she can imagine the line at the bank of phones on the base. The lucky guys with their own cell phones, talking as long as they want. The rest of them waiting to call, some poor schmo having to keep the line moving, cut the calls short.

Is he already packed? Is he hungry, is he tired, is he lonely? Is he scared of this phone call? She's scared she's gonna cry and end up not telling him . . . telling him what exactly? How do you take the stupid daily details that don't mean anything at all, like yesterday's math test and the way she just blanked out and couldn't think at all, and the new coffee Gram is trying out in the café, and what's in the news about the war and what's not in the news about the war; how is she supposed to pretend that this is all fine and normal and she can handle it when . . .

Suddenly she's angry; she's so angry so quickly she feels like her head could come off. Why is he doing this? Is there something wrong with her? If she were different, if she were better, smarter, prettier, then would he stay? Why isn't Mom enough? And Ellie and Gram and the garden and his baseball team? Why isn't any one of those things enough anymore?

The phone rings. It's exactly five, she notices, as she picks up the receiver. Mom must be stuck in traffic.

'Dad,' she says, and her voice sounds dead.

'Honey? Alice? How are you?'

'Fine.'

'Where are you?'

'The kitchen.'

'Doing homework?'

'Sort of.'

'Where's Mom?'

'Not home yet.'

'And Ellie?'

'Upstairs playing dress up with Janna.'

'We don't have a lot of time. You want to call Ellie to the phone?'

'No.'

'What?'

'I want . . . '

'Alice?'

'Don't go,' she manages to choke out.

'Alice, honey, listen — '

She hears Mom's car in the driveway.

'Mom's home.'

'Okay.'

'I'll call Ellie.'

'Wait! — Alice, are you still there?'

'Yeah.'

'We said our good-byes, remember? Let's just have this be a regular call, like hi, how are you?'

'You want to pretend?'

'What?'

'You want me to *pretend?*'

And then Mom is through the door and standing beside her.

'I just want to hear your voice, honey. To take that with me. Maybe hear you laugh. I don't know.'

'Keep talking.'

'Is Mom there?'

'Yes. But — '

'You can stay on. Or you could get on the extension.'

'That's okay. Here's Mom.'

'Sweetheart?' Angie says into the phone.

'Angie . . . '

Even Alice can hear the longing in his voice when he says *Angie* like that. She knows she

46

should leave the room; she should give them their moment, but she can hear his voice faintly, and she can't walk away from that any more than she could talk when she was on the phone.

'Are you okay?' Angie asks.

'Yeah. Fine. We're in good shape.'

'Did you get the package we sent?'

'Tell Alice and Ellie I loved the cookies. And your mom.'

'I know we don't have much time — '

'What are you wearing?'

'*Matt!*'

'I want to picture you.'

'I'm wearing that navy dress you like. With the belt.'

'And heels.'

'Yes. Heels.'

'What's Alice wearing?'

Mom holds out the phone to Alice.

'You want to tell him?'

Alice takes the phone.

'Jeans, high tops, and your blue shirt.'

'You're wearing my clothes?'

'Just your shirt.'

'Send me pictures. Okay, Alice? Send me pictures.'

He sounds so young. It's hard to think of her dad as young, but his voice, there's another note in it now. That upper layer of control that's always there is suddenly gone and he sounds like he feels, she thinks. The realization, he *is* scared, suddenly shoots through her like an adrenaline rush.

'Go get Ellie,' Angie says, reaching for the phone.

But Alice won't give up the phone. Now she's ready to pretend, she's ready to do whatever it takes to get her dad's voice back to normal.

'Dad,' she says, 'Dad — ?'

'I'm right here, sweetheart.'

Angie shakes her head and walks through the dining room to the stairs where she calls up to Ellie to come to the phone.

'Uncle Eddie is taking us to the movies, and it's only three more weeks until the equinox and the Red Wings home opener, and Henry might flunk math this term even though I keep trying to help him, and ever since you left, it's hard to concentrate, and Mrs. Piantowski might be having another baby or maybe she's just getting fatter, and Gram says . . . '

'It's Ellie's turn,' Angie says, taking the phone from Alice.

Alice sinks into a kitchen chair and pretends to listen to her sister chatter on about Janna and Janna's new bunk bed with a desk built right into the side of it, and how Ellie thinks she wants to write and draw pictures for a book about a sleepover where the bunk beds are stacked ten high and go right through the ceiling and reach up to the sky with magic ladders.

'Draw me pictures,' she hears her dad say. 'Draw me lots of pictures.'

Her mom takes the phone and shoos both girls out of the kitchen so she can have a minute alone with Dad.

Alice listens outside the door.

'Did you get your orders?'

'Yeah, we did.'

'Where are they putting you?'

'F.O.B. Falcon. For the time being.'

'Where's that?'

'Somewhere between Baghdad and Falluja.'

'I don't like the sound of that.'

'It should be pretty interesting, actually.'

'Still reconnaissance and surveillance?'

'And artillery.'

'I thought you'd be in engineering.'

'It's the surge, Angie. They need boots on the ground.'

'Or transport. Or supply. Or security.'

'You get assigned.'

'What about rebuilding roads and schools and bridges and . . . Do they know you're an engineer?'

'Of course.'

'Your CO. Does he know? Can you remind him?'

'It's the *army*, Angie.'

'I know, but — '

'Write to me, sweetheart.'

'Okay.'

'Letters are like . . . You have no idea how important they are. Mail call . . . '

'Every day.'

'Promise me.'

'I promise.'

'You're my girl and I love you.'

'Come home to me.'

'I will. You know I will.'

★ ★ ★

The doorbell rings; Janna's mother Joyce is at the door. Alice helps find Janna's back pack and sneakers, the Shrek lunch box, and her jacket and sweater, and she even manages to say the right things to Janna's mom, who is on her way home from her job at the cosmetics store at the mall and looks tired and a little frazzled.

'My feet are killing me, my cheeks are killing me, I'm so sick of smiling; I can't wait to get home and have a nice cold beer. I probably shouldn't say that in front of you kids, but a day like today? A beer is my one true reward.'

She and Janna head down the walk.

Ellie waves from the door.

'I'm gonna draw Daddy a picture right now.'

'Good idea.'

'I'm gonna draw Daddy a picture every day.'

'He'll like that.'

'And send it to him. So I can tell him my story, little by little, day by day, like we're on the installment plan.'

Ellie gets out her crayons and markers and paper and starts to draw right there at the dining room table with Alice beside her. Alice digs her math homework out of her back pocket and starts solving problems with one of Ellie's pencils. They sit there, drawing and doing math, like they're not hungry, like it's not time for dinner, like they can't hear their mother sobbing on the other side of the kitchen door.

'You want to take a walk?' Alice asks.

'Now? I'm hungry.'

50

'I know.'

'Maybe we shouldn't leave Mom.'

'Just for a little while.'

'Okay.'

In the front hall they pull on jackets. Ellie steps into her pink boots and insists on finding the matching mittens to her pink hat.

Outside it's colder and darker than either of them expected. At the end of their driveway they turn left and head away from their usual route to school on Baird Road. The sidewalks are covered with rutted, frozen slush. Ellie reaches out and takes Alice's hand. They walk for a while, not saying anything, their breath puffing out of their mouths. Alice tries to make rings with her breath but can't. Ellie tries snorting like a dragon to see if she can get steam to come out of her nose.

'Is it winter where Daddy is going?'

'Yeah.'

'Winter like this?'

'I don't know. I think so.'

'Snow and everything?'

'I'll find out.'

'I'm cold.'

As they turn toward home, Ellie trips and falls on the ice, hard. Alice picks her up before she can even start crying and feels something warm and wet on her neck.

'Is your nose bleeding?'

Ellie puts one pink mitten up to her nose, it comes away red, and she starts to wail.

'It's okay, Ellie. We'll get you fixed up at home.'

'My mittens!'

'They'll be okay.'

'No they won't!'

'I'll wash them.'

'They're my favorite ones.'

'I know.'

'Can't you go any faster? Daddy can carry me faster.'

'He's bigger than me.'

'And stronger. And nicer.'

'I'm being pretty nice right now.'

'Can I have ice cream for dinner?'

'Not that nice.'

Ellie gets heavier and heavier with every step. When Alice finally turns into their yard, she's sweating and breathing hard. They get through the front door and head straight into the kitchen. Mom is long gone. No dinner preparations in sight. Alice sits Ellie right on the sink and starts to assess the damage.

'I think you're gonna live.'

'Is it broken?'

'Not a chance.'

'You sure?'

'Split your lip, though.'

'Really?'

'And you've got a little gash on your chin.'

Alice slips off Ellie's jacket and turns it inside out so she can't see the blood. She grabs a paper towel and wipes Ellie's blood from her cheek and chin.

'You're a mess, Alice.'

'Thanks a lot.'

She tosses her own jacket on top of Ellie's.

'Give me your mittens, too. I'll get them

soaking downstairs.'

'Will you make dinner?'

'As soon as I put our jackets in the wash. I'm gonna give you some ice for your lip, okay?'

She hands Ellie an ice cube wrapped in a dishcloth.

'Hold that right on your lip. Don't press. I'll be right back.'

Alice runs down the basement stairs, turns on the washer, and fills up the sink to soak Ellie's mittens. She's secretly glad to have stuff to do. She charges back up the stairs and checks out the fridge.

'You good with grilled cheese and tomato soup?'

'Again?'

Alice gives her a look.

'Get your book and read in here to keep me company, okay?'

'Should I call Mom?'

'No, let's surprise her.'

'I could make her a tray.'

'Good idea.'

While Alice makes grilled cheese sandwiches, the slow, slow, slow way her dad makes them, Ellie gets the tray off the hall table. She finds a cloth napkin to make a little placemat, then sets the tray with the nice china from the china cabinet.

'I need a flower and a vase.'

'You could draw one.'

'And then can I stir the soup?'

'Yup.'

'And pour the milk?'

'It's really heavy, Ellie.'

'I can do it.'

Alice pulls the stool over so Ellie can stir the soup. She sets the table for the two of them.

'The tray looks nice.'

'You think Mom will like it?' Ellie asks.

'Yup.'

'I want ice cream for dessert.'

'Okay.'

'Neapolitan.'

'We'll see what we've got.'

Alice pours soup into bowls and cuts the sandwiches in triangles the way Ellie likes them, while Ellie pours the milk.

'I want to carry the tray.'

'How about if you carry the plate and I'll carry the tray with the soup.'

'I won't spill.'

'It's even hard for me not to spill.'

'Okay.'

Upstairs, neither one of them has a hand free to knock on the door to the bedroom. Ellie gives three little kicks with her foot.

'Mom?'

The room is dark. Angie has kicked off her heels and is lying on top of the bed with a cold cloth over her eyes.

'Mom?'

'Not now.'

'We brought you some dinner.'

'I'm really not hungry.'

'On a tray.'

Angie opens her eyes and sits up in bed. She reaches over and turns on the bedside lamp.

Alice sets the tray on her lap. Ellie sets the pink scallop-edged plate with the grilled cheese sandwich in the exact center of the tray.

'I split my lip on the ice,' Ellie says.

'We just went for a little walk.'

'My nose was bleeding, too. I bled all over Alice.'

'It's okay. I've got our jackets in the wash already.'

'Alice carried me all the way home and fixed me up and made dinner. I helped. I drew you a flower because we didn't have one to put on your tray.'

Angie reaches out to touch Ellie's lip. She wants to say thank you but she's not sure she can trust herself to say anything at all.

* * *

After dinner, after washing the dishes and locking up the house, Alice climbs upstairs to find that Ellie has fallen asleep with her clothes on right on top of the covers. Ellie should have had a bath, Alice realizes, but it's too late now. She pulls off Ellie's shoes and socks and sweater and manages to slide her under the covers. How can she sleep through all that? Her lip is swelling and her chin has a dark bruise.

Alice sits down at her desk by the window and realizes that none of her homework is done and she is too tired to read about the Revolutionary War now. She looks across the backyard to her dad's workshop sitting squat and dark in the moonlight. That is absolutely too sad to dwell on, so she opens the window and sticks her head out, craning her neck to see Henry's house down the block, but his window is dark, too. She looks at her dad's watch and rights it on her wrist so she can read the dial: ten o'clock.

She listens to Ellie snoring and thinks of hearing her dad's voice coming through the phone, saying: 'Angie . . . ?' Did they say good-bye? Did they ever actually say good-bye? She thinks of her mom's untouched tray, Ellie's bloody mittens, she hopes their jackets will be dry in the morning, and somewhere in there — after she gets up and gets her old stuffed bear off the shelf, which feels silly and childish but right now she doesn't care — somewhere in there, she falls asleep.

March 23rd

Alice and Henry walk Ellie to school every morning, and then instead of climbing the hill and crossing the middle school playing fields to get to the high school, they go the long way around, down Belknap Road and past the Four Corners. Alice and Henry could take the bus but they both hate the bus. Nothing good ever happens on that bus. They walk no matter what the weather so they can just *be* for twenty minutes before school. They don't talk much; some days they don't talk at all.

Henry and Alice have known each other, as their parents like to say, since they were in utero. This phraseology has become less and less charming the older they get. They've also been stuck having play dates since they were born because their families are neighbors. This was not such a big deal in grade school. Fifth grade got a little uncomfortable. If they could have gone to different middle and high schools it might've been better. But it is what it is.

The facts include things like Henry coming home from school in second grade and telling his mom, 'I'm going to marry Alice. William wants to marry her, too, but he can't.' Their mothers repeat this stuff. Still! They also got caught — of course — stealing candy from Mr. Ricci's corner store and playing doctor and locking Ellie in a closet — she had a flashlight! — and whatever else little kids get up to. And just when Alice thinks she can't stand one more day of enforced friendship with Henry, he will do something so amazing that she thinks he's a saint or something.

Henry was always small for his age. So small that his parents worried and his doctors worried and Henry had to go through all these tests and things. But in the last six months, he has grown six inches. Henry is not the same boy. At all.

Sometimes Alice looks into his face and sees that his eyes are grayer and he has these cheekbones that look about as sharp as his ankles and wrists. Everything about Henry is a little angular and over defined, like all that fast growing hasn't given his skin a chance to catch up yet. It's like he's still two people: little kid Henry and growing up Henry, and Alice is watching those two people switch places right in front of her eyes.

Henry's brother, Rob, is a lot older. He's already graduated from college in Boston and is working for a relief organization in Haiti. So his parents are older, too, and Alice's mom is always saying that Henry's the kind of kid who needs to come from a big family. He needs the noise and the friction and the company. Not that the Blisses actually qualify as a big family, but if you add Henry, their numbers start to look a little more substantial.

Today Henry is worried about baseball tryouts. He loves to play baseball, but he pretty much sucks in every position. And Alice, who goes to most of Henry's games, has seen him play just about every position. Coaches move Henry around the field, thinking if they could just harness all that enthusiasm, some talent might emerge.

Alice has spent long spring and summer evenings playing catch with Henry, trying to pitch for Henry, and trying to field for Henry. Occasionally her dad would join them and they'd toss the ball around in the spring twilight, the streetlights coming on one by one, crickets whirring, that damp, green spring smell redolent in the air around them. Something else was in the air as well; something about promise and possibility and another beginning, another summer just around the corner.

But with her dad gone, they have not been tossing the ball around much. In fact, Alice doesn't even know where her mitt is.

The whole tryout thing is one horrible round of humiliation after another for Henry. Alice is about to offer to come with him when Henry says he might not try out for baseball this year after all.

Alice is shocked at this news and possibly also a little bit glad for Henry that he can stop feeling so bad trying to do something he loves so much. But then there's this other reaction, like why the hell does everything have to change all the time?

She doesn't say any of this, of course, because what could she say? I'm shocked-sad-mad-disgusted-furious, I want to scream at you, I want to celebrate. She sounds schizophrenic, even inside her own head.

She just keeps walking, keeps her head down. She's chewing her lip and tastes blood — damn! Now that's gonna bug her all day. And then they're passing Mrs. Minty's house.

Mrs. Minty lives alone, and Mrs. Minty always comes out on her porch and waves to Henry and Alice. Mrs. Minty is old. Really old, like from another century. But that doesn't stop her from tutoring at the library, where she runs the literacy program. Teaching adults to read and write two afternoons and two evenings a week.

There she is in her tweed skirt and cardigan sweater and those dark brown tie shoes with a little heel. Her hair is in a bun. Her dad used to say, 'Mrs. Minty looks like she just stepped out of a bandbox.' Whatever *that* is.

'Good morning, Alice! Good morning, Henry!'

'Good morning, Mrs. Minty!'

Henry gives her a little wave. Henry always

gives her a little wave.

'Henry, I wonder if you wouldn't mind stopping by after school. I need some help moving a few boxes.'

'Sure thing, Mrs. Minty.'

'Alice, you come, too. I'm baking cookies this afternoon.'

'Yes, ma'am.'

Mrs. Minty is smiling at her, not some sappy, oh you poor thing smile, but just a regular spring morning smile. Alice stops. Henry is shuffling his feet and giving her all the nonverbal *let's go* signals he can think of. But Alice ignores him. She stands still right there on the sidewalk and takes a good long look.

The apple tree in Mrs. Minty's front yard is full of fat buds getting ready to bloom. And it's full of birds, too, and they're all singing. Alice didn't notice the birds before, but now she does. They're making a racket. How could she not notice this? And then she looks down into the green, green grass and Mrs. Minty's whole yard is filled with tiny white and blue flowers.

'Those are pretty flowers, Mrs. Minty.'

'Snowbells and scilla. Some of the first to bloom each spring. They'll even bloom in the snow. My husband and I planted a hundred bulbs thirty years ago. Now there are thousands.'

Henry actually takes Alice by the arm and pulls her away, giving Mrs. Minty a last wave.

Alice is thinking she'd like to just lie down in Mrs. Minty's front yard and skip school altogether, but Henry has this death grip on her elbow and before she knows it, he is propelling her up the drive to school.

They're early — as usual — so they head to the auditorium, which has the only decent piano in the school. The janitor has given Henry the key so Henry can come in and play whenever he wants. This is strictly against the rules. The janitor, Mr. Herlihy, and Henry have decided, after much wrangling and discussion back and forth, that they don't care about that stupid rule.

Mr. Herlihy, it turns out, loves music. He has a huge collection of old jazz records. LPs he calls them. And whenever he can, he slips inside the auditorium and sits in the last row to listen to that kid Henry Grover playing in the dark.

Henry rigs up his book lamp so it creates a little puddle of light, and Alice climbs up onto the lip of the stage, and angles her book into the one spot where there's almost enough light to read by. Henry plays while Alice finishes her English homework.

Henry likes this arrangement. He gets to improvise and no one makes comments. Alice never tells him to shut up or play something different. Alice lies on the stage and reads, and sometimes she puts her book down and just listens to him. Every once in a while she'll tell him she likes what he's playing, or she'll make him stop and listen while she tells him he's gonna be a great musician one day. Every once in a while he can see the music take her someplace else and he can see the old Alice, the six-year-old or the ten-year-old or even the twelve-year-old Alice.

Alice abandons *The Catcher in the Rye* and

looks up into the darkness. The velvet curtain smells old and musty, and everything around them is shrouded in shadow. She's trying not to think about her father, about waiting and waiting for the letters that are taking forever to get to them, about the too quick, too hurried call when he first arrived, with every other word breaking up on them, none of them certain that anything they were saying was actually getting through.

She scoots over until she's lying underneath the piano. Here she can feel the sound reverberating in the floor below her and in the piano above her. She closes her eyes and breathes with Henry's playing, until the notes are inside her heartbeat and the notes are in her breathing and the notes are flowing through her veins.

March 24th

After her last class the following day, American history, Mr. Herman hands Alice a blank piece of paper with her name at the top of it, and wants an explanation as to why Alice didn't even bother to try answering one single question on yesterday's pop quiz. She looks out the window, looking for an answer maybe, and sees the track team lope out onto the track.

'Do I need to call your parents?'

She drags her attention back to Mr. Herman and the blank piece of paper in her hand.

'What?'

'Your parents. Do we need to get them involved?'

'No. No. Definitely not. You don't need to call them. I wasn't feeling well.'

'You should have told me.'

'I didn't really realize until it was too late.'

'You should have come to me after class, then.'

'Can I make up the test?'

'I'm afraid not.'

She steals a quick look at him. He's being a hard-ass because he thinks she's a good student and maybe he can shock her back into line. She thinks, I used to care about this; I used to be able to care about this, when her attention is drawn back to the runners outside on the track.

'I'm gonna miss my bus, Mr. Herman.'

'Don't let this happen again, Alice.'

'I won't.'

She is released; she is walking out the door, running down the hall, and slamming through the back doors that lead out to the playing fields and the track. Dumping her backpack and jacket on the ground, she jogs over to the coach.

'Can I run?' She asks.

'Can you?'

'I don't know. I want to run.'

'What's your name?'

'Alice Bliss.'

He makes a note on his clipboard.

'Grade?'

'Tenth.'

'You have any shorts? Sneaks?'

'I've got these,' indicating her battered Chucks.

'Take it easy, okay? We're just warming up. It's our first day outdoors.'

'Okay, okay, but I can run?'

'We'll see about that.'

Alice sprints to catch up with the runners who are doing laps and falls in beside a tall redheaded girl who looks like she knows what she's doing. The girl turns her head and gives Alice a half smile. Alice in her jeans feels like a mule next to this gazelle, but it's fun to try to match her stride, to lift her head, the way this girl does, to begin to sweat. She's feeling the cool early-spring air and the clouds crossing the sun, and her body, she's feeling her body, and her legs are starting to ache and feel heavy, but it doesn't matter; she's running, she's breathing, and for a second, for a tantalizing series of seconds, she's feeling free.

That night B.D., the coach, calls her mother and tells her that maybe they should get her a pair of running shoes. And shorts and a T-shirt and a sweatshirt, too. Angie wants to know what this is all about.

Alice just says, 'I guess I joined the track team.'

March 31st

Alice makes a deal with Henry so he'll pick up Ellie and take her home with him on the days she has practice, which is turning into every day. Henry doesn't seem too happy about this, but Ellie loves it. Ellie and Mrs. Grover have started

64

to play Scrabble. Ellie is memorizing all of the acceptable two letter words. Mrs. Grover is scrambling to keep up. Their scores are going through the roof. They've even ordered competitive Scrabble playing dictionaries via interlibrary loan. Mrs. Grover has set up an extra table in the dining room dedicated to Scrabble. Don't even think about doing your homework at that table. And every day at four thirty she serves tea in real china teacups. With little cakes. And sometimes special sandwiches.

Mrs. Grover is good at doing things that really matter but nobody notices. Like being nice to eight-year-olds, or running the community drive to collect children's books for the nursery at the YMCA, or supplying the local kindergarten with craft supplies after all the budget cuts eliminated just about everything except construction paper and snub-nosed scissors. All the kindergartners love Mrs. Grover's feathers, which she collects all year long on her walks through the Mendon Woods, or around Pond View Reservoir, or out by the lake.

Today, right before practice starts, Stephie and a clutch of older girls pass Alice and the other runners on their way to the student parking lot. Alice knows that Stephie, whose new friends call her Steph, as though two syllables are just too much trouble, would not be caught dead running. Stephie is paler than usual and she's wearing one of those push-up bras and a short skirt. When Jeremy Baskin, a senior, catches up to her and runs his hand over her ass, Stephie looks over her shoulder at Alice. But she's too far away now, and Alice can't tell if that's defiance or fear.

Alice turns back to the track. Ginger, the redhead, tosses her a baton on the fly as she sprints past her. They run, one forward, one backward, tossing the baton back and forth. Ginger's hair is cut almost as short as a boy's, she has strong legs and big feet, and she never looks down when she runs, she only looks up. She plays with the baton like Ellie would, and, with her energy and her quickness, she lifts Alice into a world where running *is* play.

Alice finds herself fantasizing about being the school's top tenth-grade 400-meter runner, not that there are a lot of other tenth-grade girls giving up cheerleading or softball to be on the track team. The idea that she might have talent at such a simple thing is amazing. Henry just rolls his eyes when she talks about running sprints while B.D. screams at her: 'Breathe, breathe, *breathe!*'

But nobody needs to scream at Alice to run or to breathe. When she's running she doesn't want to stop, she just wants to keep going. She feels something she's never felt before; she feels powerful and strong, she feels like no one can hurt her. Being outdoors, getting into a groove, the freedom and the repetitiveness of her stride; she doesn't know what it is, exactly, but something settles in her head. Running for time or for distance, on the track, on the roads, through the woods, getting lost, falling, the hard runs, the easy runs, all of it, every minute of it, she's living and breathing in another world. It is an escape so profound she finds herself longing for school to end and running to begin.

★ ★ ★

Alice arrives home to find Mom and Ellie waiting in the car.

'You're late,' Ellie says.

'Late for what?'

'I have a surprise for you girls,' Angie says, as she pulls out of the driveway.

'Daddy called!' Ellie crows.

'And I missed it? Are you kidding me?'

'An incredibly quick call,' Angie says.

'Like five minutes. Super fast.'

'He's moving to a new base. And it's normal for mail to be slow.'

'Write me, he said to me; and to Mom and to you, Alice. He wants letters. Lots of letters. I've already written him two times and drawn four pictures.'

'Where are we going?' Alice asks.

'You'll see,' Angie says.

'Did he say where he is?'

'F.O.B. Falcon,' Ellie says.

'For the time being,' Angie adds.

'What's F.O.B?'

'Forward Operating Base.'

'Everything has an acronym in the army,' Ellie says. 'Like they've got their own special language. F.O.B. and TNT and HQ and IED.'

'What do you know about IEDs?'

'They keep inventing new ones: VBIED:

67

vehicle borne IED; SVBIED: suicide vehicle borne IED; DBIED: dog borne or donkey borne IED.'

'Where do you get these little tips?' Alice asks.

'Bobby DiFiori in the fourth grade likes to watch CNN.'

'And he talks about this stuff?!'

'On the playground. At recess.'

'Oh, my God . . . '

Angie pulls up to the Holschers' farmhouse and beeps the horn, like it's a prearranged signal. Edna comes out the front door and Hank walks up from behind the barn. They're both wearing muck boots and barn jackets and grinning from ear to ear.

Mom makes introductions, and Edna walks right up and takes Ellie by the hand.

'Mrs. Holscher . . . ' Ellie begins.

'Call me Edna.'

'Where are we going?'

'You'll see.'

They all follow Edna and Ellie to the barn, all the way down the central aisle to the last stall on the left.

Hank unhooks the door.

'Go ahead.'

Inside the stall, in knee deep straw is a mama goat and three brand new baby kids, nursing.

Ellie goes right to her knees, beside them.

'They were born yesterday afternoon,' Hank offers. 'Triplets. Can you beat that?'

'Can I touch them?' Ellie can barely contain her excitement.

'Sure.'

'The mama won't mind?'

'Let her see you. Go slow,' Edna says.

'What's her name?' Alice asks.

'Goldie.'

'Hi, Goldie,' Alice says, stroking her nose.

'Can I hold one?' Ellie asks.

'As soon as they're done nursing, they'll be climbing all over you.'

Ellie is petting the baby goats and Alice joins her while Angie, Edna, and Hank watch them.

'They're so cute. Can we bring one home?'

'They're gonna get big, Ellie.'

'I don't care.'

'We've picked out two names for the babies so far,' Edna says. 'Blondie and Walden. Got any good ideas for the third kid?'

Ellie considers.

'What kind of goats are they?' Alice asks.

'LaManchas. Milk goats from Spain. They're friendly, easy to handle, and great producers. You like goat's milk?' Hank asks.

'I don't know, I've never tried it.'

'I like it,' Ellie announces.

'You've never had it either!'

'I can just tell.'

'Can you tell who's who?' Angie asks.

'The gray one is Walden. The sandy colored one is Blondie. And the one with the white feet needs a name.'

'Niblets,' Ellie says.

'Niblets it is.' Hank laughs.

'Really?'

The kids finish nursing and, just like Edna

69

said, they climb all over the girls, nibbling their fingers, rubbing their heads against them. Ellie is giggling.

'I can't believe how soft they are,' Alice says.

'Hi, Niblets,' Ellie whispers into the white-footed kid's ear, as she hugs him against her.

'We've got baby lambs and new chicks, too, if you want to see them,' Hank says.

'Maybe later,' Ellie says, in a dreamy voice.

'C'mon in the house when you're ready. Just be sure to latch the stall door.'

Alice looks up and smiles at her mom; just a wide-open uncomplicated happy kid smile. Angie bursts into a laugh.

'They're great, aren't they?'

'Yeah. Really great.'

Hank puts his arm around Angie's shoulder as the grown-ups turn to leave the barn.

'I made pineapple upside down cake,' Edna calls back to them. 'And you can try some goat's milk when you come inside.'

April 4th

Matt's letters are finally starting to arrive. Sometimes in a bunch, sometimes just one for Angie. He writes Angie every day he's not out on patrol.

Ellie collects the mail from the mailbox after school and puts everything on the hall table. Alice and Ellie never open anything until Angie gets home, no matter how tempting. After work, Angie pours herself a glass of wine and they all sit in the living room to open the letter, or letters if they're lucky. If there's only one, one for Mom, she'll read the sections she feels she can share or things Dad asks her to tell them.

Tell Ellie we get M&Ms in our ration packets. Some of them are dated 1992.

Tell Eddie there's a 21-year-old kid named Lewis from West Virginia who has a 1982 Ford Mustang. He's planning on going to all the hotrod shows when he gets home. And there's this new kid named Chad. 19. Hell of a poker player. He's from Wyoming and he loves Texas Hold 'Em. He laughs and laughs every time he takes his buddies' money.

Tell Ellie I saw a blue and green parrot when we were outside the wire yesterday. Perched on a toppled date palm. Where the heck did he come from? Later that day, a dirty, dusty old tabby cat walked out of a building we'd just dropped twenty shells on. Each one big enough to end the world. Tail in the air. Unbelievable.

Tell Alice she will not believe what I have to do to get some coffee when we're out on patrol. There's no electricity and no more water than what we're carrying on our backs. After two hours of sleeping on a cement floor, coffee becomes very important. I collect packets of Taster's Choice instant coffee from the kids who are too young to be hooked on the stuff. And then I beg the powdered-cream and sugar packets we all get in our prefab rations. You open your mouth, pour in all three, toss in some water, and shake your head violently. Instant coffee. *Outside the wire. Good morning, sunshine!*

The part of the letter Angie won't read, or can't read, or can't trust herself to give voice to, says:

Angie, sweetheart,

I miss you more than I could have ever believed. I knew I was going to miss you but I had no idea how much. And it doesn't go away, it doesn't calm down, it doesn't fit inside my pocket with your letters. It's like an ache, Angie, a constant ache for you.

I can't imagine all the weeks and months ahead of missing you.

I miss our girls, I miss work, the house, the garden. Nothing like being out here to make you appreciate home.

You'll laugh at me, but I love thinking about closing up the house every night. Walking downstairs barefoot, turning out lights, locking the back door. Just that sense of easy quiet, knowing the girls are safe in bed, and that you're in our bed waiting for me. Home. I dream of home, Angie, and you know I dream of you.

Matt

Later, when Alice slips the letter out of the envelope and reads it as fast as she can, the words, no, the feelings, the impossibly intense feelings burn into her. It's like opening a bedroom door.

April 5th

Three weeks after Matt ships out Ellie gets the stool so she can reach Matt's shelf of favorite books. First up: his leather-bound college dictionary.

She brings this to the breakfast table and announces she's going to read the dictionary while Daddy is gone. Alice is thinking, *yeah, right*, as Ellie opens Webster's Dictionary, Second Edition, reads the inscription from Dad's mom wishing him good luck in college, and begins at the beginning, right there on page one. While eating Cheerios. Ellie gets up and digs a pink notebook out of her school backpack and begins noting down superfascinating words.

Ellie's current teacher is a dictionary nut. She purportedly has hundreds of dictionaries, though this does not sound remotely credible to Alice. Where do you put them? What do you do with them? What, exactly, is the point? She tries to imagine perky Mrs. Baker, who is not even five feet tall, saying to her husband, 'I'm just going to curl up with a good dictionary.'

But none of this matters to Ellie, the annoying little autodidact. She is eating up the A's like they are the elixir of knowledge, like this is a book with a plot, an action adventure, mystery, crime thriller, page turner, can't-put-it-down-exciting read.

'Ellie,' Alice can't resist saying, 'Dad *used* the dictionary, he didn't read it.'

'How do you know what Daddy did or didn't do in college?'

'If she wants to read the dictionary, let her read the dictionary,' Angie chimes in.

'You don't think it's a little — '

'Mrs. Baker says there can be ineffable joy in pursuing the absurd.'

Both Alice and Angie turn to stare at Ellie and think, simultaneously — if that's possible — where does she come up with this stuff? and, Ellie and Mrs. Baker were made for each other.

'You want to know my new favorite word?' Ellie asks.

As if they could say no.

'*Sesquipedalian*, which means '*long word*.' I'm collecting them: long, rare words.'

Angie is making sandwiches for a change, Alice notices, as she opens the paper to international news. It's just PB & J, but still. And then she sees the headline.

'Gram's taking you two for haircuts after school today.'

'Finally!' Ellie says.

Alice closes the paper, folds it in half.

'She'll pick you up here at four thirty.'

'I have practice.'

'I know exactly what I want. I have a picture,' Ellie announces.

'You'll just have to get out of practice a little early, Alice.'

'You're gonna be surprised, Mom,' Ellie sings.

'I don't need a haircut.'

'Just a trim.'

'I don't need a trim.'

'Do you know how long it took me to get the

74

two of you an appointment when Gram was available?'

'Ellie could still go.'

'You're both going. End of discussion.'

'But, Mom — '

Henry arrives, shouting, 'Good morning, Mrs. Bliss!' As they head out the door, Alice grabs the front section of the paper. She passes up Henry's invitation to come to the auditorium while he plays piano and instead sits on the front steps and watches all the students and teachers arriving at school. Does everyone have a secret life, she wonders? Is everyone carrying an impossible, unbearable secret?

Students stream up the steps and into the building past the army recruiter's table, the baseball bake sale table, and the lone ninth-grade girl passing out fliers for the pep rally. When the stream becomes a trickle she gets up, dusts off the back of her pants, and heads into school, down the hall, past the principal's office, on her way to the stairs to her homeroom. She suddenly notices that everything is worn: the linoleum, the paint on the edges of the doors, the ceiling is cracked and veined. When she glances into the principal's office she can see Mrs. Bradley; even Mrs. Bradley looks worn as she pulls her sky blue sweater over her soft stomach and then leans over to search for a file in the file cabinet. Alice is trying to remember — didn't somebody tell her that one of Mrs. Bradley's kids died of cancer when they were little? Yet here she is every day.

Mr. Fisher, who actually knows every single

kid in all four grades in the high school by name, steps out from his office to ask Mrs. Bradley for something and before he speaks, his forehead is creased in a frown. He is pinching the bridge of his nose, as though to relieve pressure or pain. Both of them look pale and drained. And there it is again: worn.

Mr. Fisher straightens his slumped shoulders, leans both fists on Mrs. Bradley's desk, and says something that makes her laugh. You can tell he used to be a football player; he's got that low to the ground swagger to his walk even though he's now too chubby and about fifteen years too old to pull that off particularly well.

Alice's legs are feeling so heavy she's not sure she'll be able to walk up the flight of stairs to her homeroom. Maybe she could just head on down the first floor hall to the nurse's office and ask to lie down. Or back out the door and down the street to Gram's apartment, or all the way home. Suddenly she just wants to lie down on the floor. She crosses to the wall and leans against a locker. She manages to slide along the wall to a seated position before she falls down. She's thinking she should bend her knees; she should fold herself up so no one will notice her, but her legs are ignoring her. She grabs fistfuls of her dad's shirt as she wraps her arms around herself, trying to hold on to something solid. She's having trouble breathing. She thinks she might scream or throw up or pass out. She thinks that not one of these options is a good one.

The National Guard and marine recruiters are folding up their tables, packing their brochures into boxes, chatting and laughing and greeting students they seem to already know by name. Their uniforms, their boots, their bearing, everything about them seems to be shouting at her to pull herself together.

Bells start ringing; she's missed homeroom entirely. How did that happen? Doors are being flung open and she can hear hundreds of feet coming down the hallways above her and all around her. She brings her hands up to her ears to drown out the sound.

A crowd eddies around her, edging closer. No one approaches her, no one kneels down to ask if she's okay. Some kids gawk and move on, others hang on waiting to see how this will play out. Alice keeps her hands clamped over her ears so she can't hear their comments.

The principal has put on his suit jacket and straightened his tie. He is moving down the hallway at the fastest clip he is capable of with the school nurse in tow, the very small, very shy Miss Lambert. They are pushing through the crowds of students, and Mr. Fisher is reminding them to *Keep moving! Get to class!* The students reluctantly break up to let him through, and most of them head off to class. A few just draw back slightly to watch from a safer distance. No one is saying much. Mr. Fisher raises his voice and sends the stragglers on their way.

Somehow Henry is there and he is talking to the principal, gesturing and standing up straight, and even from where she sits on the floor barely daring to look at him through her lashes, Alice can tell he is being very, very convincing.

But this is a fleeting impression when what floods her mind's eye is a road called Highway 10, fifteen miles west of Baghdad, a road she has Googled in the school's computer lab and watched and contemplated, a road her father undoubtedly travels on.

Henry manages to get her to the nurse's office and settled onto a cot. He's about to leave when she hands him the clipping from the *Democrat and Chronicle* that has been burning a hole in her pocket. He bends his head to read the article.

Four American soldiers, members of the National Guard from New York, were traveling in three Humvees heading west on Highway 10 toward the city of Falluja. The U.S. military reports that they were on combat patrol when their convoy was attacked by improvised explosive devices, small-arms fire, and rocket-propelled grenades. Two soldiers were burned beyond recognition, a third soldier was dragged off. When found, the body was so badly mutilated the military announced it had found the bodies of two men, not one. The body had no head, legs, or arms. Organs were removed. A fourth soldier has been declared missing. There were no survivors. One of the Humvees burned with such intensity that the surrounding trees were incinerated.

He carefully folds the paper into a tiny square and puts it into his back pocket.

'Alice, you've gotta stop reading the papers.'

'How else am I gonna find out what's going on?'

'Maybe it's better not to know.'

'I don't think so.'

'There are guys who — '

'Who what?'

'Who survive, who make it back.'

'Members of the National Guard from New York. Did you read that part?'

'There are dozens, maybe hundreds of men from — '

'Thousands.'

'Okay. Thousands.'

'He travels that road, Henry.'

'You don't know that for sure.'

'It's a good guess.'

'Reading about it will not make anything better.'

'Not reading about it makes it seem like I don't care.'

'No, Alice, that's not the way it works.'

'How do you know?'

'I know you're making yourself a little crazy here.'

'Just a little?'

'And that Ellie needs you and your mom needs you and — '

'I took the paper so my mom wouldn't see it.'

Miss Lambert sticks her head in the door to remind Henry to get to class. She waits, too, while he gets up from the edge of the cot.

'Could we just have a minute?' he asks her.

Lydia Lambert is young and thin and nervous. She is new to this job. She quit the hospital job

79

she took right out of nursing school, then floundered for a while between two local nursing homes. It was distressing to learn, after all that school and all that training, that she didn't actually like being around sick or dying people. They make her anxious, really anxious.

High school kids don't make Lydia anxious; they make her sad, with their cramps and sprains and heartache and heartbreak and above all, with their loneliness. Being young can be so lonely, she thinks; more lonely than anything.

She decides to let them be.

★ ★ ★

'Do you want to go home? I could take you home.'

'That's okay.'

'I'll come back after second period. You'll be going stir crazy by then.'

'Wait, Henry . . . '

'What?

'Don't go.'

Henry sits on the floor next to Alice's cot.

'Tell me he's gonna be okay, Henry.'

'He's gonna be okay, Alice.'

'Tell me every day, every time you see me.'

'Okay.'

'Help me believe it.'

'If anybody can make it through, your dad — '

'Yeah. Matt Bliss can do anything, right?'

'That's what everybody says.'

Alice looks around at the stainless-steel table and the cupboard full of Band-Aids and aspirin

80

and gauze pads and Ace bandages and wishes she still lived in a world where any of these things could make anything better.

'They cut up the bodies, Henry.'

'Alice, don't — '

'Why would anybody . . . ? God . . . how do you fight against that?'

'I don't know.'

Henry leans his head against the cot and inadvertently against her leg, or perhaps not so inadvertently, and straightens his legs in front of him. If she stretches her arm out, Alice can just barely reach the top of his head. It is nearly, but not quite, touch. She doesn't know why this is so important right now, but it is.

★　★　★

B.D. is not happy with Alice when she leaves practice at four fifteen and sprints for home. Another little checkmark next to her name on B.D.'s clipboard, Alice thinks. She doesn't want any checkmarks next to her name, just improving times.

Gram and Ellie are waiting in the car when she turns into the driveway. Great. Now she gets to go to the hairdressers in her running shorts and sweaty T-shirt. Ellie bamboozled Gram into letting her ride shotgun, so Alice climbs into the backseat and pulls a sweatshirt out of her backpack and over her head.

'Hi, sweetheart,' Gram says.

'You stink,' Ellie announces.

'Shut up, Ellie!'

81

Gram puts the car into gear and slowly backs out of the driveway.

'We're just going to make it.'

'Don't worry, Gram, they always make us wait.'

'Daddy called.'

'He did?'

'For two minutes.'

'And I missed it?'

'It was a terrible connection,' Gram adds. 'We were shouting.'

'He's okay?'

'He sounded good,' Gram says.

'He sounded *great*,' Ellie crows.

He's okay floods through Alice and she takes what feels like her first deep breath all day.

*   *   *

At Headlines, Alice's basic trim takes ten minutes. Ellie is furiously flipping through magazines and turning pages down.

'I need glasses,' Ellie says as she shrugs out of her coat and climbs onto the stylist's chair.

'What?' Alice asks.

'They tested us at school today. These are the ones I want,' she says, tossing Alice a magazine. Then, turning to Patty, she unfolds the picture of the haircut she wants.

'Is your mom okay with this?' Patty asks.

'Oh, yeah,' Ellie bluffs.

'You sure?'

'Totally.'

Alice gets up to take a look at the picture.

82

'You want *that?*'

'Yes.'

'I could do that at home with a bowl over your head.'

'Ha, ha,' Ellie says, not laughing.

'Who is that?'

'I don't know. Some film star from the old days.'

'Gram? You know who this is?' Alice asks.

'Louise Brooks,' Gram says. 'I think she's the one who inspired everybody to bob their hair.'

'It'll be cute on her,' Patty offers.

'You sure you want this haircut?' Alice asks.

'I love it,' Ellie says. 'Love, love, love it.'

'The bangs are really short, Ellie.'

'That's the point.'

'Okay, then.'

Alice sits down to watch as Ellie's braids are cut off. Gram sits down beside her and reaches over to take Alice's hand.

'Your mother is going to kill me,' she whispers, as she pulls out a handkerchief and blows her nose.

★   ★   ★

Patty carefully saves the braids in an envelope, knowing that Angie will probably want them. And if not, Ellie can donate them to Locks of Love. Ellie has her hands over her eyes so she can have the maximum surprise when it's all done.

'You can open your eyes,' Patty says.

Ellie takes a look; her expression is dead serious.

83

'Can I see the back?' she asks.

Patty gets a mirror.

'Okay. Can you take the cape off?'

Ellie hops off the chair. She's wearing a dress with a big skirt and cap sleeves. She twirls around and her skirt bells out around her and her hair flies out from her face and for sure, she will be the only little girl with this hairstyle, the only little girl to wear these kinds of dresses. She looks like she could leave the ground she has so much energy, her skinny arms in a blur as she twirls. And she is grinning from ear to ear.

'Love it, love it, love it,' she says, giving Patty a hug.

And then, turning to Gram, 'Can we go to the glasses store?'

'Glasses? What kind of glasses?'

'I need glasses, Gram. I told you in the car.'

'Well, we probably need to ask your mom.'

'Can we just look? I like these,' Ellie says, handing Gram a magazine.

★ ★ ★

At the eyeglass place Ellie is not happy with the selection they have for kids. She pulls out her picture and gives it to the guy behind the counter. He's incredulous, but goes to the locked cabinet with the designer frames and hands her a pair. She tries them on. The lenses are elongated rectangles and the frames are dark green plastic.

'Too big,' Gram says, thinking that will be that.

But Ellie studies her reflection in the mirror,

turning this way and that, trying to keep the glasses from sliding off her face and not having much luck. Alice suddenly has this stab of fear for Ellie. With this haircut and these glasses she will be teased mercilessly; Alice has already swallowed several choice phrases rather then throw them at Ellie. But now that she's actually looking at her she can see that Ellie is really skinny, maybe even skinnier than usual, and pale, superpale, like maybe she's coming down with the flu or something, or maybe she's not sleeping well or eating well and Alice thinks maybe she hasn't been paying attention to the right things and maybe she should be paying more attention to her sister, and how is she ever going to manage with one more thing to worry about?

'Can you order these in a smaller size?' Ellie asks the clerk.

'Sure. We can have them for you in a week.'

'How much are they?' Gram asks.

'Three fifty.'

'Three *hundred* and fifty?' Ellie asks.

A tight-lipped smile from the clerk.

'Thanks so much,' Gram says, ushering them out the door.

In the car, holding the envelope with her braids in it, Ellie is unusually quiet. Even when Gram gets to talking about the chickens she's thinking about getting and the chicken coop Uncle Eddie has promised to build for her, even though knowing Uncle Eddie, that could take another year, and how Ellie is going to be her right-hand girl in the chicken-and-egg business.

Ellie and Gram love chickens. Alice does not really find chickens remotely appealing, let alone lovable, but Gram keeps telling her: 'You just wait and see. When we get our first baby chicks . . . '

'eBay,' Ellie says out of the blue. 'Second-hand stores. We have some options.'

'What are you talking about?' Alice asks.

'I'm not giving up on those glasses.'

★   ★   ★

At home, Ellie drops her coat on the floor and twirls her dress and her new haircut for Angie. When Ellie hands her the envelope with her braids inside, Angie sits in the nearest chair and bursts into tears.

'What's the matter, Mom? Don't you like it?' Ellie asks.

'Sure I like it. It's just . . . It's just . . . '

'Don't you think it's pretty?' Ellie asks.

'It's really pretty,' Angie says. 'And really different.'

'Nobody else is gonna have a haircut anything like this. Not in my school. Not even in your school, Alice. It's unique. Unparalleled. Radically distinctive and without equal! Can we take a picture so Daddy can see?'

And Ellie does a wacky herky-jerky dance, her skinny arms pumping up and down over her head, her elbows jutting out; her feet flying. Ellie is taking interpretive dance to new heights, Alice thinks, as she tries to swallow the ache she feels looking at her sister's braids in her mother's lap.

86

April 8th

'What are you doing?'

Alice is in the front hall closet, surrounded by photo albums and photo boxes, when her mother, wearing one of her dad's old sweatshirts, interrupts.

'And are you ever going to take that shirt off?'

Alice considers which question to answer.

'I'm looking for that picture of me and Dad with the shovel and the pitchfork. The one Uncle Eddie took last October.'

'What do you want that for?'

'I'm gonna send it to Dad in the care package.'

'What about your school photo?'

'No way.'

'Daddy would like that.'

'You send it then.'

'It's you right now.'

'God, I hope not.'

Angie gives her a look. Here it comes, Alice thinks. The appearances are not everything speech. The *it's what's inside that counts* speech.

Yup. There she goes. Launches right in. With embellishments even. Alice tunes out the sounds and watches her mother's very pretty mouth forming the familiar words.

Alice does not make the appropriate murmuring noises in response, the oh, mom, thanks so much, you really understand, don't you, and instead just looks at her mother thinking, why do you do this, when we both know it's total garbage?

87

These silent looks are like a little ticking bomb.

At first Alice can see Angie thinking, in a clenched teeth sort of way, *I'm not going to rise to the bait*, but before you know it, in a nanosecond, she's furious.

'You're making a mess.'

'I am not.'

'I spent days organizing these photos.'

'Days?'

'Any order I had managed to — '

'I'll put it all back.'

'The way it was?'

'Yeah. Exactly the way it was.'

Just go away, Alice thinks. I was perfectly fine before you walked in here. Angie opens her mouth to say something else, thinks better of it, and turns on her heel and leaves.

Now Alice is thinking maybe it *is* a dumb photo. Now she's thinking about how she's not pretty and how that's probably evident in this photo. It's probably been evident forever, even in her baby pictures. Now she's thinking about this crap when before she was just looking for a photo where she and her dad were having fun and goofing around and it didn't have anything to do with being pretty.

This is why girls hate their mothers, Alice thinks, as she finds the photo.

They're in the garden, standing in the middle of their pumpkin patch. Dad is holding a pitchfork; Alice is holding a shovel. There are two bushel baskets tipped over like cornucopia, full of corn and peppers and zucchini and gourds and tomatoes. They're wearing matching Red Wings T-shirts and baseball hats, and they're both trying — and failing — to look serious.

There's another one and another one — a little series of shots she hadn't remembered. Uncle Eddie caught them laughing and making faces and pretending their biggest pumpkin was too heavy to lift.

She rifles through the box to find the negatives, pockets them, and puts the originals back exactly where she found them. She's going to send her dad the whole series.

She raids the change jar before hopping on her bike to go to the drugstore at the Four Corners to make copies. On her way out the door she tells Ellie she'll be back in half an hour max and then they can seal up the box and take it to the post office.

'Get some batteries,' Ellie yells after her. 'They all need double As!'

Alice pops back inside.

'Mom! I'm taking five dollars to get Dad batteries!'

And she's out, she's on her bike. Only now does she realize how cold it still is. There's a misting kind of rain and the roads are all slushy. She's gonna get soaked if she rides in the street. She veers off onto the sidewalk, which is marginally better but at least she won't get sprayed by the passing cars. She pedals past Mrs. Piantowski's and Mrs. Minty's and then there's Gram's restaurant, with people waiting outside even in this weather. Happens every Saturday and Sunday, people queuing up around the block.

At the drugstore she marches up to the very tall, very skinny high school boy manning the photo machine, explains what she wants, begs him to make her photos right now, this very minute, *it's urgent*, and then heads off to find batteries.

True to his word, Steven — she reads his badge — has her photos ready. While checking out, she looks at her dad's watch. Eleven o'clock. They'll just make it.

Outside Henry is standing next to her bike.

'Hey, Alice.'

'Hi, Henry.'

'You want to go sit at the counter at your Gram's and have breakfast or something?'

'I can't, Henry. I have to get to the post office before it closes.'

'After the post office, then.'

'I have to ask my mom.'

'I'll meet you at the post office. She'll probably say yes, don't you think?'

'Yeah. I gotta go.'

'Post office! High noon!' He shouts after her.

At home, Ellie and Angie have the box all ready. Alice tucks the photos into an envelope and slips in the letter she's been writing her dad all week during boring classes at school. It's a dumb letter, she knows that, a rambling, dull letter. She read the guidelines from the army: your soldier wants to hear the news from home. But there is no news in Belknap, there's just the weather and school and Mom and Ellie

90

and Gram and Uncle Eddie and running and not being able to sleep and missing him and wishing . . . But you are strongly advised to keep any and all worries to yourself. All the sleepless nights, and, let's face it, the fights with Mom, all the real stuff, you're supposed to leave that out.

Ellie hugs the box after they seal it up and plants a big kiss right on Dad's name.

They rush into jackets and boots and head to the post office. As if what they're all feeling right now will reach him, as if the hustle and the bustle will somehow cross the miles.

They stop at Gram's, where she has very carefully packed up a loaf of Matt's favorite harvest bread made with pumpkin and walnuts. She has followed the army guidelines to the letter and has real hopes this bread will make it and still taste good by the time it gets there.

Slipping inside the post office at a whisper before twelve, they're giddy because they've made it in time. The two boxes go on the scale: they fill out the customs forms and pay the postman. But then there's the walk from the counter to the door, with the postman following behind to lock up. Just those few yards and the air starts to go out of the balloon. Outside, Angie pulls her coat around her as though she could hug away the loneliness, and reaches out to take Ellie's hand.

'Let's go to Gram's for lunch.'

'I meant to ask if I could go to Gram's with Henry.'

'That's fine. Ellie and I can have a booth all to ourselves, right sweetheart?'

Alice takes a look at her mother standing on the steps of the post office squinting into the rain. She wants to say, I see it; I notice all the things we are not saying, all the moments we are silently agreeing to ignore. It's like a shadow that follows them and falls between them; this other life full of other feelings, this yawning emptiness where her father belongs.

And then Henry is there, materializing out of thin air, twirling Ellie off her feet and singing something right into her ear that makes her laugh out loud.

'Don't tell,' he whispers.

'I won't,' she grins back at him.

They walk to Gram's and for some strange reason it's pretty quiet. The line out the door is gone. Ellie and Angie sit at a booth while Henry and Alice settle in at the counter.

Sally, who is trying yet another shade of strawberry blonde, comes over to pour coffee as Gram sticks her head out from the kitchen to say hi.

'Hi, Gram!'

Ellie rushes her for a hug.

'I'll join you for a cup of coffee as soon as I can.'

Gram gives Alice a kiss and says to both of them: 'If you want to help me clean up, breakfast's on me.'

'But I wanted to . . . ' Henry begins.

He gets off the stool and whispers to Gram: 'I invited Alice, Mrs. Bird.'

'Really.'

'I've got snow shoveling money.'

'You're too young to date.'

'This is not a date. And her mother's right there.'

'Don't go getting any ideas.'

'I wouldn't.'

'Yes, you would.'

'Not in front of you and Sally and Ellie and her mother I wouldn't.'

'I could still use your help with sweeping and washing the floors and the final round of pots and pans. For that you get the employee discount.'

'Deal.'

'This is not a date, Henry.'

'Absolutely not, Mrs. Bird.'

Henry slides back onto his stool next to Alice.

'I hope you're hungry,' he says. 'I'm having the lumberjack special.'

'You are not! You can't possibly eat all that.'

'Wanna bet? Are you actually drinking coffee?'

'With a lot of milk and sugar. Wanna try it?'

She pushes the mug toward him. He sips. Considers. Hates it.

Sally sits down next to them to take their orders, leans into Henry, with a lot of cleavage, and enjoys his blush.

'You should've seen it in here an hour ago. All morning! A madhouse! We're out of every kind of bread except white and English muffins. No more eggs Benedict, no more Canadian bacon.'

'You got the lumberjack special?' Henry asks, looking anywhere but at Sally.

'Bacon or sausage?'

'Bacon.'

'How do you want your eggs?'

'Over easy.'

'Pancakes or French toast?'

'Get the French toast,' Alice says.

'French toast, please.'

'Is this a date?' Sally wants to know.

'What?' Alice asks.

'Your Gram's all worried this could be a date or something and you're too young.'

'It's not a date,' they both say simultaneously, and perhaps too loudly.

'Alice helps me with math all the time. I just wanted to do something nice for her.'

'Awwww . . . The usual for you, Alice?'

'I want my dad's usual.'

'Corned beef hash comin' up.'

There's an awkward pause as Sally shouts their order into the kitchen. Alice glances up into the long mirror over the counter and catches a glimpse of Ellie snuggled up close to Angie. Angie is stroking Ellie's hair, lost in thought.

'You can't do anything around here without everybody trying to . . . '

'I think it's really nice, Henry.'

'You do?'

'Yeah.'

'Well, that's good.'

'But let's not get weird, okay?'

'No, no, no. Of course.'

'Like you're acting nervous and stuff. And you should quit it.'

'Okay.'

He looks at her. He looks away.

'Listen . . . ' and he trails off, uncertain how to proceed.

'What?'

'You know how there's the dance coming up in May?'

'Henry!'

'What?'

'Okay. Wait a minute. Maybe I'm jumping to conclusions. Is there somebody you want to ask?'

'Duh, Alice.'

'Julie? Julie Watson?'

'Are you kidding me?'

'Her sidekick, Abby?'

'You, Alice. I want to ask you.'

'Henry!'

'What's so wrong with that?'

'We're like almost related.'

'We are not!'

'Okay, but — '

'I even asked my mom to teach me how to dance.'

'You want to dance with me?'

'Yes.'

'I think the dances your mom knows how to dance may not be relevant in this case.'

'Well, there's all the stuff about how to hold your partner for a slow dance, and not looking at your feet, and apologizing if you step on her feet, and offering to get punch.'

'Manners.'

'Dance manners. Yeah.'

Alice puts more sugar in her coffee.

'You are full of surprises, Henry.'

'Somebody else already asked you.'

'No, they didn't.'

'Are you saying no?'

'No, I'm not saying no, I'm just saying . . . '

Their food arrives.

'If it's no, tell me quick. I can't stand long drawn out no's.'

'I don't know what to say.'

'Say yes. It'll be fun.'

'Really.'

'Yeah!'

'You honestly think so.'

'Yeah, I do.'

'Have you ever had one minute of fun in that gym before?'

'No, but — '

'Maybe if it was just you and me, Henry, it might be fun. But our classmates will be there. Remember them?'

'I don't care about them.'

'Do we have to get dressed up?'

'Yes! That's part of the fun.'

'Okay.'

'Okay? Is that yes?'

'Yes.'

'And we'll get dressed up and everything.'

'And we'll send my dad a picture.'

'My mom even said she'd drive us.'

'Let's walk like we always do.'

'Really?'

'Don't you think that would be kind of cool at night?'

'Will your mom let you?'

'Probably. Can I have a bite of your French toast?'

'Sure.'

'Gram makes the best French toast in the world.' He passes her the plate.

'We could get Uncle Eddie to pick us up. In one of his retro cars.'

'That would be awesome. Maybe a convertible. Maybe he'd wear a chauffeur's hat and be the first car idling at the door when everybody comes out.'

'Yeah. Maybe he would.'

Henry, relieved, tucks into his food. Gram comes out and sits down in the booth with Angie and Ellie. Sally joins them. Alice is looking at everything. Henry with egg yolk on his upper lip, Gram tired and asking Ellie to rub her shoulders, Sally looking a little haggard, like she's got a headache, maybe left over from Friday night, maybe from more trouble with one of her boys, Angie stretched out with her head resting against the back of the booth, Ellie kneeling behind Gram working on her shoulders with her little hands.

Sally gets up and puts the CLOSED sign in the door and then flips the radio to her favorite country station. A song of lost love fills the room as Sally waltzes across the floor to start wiping down the counters.

'That Teddy Thompson's got a nice voice,' Sally says.

'That's not all he's got,' Gram adds.

'Gram!'

'I wouldn't kick him out of bed for eating crackers.'

'What does *that* mean?' Alice wants to know.

97

Angie is laughing and covering Ellie's ears.

'Means he's so fine he can break *all* the rules,' Gram says.

Henry dips his head so low it's almost in his plate. Alice turns her back on the sight of Gram, Sally, and Angie cracking up over Teddy Thompson and concentrates on composing the perfect bite: hash, egg with some soft yolk, plenty of pepper, and a dab of ketchup. She puts it in her mouth and closes her eyes and tries to let the taste bring her dad into focus inside of her. It doesn't work, not that she was really expecting it to. Mostly she thinks, not bad, but I wish I'd ordered waffles.

April 10th

Alice arrives home from practice to find Angie on the phone with Matt. Angie gives her a quick smile, then turns her back and closes the kitchen door. Alice walks in anyway.

'Is it Dad? Can I talk to him?'

Angie waves her away and closes the door behind her. So Alice stands just outside the closed kitchen door, furious. She can occasionally hear her dad's voice, but very few words. She waits a minute until her mom is distracted again and pushes the door open a crack. Now she can hear the excitement in his voice.

'C'mon, honey. It's what we've trained for.'

'You promised me, Matt — '

'It's the army, remember? They make the decisions.'

'This is what you *wanted*. Admit it.'
'Angie . . .'
There's a pause.
'How are the kids?'
'They're fine.'
'Are you getting my checks okay?'
'Two so far.'
'I know they're slow, but that's pretty good. It means we're in the system. Are you getting my letters?'
'They take about ten days.'
'But they're getting there?'
'Yeah. They're great, Matt.'
'Write me. Write me more. You don't know what a letter means.'
'I will.'
'I wrote to both girls today. Tell them, okay?'
'I will.'
'I've gotta go.'
'Matt, this is so hard.'
'I know. I know it is.'
'I wish you could call more.'
'Me, too. But we're moving around so much right now.'
'Come home to me.'
'You know I will.'
'Stay safe.'
'I love you, Angie. I love you.'

★ ★ ★

Alice lets the door close completely. She can hear Angie hanging up the receiver and then crossing to the sink where she turns on the tap.

Alice retreats to the hall table where, breaking with tradition, she picks up the letter addressed to her and tears it open, not waiting for Angie or Ellie, not waiting for anyone.

Dear Alice,
It was great to get your letter and hear about your running. I'm so proud of you. I want to meet that girl Ginger on your team. And B.D., too.
You asked me to describe Falluja. There's all the stuff you've heard about: the trash, the bombed-out buildings, the piles of white rocks, the dead wires, the burned cars. But there's so much else that doesn't make it into the news. There are kids playing soccer. There are goats, and outhouses, and even beds on rooftops. Date palms, and sand-colored buildings, razor wire, fences, blast walls. From rooftops you can see the river snaking through the city and the network of irrigation canals and the desert in the distance. The dust is so fine it coats everything: your hair, your face, your throat, your teeth. The mosques — there are two big ones — are really beautiful — green and cobalt blue domes that you can see from everywhere in the city.
Some of the market places are still thriving and the Andaloos Market, near us, is lively as anything. You can buy everything from sodas to car parts to T-shirts, sandals, scarves, soccer balls, even furniture, all along a crowded street barely wide enough for a HMMWV to pass through.
They sell delicious flatbread that marines call

100

'Muj bread.' It looks like a tortilla. Two bucks for 24 pieces. It's a deal. Great with my morning coffee. If only. Ha ha!

Write me. I love your letters. And I love you.
Dad

April 14th

There is no practice today. B.D. is sick or something. Alice feels lost.

Drifting past the high school playing fields, headed for the cut-through to the elementary school, Alice crosses the track, starts up the hill and steps in dog poop. Shit! All these people who walk their dogs here; they know the leash laws! They know that kids use these paths. Idiots! She's stumbling around trying to wipe the crap off in the grass, and looks up to see John Kimball laughing at her. The cutest guy in school who has never so much as glanced her way ever, not even once, not that she cares; now he takes a moment from doing something spectacular on the baseball field, now he decides to stop and look at her.

'Asshole!' she shouts. Which only makes him laugh louder. 'Asshole!' she shouts again and to her amazement, he drops his mitt and heads over to her.

'Hey, I'm sorry.'

'Go away.'

'Listen — '

'You're just making it worse.'

'No, that was stupid. I didn't mean — '

'Didn't mean what? You're so full of shit.'

'You're crying.'

'No, I'm not!'

'I didn't know you could cry and be mad at the same time.'

'You don't know much, do you?'

'Okay, okay,' he says, and starts backing off, still looking at her.

She looks down and can't believe her sneaker. This must've been some really big dog.

'Alice, right?' He calls out to her.

'What?'

'Your name's Alice, right?'

She looks past John and sees Stephie and Jeremy Baskin holding hands, standing with a bunch of kids, and realizes they've been watching and of course they're laughing. They're all laughing at crazy Alice Bliss.

Fuck you, Alice thinks, as she heads blindly toward the path through the woods. She's stumbling around like an idiot and tripping over rocks and careening into branches, which are lashing her face. Is that blood? Is her face scratched? Oh, who *cares*, she just wants to get this shit off her sneaker; she's madly scraping away on rocks, on roots, in the leaves and pine needles, and good god — it's almost coming up over her socks! when Henry appears.

'Alice, what are you doing here?'

Why does he sound so mad, she wonders as she grabs the sweatshirt she's got tied around her waist. She can't believe she is wiping her face and blowing her nose on her favorite sweatshirt.

'I thought you had track.'

102

She rolls up the sweatshirt and stuffs it in her backpack.

'It was canceled.'

'Why didn't you tell me?'

'What difference does it make?'

'What difference does it make?! I've been leaving band practice early every day for three weeks to pick up Ellie. Not that you've noticed! Not that you care! Not that you've ever even bothered to say thank you!'

'I didn't — '

'What is that *smell*?'

She looks at her shoe.

'Oh, my God, that's gross.'

And he turns and heads back to school.

'Where are you going?'

'Maybe if I make it through a whole rehearsal once or twice Mr. Brooks won't drop me from band and take away my clarinet solo.'

'Why are you so mad at me?'

'Jeez, Alice! You are not the only person on the planet!'

★ ★ ★

Well, I know that, Alice thinks, as she watches Henry hurry away from her. She looks at his thin back and narrow shoulders and low-slung pants and too heavy backpack, filled with homework he will actually complete, and those awful black lace-up shoes he wears just to be different. She looks at his shaggy thick hair and his beloved Red Sox hat that his brother gave him. She tries to remember the last time Henry was this mad at

103

her and thinks it might have been her birthday party when she turned seven. The two of them spent weeks planning that party, they even had a theme, the Wizard of Oz, and his mom baked one of her amazing cakes that had the characters all over the top of it, and Henry dressed up as the Cowardly Lion. And then Alice forgot about Henry completely in her excitement over all the other little girls in their Dorothy dresses.

★ ★ ★

She's late picking up Ellie, even later than she thought. The teacher who got stuck waiting — looks like Mrs. Comstock — glares at Alice as she gets into her car. The school is locked up, Ellie is sitting on the front steps all alone, and it's clear she's been crying, but she's done with that now. Now she's steaming mad. She walks right up to Alice, right up close, and takes a big breath to start yelling at her, when she smells the poop and nearly gags.

This is too much, Ellie thinks, this is insult and injury and grievous and if she were not eight years old she would figure out some way to sue her sister for damages. No, she would figure out how to divorce her sister. She would figure out how to become not-sisters. Un-sisters. Unrelated.

'First you're late! Really late. Later than ever. So late I didn't think you were coming. And now . . . and now — '

Alice looks at her shoes.

'I hate you Alice, I really hate you.'

Ellie takes another step back, farther away from the smell.

'Where's Henry?'

'Band practice.'

'I am *not* going to walk home with you.'

'But — '

'You can walk on the other side of the street. Or you could hide in the woods 'til it's so dark that no one will see you. And *smell* you!'

'Ellie — '

'Do *not*! Do not even *try* to speak to me!'

Ellie turns and walks off, heading for home. She is walking fast, as fast as an eight-year-old can walk. Her head is down and she's swinging her arms, sort of like Mom on a power walk. She's like a little engine. Running on mad.

And she's wearing a hat, Alice notices, even though it's not that cold. A hat that completely covers her hair.

'Hey! How'd everybody like your new haircut?' Alice shouts across the street.

'What do you care?'

'I bet Mrs. Baker likes it.'

'Yeah.'

'Janna?'

'Pretty much.'

'The other kids?'

Ellie is twisting the middle button on her hand-me-down plaid spring coat.

'Luke Piacci?'

The button pops off in her hand.

'Is that why you're wearing that hat?'

Ellie gulps in one of those horrible sobs where

it sounds like she's choking and wailing at the same time.

'Can I come over there?' Alice asks.

'No!'

'*I* like it,' Alice offers.

'No you don't. And neither does Gram or Mom or — '

'I bet Mrs. Grover likes it.'

'What about Daddy?' Ellie asks through a fresh burst of tears.

'Daddy's gonna love it.'

'You're just saying that.'

'You know what Daddy would say?'

'What?'

'Take off that silly hat and quit worrying about what other people think.'

They cross Belknap Road with slightly less distance between them and turn down Baird Road.

'Hey, you want to bake a cake? After I throw these stupid sneakers in the trash?'

'He said I look like an elf.'

'Who?'

'Luke Piacci.'

'Maybe that was a compliment.'

'An *elf.*'

'Well, you're a very, very cute elf, Ellie.'

'Shut up!'

They turn into their driveway. Alice carefully keeps to her own side of the drive.

'Could we make a lemon cake?' Ellie asks.

'Sure.'

'Caramel frosting?'

'Sounds good.'

'Okay!' Ellie shouts, pulling her hat off and skipping along the last twenty yards of their driveway, past Matt's grape arbor and apple trees. A wash of sunlight spills over the trees and dapples her shining cap of hair.

'Okay.'

April 16th

They get through the weekend somehow. Alice didn't even tell her mom the truth about her sneaks. She just threw them away wrapped up in dozens of Wegman's bags. She paid Ellie two bucks to keep her mouth shut and told her mom she lost them.

Which made her mom really mad.

'I just bought those sneakers!'

'I'm sorry.'

'You're not paying attention, Alice!'

'I'm — '

'How many pairs of sneakers do I have to buy, anyway? In a lifetime of being your mom . . . ? And when are you going to at least *wash* that stupid shirt?!'

So all day Saturday it's mad Mom and a trip to the hated mall and the dreaded shoe store *and* the eyeglasses store to pick up Ellie's new glasses. A compromise pair, yes, but still way too big for Ellie's little face. She loves them.

Now it's Sunday afternoon and everybody is in a bad mood as they play catch up with chores. Alice is stuck in the basement with a mountain of laundry while Ellie is upstairs 'dusting' and

Angie is what, doing the taxes? Never a good day. Then the washing machine blows a gasket or a hose and floods the basement. Now they've got wet laundry, puddles of water, and that nasty damp basement smell. Nobody wants to pile this stinking, dripping laundry into the car and schlep to the Laundromat. So Angie's terrible mood gets worse. Chores and broken appliances and they can't afford a new washer right now, goddamnit! Which is when Alice calls Uncle Eddie.

'Here comes Uncle Eddie!' Ellie shouts.

Angie can barely contain a groan.

Alice loves Uncle Eddie. Everybody else thinks he's a fuckup.

Eddie was brilliant in school when he bothered to attend, especially math and physics. Could have done anything, won scholarships, the whole nine yards. Instead he got fat and runs a garage. Uncle Eddie can fix anything. It really burns everybody that he does well in his sideline business, too, buying high-end cars at auction for a client base that stretches across the country. Just how much does it bug Angie to see fat Eddie drive up in a vintage Mercedes he's scored for one of his rich clients, smoking a big cigar, with cash in his pockets. Eddie loves cash.

All the pretty girls like Eddie. Even fat he's really handsome, with lashes so dark and thick it looks like he's wearing eyeliner. He's had scores of girlfriends. Angie doesn't like them coming over to the house anymore. What used to be fun and flashy and definitely out of the ordinary is now relegated to the despised favorite phrase of

108

all boring adultdom: 'not appropriate.'

Uncle Eddie also likes to disappear every few months for a week or so. Nobody knows where he goes. On a drunk, chasing a girl, proving he's still free and unattached and unencumbered. Or maybe he's just tracking down a vintage car he's heard about through the grapevine.

Fastidious little miss Ellie is already starting to turn her nose up at Uncle Eddie. She's imbibing Angie's attitudes and opinions apparently. But his presents always wow her. Like Uncle Eddie always knows just what you really want, not what your mom thinks you should have, like the fringed cowgirl vest from his trip to Vegas, or the red, glittery Dorothy shoes with straps he bought one time in New York City. You can watch Ellie's ambivalence play out right on her face. First, she's loving the car and then she's hating the cigar, then she's loving Eddie's booming laugh, but hating his big belly and his stubbly face and his grimy fingernails. When he picks her up and calls her pumpkin, she wrinkles her finicky little nose. He's on to her, too. 'Don't be a simp,' he tells her. 'What are you so afraid of, a little dirt?'

Angie is at the front door.

'Eddie, can you lose the cigar?'

'Hi, sweetheart.'

'Hi, Eddie. The cigar . . . ?'

'It looks good, though, don't you think?'

'Niiiice set of wheels,' Angie says.

Eddie does a little shimmy and shake. Right there on the sidewalk. Angie can't help herself; she smiles at him, covering her mouth with her hands. He's unbuckling his belt in preparation for dropping his pants.

'No! Eddie! It's broad daylight!'

'I just want to get a laugh outta you.'

She's laughing and shaking her head — who knows at who? Eddie? Herself? At the fact that she's laughing at all?

'I heard your washer's on the fritz.'

He reaches into the backseat and takes out his tool kit.

'So I'm gonna fix your washer and then I'm gonna take you out to dinner, gorgeous. Alice can babysit, right?'

'Why can't we come?' Ellie wants to know.

'Oh, so now you like me?'

'I like you,' she says, a little too slowly.

'Your mom needs to put a dress on and go out someplace where she can turn heads and drink a martini. This is my big secret, the reason so many beautiful girls go out with me. I improve their looks. Next to me they look even more gorgeous than they already are.'

And then he's inside their little house, bumping into doorjambs, knocking the pictures out of whack on the walls. When Eddie stumps down the basement stairs, the whole house shakes. Angie clucks, she actually clucks, but Alice thinks the house is doing a little happy dance, just like Uncle Eddie.

'I need an assistant!' he shouts from the basement.

Alice looks at Angie who raises her eyebrow, as in, who me? Are you kidding?

So it's Alice who clumps downstairs. It's an act, the clumping. She loves hanging out with

Uncle Eddie. Every time she sees him, there's always one shocking thing he tells her and the promise of more revelations to come.

He turns off the water and disconnects the hose. 'Pay attention,' he tells her. 'You could learn something.' Alice does not really need to be told to pay attention to Uncle Eddie.

'Okay, that's the intake, that's the outflow. My guess is, it's the outflow. Let's take a look.'

He inspects the hoses.

'Hoses look okay. You see anything I'm not seeing?'

It's a rubber gasket that's shot; that's what he figured it would be. He took the liberty of bringing a few basic supplies with him, including a gasket. How does he know these things? He takes the hose and tells Alice to pull off the old gasket.

'It's stuck.'

'Yank it! Give it a real tug.'

'It's really stuck.'

'Yeah, they get corroded.'

He zaps it with some WD-40 and it comes right off.

He hands her a new gasket: 'Fit that one on.'

She slips on the new gasket.

'Like I said, it's not rocket science. Now reconnect it.'

When he squats down to test the connection, she wishes he'd wear his pants a little higher. He turns his head, catches her looking at him, and gives his jeans a hoist.

'Sorry about that, kiddo.'

'Oh, it's nothing, I . . . '

'Nobody wants to look down an old fart's butt.'

This cracks her up.

'Actually nobody wants to look down anybody's butt. Way too much of that these days. It used to be your old man had to tell you to keep your pants on, now they gotta tell you to keep your pants *up*, too. Not that kids are listening. What did your pop tell you?'

'What do you mean?'

'Words of wisdom. Advice. That kind of thing.'

She thinks for a minute.

'I don't think we got to that phase, yet.'

'Sure you did.'

'What, like how to live my life and stuff? I'm in the tenth grade. It's a little early!'

'No. The basics. Like don't kiss a girl if you just ate garlic pizza.'

She thinks again. She can't believe she has to think about this! There should be a list, a list that comes trippingly off her tongue, of all the great things her dad told her.

'Marigolds are a natural insect repellent?'

'Apropos of . . . ?'

'How to lay out a garden?'

'Exactly! What else?'

And Uncle Eddie, unlike most adults, is not impatient for her answer. It's okay that she's taking her time. He just hangs in there.

'Let's give her a little test run,' he says, and turns the washer on.

So now they've got the snug basement and the friendly washer-filling-up sounds and Uncle Eddie is the first person to ask her a direct question about her dad, to assume, of course they'll talk about her dad, like it's totally natural to talk about her dad, no problem, bring it on.

'He told me, never sell yourself short.'

'You'll find yourself thinking of that one even when you're forty.'

'Don't let anybody make up your mind for you.'

'Yeah.'

'You're as good as anybody else.'

'Right.'

'He gave me a compass when I was twelve.'

'Cool.'

'He said when I don't know what to do, I should just stop and close my eyes for a minute and see if I can hear my inner voice. And that voice, that's my compass.'

'Your dad loves that stuff — maps, compasses . . . '

'Yeah.'

'He's a good dad.'

God bless Uncle Eddie for talking in the present tense.

'You know how you feel about your mom right now?'

'Yeah.'

'Like she's this huge pain in the ass?'

'How do you know these things?'

'She's my big sister. She's been a pain in my ass my whole life! Anyway, you're not gonna feel this way forever.'

'I don't believe you.'

'Couple years . . . it'll all be different.'

'I really don't believe you.'

'And right now, you've got a choice about how you want to feel and be around her.'

'I do not!'

'You do. I'm not saying it's easy, but you've got a choice.'

'Like what, suddenly she's gonna be nice to me?'

'Like maybe you could have a truce. A little cease-fire.'

'Did she tell you to do this?'

'Nope.'

''Cause it's really making me mad.'

The washer spins to a stop. They both turn to look at it. No leaking.

'Let's load her up.'

They both start tossing darks into the washer.

'Uncle Eddie . . . '

'Yeah.'

'It's not that I hate her . . . '

'I know.'

'I just don't love her right now.'

'That's all I'm trying to tell you, Alice. Right now doesn't go on forever.'

'You sure?'

'I'm sure.'

'Hey — that's a good piece of advice.'

'From me? Hell, no.' He grins.

Upstairs Angie has put on a silky dress and red high heels and dangly earrings and lipstick. Uncle Eddie gives Alice a little nudge.

'You look nice, Mom.'

Her mom actually smiles, after she gets over the shocked surprise.

'Thanks, honey.'

'Your mom's a party girl. I bet she never told you that.'

'Eddie!'

'Perfume, too. Wow!'

'Are you going like that?' Angie asks.

'How'd you pack so much disapproval into five little words?'

'Thanks for fixing the washer.'

'I've got a clean shirt — Ralph Lauren — whoo hoo — and a sports jacket in the car.'

'Always ready for a good time.'

'That's me. Life is short. Let's go.'

Alice watches them walk to the car, their heads close together, laughing at something she can't hear, and she thinks she doesn't really know anything about her mother. She never thinks of her mother as being a sister and that she had this whole other life in her own family, until she sees her link her arm through Eddie's arm and lean into him. Why didn't she ever see this before? She sees that her mom loves Uncle Eddie even though all she ever does is give him a hard time and complain about him. And she's happy to be going out. Putting on some high heels and going out.

'What's for dinner?' Ellie shouts.

'Come into the kitchen and help me figure it out,' Alice shouts back at her.

Ellie stomps in.

'I bet there's nothing good,' Ellie says.

'You're not helping.'

'We could call Gram. She'd come over. She might even take us out.'

'We've gotta finish all that laundry.'

Alice opens the fridge. Why is she bothering to do this? She knows she's not going to find some yummy leftover casserole, or even fresh sandwich fixings. She slams the door.

'Okay, here's what we're gonna do: Backwards dinner. In front of a movie.'

She takes inventory: one tired banana, some ice cream; she knows how to make fudge sauce. She tests the whipped cream canister; it's not full, but it's promising.

'I'll make chocolate sauce.'

'Can we make it peppermint?' Ellie asks.

'Yeah. You peel the banana and get it into bowls.'

'Can I scoop the ice cream?'

'Sure.'

'Make it really chocolaty, Alice.'

'Okay.'

'Make lots.'

'I will.'

So Alice melts chocolate chips and stirs in half-and-half while Ellie stands on a chair to scoop ice cream onto banana halves.

'I wish we had a cherry for the top.'

'How about walnuts?'

'That's what Daddy likes!'

'I know.'

'Okay! Do it like Daddy does.'

They sit down in front of *Clueless* for the five hundredth time and eat banana splits and talk back to the movie and say all the lines they know by heart. They pause the movie so Alice can go downstairs and put one load of laundry into the dryer and start the next load.

She gets back upstairs to find Ellie standing on tiptoe on a kitchen chair with the longest wooden spoon in her hand, trying to reach the popcorn maker, and finally managing to pull it toward her by the cord. Alice waits and is rewarded by the sight of Ellie, popcorn maker clutched to her chest, grinning from ear to ear.

She hands the popcorn maker to Alice and says, 'I love backwards dinner.'

'Me, too.'

'Will you make mac and cheese later?'

'If you're still hungry.'

'Lots of butter for the popcorn, okay? Not the skinny way Mom does it.'

'Okay. You do the butter.'

'Yeah?'

'I'll show you.'

They manage to fold two loads of laundry in front of the movie before Ellie falls asleep. Ellie was so proud of herself for having given up the baby habit of sucking her thumb in kindergarten, but there's that thumb now, while she's sleeping. Alice brushes the hair off Ellie's sweaty forehead. Ellie is wearing her favorite plaid skirt with pleats. Alice thinks of these clothes as throwback clothes. Maybe her mom wore a skirt like this when she was in second grade. Ellie's bony knees are scraped and scabby, and both kneesocks have scrunched down around her ankles.

When Angie and Uncle Eddie get home, the girls are both sound asleep on the couch. Uncle Eddie picks Ellie up in his arms and carries her upstairs. Angie wakes Alice. Alice was dreaming, she was dreaming about Small Point; she was dreaming about a sliver of moon hanging low over the water; she was dreaming that she and Dad were walking the beach in the moonlight; she's following in his footsteps, and he was just beginning to turn around to say something to her when her mom wakes her up.

'Alice . . . honey . . . '

When she bends over like that, Alice can smell her perfume and the faint scent of her lipstick, and maybe that other smell is a martini or two.

'Time for bed.'

'Okay.'

Alice sits up and her mom surprises her by sitting down beside her. Close beside her.

'You folded the laundry.'

'Yeah.'

'Thanks.'

'Ellie helped.'

'You guys make out okay?'

'Yeah.'

'No fighting?'

'Nope. We had backwards dinner.'

'Perfect.'

'Did you have a good time, Mom?'

'I had a really nice time.'

Uncle Eddie clatters downstairs and sticks his head in the doorway.

'We danced,' he says.

'You did not!'

'Yeah, we did.'

'Where were you?'

'That little roadhouse out by the lake. They've got a dance floor the size of a postage stamp.'

118

'And a piano and this old lady with dyed red frizzy hair who does jazz standards,' Angie says.

'How do you dance to *that?*' Alice wants to know.

'Your Uncle Eddie's a good dancer.'

'Sure he is,' Alice teases.

'He taught me everything I know.'

'I thought Dad taught you how to dance.'

'That was more like refining what Eddie had already laid down.'

'Alice, I'll pick you up tomorrow for your first driving lesson,' Uncle Eddie says.

'What?!' Angie can't keep the shock out of her voice.

'Really?' Alice asks.

'She's fifteen! She doesn't have a permit!'

'Relax, Angie. We're gonna drive around in circles in an empty parking lot.'

'You're not going to put that child behind the wheel of that Mercedes.'

'I don't think that will be a problem for Alice.'

'Eddie!'

'Gotta go, kids.'

Uncle Eddie heads out the door.

'Thanks, Eddie,' her mom shouts, as the door slams. 'He's too much sometimes.'

'He's great.'

'He put the top down.'

'Cool.'

'We drove out to the park — where the kids go to neck.'

'To *what*, Mom?'

'Make out?'

'I'll never understand how you can be so fifties

119

when you grew up in the seventies.'

'He put the top down so we could hear the water and look at the stars.'

'Nice.'

'He had a blanket in the trunk.'

'Pretty smooth.'

'You need to watch out for boys like your Uncle Eddie.'

'I'll keep that in mind.'

'I mean it.'

'Mom — !'

Angie puts her head back against the couch cushions and reaches for Alice's hand.

'It was so beautiful. We had the radio on . . . And that dumb-ass cigar of his smelled really good outside.'

'I love cigars outside.'

'He's always surprising me, y'know? Now if he'd just lose twenty-five pounds and find a nice girl — '

'Don't ruin it, Mom.'

'It would be good for his health. I worry — '

'Don't you like anybody just the way they already are?'

There's a long pause while Alice disentangles her hand.

'We didn't hear from Dad this weekend.'

'He's probably out on patrol or something.'

'You think he's okay?'

'I'm sure he's fine.'

'How can you be sure?'

'You know Dad; he knows how to take care of himself.'

'But what if — '

'Alice, let's not get into this right before bed, okay?'

'I was just wondering.'

'I know, honey.'

No, you don't, Alice thinks as she heads up the stairs. You have no idea.

* * *

Angie walks through the house turning out the lights before she heads upstairs to her bedroom. She reaches under her pillow and pulls out Matt's latest letter:

You've never seen the moon like it is here. Because the base is blacked out for security reasons and there's so little electricity anywhere else, it's truly dark. I don't know if you can experience this kind of darkness in the U.S. anymore. Whenever I'm out walking across the base — for a meeting, for a meal — I'm so aware of the night sky. And looking up, Angie, looking up kind of lifts you up, you know? Almost like praying or wishing or hitching your wagon to a star. That's an old time phrase, something my dad would say. But just sensing that mystery feels like a kind of prayer to me, even though you know I'm not much for prayers and all that.

* * *

Angie tries to think of the last time she really paid attention to the night sky. Tonight, maybe, out at the lake in Eddie's convertible. But did

121

she really see it? Or was she all caught up, as usual, in talking or arguing or giving Eddie advice he doesn't want and never heeds? When was the last time she walked beneath the moon, or sang, or danced, or held Matt in her arms under a starlit sky? Here she is, with every freedom and every convenience and she doesn't have time to notice the moon. And there's Matt, doing whatever it is he can't tell her about every day, reveling in the night sky.

My soul lifts up, she thinks. *My soul lifts up* . . . Where did that phrase come from and why is it popping into her head now? The moon, the sky, the possibility of a soul, the miles, the oceans, Matt, trying not to worry, getting through the days believing he'll come home, believing he'll be okay. It's all a prayer, she realizes, every breath, every day. Come home to me. Come home.

April 17th

They are sitting on the bed in Henry's bedroom after track practice, ostensibly working on geometry homework. Alice gets up to open the window because Henry's feet really stink. She can see into the Grovers' side yard where Mrs. Grover is taking the laundry off the line. There are robins on the greening grass and the forsythia is just beginning to bloom. Alice wants to be outside, she wants to lie down in the grass and forget about geometry and school and no news from her father and a million other things.

122

Mrs. Grover is singing. To herself, really, kind of under her breath but every other phrase or so drifts up to the window and Alice can hear it. She's singing that great Bunny Berrigan song, 'Can't Get Started.' The only reason Alice knows this song is because it is a very big song at Henry's house. Mrs. Grover has one of the original recordings on a scratchy 78 that she loves to play. She actually has a record player and she changes the spindle and puts this record on and sits down and plays it and listens to it, really leans in and *listens* to it. Alice had never seen anyone listen to music like this, so it was a bit of an event when she was around four and happened to be playing with Henry when his mother took out the old Bunny Berrigan record and put it on. And sat there. And listened.

Here she is, on a spring day, bringing in the wash and singing to herself. Mrs. Grover is no longer young; at least that's how Alice's mother would put it, and Alice's mother would think she was being tactful, not hearing the obvious criticism and condescension in the phrase. Even though Mrs. Grover wears those awful sensible shoes and has gray hair that she wears in a bun, Alice thinks that maybe Mrs. Grover is still young in the ways that are important. Like she's not so serious all the time, and she sings and right now she's teasing a cardinal. Whistling in response to its call and damn if that cardinal doesn't whistle right back. Alice's mother doesn't even have a clothesline, let alone stand outside and lift her face to the sun and sing and whistle to the birds.

123

Henry works away, oblivious, or so Alice thinks. Henry, of course, has another story to tell and not necessarily one he's ready to tell Alice. For instance, it is impossible to think when Alice is this close to him. The smell of her shampoo, the habit she has of closing her eyes and scratching her nose as she thinks through a math problem, the way he can tell she is miles away from him even though she's in the same room. She's finished her homework, as usual, and Henry is left to try to think his way through the problem on the page when he'd much rather think about, or even just watch, Alice. Which is what he's doing when she turns back from the window.

'Your mom's bringing in the wash.'

'Yeah.'

'I love the way the sheets smell when they've been dried outside, don't you?'

'Yeah.'

'You never thought about it.'

'Nope.'

'Not a guy thing.'

'Nope.'

Alice goes back to watching the clouds and the sky and thinking about her dad, but she can't stand this train of thought so she turns back to Henry. Henry on the unmade bed, Henry who is scratching his ankle until it bleeds, Henry who forgot to comb his hair this morning and all of his cowlicks are sticking up.

There are still Transformers on the shelves and the complete set of Harry Potter. She knows if she opened the drawer to her left, Henry's

124

collection of arrowheads would be there, perfectly labeled, right next to the tackle box with all his stuff for tying flies. Henry ties the most beautiful flies. He even has a Web site for selling them. And then there's his iPod — which he earned by mowing lawns — and his collection of jazz CDs. Henry is one of those kind of dorky boys with a lot of interests. But the piano is moving beyond that now; the piano has totally overshadowed the arrowheads; the piano is even starting to move the fly tying aside. Alice thinks that there is always music inside Henry's head, and right now she wishes she could have music inside her head, too.

There are no rules at Henry's house about what Henry and Alice can and can't do, where they can go, what rooms they can be in, what doors have to be open. At Alice's house the rules are probably the same rules her parents lived with. No boys in a bedroom, yours or anyone else's. In fact, no boys on the second floor. Ever. No closed doors. Feet on the floor at all times.

She turns back to the window and wonders what her Dad is listening to. Are there radio stations? Is there rock and roll? R&B? Hip hop? Rap? Does he hear the call to prayer five times a day? Is it just background noise or does he really hear it? What if Alice heard a call to prayer five times a day? And what if, instead of praying, which she only half or one quarter believes in anyway, what if she just stopped and listened five times a day? Could she hear her dad's voice? She can't remember his voice. She can almost see his face sometimes, but she can never hear his voice.

And the harder she tries to see him or hear him inside her mind the farther away he recedes. If there were music inside her head could she forget for five minutes, could she ride the sound, the voices of the instruments, just take a ride, fly away from everything she's thinking all the time?

Henry is standing beside her.

'What's so interesting out there?'

'We haven't heard from my dad in three days.'

She can feel Henry weighing his words, trying to figure out how to respond, but mostly she can feel his warm, solid presence beside her, and before Alice has time to think about what she's doing, or even know what she's doing, she kisses him. Just leans in and kisses him. Everything slows way down for a few seconds as she bumps into his glasses and stumbles over one foot and wonders, fleetingly, if she should close her eyes or not, but really doesn't have time to worry about that because time flips back to normal mode and Henry recoils in shock — or is that disgust? — she's not sure. Whatever it is, it's not pretty and it's not what she expected, if she expected anything at all and now she can feel a blush blooming from the top of her head and flushing red and hot the whole length of her body. The talking part of her brain is in panic mode: Oh, no! You idiot! Why did you do that? That was so stupid! The feeling/sensing part of her brain is going Wow, not so bad, really, if you were just a little more mellow and relaxed maybe you could get the hang of this. But Henry? What is she doing kissing Henry? From the look on his face, he's wondering the same thing.

126

Henry has turned away from Alice. His face is flaming hot and he is so acutely embarrassed he doesn't know how he is ever going to be able to face Alice again. He cannot believe that the first time a girl — and not just any girl, but Alice — makes a move, he reacts like one of those supersensitive cats who never let you get within ten feet of them. Why did he do that? What's wrong with him? Surprised. That's it. He was just surprised. Shocked even. Girls like Alice do not just up and kiss boys like Henry. At least not in Henry's very limited experience in which all sorts of girls, in fact, all girls, have handily managed to avoid kissing him. And no fair: It happened too fast. Was that really a kiss? Did he even feel it? Did their lips actually touch? The only person he can ask is Alice, and he can't ask Alice because he still can't look at Alice. Or speak.

Alice is stuffing her books and her notebooks and her jacket into her backpack. He needs to say something. Anything. It sounds like she's crying. Say something, you idiot! But Henry is rooted to the floor like his socks have superglue on them and his legs are made of lead and not one single body part is responding to his urgent, desperate commands.

Alice is at the door.

'We could pretend that never happened, okay? So it doesn't get weird and stuff.'

Too late for that! is what Henry would normally say, if Henry could find his voice, if Henry could just turn and look at her. He's thinking this is about the loneliest he's ever felt in his life, this not being able to look at Alice, this business of being glued to the floor when he wants to reach out and touch her hair or her hand or her sleeve even.

And then she's gone, and Henry finds out that loneliest is right now, after she's left the room. Suddenly his feet unfreeze and his legs start to move and he's running down the stairs three, four at a time and throwing open the front door. But Alice is already halfway down the block, jogging steadily, her backpack bouncing on her back.

He watches until she turns in at her driveway and he can't see her anymore. He sits down on the front steps, pops back up, starts down the walk, retreats to the steps. I need to do something; I need to go over there; I can't possibly look her in the face; I have never felt so stupid in my life. But mixed in with the stupid feelings and the indecision and the walking up and down, there's another feeling, a big, welling up feeling in the middle of his chest, this kernel, this diamond — okay, yes, a diamond in the rough — this fact, this incontrovertible fact: *Alice kissed me*. Then he remembers, right, her father. Three days. No contact. So maybe that wasn't really a kiss. Not a kiss kiss. More like some desperate something that looked like a kiss, that almost felt like a kiss but was not, actually, a kiss.

That would make more sense. But making sense of this turns out not to be comforting in the least. Making sense of this turns out to feel like a direct blow to the solar plexus. Maybe he's

128

wrong, maybe he could talk to her. But what would he say, exactly? Hey, Alice, explain your motives. Hey, Alice, could we try that again? The more he thinks about it the more difficult it is to get up and walk down the block. And just as he's finally getting so uncomfortable he can't really do anything else but head over there, because nothing could make him feel worse, Alice's Uncle Eddie pulls up in an old orange Dodge and blows the horn: three long blasts.

He sees Alice run out to the curb, look up the street at him, watching her. She waves and turns away before he can wave back. She slides into the seat beside Uncle Eddie and they head off. Henry walks out into the street to watch them go. He waves at her, willing her to turn around and see him, which she doesn't do. He waves at her until the old Dodge crests the hill and disappears out of sight.

He turns back and starts trudging up his driveway, staring at the scuff marks and the incipient holes in the toes of his Chucks. Until he is stopped by the sight of the toes of his mother's brown sensible tie shoes. Pointing directly at him.

Don't look up, don't look up, he tells himself! What did she see? Did she see anything? Can he never, not even once in his life do something that his parents don't know about or find out about, or stick their noses into and ruin? Like *splat*, total *splat*. Ruin forever.

'Everything all right, Henry?' his mom asks the top of his head.

'Uh huh,' he answers her shoes.

'Alice seemed like she was in a big hurry to get out of here.'

'Uh huh.'

'Do you need to talk about it?'

'Uh uh.' And he shakes his head for emphasis.

'You sure?'

'Uh huh.'

'How's the homework coming along?'

'Fine.'

'You want a snack?'

'We ate the Oreos.'

'All righty, then.'

Mrs. Grover heads back inside, the laundry basket resting on her ample hip.

Henry dares to look up only after the front door has closed with its solid *thump*. And then he throws himself on the grass, the cool, damp, early-spring grass. He can feel the wet already seeping into him, but he doesn't care. What if, he's thinking, what if that really *was* a kiss?

★ ★ ★

The orange Dodge has one of those bench seats in the front. Alice has never seen one of those before. The whole car smells like wax it's so spic and span.

'Nice car, Uncle Eddie.'

'Isn't she a beauty? Who knew an old Dodge could have so much style?'

'What's that thing on the steering wheel?'

'Necker's knob.'

'What?'

He puts his arm around her and pulls her

across the seat until she's snugged right in beside him.

'So you can drive with one hand.'

'And . . .'

'Find a country road, open the windows, drive real slow, and give your girl a kiss.'

'You ever have a car like this when you were a kid?' she asks as she slides over to her side of the seat and rolls the window down.

'I wish! I had to drive my old man's Ford. Stripped down, strictly utilitarian. Boring, boring car. How are you doing?'

She thought they were talking about cars, now he wants to know how she's doing?

'Where are we headed?'

'I thought we'd go up to the high school parking lot and just get a feel for things.'

Alice is thinking that might be a better idea much, much later in the day or in the middle of the night or some weekend when there's no game and no practice going on and really absolutely no people around to watch and make her want to hyperventilate.

'You know how there's that faculty parking lot out by the maintenance shed? I thought we'd head over there.'

Uncle Eddie can read her mind.

Next thing she knows she's behind the wheel. When they adjust the bench seat so she can comfortably reach the gas and brake pedals, Eddie is left with both knees jammed against the dash.

'No problem,' he reassures her. 'Plenty of room.'

She puts on her seat belt.

'Okay. You know the difference between the gas and the brake?'

'Gas is right, brake is left.'

'Which foot do you use for the brake?'

'Trick question! Right foot for both.'

'Smart-ass.'

She smiles at him.

'Put your foot on the brake.'

He talks her through the gears. The Dodge is automatic but the shift is on the steering column. She's never seen that before. It's cool, though, the way you grab the handle, pull it toward you, and slide the lever to 'D' for drive.

'So let's just start real slow in a nice big circle around the parking lot.'

'Okay.'

'You ready?'

'Yeah.'

'Put her in drive and then release the brake nice and slow.'

Alice does as she's told and they're moving! She's driving! Okay, so she could walk faster than this, but she's driving!

'Can I give it a little gas?'

'Not yet. Let's just focus on steering.'

She misjudges the first turn.

'Straighten out your wheels. You feel that now? You've gotta get a feel for how she handles. Every car is different, different turning radius, different responsiveness to the steering wheel.'

The second turn she drives right off the asphalt onto the stony shoulder, but pulls the car back in line a little more smoothly.

'A little more to the left.'

The third and the fourth turns are pretty easy. She's proud of herself, but she doesn't dare take her eyes off the macadam in front of her to look at Uncle Eddie and judge his response. By the third time around she's starting to feel pretty good. She actually sits back in the seat a bit and relaxes the death grip she's been keeping on the steering wheel.

'Can we go a little faster?'

'Don't get cocky. You've been driving for five minutes.'

'I'm a natural. I take after you.'

'Next time. Maybe.'

'I think I'm getting dizzy.'

'So stop in the middle and start going the other way.'

She finds the precise middle of the parking lot, comes to a full stop, puts on her blinker for good measure, and turns right.

'Who taught you to drive, Uncle Eddie?'

'Your mom.'

'You're kidding.'

'I made my old man crazy in a car. He swore he would never go anywhere with me behind the wheel.'

'How come?'

'He thought I was a hothead.'

'Were you?'

'Sometimes.'

'A lot of times?'

'According to my old man. But as you can see, I've mellowed with the years.'

'What kind of a teacher was Mom?'

'Awful. Her knuckles would be white, she'd be holding her breath and grabbing at the dashboard or the door handle for support every other minute.'

'How'd you get her to keep getting into the car with you?'

'I paid her.'

'You did not!'

'I was desperate. She would even gasp and moan whenever I did something stupid.'

'But if she hated it so much — '

'She needed the money.'

'For what?'

'College.'

'So if she was such a scaredy-cat how'd you get to be such a good driver?'

'I love it. Have you noticed? People tend to be good at the things they love.'

'She's not happy about this.'

'She's not thinking it through.'

'What do you mean?'

'It's just the two of you taking care of things while your dad's away. There could be an emergency where you'd need to be able to drive.'

'Like what?'

'To get help.'

'For who?'

'Say your mom gets food poisoning or appendicitis.'

'Wouldn't I just call an ambulance?'

'Or Ellie falls.'

'Ditto.'

'Or Gram.'

'Same.'

134

'Or something unexpected.'

'Like what?'

'I don't know! In my book it's just a good idea to be prepared. In case.'

'In case.'

'Plus, it's fun.'

'Yeah.'

'And you'll be the first one — of all your friends.'

'Except for Ashley Cooper who lives on a farm and has been driving a tractor since she was twelve.'

At which point Alice realizes that she is just cruising around the parking lot. Slower than slow, but making the turns effortlessly, like a real driver. She cranks down her window and sticks her elbow out.

'Both hands on the wheel!'

'Okay, okay.'

'Confident is good. Overconfident is not good.'

'Got it.'

Both hands on the wheel, the cool spring air coming in the window, the nose of the car moving slowly past empty fields, the utility garage, the Dumpster, the crowns of the distant weeping willows gilded by the setting sun.

'There you go, kiddo. There you go.'

Alice risks a glance at Uncle Eddie.

'Who was your first girlfriend?'

'Why?'

'Just curious.'

'Melissa Pardee. Fourth grade. I followed her around like a puppy.'

'First kiss?'

'What is this? Twenty questions?'

'First kiss?'

'Why the sudden interest in kissing?'

'Quit stalling.'

'Jessie Simons. Sixth grade. On the bus coming back from a field trip.'

Alice tries to picture eleven-year-old Uncle Eddie making his move with little Jessie Simons.

'Did she kiss you back?'

'Who knows? Probably. That was a long time ago. So what about your first kiss?'

'Are you kidding me?'

''Fess up, Alice.'

She laughs and shakes her head.

'I guess I'm one of those late bloomers.'

'Sure you are.'

'Were you ever in love?' she asks.

'Alice, c'mon — '

'Were you?'

'Lots of times.'

'No, I mean, really in love.'

Eddie looks out the window.

'Once.'

'What happened?'

'That's a long story.'

'How come you never got married?'

'What's with all the questions?'

'Well . . . ?'

'I let her get away.'

'Why?'

'Couldn't commit I guess.'

'Where is she now?'

'Married with four kids, teaching second grade

about one hundred miles from here.'

'Do you ever see her?'

'No.'

'Do you ever get lonely?'

'Geez, Alice, let's move on to brighter things. You're *driving*, did you notice?'

She completes one last circuit before pulling up in the center of the parking lot. She remembers to put the car in park, engages the emergency brake, and relinquishes the wheel to Uncle Eddie. He moves the seat back with a sigh and punches her in the shoulder.

'Good job. I can't believe we need a bigger parking lot already.'

'We could go to the mall.'

'Next week the mall.'

'For real?'

'It's a date.'

Uncle Eddie turns the radio on to golden oldies as he pulls onto Five Mile Line Road.

'Crank your window down,' he shouts over Van Morrison crooning 'Tupelo Honey.'

They both start singing along really loud.

She's as sweet as tupelo honey

She's an angel of the first degree

Normally this would embarrass Alice, normally she would be all self-conscious about how her voice sounds while at the same time scanning the streets and the sidewalks to see if anyone is witnessing her craziness. But today, she decides, she doesn't care. Here in the orange Dodge with fat Uncle Eddie, singing at the top of her lungs, she doesn't have to think, she doesn't have to worry, she doesn't have to give a damn. The day has turned to a pink dusk, and just like Henry, she's got music inside her head and all around her.

April 18th

Alice does not like being dragged to the pool with her mother while Ellie takes a knitting class in the Y's paneled, stuffy rec room. After school and track she just wants to go home.

Alice sits in the bleachers. It's hot, it's almost dripping with humidity. She hates the bleachers, she hates the chlorine smell of the pool. Underneath all that bleach there's this nasty, damp rot kind of smell.

This time slot is lap swim only, so it couldn't be more boring. Just a bunch of grown-ups and old people going back and forth, never getting anywhere. How they can put their faces in that slimy water is beyond Alice.

Here comes her mother from the showers. Her Speedo bathing suit and cap on, her goggles in her hand. She stops where Alice is sitting, sweaty and miserable.

'You don't have to sit there like a lump, you know.'

'Thanks, Mom.'

'You *do* have a bathing suit.'

Alice doesn't bother to answer.

'It's healthy.'

'Uh huh.'

'You get into a different place in your head. It's peaceful.'

138

'Okay, Mom.'

'Just once. Will you try it just once?'

'Probably not.'

'You love to swim in the summertime.'

'That's different.'

'How is that different?'

'It's outdoors, for one.'

'I was thinking this was something we could maybe do together.'

'I'll think about it,' Alice says.

Angie walks away, hops into an empty lane, pulls her goggles on, gives Alice a little wave, and starts swimming. As she warms up for a few hundred meters with an easy breaststroke, she's trying not to think about Alice and how is she ever going to reach her or even just feel comfortable with her own daughter ever again? She's trying not to think about Matt and where he is and if he's all right; she's trying not to think at all; she's trying to get to that place where she's swimming and *not* thinking, just moving her body, just making her turns, reaching into the backstroke now, her favorite stroke, and letting her mind slow and quiet and then quiet some more until, for a few sweet strokes or lengths or moments, she is nothing but body and breath and motion.

Only it's not working today. She turns and attacks the crawl as though she is attacking her anger, trying to drown it in the pool. No one talks about the anger, the rage, how the love and longing are all mixed up with these other less attractive emotions. How could he leave me? How could he leave us? This was not the deal, this is not where their lives were supposed to be heading. And that shirt, that stupid blue shirt of Matt's hanging out beneath Alice's jacket, looking grubby, looking like hell, looking like a goddamn battle flag waving under her nose: bad mother, bad mother, bad mother.

It's just a shirt, she tries to tell herself. Ignore it. Forget it. Distant daughter. Deployed husband. Another turn, and another turn. Backstroke again, her favorite stroke again. Just breathe, Angie. Just breathe.

★ ★ ★

Alice grabs her backpack and heads up to the lobby. She rummages in her pockets to see if she has enough change to buy a Coke or a snack from the vending machines. No such luck.

She peeks into the rec room and there's Ellie, sitting in a circle with four other girls. No boys of course. The teacher is this comfy-looking woman with long, scraggly hair, a patchwork skirt, Birkenstocks, and an obviously homemade sweater. She patiently moves from kid to kid, helping them work their big wooden needles, helping them find dropped or lost stitches. Ellie is chatting away like she's found her niche.

Alice closes the door quietly and heads outside. The YMCA is a relatively new building, built on the outskirts of Belknap's Four Corners. Not that there's much left to the Four Corners since they built the stupid mall three miles down Belknap Road. There's just the library, two churches, a gas station, a bar, an upholstery store

140

that always looks like it's on the verge of going out of business, The Bird Sisters, Jansen's Hardware, and the local pharmacy. Ricci's little grocery/ deli is still trying to hang on. It is the dimmest, dustiest store on the block. A 25-watt bulb would be bright in there. Maybe they don't want anybody reading the expiration dates on the canned goods. They've recently updated their penny candy aisle, even though penny candy doesn't cost a penny anymore.

Alice sits on the bench by the bus stop. She'd like to walk the few blocks to the library, but then no one would know where she is. She'd like to be sitting next to Stephie in the library doing their homework just like they used to do, passing notes and sharing M&Ms and giggling and making the librarian come over to tell them to be quiet. *Again*. She'd like to walk the half-mile home. Somehow this stupid trip to the Y is a family outing in her mom's mind. Even though Alice hates it, even though they are all in different parts of the Y. Maybe the family part is when they go out to Don & Bob's afterward for hamburgers and onion rings. Alice is counting on frozen custard for dessert.

She's trying not to think about what happened with Henry yesterday, when she sees Mrs. Minty struggling to get her rolling cart out the door of Ricci's grocery. Alice starts to cross the street to help her when John Kimball maneuvers his way past Mrs. Minty and then not only holds the door for her but picks up her cart and carries it to the sidewalk. He's holding a soda and a package of Devil Dogs in one hand and doing all this maneuvering for Mrs. Minty with his other hand.

She thanks him. She knows his name. He offers to walk her home and help unload her groceries. She declines, says the exercise is good for her heart and her bones. And then she asks him about baseball. Mrs. Minty follows high school baseball? She tells him he's a great shortstop. Mrs. Minty goes to games? Curiouser and curiouser, as another Alice would say.

Alice quickly retreats to the farthest corner of her bench and pulls out *Othello* so that John Kimball won't know she's been eavesdropping and, hopefully, won't even notice her at all. Which is when she hears Mrs. Minty say:

'You remind me of my boy. All you boys do. He was just your age.'

'What happened to him?'

'Meningitis. The local doctor didn't realize how serious it was.'

'When was this, Mrs. Minty?'

'1963.'

'What was his name?'

'His friends called him Pete. We called him Peter. After my father.'

'Did he play baseball?'

'Shortstop. Just like you.'

'Any good?'

'We thought he was marvelous. So fast.'

'Did you have any other — '

'No, no. Just the one.'

'And your husband?'

'That was the beginning of a terrible decade.

Not the sort of times you can live through with a broken heart.'

'You mean the war?'

'And the assassinations. And everything else. Jared found he couldn't keep getting up in the morning . . . The doctors say he died of heart disease. But I know better.'

'I'm so sorry, Mrs. Minty.'

'It was his time.'

That's what grown-ups always say, Alice thinks. But what does it mean? That every person gets allotted a certain number of days?

'Now how in the world did we get on this topic?' Mrs. Minty continues.

'Baseball.'

'Very diverting, baseball.'

'I have to be careful it doesn't divert me right into getting C's and D's.'

'You following the Red Wings as usual this year, John?'

'Yes, ma'am.'

'I'd love to go to the opening game.'

'I'll talk to my father, Mrs. Minty. We'll make a date.'

'That would be lovely. Tell him I expect the full treatment: beer, peanuts, hot dogs.'

'Will do.'

'The Boxford High game next week. Is that a home game, John?'

'Sure is.'

'See you there. Weather permitting.'

Mrs. Minty heads off, with a jaunty little wave, her square purse hanging over one arm, one hand firmly on her rolling basket. She doesn't

143

move quickly, but she's determined. She also, Alice notices, isn't looking down at her feet and the sidewalk, but instead, is looking up at the trees and the birds and the houses, and whatever else there is to see on her six-block walk home.

Alice is watching Mrs. Minty and trying to take in the fact that she lost her son, that she even had a son, and that he was just her age. Alice has never known anyone who died before except for her grandparents and her great aunt Charlotte. Even though she didn't know him, even though he died before she was even born, suddenly this boy, Peter, who played shortstop, is as real as real can be.

As real as John Kimball, who has materialized in front of her, and not only that, has decided to sit down on the bench beside her and offer her a Devil Dog.

'No, thanks.'

'You're not one of these crazy girls who doesn't eat, are you?'

'No.'

'Good.'

'I just heard, I couldn't help hearing, about Mrs. Minty's son, Peter, and . . . '

'Yeah.'

It's really strange, or maybe not so strange, that they just sit there for a minute, thinking about Peter, not saying anything else for a while. Normally this would make Alice squirm and fret: Should I be saying something? Like what? Should he be saying something? But she is not thinking any of these things; she is not, in fact, worrying. This is hard to believe given that it is

144

John Kimball sitting beside her and the last time she saw him she had dog shit all over her shoes. Hard to imagine that that ghastly experience might have been an icebreaker.

'He was only fifteen,' Alice ventures.

'Yeah.'

'You ever know anyone who died?'

John looks down at the ground.

'My mother.'

'Oh my gosh, I'm so sorry.'

'Yeah.'

'No, I mean, I'm really — '

'Thanks. It's okay.'

He opens the package of Devil Dogs.

'I think about it all the time,' Alice says.

'What?'

'Dying.'

'Really?'

If there were a red light in her brain, it would be flashing. Crazy outcast girl talking to the most popular boy in school. And the topic she chooses: dying. Not a good idea! Cease and desist!

'Why?' he asks, like he really wants to know.

'My dad's in Iraq.'

Why is she telling him this? It's not like they're friends, it's not like they know each other at all, really; it's not like this is the person she would choose to confide anything in, about anyone, ever. Ever!

'I didn't know.'

There's a big pause here and she expects him to push off and head down the street just like everybody else does whenever the war comes up.

'Is he doing okay?'

She looks at him. He is so not what she thought he was, at least in this moment, that she has to get a visual on him to place herself back in reality.

'From everything I read I don't know how he could possibly be all right,' Alice answers.

'I don't follow it as much as I should.'

'No, I know, most people — '

'Which kind of makes me a really big jerk, doesn't it?'

'I wouldn't say that.'

'I don't know what to say about your dad.'

'I know. Nobody does.'

'But I wish I could say everything is gonna be all right.'

She turns and looks at him again. He has a Devil Dog crumb stuck to his lip. She takes a breath. She tests the waters of this moment with this boy. Could this possibly be real? And before she has a chance to think, to stop herself, she reaches out and brushes the crumb off his upper lip. He pulls away from her, possibly just a startle reflex, possibly total aversion, she notices, as she curls her hands into fists and shoves them under her thighs. Just like Henry, she thinks.

'Hey, Alice!' Ellie yells.

She's running down the steps of the Y, waving her arms wildly, waving her knitting like a flag.

'I've gotta go,' she says.

'Yeah.'

'Okay. So — '

'I'll see you around, okay?'

He gets up and starts walking away.

She ducks her head; she knows she won't really see him 'around,' that come tomorrow they will still pass each other in the halls and she will be invisible to him and his friends — which is, of course, better than being the object of their attention and ridicule.

Funny that a bench on Main Street could be neutral territory, kind of floating in a different world with different rules where for a few minutes they could almost talk, almost see each other.

She looks up. Ellie is waiting on the steps.

'Alice, c'mon!'

John stops and turns around. He's coming back to the bench.

'Listen, you want to come to the Red Wings game with me and my dad and Mrs. Minty?'

'Are you joking?'

'No, I'll talk to my dad. It's fun. You like minor league baseball?'

She wonders: Does she like baseball? Does it matter?

'Okay,' she finds herself saying. 'Okay.'

'Great.'

And he's off, jogging down the street toward home. John Kimball did not just ask me out. This is not a date, this is probably not even going to happen. This is charity Tuesday with Mrs. Minty and that weird girl whose father is in Iraq. Okay. Good deed for the day. Pull yourself together, Alice.

She joins Ellie on the steps of the Y. Ellie with her new glasses.

'Who was that?'

'Just some guy from school.'

'What's his name?'

'John.'

'Do you like him?'

'No!'

'Yes, you do.'

'I've never even talked to him before today.'

'Is he popular?'

'What do you think?'

'I think you like him.'

'You're nuts.'

'What about Henry?'

'What *about* Henry?'

Ellie gives her one of those all knowing smart-ass teenager kind of looks. Where does she get this stuff?

'C'mon. Let's go find Mom,' Alice says.

'Did he ask you out?' Ellie wants to know.

'Did he ask me out? Are you kidding?'

'Did he?'

'To a Red Wings game. With Mrs. Minty.'

'See?'

'See what?'

'He asked you out.'

'Charity. Strictly charity. He must be getting his Boy Scout Buddha badge in compassion. Or selflessness.'

'They don't have Buddha badges in the Boy Scouts. You're making that up. Plus, he must be an Eagle Scout already.'

'Right. Eagle Scout Buddha Badge.'

'You think Mom will let you go?'

'Who knows?'

'Are you gonna ask her?'

'Maybe.'

'He's kind of cute.'

'Ellie!'

'What? He *is*.'

'How was knitting?'

'You're changing the subject.'

'Yup.'

'I'm making a scarf for Dad. I picked double rib stitch.'

'What colors?'

'Lots of colors. Mrs. Morris has hundreds of colors.'

'Will you show me later?'

Alice takes Ellie by the hand as they head to the parking lot at the rear of the building. She listens while Ellie talks about Mrs. Morris and how she smells like spices and how Dad is gonna love the scarf of many colors even if he gets it in the wrong season and how he could use it as a talisman or a good luck symbol just like the knights of old.

'You want to hear my new favorite word?'

'Sure.'

'*Hypergelast*. What do you think *that* means?'

'Sounds like extreme gymnastics to me.'

'It means someone who can't stop laughing!'

Ellie doubles over she is laughing so hard. She laughs and laughs. And Alice can't help herself; she joins right in.

April 19th

The alarm didn't go off this morning, or if it did, Alice didn't hear it and now she's late and to top it off she can't find her shirt. It's not under the bed, where she left it, carefully hidden behind her backpack; it's not in the hamper; it's not in the basement in the pile of laundry overflowing the laundry basket. Ellie swears she doesn't know where it is.

'Did you take it?'

'Why would I take your smelly shirt?'

'Did you take it?'

'No, Alice, I did not take your smelly, disgusting shirt!'

'Where's Mom?'

'How should I know?'

'I need my shirt.'

'It's just a shirt.'

'It is not just a shirt. It's Dad's shirt.'

'You are obsessed.'

'I am not!'

'How is it I can be so much more mature than you are, Alice, when I'm only eight?'

'Bully for you, Miss Goody Two-Shoes.'

Just then she hears the garbage truck screech to a halt at the curb. She looks out the window. There's her mom, *in her bathrobe*, dragging the garbage can down to the curb. Could she be any more embarrassing?

Which is when Alice puts two and two together and speeds through the front door and down the front steps and down the driveway in her bare feet.

'Mom! *Mom!*'

The garbage guy has their garbage can in his hand, he's hoisting it up and pouring it into the open maw of the truck.

'Wait! Wait! *Stop!*'

But it's too late. She doesn't actually see the blue shirt going into the grinder thing in the back of the truck. No, it's probably buried in a bag of trash and used Kleenex and carrot tops.

Angie walks up the driveway. Alice can't even look at her mother she's so furious. She's trying to control her breathing so she'll be able to speak.

'What's going on? . . . Alice?'

'Dad's shirt.'

'Oh, don't get started on that again.'

'You threw it away, didn't you?'

'You can stand out here and catch your death in bare feet, but I'm going inside.'

Angie starts to walk past Alice, but Alice steps in front of her, blocking her way.

'If it's not in the trash, where is it?'

'This is ridiculous. I'm going inside.'

But Alice won't move.

'How could you do that? And how could you lie to me?'

'I haven't lied to you.'

'You want to know why girls can't stand their mothers? It's shit like this, Mom!'

'Inside!'

'First you steal my clothes, then you lie to me and now you think you can order me around?!'

'Alice!'

Angie tries to walk around her again.

'Couldn't you just ask me, Mom? How hard is that? Just ask me!'

'I am not going to argue with you in the middle of the driveway! We can continue this

151

inside.' Angie pushes past Alice. 'Or not at all.'

'Fine! How about not at all?! That would be just more of the same, wouldn't you say, Mom?'

Alice has the satisfaction of hearing her mother slam the front door. Hard. Which is when she hears the garbage truck shift into second gear as it continues its lumbering journey down the street to Henry's house, where no doubt Henry's father had the trash down at the curb well before six a.m. No mothers running out to the street in bathrobes at Henry's house.

Where is her dad's shirt now? Part of the compost of newspapers, orange rinds, cereal boxes, last night's take out containers . . . Some of the fight goes out of Alice as her feet begin to ache they're so cold. She starts up the driveway.

Okay. She'll get another one of her dad's shirts, and maybe she'll take one of his jackets, too. And if she can wear both of those things, maybe, just maybe she'll be able to hold it together and walk out the door and go to school like she's supposed to.

As she walks through the front door, her mom pushes past with a cup of coffee.

'Alice, get ready for school. Enough of this nonsense.'

Alice does not respond.

'Alice, I mean it. Get a move on.'

Alice swallows hard and finds her voice.

'If anything happens to Dad — '

'What?'

' — it's your fault.'

'You're being ridiculous.'

152

'Am I?'

'You want to blame me. Fine. Blame me. You know who you're really mad at?'

'I don't want to hear this!'

'You're mad at Dad.'

'I am not!'

'Think about it, Alice.'

'Dad did not put that shirt in the trash!'

'Dad — '

' — Don't!'

Alice walks up the stairs and into her parents' bedroom where she takes another shirt out of her father's drawer. Angie follows her.

'I'd really rather you didn't take another one of Dad's — '

Alice's hands are shaking as she unbuttons a crisp blue and white striped shirt. Not the same, not the same shirt at all, she thinks in a kind of wild, sad desperation. One of the buttons pops off and skitters across the floor. She looks at the shirt for a moment, the stripes, the missing button, then shoves it back in the drawer, and slams the drawer shut so hard several photos fall off the dresser.

'What are you doing?'

'I'll never forgive you if — '

'Alice. For heaven's sake.'

'Can you spare one of these?' Alice asks, as she opens the top drawer and grabs a white T-shirt.

'Take five! Take six! You want them all? Take them all, goddamnit! Take them all!'

'I only wanted one, Mom. The one I had. The one he wore,' Alice replies as she slams out the door and down the stairs.

*   *   *

Angie sits on the unmade bed, the broken glass of her favorite picture beneath her fingers. She feels awful, as she always does after a fight. Couldn't she just have *washed* that stupid shirt?

She looks at their wedding photo. Matt is holding her with both hands around her waist, his head thrown back, his whole face lit up with laughter.

Lighten up, she can almost hear him say. *Don't you remember all the shit you put your parents through when you were in high school? She's just a kid, a scared kid.*

Does she have to be so annoying, Angie wonders? Does she have to wave everything right under my nose?

Stop rising to the bait. You're the grown-up here.

Easy for you to say, Matt Bliss, from nine thousand miles away.

April 20th

Alice and Henry catch the bus downtown after school, way downtown, to Pearl Street, to the cool vintage clothing store that specializes in tuxedos. They have twenty dollars to outfit Henry for the dance, and another twenty for Alice. Maybe. For Alice this is all a big maybe. The mothers wanted to take them to the mall; that was a definite no.

Unbeknownst to Alice, Henry also has another

fifty dollars in his pocket, given to him by his mother. Henry and his mother have discussed the options; Henry and his mother have outlined a basic game plan; Henry actually knows what he is looking for.

Sitting next to Alice on the city bus, however, Henry feels lost. It's a cold, comfortless day that could belong to any month from October to May. Henry follows Alice's lead and pulls out his history homework, but he can't read. Reading in cars and buses makes him sick. He sneaks a look at her. She appears to actually be reading about the Continental Congress. She does not sense him looking at her and turn toward him and begin to talk, like she usually does.

They have not discussed the kiss. Or the non-kiss. In fact, they haven't really talked at all. They are both pretending that nothing happened, that everything is the same. But of course, nothing is the same. Riding the bus isn't the same, sitting side by side so their legs almost touch is not the same, getting thrown against Alice as the bus makes the long curve up onto I-95 is not the same. Not talking is not the same. Not talking and joking and laughing. Not having to think so much about every single thing it gives you brain cramp is not the same. It's all so overwhelming that Henry falls asleep, right there on the noisy downtown bus, falls sound asleep until Alice wakes him up at their stop on Jane Street at Downtown Crossing.

They walk the two long, dreary blocks to Pearl Street in total silence. Maybe this was a mistake, Henry is thinking. Maybe this whole thing is one big, terrible mistake. Maybe Alice hates him now and maybe he's mad at Alice for ruining everything and maybe they should just go home. But there's Alice throwing open the grimy door and striding inside Rerun like she owns the place.

There are millions of tuxedos at Rerun, crammed into a long, narrow, dusty storefront on a street that has seen better days. Rerun is flanked on either side by empty stores. The middle-aged, potbellied, Hawaiian shirt — wearing guy behind the counter is eyeing them as if they are hardened shoplifters out to rob him blind. Alice starts sneezing. They don't even know what size to look for. Henry walks up to the counter.

'Hi.'

'Yeah.'

'I need a suit. Or a tuxedo.'

'Uh huh.'

'For a dance.'

'Look around.'

'I don't know what size.'

The guy whips out a tape measure.

'My name's Henry.'

Measuring Henry's waist.

'What's your name?'

Measuring Henry's chest.

'Roger.'

Measuring Henry's inseam.

'Nice to meet you, Roger.'

'The smaller sizes are on the left. Upper rack.'

'What size am I?'

'You're the size that's gonna need alterations.'

'Which is — ?'

'There might be a couple of thirty-fours in there.'

'You got anything for my friend?'

'A tuxedo?'

'Hey, Alice! You want a tuxedo?'

'Maybe,' Alice answers from the other side of a rack.

'I was thinking more like a dress,' Henry says. And then quietly to Roger: 'You know that actress in the movie *Breakfast at Tiffany's*?'

'Audrey Hepburn?'

'A dress like she wore.'

'That's a sheath, bud.'

'And maybe a hat.'

'Does the girl know?'

'No.'

'You might ask the girl.'

'That's my mom's favorite movie.'

Roger gives him a look.

'Do you have anything?' Henry asks.

'I might.'

'Is it in a vault or something?'

Roger calls to Alice. 'What size are you?'

'I don't know. Small?'

'That's a start.'

He walks to the racks of tuxedos, effortlessly extracts four of them, hangs them in a fitting room wallpapered in leopard print, and disappears through a back door.

'Am I supposed to try those on?' Henry asks.

'Yup!'

Alice plops into a lime green swivel chair to wait.

157

Henry closes the curtain.

'I think you should look at some pearls.'

'What?'

'Some long strings of pearls.'

'What are you talking about?'

'Are there hats? Have you seen any hats?'

'Henry, have you lost your mind?'

He steps out of the fitting room.

'This one's too big.'

Henry is drowning in this tuxedo. The sleeves reach his knees. He'd need stilts to wear the pants.

'Try the next one.'

'Look at the pearls.'

'What pearls?'

'In the glass case.'

'What do I want with pearls?'

'Alice could you just — '

Henry steps back into the fitting room as Roger appears with half a dozen little black dresses draped over his arm. He hangs them one by one across the back wall of a fitting room papered in faded peppermint stripes.

'I think this is what he was looking for,' Roger says.

'Those are for me?'

'I'll find you some pearls.'

'Henry . . . ?'

'Just try them on. Just for fun,' Henry says from behind the curtain.

Alice finds herself in the pink room with the peeling wallpaper taking off her backpack and her clothes and carefully pulling the first dress over her head. There is no mirror inside the

158

fitting room, so she's going to have to step outside to see what it looks like. She hesitates. This could be really embarrassing. It seems like it fits; she can still breathe after she zips the zipper. At least it's not long, and at least it's not full of ruffles and bows, and it definitely doesn't look like anything her mother would pick out for her. It's straight and close fitting but not tight, and the skirt hits just below the knee. Maybe she's gonna look like a fifty-year-old widow in this dress.

She steps outside the fitting room. She still has her socks on, but even so she can see that it's a beautiful dress. And even though she's mostly all covered up, it's also a sexy dress. It hugs her body and her waist looks tiny and it shows off her shoulders and her long neck.

'What size shoe do you wear?' Roger asks.

'Seven and a half.'

He hands her a pair of red high heels. She shakes her head.

'Do you have any flats?'

Roger disappears and reappears with a pair of black, pointy-toed flats. Alice pulls her socks off and slips into them.

Henry steps out of his fitting room in a jacket that actually fits and pants that are kind of tight but in a good way. Even just wearing a T-shirt under the jacket, Henry looks good. But Henry is not looking in the mirror, Henry is looking at Alice.

'What?' She laughs.

Roger reappears with an impossibly long string of pearls that he doubles around her neck,

159

and several hairpins.

'Put your hair up,' he instructs, handing her the pins.

Alice lifts her hair off the nape of her neck. Roger glances at Henry, raises an eyebrow. Here it is, the simplest gesture in the world: a girl lifts her hair off the nape of her neck and a boy and an old man catch their collective breath.

'There,' she says, and turns to them.

She smoothes the front of the dress, looking down at her hands, at her bitten fingernails, at her big feet in the pointy-toed shoes. This is a woman's dress, she thinks, a young woman's dress. It is not a girl's dress. It is solidly on the other side of the line outside of girlhood. It is a dress that says something big in a very quiet way; it is a dress that is talking to Alice right now, a dress that is making her feel possibilities never before considered, the possibility of perfume and pretty and dancing and boys. This dress is who she might be, only more so.

When she looks up they are both smiling at her.

'You need a shirt,' Roger says to Henry, and hustles off to find him one.

Henry almost can't bear looking at Alice. There's something happening in his stomach that could be the flu or could be just plain, pure misery and longing.

'Do you like it?'

He nods his head and closes his eyes to try to contain the intensity of what he is feeling. He closes his eyes and imagines holding Alice on the dance floor, his hands resting on the small of her

160

back; he imagines hearing Duke Ellington and a
tenor sax and knowing the tune and knowing the
words and knowing the steps, and holding Alice
in his arms, Alice in that dress, Alice with that
music . . .

'Henry . . . ?'

He opens his eyes to find Alice grinning at
him.

'What?'

'This could be fun.'

April 21st

'There are two soldiers at the front door!' Ellie
shouts.

'What?!'

'Two soldiers! Knocking on the door.'

'What are you talking about?'

'I think you should answer the door.'

'Is it Dad?'

'No! It's not Dad!'

'Nobody comes to the front door.'

'Alice! I want you to come down here right
now!'

'I'm coming!'

Alice is running down the stairs thinking,
soldier at the front door, soldier at the front
door. Her heart is flip-flopping in her chest, and
she's not really sure where her feet are and
before she opens the door she has a chance to
register Ellie. Ellie who is standing stock still in
front of the living room window, a bright blue
crayon in her left fist, staring out the window at

the soldiers who are improbably standing on the front stoop, patiently waiting for someone to open the door.

She hesitates with her hand on the knob. He knocks again, softly. Do they get training in this? How to knock? What time of day to show up?

She opens the door to a soldier in his twenties who immediately takes off his hat, revealing an extremely new haircut. He is flanked by another soldier twice his size.

'I'm Sergeant Walker Ames. This is Army Chaplain McMurphy. May I speak to your mother?'

'She's not home.'

'When will she be back?'

Alice glances at her dad's watch.

'Maybe six thirty, maybe later.'

'Can you call her?'

'Is my dad all right?'

'Can you call her?'

'Can you just tell me that?'

'I'll wait while you call her.'

He is eerily, almost creepily calm Alice thinks, as her mind races to take in all of the possibilities of what his presence on her front stoop means.

'Do you want to come inside?' Ellie asks.

'No, thank you. Please call your mother.'

Twenty minutes later Angie pulls all the way into the driveway and comes in through the kitchen door, the way they always do. As she stoops down to give Ellie a hug, Alice can see that her hands are shaking.

'I just wanted a moment with my girls,' she says, as she pulls Alice to her side.

There's that soft knock again.

Angie stands and walks to the front door. The girls are hesitating behind her. She reaches out and opens the door.

'Mrs. Bliss? Mrs. Angie Bliss?'

'Yes.'

'Sergeant Walker Ames. May I come in?'

★   ★   ★

Missing. They have almost no information other than that Matt Bliss is officially MIA.

Here's what they do know, or what the army will tell them, or what they have sanitized to put in the official letter, which is delivered by Sergeant Ames and the very bulky, very bald, and nearly tongue-tied army chaplain McMurphy.

Matt had been patrolling Falluja for six days with his thirteen-man infantry squad. On the day in question, Matt's unit rushed the roof of the tallest building in the northern end of the city. With a nineteen-year-old named Travis Boyd in the lead, the soldiers ran up the building's four flights of stairs. When they stepped out onto the roof, the enemy opened fire. Matt ran past Travis Boyd to the far side of the building where he was shot and wounded. Within seconds, everyone else on the roof was wounded.

In the letter to the family they quote Travis Boyd: 'We tried to get to Matt. I could see he was still alive. But the insurgents dragged him away with them.' Boyd was hit with shrapnel and suffered a concussion, earning a Purple Heart.

They do not know where Matt is being held or why. Sergeant Ames is talking about hope, telling them of other cases where missing soldiers have been found, or rescued. He advises them to be patient, not to watch the news, to go about their daily life as usual.

The army chaplain is doing considerably less talking. He does manage to ask them to call him, any time of the day or night. He hands Angie his card. Ellie wants one, too.

'Girls, I want you to go to your room.'

'But, Mom — ' Alice says.

'Alice, take your sister upstairs, please.'

Alice turns to Sergeant Ames.

'Did you say he was on a roof?'

'Yes.'

'He was ambushed and wounded on a roof?'

'Yes.'

'Alice, I'd like you to go upstairs now please,' Angie says.

The girls go, reluctantly. Alice sits on the upstairs landing to listen as best she can with Ellie sobbing in their bedroom.

Angie asks to speak to Sergeant Ames alone. McMurphy heaves himself out of Matt's favorite chair and leaves the house, shutting the door very quietly behind him.

'The army recovers her own, ma'am.'

'Dead or alive?'

'We always work toward the best possible outcome.'

She looks at him.

'Believe me. We are on top of this. We will be the first to know if there is any intelligence.'

164

'Are you actively searching for him?'

'I'm afraid that's classified.'

'Is that really all you can tell me?'

'Steps are being taken.'

'When will we know more?'

'It is my duty to keep the family informed, ma'am.'

'Do you have any idea why they would take Matt like that?'

'It happens occasionally.'

'But why?'

'Ma'am — '

'I'm thinking the worst here, Sergeant. Some real information would help.'

'Intelligence is usually the motive for any capture.'

Angie takes a deep breath.

'And how often do you recover soldiers alive?'

'I don't have an exact number, ma'am.'

'I don't believe you.'

'It's a small number.'

'Is it zero?'

'No, ma'am.'

'Are you going to make me guess, Sergeant?'

'Less than twenty percent.'

'Thank you.'

Angie looks out the window at the weak April sunshine shading into evening.

'Is he likely to be tortured?'

'There's no reason to give up hope.'

'You didn't answer my question.'

'Reports vary widely.'

The careful management of information, or lack of information, is making Angie furious.

'My husband has been wounded — we don't know how gravely — and dragged away by insurgents. He is presumably without medical care.'

'He's strong, he's fit; he's well trained.'

'Do we have any idea how badly wounded he was? Or where he was wounded? Can you contact Travis Boyd with our questions?'

'I will make every effort to do so, ma'am.'

'My name is Angie. Please call me Angie.'

'We are instructed to — '

'Every time you call me ma'am I feel like a widow.'

'Yes, ma'am.'

Sergeant Ames with his raw haircut and bad skin ducks his head, embarrassed.

'Is there anyone I can call to find out more? Is there anything I can do for my husband?'

'You have my number. And the number for the chaplain.'

'Can I talk to a soldier who was there with him?'

'I'll look into that.'

'Where is Travis Boyd now?'

'He's at the army hospital in Landstuhl, Germany.'

'Will he recover?'

'Yes, ma'am, he will.'

'I'd like to speak to him.'

'I'll do my best.'

'When, Sergeant? How soon can I speak to him?'

'I'll make it my priority, ma'am . . . May I make a suggestion?'

166

'Yes.'

'Go to work. Go to school. Go to church. Continue with your daily lives.'

'I'm not sure . . . '

'Sitting in your house for days or weeks can be demoralizing. Call your family. Call your priest or your pastor.'

'Are you telling me to pray, Sergeant?'

'I don't know what your beliefs are, but most people find it a solace. We can also connect you with another family who has gone through this.'

'Thank you.'

'Shall I contact someone then?'

'I don't know. Not yet. I don't know . . . '

'With your permission, I'll call on you tomorrow.'

'Yes. All right.'

Now that he is at the door Angie finds she doesn't want him to go. She doesn't want the next minute and the next to begin.

'Hope is a powerful thing, ma'am.'

'Thank you, Sergeant.'

Angie stands at the door watching Sergeant Ames as he walks down the driveway and gets into his army-issue Ford sedan. McMurphy is slumped low in the passenger seat, waiting. She notices that Ames is painfully thin and too pale and that he walks with a limp. What has he survived, she wonders? What have we put this boy through? What does he do to prepare himself to bring this news to grieving families? Is this kind of duty something you choose or something you are assigned to? How in the world does he bear it?

Be strong, she hears Matt saying inside her head. *Be strong, Angie.*

If he's still talking to her, if he's still bossing her around, if he's still driving her crazy by holding her to a higher standard, even if it's just inside her own head, then he must still be alive. Matt, she thinks, Matt . . . Be there for me. I need you.

In the sudden quiet after the door closes on Sergeant Ames, Alice sits on the landing and closes her eyes and tries to imagine a rooftop in Falluja.

★   ★   ★

She's nine years old the first time she goes on a roofing job with her dad. Her mom is at the library studying for her state licensing exams to be an insurance agent and examiner. Ellie is in day care and Alice is on spring break and therefore at loose ends. So Matt enlists her as his helper.

This all sounds like a good idea when they're in the kitchen making sandwiches and pouring strong hot tea into Matt's special work Thermos. Fun project with Dad. Dad and Alice on an outing. No interruptions from baby Ellie.

But then they get to the house in question, with the roof in question, and Alice's stomach takes a nosedive. The house is high on a hill. On top of that, it's a tall house. With a tower. There's an extension ladder and a kind of scaffolding built into the roof. Alice stands at the foot of the extension ladder and looks up. The roof is a million miles above her. And it's really, really steep. She's in the midst of changing her mind and coming up with a plan. She could stay in the car, or near the car, she promises not to be any trouble, not to interrupt him or complain about being bored.

'Okay. Let's go.'

'I think I might be afraid of heights.'

'I don't think so.'

'I didn't think it would be so high.'

'It's not that high.'

'It looks high.'

'Let's go.'

'I could stay in the car, I could — '

'Alice — ' he says in that tone. That tone that says there's no sense arguing, don't be a wuss, and don't disappoint me. She hates that tone. More than she hates that roof? It's a toss-up.

When she starts up the ladder she's fine, but half way up one of her legs starts to shake. She is not making this up. It's weird.

Matt is right behind her, his hands gripping the rungs on either side of her.

'It's okay. You're not gonna fall.'

'But — '

'I've got you. Take a breath . . . '

She breathes in.

'Don't hold your breath, Alice. Blow it out.'

'Okay.'

'There's nothing to be afraid of. It's just a ladder.'

She climbs two more rungs.

'Daddy — '

She can't move. Her legs are now shaking so

169

badly she can't trust them to hold her up. Matt puts his palm against her lower back.

'Just breathe. You're okay.'

She tries that. Her hands are starting to go numb because she's holding the ladder so tightly. She makes the mistake of looking down.

'Dad! I need to go down. I can't do this.'

'Yes, you can.'

'No, I can't!' I will not cry, I will not cry, she says inside her head.

'You're safe. I won't let you fall.'

'I'm so — '

'I know you're scared. It's okay to be scared. You just don't want to give in to it. Don't let it get bigger than you, Alice. It's just a feeling.'

She starts to sniffle. She can't help it.

'Crying is not going to help here.'

'I know.'

'Look up. Four more steps and we're there. You can do it, Alice, I know you can.'

She takes another step.

'It's really beautiful up there, Alice. You can see all the way to the lake.'

'Really?'

'You're gonna love it.'

And another step and another and now there's a new problem, how do you step out onto the roof? That is the scariest step of all.

'Don't think about it. Just reach for the scaffolding and hold on to that.'

She closes her eyes.

'You can do it, Alice.'

'Are you sure?' she says in a very small voice.

His lips are right next to her ear so she can feel

the warmth of his breath as he says: 'I'm totally sure. I'm so sure I'll bet you a dollar.'

'Dad?'

'Don't think. Just go.'

She reaches one hand out and grabs the scaffolding and steps off the top rung of the ladder and onto the roof.

'Now what?' She can feel the breath catch in her throat.

'You see where it looks like a bench? Just step on the braces — there are two — that's all you need to do — and sit right there on the bench.'

Her hands are hot and sweaty and slippery and she thinks that sharp tang in the air is her own scared sweat.

'You can do it.'

She wants to close her eyes. She wants to be back on the ground. She wants to be home alone. She wants to be anywhere rather than here.

'Two steps. That's all.'

She puts her left hand against the roof shingles, as if that could help.

'You've got it.'

And she does have it. Two steps and she reaches the bench built into the scaffolding. She sits and grips the edge with both hands. Her stomach is roiling but she is determined not to throw up. When she finally looks up after what feels like a hundred years, her father is grinning at her. He's looking at her like she just hit a home run, which she has never done in her life.

'Way to go, champ.'

She tries to smile and feels the bile rise in her

171

throat again. She closes her eyes, her knuckles white.

'Look around,' he tells her.

She can't take her eyes off his face. Keeping her eyes glued to her father is what will keep her from falling off this roof.

'I can't.'

'Okay. But you're missing the best part.'

She closes her eyes, and she can feel her heart pounding and hear her breath rasping in her ears.

'Breathe, Alice . . . Breathe deep. And then open your eyes and look. Just do it.'

They're above the trees; they're above the power lines; they're above everything. She can see the sun shining on the lake and big, puffy cumulus clouds hanging in the sky. She can see more blue sky than she can see from her house or her yard or her street. She can see the curve of the beach at Loudon Pond Park and the old-fashioned bathhouses still closed up for the winter. She lets out a breath and realizes she's been holding her breath for what seems like forever. She dares to turn her head to see where her dad is and Matt Bliss is walking all over the roof like it is a flat surface just above the ground. He looks like he's walking around his own kitchen. She watches him, amazed.

'You'll get the hang of it.'

I don't think so, she wants to tell him, but still isn't sure she can safely open her mouth.

'When you're ready, you can start handing me shingles. You see the box? To your left?'

She nods.

'Just one at a time, kiddo.'

'If I were a boy, would I be better at this?'

'How many boys do you know who are brave enough to climb up here?'

'I don't know.'

'Henry?'

'He's afraid of heights.'

'See?'

'Do you wish you'd had a boy instead of me?'

'Never.'

'Do you wish I was good at baseball?'

'Yes!'

'Me, too!'

'Okay. You can start with the shingles.'

'Now?'

'Yes.'

'Already?'

'Now's a good time.'

She cautiously reaches for the shingles and just as cautiously reaches out and hands them, one at a time, as he needs them, to her father. At first this takes every ounce of concentration she has, all she can do is look at the roof, and the box and the shingles and his reaching hand. Just as she starts to get used to it, Matt finishes a section. And then he wants her to move to another section of scaffolding and another makeshift bench and another box of shingles. At first these moves reignite the terror inside of her, but by the fourth or fifth time, she's found her roof legs and she is — cautiously — moving a little more freely. And she's able to look up every now and then and take in the new view from a new section of the roof.

173

'You hungry?'
'We're having lunch up here?'
'You want to go down and come back up?'
'No!'
'Okay, then.'
He sits beside her and pulls out the lunch they packed together. Pita pockets and carrot and celery sticks and apples and brownies.
'What if you have to pee?'
He looks at her and raises an eyebrow.
'You do not!'
He shrugs.
'In broad daylight?'
'I face away from the street.'
'What about the neighbors?'
Another shrug.
'What am I supposed to do?' Alice asks.
'Skip the apple juice would be my advice.'
He lies back against the roof, stretches out like he's at the beach, and closes his eyes.
'You're napping?!'
He hands her his watch.
'Wake me up in ten minutes.'
'You have to be kidding me. You could — '
'But I won't. Try it. Just lie back.'
'Dad — '
'Try it.'
She lies back against the shingles, bracing her hands flat against the roof, her fingernails digging into the asphalt, her feet positioned solidly on the scaffolding. She takes a shaky breath. After the first disorienting moment, it's pretty nice actually. She looks over at her father and he's grinning at her again.

174

'You're showing off, aren't you, Dad?'
'I might be showing off a little.'
'You always tell me not to show off.'
'Sometimes I guess it's irresistible.'
'You really like it up here.'
'I love it up here.'
He closes his eyes.
'Ten minutes, okay?'
Alice carefully takes one hand away from where it is trying to grip the roof beside her and brings her arm up to where she can see her dad's watch hanging loosely on her wrist. She notes the time: 12:01. At exactly 12:11 she will wake him up. If he's really asleep. If he's not just faking it. She likes it that he's trying to impress her. She likes it that he cares about her opinion. And now that she's not absolutely slick with fear, she's almost glad he got her up here. On top of the world.

* * *

The girls come downstairs slowly, not knowing what to expect. Angie is still at the front door looking out at the street. She wants to get on a plane; she wants to call her senator, her state representative, and her congressman; she wants to call her mother. She wants to fall apart and have someone else take care of things. But that would not be the way Matt would handle this. He would take steps. He would hold it together.

Before he left she was under the illusion that they had talked about everything, every possible scenario; if he were wounded or killed. But this

175

. . . this was never part of the picture. They didn't plan for this.

She can feel the girls waiting behind her, waiting for her to turn around, waiting for her to know what to do, waiting for her to come up with a plan.

'Mom . . . ?' Ellie ventures.

Angie turns away from the street and looks at her girls. When she sees how frightened they are, her own fear threatens to rise up out of her in a howl.

One step at a time, Angie. Don't think about tomorrow. Don't project into the future. Take care of today. Take care of the here and now. Take care of the girls.

'Okay. Here's what we're going to do. We're going to ask ourselves what Daddy would want us to do. And then we're going to do it.'

'Will he be all right?' Ellie asks.

'If anybody can come through this, Daddy can.'

'Do you believe that?' Alice asks.

'Yes,' Angie answers. 'Yes, I do.'

'I want to help him,' Ellie says.

'How? I don't see how,' Alice says.

'We can imagine our way to being near him,' Angie says. 'We can imagine healing him, comforting him. Think about him. Believe in him.'

A flash of anger sears through Alice. Does her mother actually *believe* this crap? And then she looks at Ellie. Ellie is soaking this up. Suddenly Alice's anger deflates and she wishes she could be eight again.

'I need something to *do*,' Ellie says.

'Go to school. Help at home. Make Daddy proud.'

'I don't see how going to school will . . . ' Alice trails off, uncertain.

Ellie closes her eyes.

'I'm thinking about Daddy right now.'

'Good.'

'Mom — '

'I'll make dinner,' Angie says. 'You girls can do your homework.'

'You're making dinner?'

'Don't look so surprised.'

'And you expect us to do homework?'

'Yes.'

'Are you serious? It's Friday night.'

'Homework tonight and work and school on Monday.'

Ellie obediently gets her backpack and sits at the dining room table. Alice joins her reluctantly, pulls out her planner, opens it, but when she tries to look up today's assignments she has trouble focusing. She finds a pen and opens a notebook so she'll look busy and then just sits there as Ellie actually completes her grammar worksheets and moves on to writing a story about honeybees.

'You're ploitering,' Ellie announces.

'I'm what?'

'Ploitering. 'Working to little purpose.''

'*Loiter* with a *p* in front of it?'

'Yup.'

'You made that up.'

'Nope.'

'Are you sure?'

'Honeybees never ploiter.'

'Are you working that into your story?'

'Extra credit vocabulary words.'

'What do you need extra credit for? You already get all A's.'

'A plus is possible. A plus is within my reach.'

'Are you illustrating your story?'

'Of course.'

'Hey, maybe you could have one honeybee who ploiters. A renegade. It could add to the drama.'

'I'll think about it.'

Ellie never incorporates Alice's suggestions into her stories. Ever.

Alice shifts her chair so she can watch her mom in the kitchen, an apron over her dress, going through the motions of making dinner. Shortly afterward, they all go through the motions of eating dinner, washing dishes, giving Ellie her bath, and finally going to bed.

★ ★ ★

After tossing and turning for what feels like forever, Alice gets up to go downstairs. She wishes she could go for a run. She wishes it were Monday so she could go to the computer lab at school to Google Earth Falluja's streets and houses and, hopefully, find aerial views of rooftops.

She's surprised to find her mom in the kitchen making tea with honey and rum. Angie looks up.

'I couldn't sleep,' Angie says.

178

'Me neither.'

'You want some?'

'You're offering me rum?'

'A teaspoon in some tea.'

'Sure.'

'It'll help you sleep.'

Angie gets another mug from the cupboard, pours a second cup of tea.

'Have you told Gram?'

'Tomorrow. Let her have one more good night's sleep.'

'And Uncle Eddie?'

'Same.'

She adds honey and a small splash of rum.

'I think if I talk about it, if I tell people, that will make it real,' Alice says. 'Right now, my mind knows it's real, but no other part of me can really . . . '

'That's shock, honey. That's how the body protects us. We can only take it in a little at a time.'

'I don't want to take it in.'

'I know.'

Angie hands Alice her tea.

'Careful — it's hot.'

'I need more honey.'

'Help yourself.'

Alice adds a lot more honey.

'It's pretty good.'

'Gram used to make this for me when I had a cold.'

'When you were little?'

'Not that little.'

Alice gathers her courage.

179

'Mom . . . '

Angie doesn't answer. She looks away.

'I need to know.'

'Let's just drink our tea and slow our minds way, way down so we can get some sleep. We'll talk tomorrow. Okay, Alice? Tomorrow.'

And Alice thinks wounded and Alice thinks captured and Alice thinks torture. She sips her tea and feels the slow seep of warmth spreading through her limbs. She feels her body slowing down even while her mind is still racing.

Angie looks at Alice, watches her get lost in her thoughts, sees her chapped lips and her tangled hair and the ancient Grateful Dead T-shirt of Matt's that she wears to bed. It's so old the jersey is disintegrating away from the seams.

'C'mon, honey. Let's go to bed.'

Angie puts her arm around Alice's waist. She can feel ribs under her fingers and Alice's cool, smooth skin. Alice lets herself be held, almost, for a brief second, before pulling away.

They walk upstairs, one behind the other now, each carrying her mug of tea like a lantern in the dark.

April 24th

Alice sits in school on Monday and closes her eyes and tries to feel whether her father is still alive. Does the body know before the mind does? Can she feel the connection she has always felt or has it snapped? She wants to know where he

180

was wounded, how badly, could he still walk and talk? What the hell was he wearing all that protective gear for if it couldn't really protect him? And what if his gear did protect him — and he was just stunned, not wounded — does that increase his chances of surviving? What if he was hit in one of the few exquisitely vulnerable places that the gear can't cover? Like his neck or his face and now she imagines a bullet ripping through an artery in his wrist or his thigh.

While waiting in the band room for chorus rehearsal to begin, Alice overhears Jennifer White and Melissa Johnson talking. She's trying to ignore them, but they're loud like they always are, and words and phrases keep hitting her like a punch to the gut.

'How could he do that?'

'I hate my father. I really hate him.'

'I can't believe he did that to you.'

'He's such an asshole.'

'Grounding you for two weeks . . . '

'I wish he'd go away, I wish he'd die, I wish . . . '

Before she can think, Alice shoves Jennifer White. She meant to just give her a little push, but it's like she's so upset she's got this superhuman strength, and that little push hits Jennifer White so hard she stumbles, loses her balance, and falls to the ground. And gets a bloody nose and starts wailing. Alice looks up in time to see Stephie glance at her and then look away, shaking her head. No sympathy from that corner. Melissa Johnson is about to retaliate when Mr. Brooks, the music teacher, pushes his

181

way through the crowd with his immense bulk. And even though Jennifer White gets a bloody nose if you just say boo to her, this looks really bad.

Next thing you know Alice is in the principal's office. Mr. Fisher wants to know what happened, he wants to talk about it; but Alice can't talk about it, she can't answer his questions, she can't tell him her side of the story. She just sits there staring at her hands or out the window. And while the principal is trying to be understanding, the longer she stays silent, the more wound up he gets until he's forgotten all about her father and has convinced himself she's being disrespectful and obstreperous and that she needs a nice little suspension to get her attitude in order.

When he picks up the phone to call her mother at work, Alice gets up to leave the room. He angrily waves her back to her seat just as the lunch bell rings. She knows he will not make himself ridiculous by actually chasing her, so she makes her escape in the general lunchtime melee and walks out the back door of the school and heads for home. Henry follows her for a ways but she can't talk to Henry right now, she can't talk to anybody.

Halfway down Highland Drive, where is she *going* anyway?, B.D. pulls up beside her in his old Chevy. The backseat is filled with orange plastic cones for practice, out-of-date running magazines, and empty coffee cups.

'Alice, where are you going? We've got practice this afternoon.'

'I can't come today.'

'You want to be on the team, you come every day.'

'I'll make it up. Tomorrow. I can make it up tomorrow.'

B.D. doesn't say anything. He's just looking at her.

'And I can run tonight. From home. Give me the workout.'

'You want to be on this team, or what?'

How can he ask her this? How can he not know?

'Yes!' she says too loudly.

'Did something happen, Alice?'

She can't answer.

'You okay, kid?'

Alice is clenching and unclenching her hands. Her legs are so tense that her right knee is vibrating.

'You need somebody to talk to?'

'No.'

'You sure?'

'I'll be okay.'

'You need a lift somewhere?'

'No, thank you.'

'Where are you going? Aren't you supposed to be in school?'

'I couldn't . . . I can't . . . '

He rolls his window all the way down, leans out.

'I'll let it slide this time, Alice. But come and talk to me, okay?'

'Are you gonna give me the workout?'

'Kid, you hardly look like you can stand up, let alone run.'

'*I can run!*' bursts out of her with more
vehemence than she intended.

B.D. reaches out to touch Alice, her hand or
her shoulder, and then thinks better of it.
Nothing is simple anymore, he thinks, not even
reaching out to a girl who is falling apart in front
of your eyes.

'You need me to call somebody? A teacher?
Your mom?'

'*No!*'

He thinks about his own kids, lost to him
following his divorce, the look they get in their
eyes, the faraway look, the fear, the anger, the
tough protective layers they build up around
their hopes and their losses.

'Alice — '

She looks at him.

'I'm not the enemy, okay?'

She hesitates, then nods and turns away.

B.D. grinds the Chevy into gear.

'Come and see me tomorrow, okay? Alice?'

'Okay.'

'I mean it.'

B.D. lurches away, tailpipe rattling, looking at
Alice in his rearview mirror.

★   ★   ★

She breaks into a run, and even though she has
no idea where to go, she's suddenly like some
sort of homing pigeon, and in short order she
finds herself at Uncle Eddie's garage. He slides
out from underneath the 1979 BMW he's
working on.

'Hey, Alice, what are you doing here?'

She looks at her feet. She didn't think she'd have to explain to Uncle Eddie.

He looks at his watch.

'Aren't you supposed to be in school?'

'I . . . It's just . . . '

He grabs a set of keys.

'You want to drive? Take your mind off things?'

'Okay.'

'We could head out to the lake. Back roads. Nice and slow.'

She nods, uncertain of her voice.

'I'll drive us out to the golf course, then you can take over.'

Eddie leads her around back to the little parking lot behind the garage and opens the passenger door of a restored 1966 Mustang. In the back corner of the lot, Matt's truck sits up on blocks, covered with a tarp. Alice hesitates. The tarp looks like a shroud. Don't think like that, runs through her mind. It's just a truck; it's just a tarp.

'C'mon, Alice, let's go.'

She turns back to Uncle Eddie and the Mustang.

'Uncle Eddie, I can't drive this car.'

'Why not?'

'It's . . . it's . . . '

'Spectacular, isn't it? Hop in.'

The seats are deep, buttery leather.

'Don't you feel cool just sitting in this car?'

Alice smiles, she almost laughs.

'If I could afford it . . . man, I'd love to have a car like this.'

185

'Who owns it?'

'Some Kodak CEO. Nice guy. For a CEO. He's got good taste in cars, at least.'

'How much longer do you get to play with it?'

'We're done. He's picking it up tomorrow. Lucky us he's busy in Washington right now. This is my good-bye drive. And I'm sharing it with you, you lucky girl.'

Uncle Eddie rolls down his window and cranks up the radio.

'Put your window down,' he shouts.

She rolls her window down, sticks her arm out, flaps her hand in the wind. Uncle Eddie fiddles with the dial until he finds the classic oldies station and the Rolling Stones: 'Satisfaction.' Perfect. He turns the volume up so loud the floorboards are vibrating under their feet. Uncle Eddie shouts along with the music.

But I try, and I try and I try and I try-y-y . . .

He drums on the steering wheel.

I can't get no!

More drumming.

No satisfaction!

He looks at her and grins. What can she do? She grins right back.

They change places and moderate the volume just a bit in the parking lot of Silver Lake Golf Course. Alice adjusts the seat and the mirrors under Uncle Eddie's watchful eye.

'You ready?' he asks.

She nods.

'I figure we've had enough practice in parking lots.'

'Only three — !'

'That's plenty. You're a natural.'

'I am?'

'Time for the open road, girl.'

As she eases the Mustang out onto Blossom Road, she thinks, thank God there's no traffic because it sure feels like she is driving down the center of the street.

'A little to the right,' Eddie suggests.

She oversteers onto the verge, and then overcorrects, and finally gets the car centered in the lane. It's harder than it looks.

'There you go. You're getting it.'

Alice makes it through six miles of open road, she manages the four-way stop at Lakeshore Boulevard, and Uncle Eddie talks her through the tricky intersection right before they get to the lake.

'Hang a left on Seabreeze. Let's get some ice cream.'

This is easy, she thinks, until she almost clips the guardrail making her turn into the frozen custard place.

'That was a little close.'

And then she hits the brakes too hard as she pulls into a parking spot.

'Sorry! Sorry!'

'You're doing fine. What flavor do you want?'

'Chocolate almond.'

'Keep count of how many boys try to pick you up while I'm inside.'

'Uncle Eddie!'

'Just keep count. I'm telling you.'

'I'm *fifteen!*'

'You're in a Mustang, baby. Count the boys.'

187

Instead she cranks up the radio again and closes her eyes. Driving is almost as good as running, she thinks. Maybe she could just get in a car and drive forever. She could drive from park to park and run at every lake and beach and woods from here to . . . Maine, she thinks. From here to Maine.

★ ★ ★

She remembers how she would stay awake to keep her dad company on the drive to the campground at Small Point, along the two-lane road that bisects the Phippsburg peninsula, the woods reaching to the sky, the moon shining like a flirtatious girl running in and out of the trees, in and out of sight, making stripes of white on the road ahead of them. She remembers opening the windows, gulping the piney air, breathing in the first hint of salt water. You can almost taste it: the salt and the pine and the cold air exhaling from the woods. She doesn't look behind. There is no need, yet, to look behind, to watch over her shoulder, to shore up moments and memories against future loss. There is only her dad and the car and the road and the turn off to Small Point at the far end of the peninsula. Here it is, the narrow bit of sand that passes for a road at low tide. Mom and Ellie asleep in the back. Alice and Matt awake, the first ones to see the Kelp Shed, the first ones to see the new speed bump, to take the sharp left turning up to the dirt roads and the campsites. Ocean side. They are ocean side, not bay side campers. Number 39. On the bluffs. Over the rocks. Set apart, but not too far to the showers.

* * *

There's a knock on her window and Alice nearly jumps out of her skin. There are four teenage boys and two older guys clustered around the Mustang. Wanting to touch it, to run their hands over the bright red curves, pushing each other and their bodies closer and closer. This one guy leans right in her window after she opens her eyes.

'Hey, beautiful.'

They jostle each other to get close to the window.

'Goin' my way, honey?'

'Where'd you get this gorgeous car?'

'What's your name, baby?'

Uncle Eddie appears with an ice cream cone in each hand.

'Back off, boys. She's my niece. She's fifteen.'

'Just admiring your car.'

'No harm meant.'

'She's a beauty.'

The men and boys disperse as Uncle Eddie hands her the ice cream.

'Six,' he says, 'I counted six.'

'It's the car.'

'Of course it's the car. It's also, I'm telling you, every man's fantasy: a beautiful girl in a beautiful car.'

They change places so Uncle Eddie can drive them out to the lake. Driving plus eating ice cream is a lesson for another day, apparently, or another car. He parks where they can watch the water and the birds.

'You want to talk?' he asks.

The cooling engine ticks away like a clock running down.

'I don't know.'

'How's your mom doing?'

'She's kind of wrapped in cellophane or something.'

'What about Ellie?'

'I'm not sure she gets how serious it is.'

'Maybe that's good.'

'Maybe it is. But she wet the bed last night. And she's sucking her thumb again.'

'Wouldn't it be nice if we could press rewind and go backward a couple of years. What about you?'

'I might be suspended.'

'Really?'

'I shoved some dimwit girl and she fell over like a . . . she fell over and got a bloody nose.'

The ice cream is freezing inside her chest.

'Why'd you hit her?'

'She was talking some dumb shit about hating her father and wishing he were dead. Because he *grounded* her.'

'Wow.'

'And then the principal was trying to be decent and wanted to give me a chance, wanted to hear my side of the story, only I couldn't talk, so he just sat there getting madder and madder, because it probably seemed like I was doing it on purpose, and then he got so mad he decided to

190

call Mom and suspend me. Which is when I walked out.'

'You walked out?'

'Yeah.'

'Really?'

'Yeah.'

'Go, Alice!'

'Probably not an appropriate response for a grown-up, Uncle Eddie.'

'Who cares? That takes guts.'

'You're crazy.'

'Besides, who says I'm a grown-up?'

Alice looks away.

'It's just . . . ' She can't continue.

Eddie waits. He's thinking that ice cream was probably a dumb idea, but what else can you do for a kid?

'The odds aren't good, are they?' she asks.

He looks out at the lake, considers.

'Probably not for most people. But for your dad . . . '

She tries to hold her voice steady.

'Thanks for not lying to me.'

Alice shivers as a bank of clouds obscures the sun. Uncle Eddie reaches out and puts his hand on the back of her head. Leaves it there for a moment. And finds himself thinking about his father, so much like Matt in so many ways. The way he could be quiet with you, the way it seemed like nothing frightened him, that he knew his measure as a man, as a husband, as a father, the way some men are just solid, without making a big show of it. All the things I've been running from, Eddie thinks, like it's possible to

191

take a pass on facing up to who or what you want to be, or who you are.

'What do you say we take Lakeshore Boulevard all the way to Sodus Point and then head home? You find some mellow tunes. We'll cruise.'

She turns the radio on; there's Van Morrison again: 'Brown Eyed Girl.'

Do you remember when we used to sing?

'Some smart boy is gonna woo you with that song.'

Sha la la la la la la la la la la te da.

'I doubt it, Uncle Eddie.'

'You wait and see, girl. It's *classic*.'

'The song or the tactic?' She wants to know.

'Both.'

★ ★ ★

Alice pushes open the door of her dad's workshop. It used to be the garage until Matt went into business for himself. Back then the plan had been to put an addition onto the garage for Matt's workshop, but he was always too busy to work on his own house. So her mom's car sits outside in the driveway. A bone of contention with Angie all winter long; but it's an old bone now so mostly nobody notices it anymore. Except Angie when she's scraping ice off her windshield.

The garage sits directly behind the house on the skinny part of their oddly shaped lot. Beyond the garage the lot opens up to the garden, the three apple trees, two cherry trees, and Matt's grape arbor. Matt installed windows along the back and side walls that look out on the garden. He had plans to put in more windows, too. Capture the view! The second-hand woodstove went in his first winter. A necessity. Can't do much with mittens on, he'd say.

It's four o'clock. Mom's still at work. Ellie's on a play date at Janna's house. It took Alice an hour to decide to come out here, after Uncle Eddie dropped her off, and another ten minutes outside the door gathering the courage to open it. Now she has to walk in.

The late afternoon sun breaks through the thickening clouds to shine through the back windows; dust motes dance in the weak shafts of light. She breathes in. It smells like wood and turpentine and linseed oil. The workshop is cool and a bit damp; it feels as though the room exhales when she opens the door. She closes her eyes; she can almost picture her dad standing at his workbench, sanding the curve on a new piece of wood to make it look old; she can almost hear the rasp of the sandpaper.

She stands in the middle of the space. Her eyes adjust to the dim light. Aside from the dust, the place is as neat as a pin. Every tool has its place to hang, every kind of nail and screw and fastener has its own jar. She crosses to his big wooden tool chest and opens it. This is the chest he built for the tools that never leave the workshop. His father's hammer, his grandfather's awl and plane and C-clamps. The chest is full of ingenious cubbies and sliding doors and drawers opening beneath other drawers. On the inside of the lid there are five photos. Front and center is the four of them the day they brought Ellie home from the hospital. Matt is holding the baby and Mom and Alice are holding on to Matt. The grin on his face is so big it looks like it could lift him off his feet. Then there's Ellie on her trike, Alice on horseback, a romantic picture from their wedding where Matt has lifted Angie off the ground and you can tell he is kissing her like crazy, and an old photograph of Matt's parents.

It starts to rain and the wind kicks up, blowing rain through the open door. She grabs her dad's work jacket, which hangs on a peg behind the door, along with a few baseball caps, overalls, and work boots. Shrugging into his jacket she almost loses it. Listening to the rain tapping out some sort of code on the roof, she closes her eyes and tries to see him. But what she sees is either the family photo in his tool chest or an image of a soldier lying face down in blood-spattered dust. The two impossibilities flash one after the other across her inner eye.

She opens her eyes as the storm begins its crescendo. The rain on the roof has grown loud and the wind is thrashing the lilac bushes outside the south window. She shoves her hands into the pockets of the jacket and finds a stub of pencil and a folded square of paper in the right-hand pocket, a level, a receipt from the paint store, and a pair of keys in the left-hand pocket. She lays them all out on the workbench.

She unfolds the square of paper. It's a note and a drawing from Ellie, maybe from kindergarten when she was first learning to make her letters. It's a series of colorful squiggles. And on the bottom in block letters, some of them backward:

'ELLIE LOVES DADDY'

She smoothes out the creases with her palm and props the note up on the windowsill where he'll be able to see it when he gets home.

Even with the jacket on she's shivering, and she's not really sure if it's shivering or shaking or all the tears she's trying not to cry; so she gets up, grabs a broom, and begins sweeping. The sweeping and the rain and the distant rumble of thunder and the wind sending sheets of rain through the door all feel like they are happening inside of her. Ellie loves Daddy, she thinks. Ellie loves Daddy. And wonders if that will make a difference. If love and caring and needing enter into the equation of what will happen to her father and her family at all.

As she sweeps, she hatches a plan. She'll get one of the air mattresses from the basement and the old Coleman lantern. And she'll bring out her books and her sleeping bag and some old pillows and she'll do her homework out here. Maybe a candle and some CDs, and the rocking chair from her room, and before you know it, Alice is imagining living in the garage and getting some books out of the library so she can learn how to put the windows in that Matt always wanted. She's pretty sure Uncle Eddie would help her. Matt already has the windows, stacked neatly against the far wall. All the windows for the workshop are castoffs he finds in the street. Old windows with lots of panes. The windows for the west wall are long and thin. There is a pair of them, and Matt wanted to install them horizontally. He just thought it would be cool. Alice wonders if there will be instructions for that in a library book; she hopes so.

She knows this is a good plan. She knows her dad would like it. She also knows that her mom won't like it. Especially when Alice starts sleeping out here. Or maybe she'll keep being so busy she won't even notice.

Inside the house she grabs dust cloths, the bucket, the mop, and Mr. Clean. Half an hour later, Alice finishes mopping the workshop floor. She's not sure this floor has ever been mopped before. She had to change the water in the bucket three times, and it was obvious the rafters had never been dusted. She tackles the windows next. Inside first. The outside will have to wait until it stops raining. The stepladder is just tall enough. She starts to imagine what it's going to look like when they install those two long, skinny windows.

It's growing dark by the time she finishes. She knows she should just head indoors and start dinner like her mother asked, but there's something about the busy-ness of working out here that is keeping her going, in spite of both shirtsleeves being soaked, in spite of feeling really cold.

She sits in the lawn chair and makes a list of what she needs to get from the house. Of course there are sharpened pencils in an old peanut butter jar and pads of paper right on the workbench. She uses block printing just the way her dad does:

Air mattress
Sleeping bag
Pillow
Fleece jacket
Milk crate
Bedside lamp
Extension cord
Flashlight
Books
Rocking chair

Maybe she can pop Jiffy Pop on the woodstove. And heat water for instant hot chocolate.

As soon as the rain lets up she will start moving stuff in. She'll fill the wood box next to the woodstove, and the kindling box, and she'll ask Uncle Eddie to find her a wooden pallet or two, so she can keep her air mattress off the floor.

She looks around at Matt's power tools, shrouded in canvas tarps, arranged carefully along the east wall. The way he cleaned up and organized, it's almost like he knew she was going to want to be out here. There's all this space in the middle of the workshop that is usually cluttered with lathes and power saws and sawhorses.

There's something nagging at her, she's not sure what, until she looks up in the rafters she's just dusted and sees a shoebox stuck up there. She gets the stepladder out again, climbs up, and pulls out the box. It has her name on it.

She steps off the ladder and sets the box on the workbench in the watery light coming through the rain slick windows.

What has he left for her? Sand dollars? Shells? Seed packets?

She lifts off the top and looks inside:

Dear Alice,

I wrote you a few letters. They're not really for right now. They're for just in case I have to miss anything important.

I love you, sweetheart. Never forget it.

Dad

Inside, there's a stack of envelopes, each with his precise writing, each with a date or an event: Graduation from high school, from college, the first time she falls in love, the first time she gets her heart broken, her wedding day, the birth of her first child, the death of her mother.

There's a series of letters with the heading 'the little moments that make up the big moments, that might get forgotten.' The subheadings in this group are: 'the moment you realize you want this boy to kiss you,' 'the moment you realize you don't love this boy anymore,' 'the moment you realize you're going to leave home and never really live there again,' 'the moment you realize you're more like your mother than you want to be.'

Alice puts the lid back on the shoebox and centers the box in her lap and puts her hands on top of it. Then she carefully climbs the ladder again and stows the box in the rafters.

There, on the top rung of the ladder, she hears his voice: *Don't look down. Look up, Alice. Look up.* And hope — where does it come from, she wonders, just the sound of his voice? — stirs to life inside of her.

Maybe, she thinks, maybe he'll be home in time for cucumbers, and if not cucumbers, then for tomatoes, and if not tomatoes, then surely in time for corn. Maybe they could go camping in Maine in August, like they always do; maybe, maybe, maybe . . .

She'll take care of the workshop; everything will be ready for him when he gets home. And if he needs help, or needs more time to recover, Alice can be his assistant, she can be his right-hand man, she can be his girl Friday; she can be anything he needs her to be.

April 25th

Taking advantage of her suspension, Alice sleeps in, tries to catch up on some homework, and then shows up at Uncle Eddie's garage for her first lesson in basic car maintenance. Today: the oil change. She has plans to surprise Angie by changing the oil and filters in their Camry.

Uncle Eddie already has somebody else's Camry up on the hydraulic jack.

'Okay, here's what you need for this job,' Uncle Eddie says as he gathers the necessary tools. 'Socket wrench, oil filter wrench, drain pan, four quarts of oil, car filter, and a drain plug gasket. Your dad will have the wrenches, and I can give you the drain pan, filter, gasket, and oil.'

Just as he starts to walk Alice through the job, Janna's mom drops Ellie off. Ellie, who has no interest in cars or car maintenance, waves hi and heads straight to what passes for a waiting area: one bench seat from some old car, a derelict coffee pot, and a mini fridge.

Alice is struggling with the socket wrench and the drain plug and hoping she's not going to have oil pouring down on her head. But Uncle Eddie is right there with a bucket to catch the oil. She pulls out the old gasket with her fingers and watches as Uncle Eddie removes the old filter with the oil filter wrench. Alice installs a new oil filter under Eddie's watchful eye, and replaces the drain plug gasket. All of this is so messy and absorbing that neither of them notice when Ellie leaves the garage.

'Tighten the new filter hand tight. Just use your fingers. That's it. You don't want to overtighten it.'

He hands her a rag to wipe up any spilled oil, she puts their tools away, and he returns the car to earth so she can pour in four fresh quarts of oil.

'That was easy.' Alice is grinning from ear to ear.

'It's not rocket science.'

'Thanks, Uncle Eddie.'

'You feel okay doing this on your own at home?'

'Sure.'

'Jacking the car up? Sliding under there?'

'Piece of cake.'

'Be careful with the jacks. You ever done that before?'

'Dad taught me how to change a tire when I was twelve.'

'Figures. I could come by on Saturday if you want. Just to make sure the jacks are safe and everything.'

'Sounds good.'

'Next time I'll show you how to rotate your tires and check the brake systems.'

'Cool.'

He tosses her a grimy rag. She wipes her hands.

'You doing okay?'

'Yeah.'

'Anything I can do?'

'You're doin' it.'

'Ha!'

'Hey, Mom said you might have met somebody.'

'Angie and her big mouth!'

'I heard her talking to you on the phone last night.'

'It's a long shot.'

'She from around here?'

'I'm not ready to share details.'

'Oh, c'mon — '

'She's a teacher. That's all I'll say.'

'Not at my school — '

'No, not at your school.'

'You promise?'

'Absolutely.'

'How many dates?'

'Two.'

'And she still likes you?'

'No accounting for taste.'

Alice looks into the empty waiting room.

'Where's Ellie?' Alice asks.

'She was right there.'

'Ellie . . . ?'

'Did she walk home?'

'No, her backpack's still here.'

'Ellie . . . '

'The bathroom?' Eddie suggests.

'You know how Ellie feels about that bathroom.'

Alice starts to panic, and then closes her eyes.

'I think I know where she is,' she says and heads for the door.

Eddie follows Alice to the parking lot out back where Matt's truck is up on blocks. Sure enough, the tarp has been loosened next to the driver's-side door.

'I'll get her,' Alice says.

Crossing the parking lot, just those few feet to her dad's truck, Alice almost can't feel her feet touch the ground. When she opens the door and finds Ellie asleep on the seat, relief washes over her and threatens to spill over into tears. She waves at Eddie to let him know they're all right and climbs up into the cab.

Ellie has a snapshot under her cheek and her thumb in her mouth. Alice looks at the photo: it's a picture from Ellie's birthday party last year, the one with the princess theme. Only Ellie doesn't look like one of those perfect little princesses, she looks slightly possessed. She's wearing a pink tutu and bright yellow tights and her red Dorothy shoes that Uncle Eddie gave her. And a fluffy white sweater and crooked homemade angel wings and long white gloves and a striped ski hat with a long, pointy top and a pom-pom. It's a photo to make you laugh. It must have been in Matt's visor. What else is up there?

Alice pulls the visor down and finds a whole collection of birthday photos. The year he and Angie made the dragon cake, the year they made the volcano cake; the silly hats and the candles and the wishes.

She pulls down the other visor and there's a photo of Matt and Angie in bathing suits, with a Frisbee, laughing. Before kids, it looks like. She opens the glove compartment. A mini road atlas, a first-aid kit, a flashlight, a level, a tape measure, a packet of gum. She pulls out a piece. Not too stale.

Ellie opens her eyes, jerks her thumb out of her mouth, sits up, and grabs the photo from Alice.

'You okay?' Alice asks.

'I like it in here.'

'Me, too.'

'I wish you could drive it.'

'That would be cool.'

'Maybe one day.'

'When Dad gets back.'

'I heard on the radio, in the car, with Janna's mom . . . '

'Don't listen to the radio.'

'Car bombs and casualties. They give the numbers but not the names.'

'That's in case the families don't know yet.'

'Do you know, Alice?'

'Do I know what?'

'Is Daddy still alive?'

'Yes, he is.'

'You're just saying that. Like if I asked you is there really a Santa Claus.'

'Ellie . . .'

'But you don't really know, do you?'

'Nobody knows. But that's what I believe.'

'Honest?'

'Honest.'

'Don't lie to me.'

'I wouldn't.'

'I wish we could just drive over there and pick him up.'

'Yeah! A couple of oceans and nine thousand miles, but *yeah* . . .'

'Today. Right now. I wish we could — '

'Me, too.'

Alice puts her arm around Ellie.

'Close your eyes.'

'Why?'

'Just close your eyes,' Alice says, closing her own eyes. 'Now breathe in,' she says. 'What do you smell?'

'Oil.'

'Try again.'

'That nasty tarp.'

'Yeah. What else?'

Ellie wrinkles her nose. Alice waits.

'Daddy.'

April 26th

Angie had not been as freaked out by Alice getting suspended as Alice thought she would be. She even talked to the principal, she even defended Alice, and they agreed to reduce her suspension from two days to one. Alice has had to write a lengthy apology to Jennifer White *and* her parents, *and* Mr. Brooks, *and* Mr. Fisher. She is also now a provisional member of the track team. Sort of like being on probation. If she has another infraction, she's off the team.

So she's back in school. Not so great. And back on the team. Much better. Ginger, Alice now knows, is the team's long-distance star, and for some unknown reason she has taken Alice under her wing.

At the start of practice, Ginger hands her a polypro T-shirt.

'This will keep you warmer. And cooler. And *drier*.'

'Wow. Thanks,' Alice says, pulling the T-shirt over her head.

Ginger hands her a pair of socks.

'Try these. They're the best I've found.'

'Hey, I can't take all this stuff.'

'My mother's a little compulsive in the shopping department. I have dozens.'

Alice hesitates.

'Really. Try 'em.'

Alice sits down in the grass to put on the socks.

'Hurry up!' Ginger is dancing around on the grass.

205

'Okay!'

'Let's go!'

And Ginger is off with Alice in pursuit.

'Do you know the route?' Alice shouts at Ginger's back.

'Pretty much.'

'And if we get lost?'

'It'll be fun.'

Keeping up with Ginger is a tall order, but Alice is determined not to lose her as they make their way around the course through the Mendon Woods. Alice's endurance is improving and so are her times. Running is the only place where she can forget what's going on in the rest of her life. She loves falling into a rhythm, starting to know her reserve, and pushing it, the steady driving forward. She sings inside when she runs, sings like an airplane, like a motorcycle, like some kind of powerful engine, humming along.

★ ★ ★

She gets home after practice to find Gram in the kitchen, standing on the top step of the stepladder.

'Gram, I don't think you should be on that ladder.'

'Well, look who's here!'

Alice drops her backpack on the floor.

'What are you doing up there?'

'Where's Ellie?'

'She's coming a little later. They had band practice.'

'Band?'

'Yup.'

'She plays an instrument now?'

'The recorder. They all have recorders. You remember. You bought it for her.'

'I did?'

'In the fall.'

Alice hangs her jacket over one of the kitchen chairs.

'Hand me that piece of shelf paper.'

'What are you doing?'

'Cleaning out your mother's shelves. They were . . .'

'A big mess. I know.'

'Lots of people don't care about cupboards. Close the door, forget about it. I like to know they're fresh. It's a simple thing. A little lift in the spring.'

'I'm worried about you up on that ladder.'

'I'm fine.'

'You could cut the pieces and I could lay them down.'

'I am actually very skilled at this. After all these years. Good old Con-Tact paper.'

'Are you implying I'd make a mess of things?'

'Not at all. I could show you. Experience, however, is the best guide.'

'We were going to bake cookies.'

'I know! I'm almost done. I've got the butter softening. Did you pick what kind you want to make?'

'I say molasses; Ellie wants chocolate chip.'

'We can do both. Get some more butter out of the fridge.'

'Gram!'

'What?'

'You went shopping!'

'I did.'

'You cleaned out the fridge.'

'I did.'

'Have you been here all day?'

'Ginny's covering for me at the cafe. I went to the market at eight, got here by nine, which left me plenty of time to clean out the fridge.'

'Wow! And the freezer — you can tell what's in there!'

'A little organization goes a long way. What has your mother been doing?'

'Take out. Breakfast for dinner. If we're lucky. Or I cook.'

'Okay, so she's had other things on her mind. Now you can have some real food. It's not so hard. Take some mental notes. These are useful things to know. Not like I could ever get through to your mother.'

Gram's got the radio tuned to the country station and every now and then she hums along, or sashays her hips a little. She's wearing slacks and an old denim shirt with the sleeves rolled up and sandals. 'Just giving my feet a little vacation,' she'd tell you, if you asked.

Alice pours herself a glass of orange juice.

'I had to throw a lot of stuff out,' Gram continues.

'Good move. I've been trying — '

'Easier for me, I think. I'm not worried that your mother might really want that two-week-old spring roll.'

'Yeah.'

'You gonna tell me how things are?'

'Gram, you seem a little hyper.'

'Me?'

'Yeah.'

'I'm thinking about spending a few nights here each week. I could get things squared away, prepare some meals, do some laundry . . . '

'Gram, you don't have time to run the restaurant and take care of us, too.'

Gram gives Alice a look over the top of her glasses, like, *are you kidding me?*

'Okay, let's get the bread started. Then we can make the cookies while the dough rises.'

'There's just one thing.'

'What?'

'Mom's not big on bread.'

'Since when?'

'Since about two months ago.'

'The staff of life!'

'I know, Gram.'

'It's not normal to be afraid of food!'

'Just one food group.'

'I'm telling you, it's not normal.'

'Gram . . . '

'Okay. No criticism. But you like bread.'

'Yes!'

'And Ellie . . . '

'Loves it.'

'Let's see how long your mom can resist toast. Let's make toast till she can't stand it. Hand me that big bowl, would you?'

'Where's the recipe?'

'You don't really need one. This oatmeal bread

is very simple and very forgiving. And when we start toasting slices? Your mom is gonna go nuts.'

With the yeast proofing, Alice beats butter for the first batch of cookies. Gram chats about this and that and lets her be. Gram knows how to wait for Alice to talk, how to be interested but not too aggressive. She doesn't ask the same old same old questions either — like what's your favorite subject, who's your favorite teacher? She asks where you sit at lunch, what you're reading, what you think about when you're alone.

The bread is fun: the measurements are a 'big glub' of molasses, a cup or two of oatmeal, a pinch of salt, 'enough' flour to form a soft dough. And the kneading part? Really you just get to beat the dough up. Slap it and punch it and squeeze it and pick it up and throw it down. Alice is making clouds of flour and Gram is laughing and egging her on.

When the dough is a smooth, sweet-smelling bundle Alice almost wants to pick it up and rock it like a baby. But they put it back in the clean, oiled bowl, turn it once, cover it with a dishtowel, and put it to rise on the back of the stove.

Alice goes still for several long moments and stands looking at the floor. When she raises her eyes Gram is there waiting for her, not flinching, not suggesting she get over it, go to her room, start her homework, et cetera. For the first time in she can't remember how long, Alice lets herself get pulled into a hug, and at first, right at the beginning, it feels so good. Gram is wearing Matt's apron and has flour on her nose and smells of the lemon verbena she keeps in her drawers. But then Alice pulls away and stumbles out of the room.

She locks the door in the bathroom and sits on the sink, kicking one heel against the cabinet. She can sense Gram on the other side of the door.

'Alice, you don't need to talk to me. I'll leave you be. If you can just tell me you're safe in there.'

'I'm okay.'

'You take your time. I'm here if you need me.'

'Okay.'

'Can you unlock the door?'

'Not yet.'

'Ellie can help me punch the bread down and form it into loaves if you don't want to. Or we can leave it another twenty minutes so you can do it.'

'Okay.'

'Okay, leave it?'

'Yeah.'

Turning away from Alice and that locked door would be impossible if Ellie weren't banging through the back door shouting: 'Graaaammm!'

Ellie squeals when she finds out they are making *two* kinds of cookies. Alice can hear the fridge and freezer doors opening and closing, she can hear every cabinet door opened and then slammed shut. Ellie is hooting and hollering about how great everything looks. Ellie is little miss neat, Ellie color codes her socks, so this move toward organization is right up her alley. Then there's quiet for a bit, and then there's

211

Ellie, playing her recorder. Must have been a request. Gram is nice like that.

Alice lies down in the tub and listens to Ellie squeaking away. There's a drip coming out of the tap, a very slow drip. Using her foot, she messes with the handle until the cadence of the drip is a little faster. Then she sticks the hole in her left sneaker right under the faucet and feels the steady drip drip of the water filling up her sock and her shoe.

What if, starts to fill her mind. What if I flooded the bathroom and the hallway and it leaked downstairs and flooded the kitchen and the living room and even the porch. What if, what if, what if . . .

She falls asleep. Gram's urgent knocking wakes her up. She actually fell asleep in the bathtub! How weird is that?

'I'm okay, Gram!'

But is she? Her arms and legs feel like lead. Sitting up, her ears are buzzing and she feels dizzy. Maybe she needs something to eat.

'Alice . . . ?'

'I'm coming, Gram.'

When she steps out of the tub she feels like she's a hundred years old. Everything hurts and every bit of her, everywhere, inside and out, is tired. Her nose and her eyes and her shins and the backs of her hands. She unlocks the door and can hear Gram's sigh of relief. Stepping out of the bathroom she steps into Gram's waiting arms.

'It's okay, honey . . . It's gonna be all right.'

Just that, her grandmother standing there with

her arms open to her. Not asking her anything, not yelling at her, not pushing, pushing, pushing.

'We waited to punch the dough down until you . . . '

'Ellie can do it.'

'We need to make three loaves. You can both do it.'

'Okay.'

'Honey?'

'Yeah.'

'Look at me.'

She takes Alice's chin in her hands.

'We're gonna be okay.'

'Okay, Gram.'

'I mean it.'

★ ★ ★

In the kitchen Ellie is standing on a chair with a huge mound of dough in front of her.

'That's our dough?!'

'See what yeast can do?'

'Wow!'

Ellie is dancing on the chair; Ellie is deciding to be magnanimous.

'You can take the first punch, Alice.'

'Okay. Stand back!'

Alice lets one fly and then Ellie is pummeling away like a fifty-pound fury. Flour is flying, the dough is elastic and warm in their hands. Ellie starts to laugh. Alice closes her eyes and takes a deep breath. Yeast and molasses and flour and the hot stove and her grandmother's perfume and Ellie's fresh little kid smell. Don't think

213

about anything else. Just this. Right here. Right now.

Gram shows them how to form the dough into loaves. They plop their babies into bread pans and brush them with butter, and put them to rest and rise one more time on the back of the stove. Cookies next. Gram leaves them to it and never once tells them to quit eating the dough while she starts dinner.

Alice knows that Gram is just as scared as she is — well, maybe not just as scared — and that cookies and toast and honey and molasses are not really going to make things right. But they're all we've got. Just the everyday things: the forks and the spoons and the plates and breakfast and lunch and dinner and homework and playing Scrabble with your sister. That's all anybody's got when you get right down to it. Some people not as much, some people lots more. But this is what is right in front of her; this is what she's got right now.

Gram sets out a plate of cookies and two tall glasses of milk. Then she pours herself a nice stiff scotch on the rocks and sits down with her girls. She and Ellie talk about Easter and shopping and will Gram teach her how to play Mah-Jongg after dinner? Gram is saying yes and yes and it's cozy in this corner with the light hanging over the table, the kitchen full of the smell of baking bread, the emptiness and the darkness pushed back, pushed aside. Alice puts her head down on the table and studies Gram's hands. Her rings, the pale skin, nearly translucent. She closes her eyes and she's gone. Gone away, Gram's voice and Ellie's voice fading out like a radio from the house next door. For a moment the tick of the kitchen clock is filling her head and she feels Gram's hand stroking her hair. Another breath and she is fast asleep, blessedly asleep.

* * *

Hours later, Alice wakes up, surprised to find herself in bed, stripped down to her underwear. Gram or Mom must have done it. She looks at her dad's watch: almost midnight. She grabs a sweatshirt and pads down the hall to the kitchen to get something to eat. She's slicing a big hunk of bread when she hears voices and realizes Gram hasn't gone home. She slathers the bread with butter and jam and walks back upstairs to her mom's room. The lights are on, the door is closed. She stands there, eating bread and licking jam from her fingers.

'It's not forever,' Gram says.

'I know.'

'We don't know when Matt . . . '

'I *know*.'

'I'm not here to make comments. I'm just here to help.'

'You can't help yourself, Mom.'

'I'll tone it down.'

'Sure you will.'

'My comments are the least of your worries!'

'We're doing fine.'

'Angie . . . '

'We *are*. I get to work every day, the kids get to school, we eat.'

'I'm just saying I could do the marketing and cook ahead so all you have to do on weeknights is reheat. I could teach the girls a few things.'

'They love it when you cook with them.'

'Sometimes these things skip a generation.'

'I can cook!'

'I know.'

'I don't want you to move in, Mom.'

'For the girls, then — '

'You're just down the street! If I need you I can practically holler out the front door!'

'But — '

'We don't do too well living together, remember?'

'It could be different.'

'It won't be different.'

Alice slides down the wall into a sitting position.

'You can stay tonight.'

'But not on a schedule? Something regular for your girls?'

'We can't need you, Mom; we can't be falling to pieces, because Matt can't be missing.'

'That's wishful thinking, honey.'

'I don't care! Bring on the magic, bring on the shamans, the charlatans, I can't — '

'I know.'

'You don't know!'

'Matt Bliss comes through. He always comes through.'

'If one more person says that to me . . . '

'Don't give up on him, Angie.'

'Oh, Mom . . . ' Angie blows her nose. 'Nothing makes sense anymore. Nobody's telling us the truth, there is no way to find out where he is or how hurt he is or what the odds are or if it's even possible to survive.'

Alice realizes she's stopped breathing. How do the grown-ups keep taking in this information and walk and talk and act normal? Is she the only one who feels like her skin is going to split apart, her head is going to crack open?

'Sergeant Ames called me at work. They found Matt's ID. *Recovered* is the word they use. Is that good news? Bad news? What does it mean?'

'It means they're looking for him. They're actively looking for him.'

Alice curls up on the hallway floor, her toast forgotten. The voices in her mother's room are softer now. She puts her hand into the sliver of light spilling from under the door as if the light could warm her. She closes her eyes and imagines that the murmur of voices is her mom and dad, and Ellie is three and she is ten and none of this has happened, none of it is going to happen. And then she sees him. Clear as day. Sees him traversing a hillside, wearing fatigues, carrying a gun, his boots gray with dust; his face filthy, his hair matted. He looks thin and tired. He is smoking a cigarette and there are soldiers in front of and behind him. It is early dawn and they are moving quickly, or as quickly as they can given the rocky footing. She wants to yell at him to put his helmet on. Is it a vision? A memory? A dream? Is he alive? Is that what this means? If only he would turn and speak to her, if only . . .

The door opens and Angie nearly falls right over her.

217

'Alice!? What the hell? What are you doing here?'

'I heard you talking and — '

'There's toast and jam all over the carpet! Could you be any more — ?!'

Gram pulls Alice to her feet and heads down the hall hand in hand with her.

'I've won the skirmish but not the battle. I can stay the night. Maybe that will give me a little toehold. Think about what you'd like me to make for dinner tomorrow night. Something your mom and Ellie really love, okay?'

Alice slides into her sleeping bag on the floor as Gram climbs into Alice's bed.

'You okay on the floor?'

'Yup.'

'This is cozy.'

'Yup.'

'Ellie can sleep through anything.'

'Just about.'

'Good night, Alice.'

''night, Gram.'

Alice stares up into the dark.

'Gram . . . ?'

'What, honey?'

'I saw him.'

'Where?'

'In my mind, I think . . . He was walking across a hillside, smoking a cigarette, other men spread out on the hill around him. How could I see that?'

'I don't know, Alice. You're very connected to your dad.'

'That's not rational, Gram.'

218

'Love isn't rational.'

'Was it a dream?'

'What do you think?'

'It was so real and so strange. Not like anyplace I've ever seen before. And Dad was different, too. Dirty and thin and . . . '

'He's probably thinking of you just as hard as you're thinking of him.'

'But — '

'The mind, Alice, there's still so much we don't know. Think about that. All that mystery, all that unknown territory right between your ears.'

'You're funny, Gram.'

'He loves you, wherever he is.'

Alice finally lets herself cry, the stupid tears falling right into her ears. Gram doesn't say anything, just reaches out and takes her hand. Then Ellie rolls over on her back and starts to snore and they both laugh. Five minutes later — or so it seems — the alarm is ringing.

April 27th

Alice has the woodstove in Matt's workshop going full blast. She's wearing his work jacket and a fleece vest and a hat and a scarf. It's sunny but unseasonably cold with a watery blue sky and a wind fierce enough to rattle the panes of the windows. Will spring never ever come?

First she built a fire, then she refilled the kindling pile and the stack of firewood, and then she hauled her stuff out of the house in two old

219

duffel bags and a milk crate she found in the basement. She blows the air mattress up and hangs her sleeping bag on the clothesline to air out, which shouldn't take long in this wind. She unpacks the milk carton full of books and photographs and sets the crate next to her bed with a small reading lamp on top.

The photographs go on one side of the workbench, so she can see them from her bed. She has collected her favorite framed photos of her dad from all over the house, rearranging desktops and bureaus so her mother won't notice which ones are missing. She adds votive candles in old jelly jars. Three doesn't seem like enough. She'll have to get more.

She lights the candles. They look nice, she thinks, but there should be twelve at least. Maybe dozens and dozens; maybe she should light a new candle for every day that Matt is missing.

The books, which are Matt's books, from his 'favorite books' shelf, get stacked neatly inside the milk crate: *The Art of the Stone Wall*, E. B. White's *The Points of My Compass*, Wendell Berry's *A Place on Earth*. These are the books Alice is planning to read every night, if she gets scared staying alone out here. If she can't sleep. If she can't stop thinking about her dad.

Her plan was to get everything set up before Mom gets home from work. A done deal. Not worth arguing about. What she hadn't planned on was Ellie.

Who is now standing in the doorway, her knitting in one hand, her other hand bleeding and held away from her like an accusation, like whatever happened to Ellie, alone in the house, is definitely Alice's fault.

'What happened?'

'Splinter. A big one.'

'The kitchen bench again?'

'Yup.'

'It's huge.'

'It *hurts*, Alice.'

'Let's see if I can get it out. Come over to the window where I can see better.'

Alice leads Ellie over to the window.

'How can you knit and get splinters at the same time?'

'*Hurry up!*'

She finds her dad's finest pair of needle-nosed pliers.

'You ready? Hold still.'

Alice pulls out the splinter.

'There you go.'

Ellie, with her finger in her mouth, takes a moment to survey the workshop.

'What are you doing?'

'I'm moving in.'

'You're gonna stay out here?'

'Yeah.'

'Alone?'

'Yeah.'

'All the time?'

'No, I'll shower and eat and change inside.'

'You're gonna *sleep* out here?'

'I was thinking — '

'Every night?'

'Well — '

'You're *leaving* me?'

'No, Ellie — '

'How can you do that?'

'You could stay out here with me sometimes.'

'No, I couldn't.'

'It'll be fun.'

'No, it won't.'

'It'll be like camping.'

'You and Daddy are the only ones who like camping. I *hate* camping.'

Ellie looks at Alice for a long moment.

'What about Mom?'

'What about her?'

'Who's gonna stay with Mom?'

'Ellie, it's just the backyard.'

Ellie starts to cry. Alice sits down on the air mattress, pulls Ellie down beside her, and puts her arm around her shoulder.

'Ellie . . . I — '

Ellie cries harder.

'It's one hundred feet away. It's — '

Ellie looks at Alice. Stares at her. Waits.

'Okay, so maybe I could just be out here sometimes.'

'Like when?'

'Like in the middle of the night when I can't sleep. Or after school. When you're at Janna's.'

'Alice, if you're not in our room at night — '

'I know.'

'Right where you always are — '

'I wasn't thinking, Ellie. I'm sorry.'

Ellie blows her nose.

'You want to help me set it up? I'm open to suggestions.'

'If you make it all wonderful you're gonna want to be here all the time. Besides, it's *Dad's* workshop. I don't think you're supposed to, like, mess it up or make it all yours and stuff. Like, exclusively. Yours.'

'You can come out here anytime.'

'You're just saying that.'

'No, I'm not. I mean it.'

Ellie wipes her eyes with the back of her hand.

'Mom's not gonna like it.'

'I know.'

'Is it secret?'

'It doesn't need to be secret. It's just an air mattress and a sleeping bag and some books.'

Ellie gets up and heads for the door.

'Where are you going?'

'I'm not going to help you leave me.'

'Ellie — Ellie — ! Wait — !'

Which is when Mom drives up from work and Alice thinks, oh, no, here we go, this is all going to fall apart. What a mess. Of course Ellie tells her all about it; Alice can see her making her case right there in the driveway. And then, yup, here comes Mom. Alice braces herself for a shouting match, but Angie steps into the workshop, looks around, and in a normal tone of voice, says:

'I don't really want you sleeping out here.'

'But, Mom . . . '

'And no boys, Alice.'

'Mom!'

'The deal is, you keep your grades up . . . '

'The whole point of this — '

'Is what, exactly?'

223

'You know what, Mom.'

'No, I don't, Alice.'

'The whole point is . . . '

Angie waits.

'I feel like I can . . . ' Alice begins.

'What?'

'Hold on to him here.'

'That's . . . '

'Or that I can still find him here.'

'Oh, honey,' Angie softens.

'Do you know what I mean?' Alice pulls Matt's jacket closer around her.

'Yes. I think I do.'

'I want it to be perfect when he gets home. I got a book out of the library so I can learn how to clean and oil all his power tools. I mean, I know it's already totally organized, but I thought . . . '

Angie looks at Alice: Her cheeks are flushed and the tip of her nose is bright red. She is swamped in Matt's jacket, it nearly reaches her knees. She looks like a kid again, a little kid.

Angie wishes she could reach out and touch Alice, but with just that thought, just that impulse, she can feel Alice pulling away.

'I didn't think about Ellie. I should have thought about Ellie, but — '

'She needs you.'

'I know.'

'More than ever.'

'What about what I need, Mom?'

'We'll work it out, okay?'

'I don't see how.'

'Have a little faith.'

224

'I just want — '

'She'll be at Janna's, there will be sleepovers, there's a week of Nature's Classroom coming up in May.'

Alice crosses to her dad's workbench.

'You're not mad that I brought some pictures out here?'

'I'm not mad.'

'I want to light a candle for every day he's missing.'

'Good idea with the jelly jars.'

'Yeah. I don't want to burn the place down or anything.'

Angie looks around the workshop again: the clean floor, the sparkling windows, Matt's orderliness echoed in Alice's neat stack of books, clothes hung on pegs, the wood basket, the kindling.

'You cleaned up in here. It looks nice.'

'You know how Daddy had plans to put those windows in the west wall? I'm gonna figure out how to do that before he gets back. I'll ask Uncle Eddie to help me.'

'Matt was so excited the day he found those windows.'

'It'll open things up. More light.'

'And a view of his apple trees.'

Angie reaches out and straightens Alice's collar.

'You're wearing his jacket.'

'It was cold. I — '

'It's okay, Alice.'

Angie sits down in the lawn chair near the woodstove. Alice stands nearby, uncertain what to do or say.

'Can I have it?' Angie asks.

'What?'

'The jacket. Just for a bit.'

Alice unbuttons the jacket, hands it to her mom. Angie hugs it to her, inhaling its scent.

'Mom . . . ?'

'Throw another log on the fire, would you?'

The fire is blazing, but Alice adds another log anyway.

'Can you open the doors so I can watch it?'

Alice opens the doors of the woodstove, props up the temporary screen.

'That's what Dad likes to do.'

She hears her mom take in a quick breath.

'I'd like to stay out here for a little while by myself, if that's okay with you.'

'Yeah. Sure.'

Alice starts backing toward the door.

'I'll be in soon.'

Alice hesitates.

'Don't forget to close up the stove, Mom.'

'I won't.'

Alice closes the door behind her and wishes she could look through the door to see her mom. Maybe she could replace the solid wood door with a glass one or put windows in on the sides. She's thinking about windows because it is frankly too strange to think about her mom in her dad's space like this, in *her* space, everything turned upside down, Alice outside in the chill wind, her mom by the fire. How did this happen?

But as of right now, right this instant, Alice has a new plan. She has decided to only think positive thoughts, to stop dwelling on all the terrifying *what ifs* that haunt her. She will keep those thoughts to herself and instead prepare for her dad's return. His certain return. She will be the one to believe in him, believe in his strength and his ingenuity, his ability to talk to, to persuade anyone about anything, anywhere, anytime. She thinks about the way he can coach you so you don't even realize he's doing it, whether it's how to throw a better pitch or how to strike a cleaner, stronger hammer blow.

When he comes home, if he's still recovering from his wounds, or so badly hurt that it will take months to recover, then she will be the one to do things for him. She'll drive him to the doctor's because she'll have her permit by then. When he's ready to go back to work she'll be his assistant, handling the things he's not quite ready for, or the things that are too tough by the end of the day when he gets tired. She'll fill his Thermos and pack his lunch. She'll load the tool chest and the truck. She knows how to do these things, she's been watching him and getting in the way her whole life.

It occurs to her that if, no, when, they find him, they'll probably send him home as soon as they can debrief him and stabilize him at the hospital. So the garden has to be perfect. There will not be a weed anywhere, the successive plantings of red and green lettuce will be beautiful, the corn will be knee high, the tomatoes will be staked; she will pick and make him his favorite chopped salad every night. Beets. She should plant some beets.

And if he's too tired to talk about what

227

happened, she promises herself she'll wait until he's ready to tell her the story, the true story that she can hold on to instead of the horror story she plays in her head every night.

Will she tell him about Henry? There's nothing to tell. Or John Kimball? Really nothing to tell. Or Stephie or what it was like to feel so alone the whole time he was gone, the way nobody knew how to talk to her, or how to talk about the war or her father, and it seemed like people just wanted to avoid her. The part about not getting along that great with Mom she can keep secret. Running, she can tell him about running, and B.D. and the way he's fair with everybody, just the way Matt is, and Ginger and her long legs, and how it's looking like Alice might really be a long-distance runner, might have some actual talent in that department. Can she tell him about the miles and miles she runs in practice and learning to believe you've got something left for the end of the race, that believing it is just as important as running it? Will it still be okay to run like that if Matt's legs have been shattered? If only she knew where he'd been wounded, but she's promised herself not to think about that. Just think about him getting out and getting home and being here and being Dad, that's all, just being Dad.

★ ★ ★

Alice heads inside to see what she can do to start dinner only to discover that her quarterly report card has arrived. Along with a letter from Matt, addressed to Ellie. A letter sent ten days ago. Maybe it's a sign. Maybe it's a good sign.

She hesitates for a nanosecond and then rips open her report card, even though it's not addressed to her, but to her parents. It's bad. No, it's really bad. Every single subject is in the low seventies, having fallen from the nineties. It's not failing. Not yet. But it will be. Each and every teacher makes a note of missing tests and missing assignments and how this just isn't like Alice. There's a special blue slip requesting a conference.

What is she going to do with this? Hide it? Put it in the trash? Hope that Angie is too distracted to notice that it never arrived?

Once again, Alice forgot the Ellie factor, because here's Ellie, having padded into the hall on her little stealth feet to read along right beside her.

'You're in trouble,' Ellie says, with a certain gleeful satisfaction. 'You're in *big* trouble.'

'Want to pretend like this never arrived?'

'Fat chance, Alice.'

'Ellie — '

'What are you doing in school? Aren't you even trying?'

'Hey, I don't need you to — '

'What would Daddy say?'

'Listen — '

'You can't just move out of the house and let every single thing go, Alice. That's not what Daddy would do.'

'Okay, okay! You can just back off, Ellie!'

Mom walks in the door and takes the report

card and strangely, oddly, says nothing. Not now at least. She picks up Ellie's letter and looks at the postmark.

'Oh, this is so strange.'

'Maybe it's a good omen,' Alice says.

'This was mailed ten days ago.'

'There could be more on the way,' Ellie says. 'Lots more.'

Angie holds the letter against her chest for a moment and closes her eyes. A silent wish, or a prayer, Alice thinks, as Angie hands the letter to Ellie.

Ellie rips open the envelope right there in the hallway.

'Wait,' Alice says, an edge of panic in her voice. 'Let's do it the same way we always do.'

So they gather on the couch, where Ellie climbs into Angie's lap and reads her letter to herself, Angie and Alice both pretending they are not trying to read over her shoulder.

'Read it,' Alice begs.

Ellie pushes her glasses into place and begins:

Dear Ellie,

You asked me what I miss:

You. Being near you. And Mom and Alice and Uncle Eddie and Gram.

I miss just hanging out with you. To do anything. Or nothing. Sit on the couch. Play chess. Drop you off at school.

I miss your drawings. I miss braiding your hair. I miss your crazy outfits. I miss tickling you. I miss that spot behind your left ear that smells like vanilla.

I miss fresh milk. The stuff here is in little squeezable plastic containers and it always tastes sour to me.

Gram's coffee.

A movie. In a theater. With popcorn!

Libraries. Book stores.

Your laugh.

Walking down a quiet street at dusk with the lights on in the houses and kids doing homework or playing on the lawns. That happy noise. Spring nights when nobody wants to come inside.

Baseball. Playing with my team, playing catch with Alice and Henry, pitching for Henry, trying to get you to play with us.

Trees. Grass. I miss green. I miss mountains and birch trees and evergreens. Let's go for a hike in the Adirondacks when I get home.

My truck. To get in, turn the key, turn on the radio, find some tunes, roll down the windows and just drive. No more body armor. No more Kevlar helmet!

Home cooked food. Hamburgers on the grill. Making sundaes with you and Alice.

A real bathroom. A bathtub. Lots of hot water. A 'combat shower' is so fast you blink and you could miss it.

Breakfast at The Bird Sisters, lunch on a roofing job, dinner at home with my three girls.

You. I'll begin and end with you. I miss you, Ellie.

Love,
Daddy

Ellie, of course, begins to cry as she reads the letter, and when she finishes, she curls into Angie's arms, as though she could burrow inside of her mother, and sobs. Alice can see Angie start to lose it and then pull herself back from the edge so she can take care of Ellie.

'Ellie,' Angie says, 'Daddy's gonna be okay. He's missing you and loving you — and all of us — right now.'

'You promise?' Ellie asks.

Angie meets Alice's glance over Ellie's head.

'I promise.'

April 28th

After practice, a long run at Mendon Pond Park, where Alice actually kept up with Ginger for the 3.5 mile course and almost caught her as she made her move up the last hill, Alice helps Uncle Eddie unload the rototiller from the really cool old Ford truck he's driving with wooden running boards and side panels. Red, of course. Eddie muscles the rototiller through the yard, out past her dad's workshop and up the small rise to the garden.

'You sure you want to do all of it?'

'Yup.'

'It's pretty big, Alice.'

'That's okay. We do corn, remember?'

'What's that smell?'

'Bailey's delivered a load of horse manure.'

'Glad I wore my boots.'

Uncle Eddie fires up the rototiller and takes

232

off along the outer perimeter of the garden, chewing up and turning the soil. Alice walks behind him picking up and tossing aside any stones that get uncovered. The soil is still pretty heavy and wet, but Eddie and his machine are slicing through it like butter. Every now and then Alice misreads the angle or direction of the rototiller and bends down to grab a stone and gets a faceful or shirtful of dirt for her trouble. Even wearing boots she and Eddie are both getting soaked with water and caked with mud. Halfway through the job Alice is dirtier than she's ever been in her life.

Uncle Eddie's approach is a lot faster and definitely more slapdash than her dad's. He's driving the rototiller, rather than carefully guiding it. He's finding out just what this machine can do, how fast it can turn, what happens when you give it maximum gas. These experiments keep plastering both of them with dirt. Alice has to jog sometimes to keep up. Uncle Eddie's got this thing going top speed and he's whooping and hollering as he slides through the corners, using all his body weight to turn the rototiller, skidding on his heels, and laughing.

This job, which Alice usually hates for its careful, dull, noisy slowness has been transformed into a road race and a mud-pie session all rolled into one. She had dreaded every plodding step as some sort of penitential slog through missing her dad. Instead, Uncle Eddie has turned this task into a game and released her by changing the unwritten rules.

He stops before their last pass around the

perimeter and hollers at her over the engine noise:

'You want to drive it?'

'No.'

'You scared?'

'No!'

'Yes, you are!'

'I am not!'

'Then come on up here. We'll do it together.'

She takes the handles, adjusting the speed. Uncle Eddie walks beside her in case she needs a hand. She's taking it slow, really slow, slow enough to lift her face from looking down at the dirt and take in the whole gentle swath of the garden; the earth turned up, the wet mushroom-y smell of dirt in the spring, full of loam, and promise and possibility. She can do this; she *is* doing this.

Fifteen minutes later she's helping Uncle Eddie drive the rototiller up two planks and into the bed of his truck.

'You want to come in for a beer or something?'

'Like this? Your mom would kill me. She's already gonna kill you.'

'I could bring one out to you.'

'That's okay, kiddo, I promised to get this baby back to the rental place before five.'

'Thanks, Uncle Eddie.'

'Anytime.'

'I wish I could get a picture of you.'

'Wait until you see your own dirty self. We should've made a video. I think it could be a big hit on YouTube. In the farm states.'

Uncle Eddie peels out and leans on the horn

as Alice turns toward the house. She kicks her boots off outside and goes in the back door and directly down the basement stairs where she strips off all her clothes and throws everything into the washing machine. Every stitch is soaked, even her underwear. She grabs a towel out of the dryer and heads upstairs. Now she can see her dirty footprints on each step. And her path from the back door to the basement is muddy as well. Her big muddy handprints are all over the back door and the basement door. She can't believe it. If it weren't so cold outside she'd go wash down with the garden hose. Now she has to track and drip all the way up to the shower, too. Her mom is gonna kill her. She grabs paper towels and scrubs the bottom of her feet.

She sidesteps her way up the stairs so she won't touch the walls. She turns on the shower and steps in. The water coming off her is black with dirt, her hair is gritty; there's even mud down her back. She leans against the wall of the shower, letting the hot water wash over her. She's feeling better than she's felt in days. They got the job done. She's going to have her garden no matter what her mother says, just the way she planned it with her dad. Exactly like last year. Sunday she'll plant peas and radishes and the earliest lettuce and spinach. Sunday she'll be in the garden, down on her knees with stakes and string and seeds.

'Alice!? Alice! Get down here right this minute!'

Oh, shit, here we go, she thinks, as she steps

out of the shower, slips on a pair of jeans and a T-shirt, and heads downstairs.

Her mother has a bottle of Fantastik in one hand and a big pink sponge in the other. She shoves them both at Alice.

'Here. It's your mess. You clean it up.'

Without a word, Alice sets to work.

'I thought we discussed this. I thought I made myself perfectly clear.'

No answer from Alice.

'Why are you insisting on — ?'

'I promised Dad,' Alice mumbles into the floor.

'What? I can't hear you.'

'I promised Dad,' Alice enunciates slowly and clearly.

'Well he's not here now, is he?'

'That's the point, Mom.'

'What did we agree on last night?'

'We didn't agree on anything last night. You made some pronouncements, I kept my mouth shut.'

'We agreed that *if* you get your grades up where they belong *then* you can do the garden.'

'I didn't agree to that.'

'That's the deal.'

'I can't accept that.'

'You're going to have to learn how to accept it. If your father were here — '

' — We wouldn't be having this discussion.'

'If your father were here — '

' — Don't go there, Mom.'

Alice stands up, puts the Fantastik under the

counter, rinses the sponge in the sink, and walks out of the kitchen.

'Just where do you think you're going?'

'To do my homework.'

Alice hears a cabinet door slam as she crosses the yard to her dad's workshop, where she will most likely not do her homework, where she will most likely sit there wishing she could write a letter to her dad about fat, fast Uncle Eddie and the garden and the muck and the mud, and the way the machine was roaring under her hands as she guided it through its last pass around the garden.

* * *

She closes her eyes and it's a September afternoon. Clear blue sky, bright sun, cool breeze. She and Matt are in the garden picking tomatoes. He finds a flawless Brandywine, wipes it clean with his shirt and passes it to her. He finds another one for himself, polishes it, and takes a bite, like it's an apple. He pulls the kitchen salt shaker out of his pocket, sprinkles on some salt and savors every last bit of it, tomato juice running down his chin. Nothing has ever tasted better. The sunwarmed flesh of the tomato, the sharp, acidic tang of the first bite, the kick of the salt intensifying everything. This is a ritual with them. The finding, the picking, the perfect late summer beefsteak tomato, the salt shaker stolen from the kitchen, the hum of the crickets heralding fall, and the explosion of flavor in their mouths. No words required.

April 29th

It's the Red Wings' home opener against Syracuse. Alice is sitting in the bleachers with John Kimball, his father, his kid brother, Joey, and Mrs. Minty. A very short and very chubby high school girl from Mendon with beautiful long, dark hair has just sung 'The Star-Spangled Banner.' How is it possible to belt out notes that high? The team sprints out onto the field to take their positions as the announcer introduces them. They get a welcoming standing ovation. Rochester loves its Red Wings. Not that Frontier Field is full; but it's a respectable crowd. Rowdy, too.

It's cool and windy but John and his father know where to sit to get some shelter from the wind and to take full advantage of whatever sun there is. They've got peanuts in the shell and, true to his promise, John has gotten Mrs. Minty a hot dog with all the trimmings.

Mrs. Minty is wearing her usual skirt, blouse, cardigan sweater, and tie shoes, but over this she has layered an extra sweater, her winter coat, and two scarves. She has also brought fuzzy mittens that look homemade, and to top it off she is sporting a well-worn Red Wings baseball cap. They are all wearing Red Wings baseball caps, which makes Alice feel slightly ridiculous.

Mrs. Minty has already purchased her season player roster and she has not one but two sharpened pencils in preparation for keeping up with the box scores. This is more baseball ephemera than Alice and her dad usually indulge in, though her dad reads the box scores every morning in the paper. Or used to.

She leans over to John.

'Do you understand box scores?'

'Yeah.'

'My dad explained it to me once, but honestly, I stopped listening after about two minutes.'

'I wouldn't worry about it.'

Everybody's a little stiff and formal, except for Joey who is happily dashing up and down the bleacher steps following one of the vendors around. Is this because none of them know one another well, or because Mrs. Minty is there and they're all trying their hardest to be polite and not yell and swear, or is it because John is wishing he'd never invited this weird girl to a baseball game and John's father is probably wondering what's going on because he thought John already had a girlfriend? That Melissa Johnson who calls every night and wants to talk on the phone till all hours.

Joey is back, panting.

'Dad! Dad! I want to sell peanuts. Can I sell peanuts?'

'I think you have to be fifteen.'

He's crushed. For a moment.

'Dad! Dad! Can I sell peanuts when I'm fifteen?'

'Sure.'

'How long 'til then?'

'Eight years.'

'You think I could be an assistant before then?'

'Ask him!'

'Ask who?'

239

'The kid you've been running after.'

'He wouldn't have to pay me.'

'Don't tell me, tell him.'

Joey sprints off, in pursuit of the fifteen-year-old demigod selling peanuts.

Mrs. Minty begins a discussion about the new shortstop, Rich Gelbart, and what the pitching coach is saying about him. John listens carefully but doesn't say much as his dad and Mrs. Minty assess Gelbart and his strengths and weaknesses, until Mr. Kimball turns to John and says:

'You could be there, son. You work hard and you could be there. Right on that field.'

'Dad . . . '

'You're quick, you can hit, and you're not afraid to push yourself. Best shortstop Belknap High's seen in fifteen years. Sounds like Peter, doesn't it, Mrs. Minty?'

'Oh, yes. Yes, it does.'

There's an awkward pause.

'Thank you for speaking about Peter, Jack. It's a comfort to me to hear his name.'

'I know it is.'

John turns to Alice.

'Mrs. Minty was my dad's high school English teacher.'

'She was not!'

'And she came to his games. Just like she comes to mine.'

'Mrs. Minty, I didn't know you were a teacher,' Alice says.

'I gave it up for a while when Peter was young. But I went back to it after my husband died.'

'I heard you came back to teaching just so you

could torture my dad,' John teases.

'I wouldn't call it torture,' Mr. Kimball says.

'Were you hard on him?' John asks.

'I had high expectations for all my students.'

'Even the ones who didn't give a . . . who didn't care?'

'A climate of expectation fosters the possibility, even the near certainty, of achievement. If I believe in you, and I communicate that to you, you will find things in yourself you never knew were there.'

'Is this a theory, Mrs. Minty,' Alice asks, 'or has it been proven?'

'Ask John's father.'

'Mr. Kimball?'

'I wouldn't have finished high school without Mrs. Minty. Well, Mrs. Minty and baseball.'

'Why not?'

'It's a long story.'

Mrs. Minty gives him a look.

'Go ahead, Jack,' Mrs. Minty says.

He looks out across the baseball diamond as though he can see into the past and says:

'My father had a massive heart attack my sophomore year in high school.'

'He *died?*' bursts out of Alice's mouth.

'At Gleason's. On the factory floor. He was forty-five years old.'

Mrs. Minty is completely present; her attention is like a pair of strong hands resting on his shoulders.

'My mom was overwhelmed trying to take care of things and hold on to the house and find a job and feed four kids. I hardly went to school

241

for the rest of sophomore year and barely passed my exams. That summer I worked on Gentle's farm and played on the town baseball team. I was trying to help my mom, but I met older kids on the job and that wasn't good for me.'

'Why not?' Alice can't help asking.

'Older kids with licenses, and fake IDs, and money for beer, and nothing better to do.'

John and Alice look at each other, taking this in.

'It was a mistake they put me in Mrs. Minty's class. She taught the honors section. I didn't know any of the kids in that class — their parents were the doctors and the lawyers in town — and I was in way, way over my head.'

'I asked for you to be in my class,' Mrs. Minty says.

'Why would you — ?'

'I knew your mother. I knew you were in trouble. And I thought I could reach you.'

'So you were my angel, Mrs. Minty,' Mr. Kimball smiles.

'Gloria's your angel, Jack.'

John's father nods and ducks his head blinking furiously for a moment, as he thinks about his wife.

There's an uncomfortable pause.

'Lovely day to open the season, wouldn't you say, Jack?'

'Yes, ma'am.'

'I predict that Gelbart is going to have such a good season we're going to lose him to the majors.'

'You could be right, Mrs. Minty.'

242

'I might even wager a small sum on that supposition, if you were inclined to take a gamble.'

'Five bucks suit you, Mrs. Minty?'

'Right down to the ground.'

John reaches over and takes Alice's hand. She can't stop herself: she turns to look at him in stunned disbelief, but he is not looking at her, he is watching Gelbart, on an 0 and 2 pitch, hit a line drive deep into left field.

She leaves her hand in his. His palm is calloused but his hands are warm, warmer than her hands. But what is he doing? He has a girlfriend. Does this mean he's kind of a bum, seeing what he can get away with far from the prying eyes at school? And what about her? Two weeks ago she kissed Henry. Sort of. If that was really a kiss. Now this. What is this? She looks at him. He won't look at her. She pulls her hand away.

Now John looks at her; he smiles at her, even more confusing, and takes her hand again. She glances over at Mrs. Minty who misses absolutely nothing. She doesn't have the nerve to look at John's father, so she sits there, holding hands with John Kimball and watching the season opener at Frontier Field in the weak but promising April sunshine. Until Joey returns, takes in the hand holding situation, exchanges a glance with his father, and then worms his way between them, laughing and chanting:

'John's got a girlfriend! John's got a girlfriend!'

'Shut up, you little twerp.'

John grabs Joey's hat and sails it into the

bleachers below. When Joey flies down the steps to retrieve his hat, John does not take Alice's hand again. Which is a relief. Kind of. She shifts away from him.

'I thought you were going out with Melissa Johnson,' Alice says quietly, as Mrs. Minty and Mr. Kimball discuss the Red Wings' new outfielder.

John pays extra close attention to the pitcher.

'Well?'

'It's complicated.'

'I think that's pretty much a yes or no answer.'

It's a full count.

Is this why twelfth-grade boys troll for ninth- and tenth-grade girls, thinking they'll be too wowed to protest or complain about anything as immature as cheating?

'Maybe you're just trying to be nice to me. But I don't really know you because I've never really even talked to you so . . . '

He turns to look at her.

'We've talked.'

'Hardly.'

'More than I talk to most girls.'

'That's not possible. I see you with girls all the time.'

'That's not really talking.'

'It looks like talking.'

'It's *just* talk. It's not anything real.'

'But . . . '

Gelbart steals second. Under the cover of the crowd's roar he says:

'I like you, Alice.'

'You do not.'

'Why is that so hard to believe?'

'It just is, okay?'

'Why?'

'It's impossible.'

'Why?'

'For one thing, you're a senior.'

'So?'

'It's confusing.'

'I thought when you said yes to coming to the game that maybe . . . '

'I figured you were just getting all your good deeds for the year over with in one fell swoop: you know, old lady, sad girl from school,' Alice says even more quietly in case Mrs. Minty overhears.

'That's not why I asked you.'

'And what about Melissa Johnson?'

'What about her?'

'I heard she spent a lot of money on her dress for the spring dance.'

'Which is why I can't break up with her before then.'

'Because of a *dress*? That's insane.'

'Yeah. But what kind of jerk would I be to break up with her now?'

Gelbart gets to third on a sacrifice bunt.

'I wanted to ask you to go with me,' John says.

'You're just saying that.'

'No, I'm not.'

Alice looks at him, thinking, I don't know you at all, and what I thought I did know about you turns out to be completely, totally wrong.

'I already said yes to Henry anyway.'

'Henry Grover?'

'He's my best friend.'

'But do you . . . ?'

'Do I what?'

'Do you like him?'

'Of course I like him!'

'You know what I mean.'

Sammy Marston hits a double deep into left field, sending Gelbart home.

'Save me a dance, then,' he says.

'What?'

'One slow dance.'

'Wouldn't that be . . . ?'

'It's just a dance.'

'Melissa Johnson won't think it's 'just a dance.''

'Fair enough.'

They go back to watching the game.

'What happened to your mother?' Alice asks.

'Breast cancer.'

Alice registers that she has never heard a seventeen-year-old boy say *breast* before.

'I'm sorry. I can't imagine . . . '

'Yeah.'

Why is this so hard to talk about?

'You must miss her.'

'All the time.'

'How old was Joey?'

'Four.'

'Does he remember her?'

'Sort of. But I think his memories get mixed up with all the pictures we have.'

Alice pulls off her Red Wings hat.

'I can't remember my dad's voice.'

'Doesn't he call all the time?'

'He's missing in action.'

He looks at her.

'You didn't say anything.'

'I never know what to say.'

'How long has it been?'

'Eight days.'

She looks at her hands.

'Alice . . . '

She can't look up.

'He'll be okay.'

She wants to believe that. She wills herself to meet his gaze.

'Let's not talk about it anymore,' she says. 'Let's just . . . '

He's still looking at her

'Are you close?' he asks.

'Yeah . . . Yeah. We are.'

He takes her hand again and Alice thinks, don't ask me if I'm all right or I am going to totally lose it.

After a long pause he says, 'I'm thinking of enlisting.'

'What?'

'I've been talking to the recruiters at school. I want marines, I think.'

'What are you talking about?'

'I'll get all this training. They'll pay for college. And it's really great experience. Plus, with my dad on his own, we can't really afford — '

'What about baseball?'

'That's a one in a million chance, Alice. You know that.'

'But you're really good.'

'Thanks, but — '

'I don't know what to say.'

'I turn eighteen next month. I can enlist on my birthday. And head off to basic training right after I graduate.'

'Does your dad know?'

'Yeah.'

'I can't believe you're doing this. They'll send you overseas.'

'Probably.'

'Oh, God . . . '

'I thought . . . '

'Isn't there any other way — ?'

'It's an incredible opportunity.'

'You can't be all you can be if you're dead,' she blurts out and can't believe how much she sounds like her mother.

Mrs. Minty and Mr. Kimball both glance over.

'I thought you'd understand,' he says.

'I understand that there are a million things that could happen to you, a million things that could go wrong.'

'C'mon, the war could be over by the time I'm done with my training.'

'You don't actually believe that, do you?'

He focuses on the game again.

'Don't do it. Don't sign your life away. Don't go,' she says, suddenly afraid he's going to laugh at her intensity.

'Are you saying we could start something?'

'What? What do you mean? No — '

'And I could stay in Belknap and live at home and work in a garage, learn how to be a mechanic, or work at Gleason's like my grandfather did, or get my electrician's license

248

and go into business with my dad.'

'No, I — '

'Marry my high school sweetheart and have three kids before I'm twenty-five, divorced by thirty.'

'That's not what I'm saying.'

'I want to get out, Alice. I want something more.'

'You sound like my dad.'

She has to let go of his hand to steady herself. She's holding on to the bleachers with both hands and looking down trying to quiet the tumult inside of her when Benny Benjamin hits a home run and the hometown crowd is on its feet yelling and cheering.

A home run on opening day, she can hear her dad saying, *that's a good omen, sweetheart. That's a good omen for the season to come.*

April 30th

All day long Alice has been trying to get out to the garden to start planting. In the morning they had a dusting of snow, which melted when the temperature soared to fifty-five and the sun came out. Now it's drizzling.

Her mother keeps piling on the chores and she's suddenly obsessively interested in Alice's homework and is demanding to see her planner. Only Alice's planner is pretty blank because Alice doesn't have many plans when it comes to schoolwork. Somehow her mother wheedled some information out of Henry's mother. Alice can just picture poor Mrs. Grover standing there asking Henry if they do, in fact, have a research paper due tomorrow? Three pages on the Continental Congress. So then it's off to the library. Why is the library even open on Sunday, Alice wants to know, doesn't anybody ever get a day of rest anymore?

Now she's got three books to skim through and three pages to write. She calls Henry.

'I need a topic sentence.'

'That's cheating, Alice.'

'Give me one of your discarded ones. I know you have at least five topic sentences up your sleeve.'

Henry considers.

'Okay.'

She can hear him take a piece of paper out of his wastebasket and uncrumple it.

'Was Jefferson the sole author of the Declaration of Independence?'

'That's a question.'

'It's a teaser. Here's the rest: While we often think of Jefferson as the sole author of the Declaration of Independence, John Adams edited it, and he defended it to the rest of the Congress and helped get it passed.'

'This is a *reject* for you? Geez!'

'I got interested in the role that Franklin played.'

'You should quit worrying about math, Henry. You're a genius. Thanks a lot. 'Bye.'

'Wait, Alice — '

'Gotta go, Henry.'

'Did you — ?'

' — What?'

'I heard — '

' — *What?*'

'John Kimball.'

There's an uncomfortable silence.

'I need to write this paper, Henry.'

'Alice — '

'We just went to a baseball game. With Mrs. Minty. *And* his father. *And* his brother.'

'Why didn't you tell me?'

'There's nothing to tell.'

'Do you like him?'

'I don't know.'

'You do like him.'

'I don't even know him.'

'Did he kiss you?'

'No!'

'He did, didn't he?'

'*No!*'

'He already has a girlfriend.'

'I know that!'

'Can I come over?'

'No. I have to write this paper.'

'I'm coming over.'

'Don't. I'm having a terrible day.'

'I need to talk to you.'

'I will be horrible to you if you come over here.'

'Alice — '

'Everything is going wrong today, Henry. I don't want to have a fight with you, too.'

'Could you just tell me — '

'What?'

'Never mind.'

'Henry, you're my best friend.'

'Okay.'

'See you tomorrow?'

'See you tomorrow.'

She hangs up and finds that she is actually grateful to get lost for a few hours in the prickly lifelong relationship between Jefferson and Adams, which turned into this amazing friendship in the last years of their lives with hundreds of letters written back and forth. And then they died on the same day: July 4, 1826. You can't make stuff like that up.

She finishes her paper and looks up to see the rain still falling. Is it ever going to stop?

She heads downstairs only to get roped into helping her mother make dinner. Her mother hasn't cooked in weeks, and today she's making pot roast? So Alice is at the sink peeling carrots to throw in with the roast that is already bubbling away inside the stove, and potatoes for mashed potatoes. Her mom is making a pie. A pie! What is going on? Okay, so it's the Pillsbury roll-out crust, but it's also cherries, real cherries that they freeze every year from their own trees.

'It's Sunday,' her mom offers, by way of explanation.

'So . . . ?'

'Uncle Eddie is coming over and so is Gram.'

'I need to get out in the garden, Mom.'

'I thought it would be nice to have a family dinner. Gram is bringing her green bean casserole.'

'It's not like it's Thanksgiving.'

'Just some family time.'

252

'Dad and I always plant on this Sunday. Some people go by the equinox, we go by the Red Wings opening game. The Sunday after. It's always the Sunday after the home opener.'

Angie carefully unrolls the crust from the package.

'Mom?'

The squeak of the rolling pin.

'Mom? Are you trying to keep me from planting the garden?'

'No.'

'Well, good. Because you can't.'

'I just thought — '

Angie stops rolling out the crust for a minute and puts the heels of her hands over her eyes. She's wearing Dad's apron, Alice notices. Everybody's wearing Dad's apron lately.

'This is your dad's grandmother's pot roast recipe. And cherry pie is — '

'Daddy's favorite.'

'Exactly.'

'So?'

'I just want my family here with me.'

Okay, Alice can understand all of this and she can even like it that her mom is cooking dinner for a change and that Uncle Eddie and Gram are coming over, but why did this have to happen today?

'Will you set the table when you're finished there? With the good china?'

'Couldn't Ellie do it? And I could at least stake out the first half dozen rows — '

' — Alice — '

She can't exactly slam down the good china

plates, though she would like to drop them in a big heap. Her mother pokes her head in the door.

'Not that tablecloth.'

'Why not?'

'The other white one.'

'What difference does it make? They're both white.'

'Thanks, honey. And cloth napkins, please. Can you fold them?'

This is like torture, Alice thinks. Drip, drip, drip. All day long. And there goes the sun, a tiny sliver managing to peek out from the rain clouds, there goes the sun disappearing from the sky. Along with Alice's plans. This is not how today was supposed to go. Dad would not have let this day get away from him, no matter what Angie had planned. He would have known how to work around her or ignore her or tease her into going along with him. Grown-ups have more options in that department, Alice thinks. She would like to just say no to her mother; in fact, she has been trying to do that all day.

'Mom!' she shouts. 'I need to plant the garden!'

'That's just going to have to wait for another day, Alice. How many times — ?'

' — How many times do I have to tell you this is the day! Today, Mom! Not yesterday! Not tomorrow! Today!'

'I don't understand what the big deal is.'

'You're not listening to me. This is the day. Same day. Every year. Tradition. Me and Dad. Tradition.'

254

'I don't see what difference one day more or less makes.'

'*Mom!*'

Alice is so frustrated she is almost crying, which she has vowed never to do in front of her mother ever again.

'Alice, you're just going to have to give in on this one. Can you finish setting the table, please?'

'Why can't Ellie help you? Why can't — ?'

' — *Alice!*'

Uncle Eddie appears, having let himself in the backdoor.

'Would you just lay off the poor kid?'

'Stay out of it, Eddie.'

'I'm just saying — '

'What do you know about raising kids?'

'I thought you were talking about the garden.'

'What sacrifices have you ever had to make?'

'Is this a contest? You win, Angie. You've made more sacrifices than I have. What does that have to do with anything?'

'This is none of your business, Eddie.'

'Angie, c'mon . . . She just wants to plant the garden.'

Alice considers stepping into the fray and then thinks better of it when Angie's next tirade turns into tears, and Uncle Eddie takes her in his arms. Angie's sobs are so loud and so ragged Alice would like to put her hands over her ears or turn on the radio to drown out the sounds and the feelings, but she can't move. It's kind of like watching a car wreck, only scarier.

When Angie finally pulls herself together, Alice turns away and very carefully, very quietly finishes setting the table.

And then it's as though they all make a silent pact to pretend that everything is fine, everything is perfectly normal as they navigate the minefield that is dinner.

★　★　★

After dinner, Alice stands next to Gram at the sink drying dishes while Mom and Uncle Eddie smooth things over with a bottle of wine in the living room.

'Good pie, huh?' Gram says.

'Yeah,' Alice agrees, looking out the kitchen window through the rain, squinting to see the garden.

'Maybe a bit too much sugar.'

Alice hands the pie plate back. 'You missed a spot.'

'I did not!'

'Right there.'

'You remember Grampa?' Gram asks.

'Of course!'

'From before he got sick?'

Alice thinks of the hospital and the blue-striped bathrobe he insisted on bringing from home, but then she remembers sitting on his lap on the maroon velvet couch in the big old house and Grampa reading to her, *The Girl of the Limberlost*, she thinks it was.

'He'd do all the voices when he read to me.'

'That's right.'

'And he always smelled good.'

'Bay rum.'

Gram hands her a mixing bowl to dry.

'He was a good-looking man.'

'Gram!'

'What? He *was*.'

'Are you twinkling, Gram?'

'And lovable; he had this sweetness.'

'Sweet as pie?'

'Maybe that's why Char always wanted more sugar. If she could've had Grampa, she'd have been waking up with sweetness every day of her life.'

'Wait a minute — '

'Her whole life that girl loved sugar. Spoonfuls in her coffee, on her oatmeal. It makes my teeth ache just thinking about it.'

'Maybe that's what made her so sweet.'

'Ha! My sister was a barracuda!'

'She was not!'

'Get in between Char and what she wanted and watch out!'

'What did she want?'

'Oh, that's ancient history.'

'C'mon, Gram.'

Gram hands Alice the roasting pan.

'Grampa. Before he was Grampa, of course.'

'What?'

'Stopped speaking to me for nearly a year when James fell in love with me.'

'You're kidding me.'

'And then she married his brother Bobby. And never, ever stopped flirting with James.'

'But you loved her — '

'Of course I loved her. She was my little sister. Doesn't mean we didn't have our issues.'

Ellie walks into the kitchen and pulls her recorder out of its case.

'Check this out,' Ellie says, unfolding a list of words. '*Cabbaged* and *fabaceae*, each eight letters long, are the longest words that can be played on a musical instrument.'

And then she plays them on her recorder.

Alice looks at Gram and bites her lip to keep from laughing.

'What does *fabaceae* mean?' Gram wants to know.

'Of, or consisting of beans,' Ellie says as she pushes her glasses up on her nose.

'Who knew?'

'Seven-letter words you can play on a musical instrument include *acceded, baggage, bedface, cabbage, defaced,* and *effaced.*'

'*Bedface?*' Alice asks.

'It's in the dictionary,' Ellie says, as she plays the seven-letter words.

'It's not exactly a tune.'

'No, it's an oddity, an aberration, an anomaly . . . '

'Okay! Okay!'

'What's your new favorite word?' Gram asks.

'I have two: *Acnestis.* Noun. On an animal, the point of the back that lies between the shoulders and the lower back, which cannot be reached to be scratched. And *pandiculation.* Noun. The stretching that accompanies yawning.'

'How about *procrastinate?*' Alice shoots back. 'Or *perseverate?* Or *temporize?* Delay! Delay! Delay!'

'What are you talking about?' Gram wants to know.

'I'm supposed to be planting the garden. It should be done. Finished. Put to bed.'

'Too late now,' Ellie says.

'Thanks a lot, sport.'

'Maybe it's just as well,' Gram offers. 'We're supposed to be getting more sleet tomorrow.'

'These are the cold weather crops. Cold weather crops *like* the cold.'

Alice finds herself close to tears, yet again. Why is it no one will listen to her today?

'Ellie! Time for bed!' Mom calls from the living room.

'That's my cue,' says Gram. 'Eddie, I need my coach and four!'

The next thing you know, Gram and Uncle Eddie are on their way home, Ellie's in the bathtub talking a mile a minute to Mom, who is perched on the edge of the tub, and Alice is out the door. In the workshop she puts on her dad's jacket, work gloves, and a hat. She slips into her rubber boots, then gathers what she needs: a hoe, string, stakes, seeds, the Coleman lantern. And finally, finally she is in the garden.

She goes back into the workshop to get the stool for the lantern so that, elevated, it can shed more usable light. In the cold, drizzling rain, in the dark, she stakes her rows one by one. Leaf lettuce, red and green, spinach, beets, radishes, peas, carrots. She hears her dad's voice reminding her to alternate the red and green lettuce. They look so nice like that. *Short rows, Alice. Stagger the planting over two weeks.*

259

She stops for a moment to listen to the wind in the branches and the steady drip of the rain, and then bends to work with the hoe, making her furrows. Not too deep. The soil is wet and heavy but she takes her time, just the way her dad does, and her rows are true.

She has to take her gloves off to handle the seed packets and the seeds. Her hands are freezing as she tears open the first seed packet.

'Alice?'

It's her mom. In a raincoat and rain boots and holding an umbrella.

'Half an hour, I'll be done.'

'Can I help?'

'Not with that stupid umbrella.'

Angie closes the umbrella, pulls a hat out of her pocket, and waits for Alice to tell her what to do.

'Dad and I work in from the outside. So we don't get in each other's way.'

'Okay.'

'Can you see the last row? Beets.'

She hands her the seed packet.

'Be patient. Don't over seed.'

'Just one row?'

'I'll see how you do and then decide if you get to do another one.'

They work in silence except for the slight hiss of the Coleman lantern and the steady drip of the rain.

'It's raining down my neck!' Angie complains.

'You'll live,' Alice says.

Alice is down on her hands and knees, carefully mounding soil over the seeds.

'Sweetie, I'm not really dressed for kneeling in the dirt.'

'I'll do it. You just do the seeds.'

Angie straightens up from the row of beets.

'Good enough?'

Alice checks out her mother's work, as well as she can, given the limited light.

'I guess I'm gonna have to trust you on this one.'

'What's next?'

Alice hands her a packet of carrot seeds.

'How do you keep your hands from freezing off?'

'You don't.'

Alice finishes the spinach and the radishes and the peas in the time it takes Angie to finish the row of carrots, and then she's on her knees, mounding the soil over the seeds. She is rewarded with her dad's voice again: *Tamp it down a bit. Not too tight.*

The soil is cold and wet and she is thinking of the days to come, the sunny days to come when she will plant peppers and tomatoes and beans and corn and squash and the soil will be warm in her hands. She can hear her dad rattling off his favorite varieties of tomatoes: *Early Girl, Brandywine, Big Rainbow, Mr. Stripey, Nebraska Wedding.* She'll plant them all.

'Is that it?' Angie wants to know.

'That's it.'

'Okay. Let's get you into the bathtub.'

'I'm gonna stay out here for a bit, Mom.'

'Alice . . . '

Alice looks at her mom; she notices that her hair is plastered to her neck. Then she looks out over the dark mass of the garden.

'Sometimes I can hear him,' she says. 'Not like in a crazy way or anything. I can hear the things he's said to me. How to do things and stuff.'

'It's really cold, honey.'

'We'd always just sit here for a few minutes when we finished planting.'

Alice picks up the lantern and wipes the rain off the stool for her mom. Angie hesitates and then sits. Alice sets the lantern down and then kneels in the dirt. She pulls a Snickers bar out of the jacket pocket, unwraps it, and hands half to her mom.

'Snickers?'

'Dad's favorite.'

'Really?'

'You didn't know that?'

'Nope.'

They eat the Snickers.

'Normally, when Dad and I would do this the sun would be shining and some birds would be singing and . . . '

'I know, I know . . . '

'And you'd just sort of feel things beginning and things continuing . . . the way some things get to continue . . . because it's the same things that are beginning every spring . . . and it's like . . . so full of hope, you know? To put those seeds in the ground every year.'

Alice hasn't said this many words in a row to her mother in a long time. She wonders if it's the dark that is letting her talk like this. Or the fact

262

that Angie has entered Alice's world for a change.

'Can you smell that smell?'

Angie sniffs, skeptical and dubious that there could be something out here she would actually like to smell. Because while she may like big animals and barns and farmers and farmers' wives, she does not, in any way, shape, or form, like dirt.

'Which smell?'

'All of them.'

'Honey, the garden isn't really — '

'Ellie told me a new word today. *Petrichor.* The loamy smell that rises from the ground after rain. Isn't it cool that there's a word for that?'

'Ellie and her dictionary.'

'It's there. Just like she said. It's there.'

Water is now dripping from Angie's neck down Angie's back and she is wishing she could enter into the spirit of all of this with Alice a bit more fully, that she could just inhale *petrichor* like a really good sport, but just as fervently she is wishing she could get inside her nice, dry house.

'So . . . is that enough communing with nature for one night?'

Alice laughs.

'You go in. I'll put the tools away.'

Angie picks up her umbrella and heads back to the house. She's washing her hands at the kitchen sink and looks up to see that Alice is still in the garden, still kneeling in the dirt. The light from the lantern barely illuminates her. Angie turns out the kitchen light and returns to the window, thinking she might be able to see a little better. What is she waiting for? Her father's voice? A miracle? Is she praying?

Angie realizes that she has no idea what Alice is thinking and she suddenly sees just how hard it is to know anyone, ever. But is there anything more difficult than trying to know your adolescent daughter? No one warned her that you can go from feeling like a really good mother to a really clueless and crappy mother the minute your daughter turns twelve. Or was it eleven?

Alice stands and stretches and picks up the lantern to walk the six rows, making sure everything is as it should be. Just the way her dad does it.

Alice is taller, Angie realizes, she suddenly looks more like Matt than ever; she has even started to move with Matt's easy grace and confidence.

Angie watches her, sees her care and her competence and the threads that connect her to Matt. Each string stretched tight over each row, each careful furrow, each seed in the dark earth weaving a web of connection and memory.

Alice, satisfied, puts the hoe over one shoulder, picks up the stool and the lantern, and heads to the workshop.

Angie calls out the backdoor.

'I'm drawing you a hot bath.'

'Five minutes, Mom. I have to clean the tools.'

Just like Matt: meticulous with his tools. In the last thirty minutes Angie has suddenly found herself face-to-face with a whole slew of things Matt has taught Alice. Angie wonders what she has taught her daughter, and feels like that list is woefully short. In this moment she cannot think of one truly valuable thing to put on that list. How to do laundry? Fry an egg? Not in the same league.

How in the world is she going to fill in for Matt? Not that anyone could ever fill Matt's shoes. But for Alice, for Alice . . . she gets a sudden and dizzying glimpse into the size of this loss. If Matt doesn't come home . . . No, she can't go there, she can't think that. He will be found. He will return. She has to believe this. She has to.

Alice walks in the backdoor, soaking wet and muddy, her dark hair dripping down her back.

'C'mere.'

Alice visibly recoils.

'Mom, I'm a mess.'

'I don't care.' And Angie opens her arms. She opens her arms to her daughter, hoping beyond hope that Alice won't turn away.

There's a long moment before Alice can bring herself to walk into them, and when she does she's stiff and cold and uncertain. But for once, Angie is not worrying about getting wet or dirty or what she has to do next. For once, Angie just holds on and holds on, until she can feel Alice melt into her, until she can feel Alice's head sink onto her shoulder, until she can feel Alice's arms go around her.

'I've missed you,' she says into Alice's damp hair.

May 4th

Four days later, when Sergeant Ames, accompanied by a second soldier, appears again at their front door there is no need for Angie or Alice or Ellie to say a word. They all know why he is here; they know what the letter he holds in his hand says. They stand in the open doorway and attempt to listen as Sergeant Ames does his duty and recites his script about a grateful nation.

'On behalf of the President and the Commandant of the Army, it is my unfortunate duty to inform you . . . '

It is a beautiful, balmy May day and the air is rich with new earth smells and fresh cut grass. They can hear the Peterson twins down the street as they shoot baskets in their driveway.

How many other screen doors open when Sergeant Ames drives up the street? How many of their neighbors are looking at his brown Ford sedan and knowing exactly what it means? The distant war suddenly brought close, suddenly right here in their driveway, right here on their front stoop, right here and right now on East Oak Street.

Sergeant Ames seems hesitant to leave. There are details: the return of the body, the return of Matt's effects. These will be handled by the military. Sergeant Ames promises to come back in the morning to guide them through the process and the decisions.

They watch him drive away and then step back inside the house and close the door. They sit on the couch, Angie in the middle, Ellie and

266

Alice on either side of her. Angie holds the letter with the official army seal in her hand. They are not screaming, they are not wailing; they are barely breathing. It is so quiet Alice can hear her dad's watch ticking on her wrist.

The phone starts to ring.

'We need to call Gram,' Angie says. 'And Uncle Eddie.'

The ringing phone is like a crying child; but Angie does not get up to answer it. Angie seems paralyzed.

'I'll call them,' Alice says.

Angie can't seem to focus.

'Mom . . . ?'

'Okay.'

Alice gets up and heads for the kitchen, the ringing phone getting louder and louder. She turns to look back at her mother. Ellie has climbed into Angie's lap and Angie is rocking her back and forth. In between 'I'll call them,' and 'Okay,' Alice has crossed an invisible line. She was expecting Angie to say, 'No, no, that's all right, honey; I'll take care of it.' She was expecting Angie to hold on to her, to hold on to both of her girls. But here she is on the outside of the circle, steeling herself to break her grandmother's heart. What is this longing to be touched and held and six years old again, to go backward in time, to be smaller than Ellie, to be the only one, to be held by her mother and her father?

She turns to look at her mother once more, thinking: *Call me back. Call my name. Reach out to me.*

But Angie is holding on to Ellie too tight, too tight. She is thinking that her heart is going to burst or stop beating. She wants to sink through the sofa and the floor and into the earth, to be with Matt, nowhere else, not to go on, not to put one foot in front of the other, not to be brave and true, but to let go, to surrender, to join him wherever he is.

The phone stops ringing. Alice picks up the receiver and punches in Gram's number. She notices that her hand is shaking. She notices that the breakfast dishes are still in the sink. She notices that the linoleum floor could use a good scrubbing. There's no answer at the apartment. She calls The Bird Sisters.

'Gram?'

'Alice? Are you all right?'

'It's . . . '

And she can't say 'Dad,' she can't say his name.

'I'll be right there. And I'll call Uncle Eddie. Is your mom there?'

'Yes.'

'I'm on my way.'

Alice hangs up the phone and sits in a kitchen chair.

Henry shows up at the back door and lets himself in.

'I saw the car.'

She closes her eyes.

'Alice . . . ?'

She nods her head. He pulls a chair up and sits beside her.

'Did you call your Gram?'

She nods.

'And your Uncle Eddie?'

Another nod. That's all she can manage.

'Okay, then.'

He takes her hand.

'We'll just wait.'

* * *

They wait. Wait for the news to sink in, for the tears to begin, for a telegram telling them it was all a mistake. That night Alice waits and waits for sleep to come. She finally gives up and goes downstairs. She finds the photograph album she is looking for and quietly steps outside the back door and crosses the grass to the workshop.

She climbs into her sleeping bag, turns on her flashlight, and opens the cover of the photograph album. It is the summer of 1997; she's six years old. This is the summer she finally learns to swim on top of the water, like the big kids do. There are dozens of photos of their week's vacation camping at Small Point. Ellie hasn't even been born yet. Angie and Matt look so young. There are photos of a dinner — was it a birthday? An anniversary? There's a bottle of wine and a jar full of wildflowers on their picnic table. There's a photo of Matt, grinning at Angie as he holds two live and kicking lobsters over the pot boiling on their propane stove. In the next photo Angie has her hair up and a skirt on and Alice can see in the photo how pretty Angie is as she turns to smile at Matt taking the picture; and she can see how her father is looking at Angie

269

and loving her; she can see right there, in this photograph, right there in that moment, that they are in love.

She turns another page and there she is, in her red and white gingham checked bathing suit. That was her favorite bathing suit of all time. She never wanted to outgrow that suit. She wonders what happened to it, if it is still in her bottom drawer. She doesn't remember Ellie ever wearing it. She can't imagine she would ever, ever let her mother give it away.

★ ★ ★

It's a long walk for a six-year-old, all the way across the island. Mom is back at the campsite reading her book while Alice hikes with her dad. At first she was dawdling because she was distracted by the trees and the ferns and the sounds of animals in the woods. She has been practicing walking like an Indian, so she doesn't disturb anything: not a pine needle, not the carpet of leaves and hidden stones. It's really hard! And really slow. It is driving Dad nuts. He keeps turning around to find that she is not, in fact, behind him because she has stopped to investigate some new discovery.

'Alice, get a move on!'

'Alice, look up!'

'Alice! You're missing everything while you worry about your feet!'

How did the Indians do this, she wants to know as she trots to catch up with her father.

They're out of the woods now and climbing

over a rise along a ridge of granite and moss. At the top of the ridge they can see the other side of the island and their destination: Sand Dollar Beach.

'Race you!' Dad calls out as he takes off down the trail. Of course he lets Alice catch up with him and pass him and then fakes running out of breath and falling behind. When she starts to slow down he runs circles around her.

'Come on, come on, come on! We're almost there.'

And then there it is: a perfect crescent of a beach tucked away between the rocks and the trees. Deserted.

'Last one in is a rotten egg!'

He drops their backpack to the sand and pulls off his T-shirt and his hiking boots and pants and sprints into the water, jumping over the waves and then diving headfirst into a big breaker. He surfaces and swims hard for a few minutes before turning back to check on Alice. Who is stuck on the beach, one boot on, one boot off, trying to get a knot out of the lace of her left boot.

'I beat you!' Dad crows.

'There's a knot!' she tosses back. 'No fair!'

'Slowpoke!'

He flips over on his back and spouts water like a whale.

She tries wriggling the knot back and forth to loosen it up and finally gets it undone. She kicks her boot off, pulls off her T-shirt and her shorts, and heads down to the water.

She's wearing her new red and white checked

bathing suit and wondering if Dad will like it, when she steps into the water. How can it be so cold? Dad is out there lolling around like it's a bathtub and the water is so cold it makes her teeth hurt.

'It's cold!'

'Run. Don't walk. Just go.'

She hesitates.

'Alice! Just go!'

She runs through the little waves and dives into the first big wave and swims underwater to her dad. She has her eyes open even though the salt stings, and she's kicking as hard as she can and pulling with her arms with all her might. He picks her up and throws her into the water, over and over. With variations. Backward. Sideways. She stands on his legs and pushes off as he throws her. She stands on his shoulders and jumps in. She's laughing and swallowing water and coughing and sometimes choking but always coming back for more.

That's my girl, Matt thinks. Not afraid, not cold, not complaining, not hesitating. Jumping in.

They leave the water and lie down in the sand. They forgot towels. Mom would not have forgotten towels. But it doesn't matter. They lie down in the sand side by side. Alice looks at the sun through her lashes and half-closed eyes, even though she's not supposed to. It's directly above them in a deep blue sky. She can hear the waves and the fir trees that line the shore moving in the wind. She can see the sun glinting, she can even see the sun when she closes her eyes. How can *that be? She can hear her dad's breathing change as he drops into sleep. And as her skin dries she feels it contract with the sun and the salt. She thinks she's gonna get a burn. They forgot sunscreen. Mom would have remembered sunscreen, too. Alice thinks it's nice to forget things sometimes. To lie in the sand with nothing but her dad and the sun and the water and the trees.*

★   ★   ★

There's a knock at the door, which startles her.

'Alice . . . ? It's me. Henry.'

'It's open,' she calls out to him.

Henry steps inside the workshop.

'I saw your light. You okay?'

It's two o'clock in the morning and it turns out that Henry has been sitting up with her. She puts the flashlight on the floor; its beam casts a light across the workshop.

'Pull up a chair.'

Henry grabs the lawn chair, brings it near Alice, sits. He's wearing old gray sweatpants that are too short, and an ancient sweatshirt that must have belonged to his brother. His hair is even more shaggy and rumpled than usual.

'I can't sleep.'

'I figured.'

'I've been looking at pictures.'

She hands him the photo album.

'From when I was six.'

He opens it.

'That was my favorite bathing suit,' she says.

273

'I remember it.'

'You do?'

'You wore that in the sprinkler and when we went to the high school pool for our swim lessons.'

'I can't believe you remember that.'

Henry wants to tell her that he remembers everything, but when he tries out the phrase inside his head he sounds like an idiot.

'Alice — '

'Henry,' she interrupts.

'What?'

'Would you — ?'

' — What?'

'I don't know how to say this — '

'That's okay.'

'I think if you could . . . maybe . . . I don't know . . . hold me . . . '

She hesitates.

'I might be able to fall asleep.'

Henry has no objection to this idea, and he would like to play it cool, like, oh sure, what the heck, I get this request all the time. Hold you? All casual like. You bet. No problem. But really he is pumped full of the jitters, which is making it especially difficult not to let his hands and his feet sort of do their own nervous dance, and right away he is thinking logistics, like how is this going to work on that skinny little air mattress with a sleeping bag. But Alice has already figured it out. She unzips the sleeping bag so that it can go over them like a quilt.

'I think if we lie on our sides we can both fit.'

So Henry finds himself taking off his shoes

274

and his sweatshirt and lying down next to Alice. She lies with her back to his chest. There's a momentary question about what to do with their arms, but they figure it out.

'I'm gonna leave the light on, if that's okay with you.'

'Sure.'

Her head is tucked beneath his chin, her body curves into him, his arms are around her. He inhales the heady perfume of her hair, mixed with the workshop smells of woodsmoke and linseed oil. He listens to her breathing. He can feel her breathing.

'Henry . . . ?'

'Shhhh . . .'

'Don't let go.'

'I won't.'

'Promise me.'

'I promise.'

They are quiet for a while.

'Henry . . . ?'

'Go to sleep, Alice.'

'I wish . . .'

'What?'

'I wish we could stay like this forever and ever and tomorrow would never come.'

He begins to sing to her, very softly, almost not singing at all, just a whisper of a tune. He spins out the tune like it is a tale he is telling her, until he feels her body relax, until he feels her falling into sleep. He sings to let her know he's there, to stay anchored to the earth, to keep from laughing or crying in amazement that he is lying with Alice in his arms, he sings as if music could keep her alive, as if music could feed her soul, as if music could weave a protective spell around her to survive these days and these weeks and these months and these years, he sings as if he could give her a piece of himself, which will ring inside of her like a bell, like a promise, like hope whenever she needs him; and in his singing, he promises her every single thing he can think of, and more.

★   ★   ★

Inside the house, Angie falls asleep from sheer physical exhaustion and then wakes into fresh grief as she returns to consciousness and remembers. She swims up from sleep to the knowledge that Matt's death is not a dream, it is not a nightmare, but more real than anything else that has ever happened to her, more real even than the birth of her children. She comes downstairs to make tea or toast or maybe something stronger and looking out the kitchen window she sees the dim, unexpected glow in the workshop.

She checks the clock. Three a.m. What's going on?

When she crosses the lawn and opens the door, her first thought is: What the hell are they doing? They're fifteen years old for God's sake! Now she has to deal with this, too? Alone. Without Matt. Years of this. And then she sees that they both still have their clothes on. And remembers that the door was not locked. And the flashlight is on. Thank God. Henry turns his head to look at her and puts his finger to his lips.

'She couldn't sleep,' he whispers.

Angie nods. And frowns. As frowns go, it is a loud frown.

'I promised to stay with her.'

He waits for a response.

'Is that okay?'

'Does your mother know where you are?'

'Not exactly.'

'I'm not happy about this, Henry.'

'It's not what you think.'

'Keep it that way.'

'Okay.'

'No funny stuff.'

'No, ma'am. Absolutely not.'

'I'm not kidding, Henry.'

'I know.'

Henry is getting a crick in his neck from trying not to look like he is plastered against Alice.

'When you wake up, get up. Come in for breakfast. No lollygagging in the damn sleeping bag.'

'Okay.'

'Eight o'clock. I want you in the house.'

'Okay.'

'Do you have a watch?'

'I can see the clock.'

'One minute past eight I'll be out to check on you.'

'Okay.'

Henry attempts a reassuring smile.

'You're way too young to be sleeping with my daughter. No matter what she's going through. Do we understand each other?'

He nods.

'This is special dispensation for one night and one night only.'

Another nod.

'You do understand that now *I* will not be able to sleep for the rest of the night?'

'Why not?'

'Because . . . oh my God . . . do I really have to explain this to you?'

'Shhhh . . . shhhh . . . we don't want to wake her up.'

'Maybe I should just stay out here with you.'

'Mrs. Bliss . . . '

'What?'

'You can trust me.'

'Henry, you're an adolescent boy.'

'So?'

'There are forces at work here that are bigger than both of us and both of you.'

'I don't know what you mean.'

'You will,' Angie says, as she turns and leaves her daughter in the arms of this boy, in the safe haven of her father's workshop, in a world turned upside down and inside out, as she turns to go back to . . . what? Her empty bed? A stiff drink? To crawl into bed with Ellie, to steal comfort from her eight year old? None of these choices were even a remote part of her life when Matt was alive. Stop thinking, she admonishes herself, just make some tea and curl up on the couch with a blanket to wait for eight a.m. Matt would be beside himself if he knew she was letting Alice sleep with Henry. In the same bed, in a separate building, with no supervision. She can hear Matt hollering, *What are you thinking?!* But Matt hasn't met this moment, Matt hasn't met these nights and these days with this pain and dislocation and the sense that they will, all of them, have to find their comforts and their safe places and their moments of peace and rest and respite wherever and whenever they can.

★   ★   ★

Henry wakes to find the sun up and Alice gone. It is 7:27, he notes, according to the clock over Matt's workbench, so at least he hasn't broken any promises to her mother yet. The pillow is squashed from Alice's head, the sleeping bag is still warm from her body, but where is she? His mouth feels like sandpaper, which probably means he was snuffling and making strange noises all night long. He would like about a quart of orange juice and a salad bowl full of Cheerios, but what is he supposed to do now? Look for her? Go into the house and have breakfast? Disappear down the street to his own house as though he was never here in the first place?

He throws off the sleeping bag, gets up, and crosses to the window overlooking the garden and what do you know, there she is, in her pajamas and his sweatshirt and a pair of too-big rubber boots, hoeing away. What does she think she is, some kind of farmer? She has braided her hair to keep it out of her face. She is hoeing very carefully, turning over the soil, loosening the clods.

279

Every row is planted now, except for the tomatoes, which have to wait for Memorial Day, or so he has been told on innumerable occasions. Soon there will be a pale green fuzz to the garden, a green, hopeful, babyish fuzz of barely born, half-baked plantlets all in straight rows. Alice finishes hoeing and heads back to the workshop. She opens the door, hangs the hoe on its hook, and asks:

'Want some breakfast?'

And that seems to be that. Like last night never happened. Like he hasn't been holding her in his arms for hours, watching her and listening to her breathe. He had been determined to stay awake all night, but something, who knows what, happiness maybe, stole him away and took him off to dreamland.

'You coming?'

'Maybe I should go home.'

She considers this.

'Okay. If you want.'

'Your mom came out here last night.'

'She did? Was she mad?'

'Yes and no.'

'Did you talk to her?'

'Well, yeah. Sort of.'

'And she let you stay?'

'Yeah. Kind of.'

'What do you mean, kind of?'

'She established some ground rules.'

'Like what?'

'The usual.'

Alice turns toward the house.

'You coming in, or what?'

'My parents might be worried.'

'Okay.'

'But I left a note.'

'So they're fine, then.'

She starts across the lawn.

'Alice — '

When she turns to look at him, the rising sun catches her square in the jaw and she steps back as though it is a physical blow. And now the birds. As he tries to find words, as he tries to find what to think and what to say he can suddenly hear the birds, dozens of them in the apple trees, dozens more in the lilacs.

'C'mon. Let's go,' she says.

He follows her across the lawn and toward the house, like a guilty party, like a hungry man, like a frightened boy, and he is full of words and feelings and confusion and a rumbling belly and somewhere important something hurts and aches and he can't tell if he is aching for Alice or if he breathed in her grief with the smell of her shampoo.

Henry pauses at the kitchen door. Alice is already pouring juice into jelly jars. When he steps into the kitchen it is unnaturally quiet, as though the house itself is holding its breath. And he suddenly knows that the millions of changes no one wants and no one can prevent, the avalanche of change falling down on Alice and her family, is just beginning.

She hands him his glass of juice as her mother steps into the kitchen.

'Right on time,' she says, looking at the clock.

'I was just leaving,' Henry says, and makes his

281

escape out the door.

He turns to wave at Alice, walking backward, waving at her through the doorway. He wants to make her smile somehow; but she seems lost to him, so he doesn't even dare flash a goofy grin. She raises a hand to him, like a salute, and inside his head he thinks, be strong, Alice, just as inside her head, she hears her father's voice: *courage, Alice, courage.*

May 6th

Within twenty-four hours every neighbor has brought a casserole or a cake or a plateful of cookies. Mrs. Grover arrives with stacks of paper plates and cups, plastic forks and spoons, and a fresh apron. She has quietly installed herself in the kitchen to take care of the food and the family.

Gram has left the restaurant in Sally's hands. Sally, Ginny, and Dave have rearranged their schedules to be there for the duration, as everyone is calling this.

Gram and Uncle Eddie have made all the necessary calls to friends and family. Uncle Eddie is shuttling back and forth between their house and his garage, trying to keep a lid on things. He's installed coolers on the back porch crammed with ice and soda and beer.

Sergeant Ames has called to tell them Matt's body will be arriving stateside, with a military escort, in two days. Do they want to meet the body in Delaware? Do they want to view the

282

body before the autopsy? Which will take two more days. At which point Matt will be placed in a coffin in his military dress uniform, unless they choose cremation. Have they chosen the coffin? Do they want to accompany the body home along with the military escort? Commercial or military plane? Do they want an honor guard at the burial?

Angie doesn't want an autopsy; she won't even allow the word to be spoken in front of Alice and Ellie, but of course, they've both heard it. Angie and Sergeant Ames have been around the block several times on this issue. Angie is furious and adamant and she's even called her senator's office to ask for help. When the senator herself calls back, Angie has a wild moment of hope, but all of the senator's sympathy and gratitude cannot change army policy.

The funeral director, lugging two sample cases, is knocking on the door with his own long list of impossible questions and impossible choices to be made. Only it's not a he, it's a she. It's a beautiful young blonde with a soft voice and soft hands and just why is it so unsettling to think of this lovely young woman dealing with the dead? How can she do it, Alice wonders? And Angie is thinking, isn't it just like Matt to have a beautiful girl taking care of him, even now.

Allison Mahoney, of Mahoney and Sons, suggests that they sit at the dining room table to go over things. Gram whisks Ellie upstairs for a game of Scrabble while Angie and Alice follow Ms. Mahoney into their own dining room.

The sample cases contain very glossy photographs of all kinds of coffins, shown open and shut. There are samples of too-shiny satin in lurid colors, fancy turned brass handles, all of which can be mixed and matched, like picking an outfit. Urns, should they go that way, large and small, plain and fancy, some are blown glass, some are hammered brass. There are pages and pages of choices for the registry book, for cards and prayer cards, and Mass cards, and preprinted thank-you cards.

'Who will be writing the obituary?' Ms. Mahoney asks.

They make their choices and their decisions, one by one. Angie is numb; Alice just wants to get away, to get outside, to go running, to think about, to feel something, *anything* else.

When Ms. Mahoney finally leaves, Mrs. Grover and Gram serve dinner. They all pretend to eat. Uncle Eddie and Henry are pretty successful at it. Afterward, Alice heads to the kitchen to help Mrs. Grover clean up.

Henry is taking out the trash. Mrs. Grover is trying to keep Alice up to date with the food and the leftovers and what they should keep on hand and what they should freeze. Alice wants someone else to keep track of this. But she is trying to help; she is trying to focus on what they should do with the leftover green beans and will anyone want any more of Stephie's mom's Jell-O salad? Which Stephie delivered herself while Alice was out in the garden.

'Mom, you decide,' Henry says as he carries another trash bag out the backdoor.

Angie has gone upstairs to lie down, Uncle Eddie has gone to the garage to check on things, and Ellie is giving Gram a foot massage in the living room.

Mrs. Grover fills the sink to wash the dishes. Alice grabs a dish-towel. This she can do.

'Any more trash?' Henry wants to know.

'That's it.'

He sits down at the kitchen table and grabs another molasses cookie. Alice pours him a glass of milk.

'You could still go tonight, you know,' Mrs. Grover says.

'Go where?' Alice asks.

'To the dance.'

Uh oh, Henry thinks, not a good idea.

'It's not a crime or anything. You could ask your mom, Alice.'

'But — '

'I don't think your dad would mind.'

'I don't feel like — '

'It might do you good.'

'I don't — '

'That's okay, Alice. I don't mind, really,' Henry says.

'You could still go, Henry.'

'Without you? Forget it.'

Alice looks out the kitchen window to her dad's workshop and the garden beyond. The last of the sunset is still coloring the sky. The last thing in the world she feels like doing is going to the school gym to see all those people, to know that they all know what's happened, but they don't know, can't know what to say.

285

'We wouldn't have to go inside, even.'

Henry, it seems, can read her mind.

'You know how there's that grassy area outside the gym, where the big maple tree is?'

'Just watch, you mean?'

'Or just listen. Maybe dance a little on the grass.'

Alice dries another plate.

'I mean we could go in if you want to, if you change your mind or anything; I'm just saying we don't have to . . . Not to pressure you or anything.'

Alice continues to stare out the window. Mrs. Grover dries her hands on her apron and puts her arm around Alice's shoulder.

'You do what feels right to you, honey. It was just a suggestion.'

Alice puts her arm around Mrs. Grover's soft waist in her paisley dress. Mrs. Grover feels so different from Alice's mother.

'I know your dad would like to see you in that dress.'

'No, he'd think . . . '

'He'd be wondering how you grew up so fast and got so pretty. He'd be wondering how it is he hadn't noticed all kinds of things about you while you were right under his nose.'

Alice, embarrassed, pulls away.

'You go change. I'll help Henry get ready.'

'I have to ask my mom.'

'I know. I'll pick you up about . . . '

'We wanted to walk.'

'That's fine, then. Henry will be back to pick you up in thirty minutes. If all you do is walk to the corner and back, that's fine, too.'

'Okay.'

'But stop by afterward and let me see you in that dress.'

Henry and Mrs. Grover are out the door and Angie has said yes, it doesn't matter, yes, it's all right, and now Alice is slipping into the dress and lifting her hair off her neck and twisting it and using too many bobby pins to try to hold it up. Maybe a ponytail would be easier. And stepping into her pointy-toed flat shoes and asking her mom if she can borrow a sweater and yes, she'll be warm enough.

Angie turns and looks at Alice. And finds herself looking straight into Matt's blue eyes.

There's a pause while Angie tries to get her voice under control.

'Daddy would like that dress.'

'Really?'

'Absolutely.'

Matt should be here, she is thinking, Matt should see this, Matt would . . . Oh, when did she get to be so lovely?

'I tried to put my hair up, but . . . '

'Let me help.'

Angie deftly pins up Alice's hair.

'Ask Mrs. Grover to take some pictures.'

'We won't stay too long.'

'Who's driving?'

'We wanted to walk.'

'Call Uncle Eddie if you want a ride home.'

'Mom, we don't have to go, I'm not even sure I really want to go . . . I could stay here with you, I could . . . '

'Go.'
Angie kisses Alice.
'Go.'

*   *   *

Gram and Ellie make Henry come inside when he knocks on the door, Henry who has opted to wear a T-shirt with the tuxedo pants and jacket, Henry who has showered in under five minutes, and slicked back his hair, who is looking older and cooler and somehow also even dorkier than he ever has in his life, Henry who, among other things in the last half hour, has learned how to spit polish his shoes to a mirror shine.

Henry stands just inside the door ready to cut and run at the slightest sign of a critical glance. He is feeling hot and nervous until Alice comes down the stairs in that dress and an entirely new mash-up of feelings starts to slosh around inside his stomach. Alice smiles at him, or at least her mouth smiles at him. Her eyes are still wary and desperate. Henry would like to kiss her eyes, but at the same time wonders just what kind of an idiot goes around wanting to kiss other people's eyes?

Which is when he notices that Ellie is staring at him.

'If you must osculate,' she says, 'please refrain from cataglottism.'

'What?'

'Leave Henry alone, Ellie.'

'But what did you just say?'

288

'If you must kiss, please refrain from kissing with the tongue.'

'Ellie!'

Gram makes Ellie find the camera, in spite of Alice's protests. After a significant spell of photographic torture by the front door, Gram lets them go and Alice and Henry find themselves walking down the sidewalk in the near dark of late twilight.

'You sure you're okay with this?'

Alice doesn't say anything in response, she just reaches out and takes his hand. Henry thinks if she keeps doing things like this, which make him feel as if his stomach and his heart have changed places, all of his internal organs are likely to get completely mixed up and rearranged.

Lights are starting to come on in the houses they pass. It's the after-dinner pause and the streets are unusually quiet. The breeze kicks up and stirs the new leaves in the trees arching over their heads.

They are going the long way to school, down Baird Road to Martin Street instead of cutting through the playing fields; they are passing Mrs. Minty's house and Mrs. Piantowski's house and The Bird Sisters and the Four Corners. Henry is worried that his hand is probably all sweaty and slick and gross, but if it is, Alice doesn't seem to notice. Alice has closed her eyes against the well of sorrow that is always there, rising and falling like a tide, but with her eyes closed she is suddenly hearing and smelling the world around her; hearing the leaves rustle and the branches scraping against each other, hearing their

289

footsteps on the cement sidewalk, the scuffing sound Henry makes in his unaccustomed fancy tie shoes, the *click, click* of her little flats, and then there it is, yes, there it is, the spring smells layered one by one, of new grass and clean dirt and somewhere in the twilight there are narcissus spilling their perfume into the night.

'Alice?'

'Yeah?'

'I'd really like to dance with you.'

'Okay.'

'A slow dance.'

'Okay.'

'And then we can go home . . . Unless you want to stay.'

Alice takes a breath.

'I sort of promised John Kimball I would dance with him.'

'What?'

'It seemed so far-fetched at the time that I never really thought — '

'He asked you — ?'

'What about Melissa?'

'That's what I said.'

'Do you want to dance with him?'

'I don't know. I mean, no, I mean . . . Henry, it's not like a lot of people have ever asked me to dance.'

She looks at him.

'It was nice to be asked.'

'When did this happen?'

'At the Red Wings game.'

'I figured.'

'And then it was awkward and I didn't know

how to tell you, or if there was anything to tell. Which there isn't. Okay?'

'Okay.'

'Can we just forget it now?'

Approaching the high school they can hear the deep bass notes thumping and vibrating all the way from the gym. The principal is at the entrance to the school, his tie loosened, talking to the police officer whose cruiser is idling in the street. He looks up and sees Alice and Henry heading to the back of the building.

'You two have tickets?'

Henry sprints over and hands him their tickets.

'Come on in.'

'We were planning to just hang out on the grass for a while.'

'You're supposed to go inside so we know who's who, what's what, and who's where.'

'Mr. Fisher,' Henry starts to explain —

'Alice, I'm so sorry to hear about your dad.'

'Thank you,' Alice says to the asphalt in front of her.

'Mr. Fisher, we don't want to go inside, we just — '

' — You just what?'

Henry steps up close and speaks quietly for a moment. Mr. Fisher considers.

'If I make an exception can you stay out of trouble?'

'Yes, sir.'

'I mean it, Henry.'

'I know you do, Mr. Fisher.'

They give the school a wide berth as they walk

291

around to the back. Behind the school the double doors to the gym are propped open, spilling music and light onto the parking lot and the edge of the playing fields. The dance committee has hung disco balls from the basketball hoops at either end of the gym floor. There's a DJ at one end and a table full of cookies and punch at the other.

Alice and Henry skirt the edge of the light as they make their way to the lone maple tree behind the school. There are several boys hanging out at the doors who seem to catch their scent and gather, in a body, to begin some kind of taunt. But then they recognize Alice, or one of them does, and they decide to leave them alone.

It is dark enough now to see the stars, dark enough and late enough for the DJ to start to slow things down. Alice sees John Kimball come to the doorway, talk to the boys who are still there, look her way, and head back inside. He seems so far away. It all seems so far away. The baseball game seems like it happened in another lifetime to another girl.

A slow song begins. Henry turns to Alice and puts his hands on her waist. She puts her hands on his shoulders and then he draws her close and she puts her arms around his neck and suddenly without thinking about it too much or having a chance to mess it up, they are dancing. Henry feels the music like his own heartbeat and moves Alice gently over the rough ground as though they are gliding on a polished floor. Alice had been afraid she would not know how to do this, or that she would do it badly or trip or step on his feet. But Henry relaxes into the music and Alice relaxes into Henry and it is so lovely and so unexpected that she allows herself to rest her head on his shoulder. She closes her eyes and she is floating in space, she is riding the music with Henry; she is trusting her body and her feet and she is not thinking about anything but this.

One part of Henry, the dancing part, is inside the music and wants to stay there because that's what he knows, that's where he can just move and hold Alice. But when she puts her head on his shoulder and he takes one hand from her waist and puts it on her head, his fingers in her soft, soft hair, it takes his breath away. He stumbles in that moment and steps on her toes, but they right themselves, they take a breath, together. Henry inhales the perfume of her skin, Alice feels the delicacy of his neck, the new strength in his shoulder; Alice feels the steps, the music, the letting go, the holding on.

The song ends and they separate. Alice does not want to come back to the world; Alice would like to stay lost in the music and the night sky and Henry's arms for a little while longer, maybe forever.

She looks up to see John Kimball at the gym doors again. He takes a step toward her; she waves to him, and then Melissa Johnson is there to reach out and take him by the hand and pull him back inside. Stephie disentangles herself from Jeremy Baskin and comes to the door. Before she can wave, Alice and Henry retreat farther into the dark beyond the maple tree and decide to cut through the Baldwins' driveway to Martin Street so they don't have to see everyone coming out of the school and laughing and talking and waiting for their rides.

In the dark of Martin Street, holding Alice's hand, Henry wants to kiss her. That rogue thought has been zinging around inside of him for weeks now, waking him at odd or inconvenient moments, startling him at breakfast or in the middle of a math test or at the piano. But this feeling in the dark of Martin Street is like a runaway car careening out of control; his blood is doing a jig in his veins, his heart is pounding, his knees feel all watery and weird, and his feet feel like they've grown six sizes. How in the world will he keep from tripping and falling? He is on the edge of falling every single second.

'Henry, are you okay?'

'What? Yeah. Fine. Why?'

'Well, you're kind of breathing funny.'

Breathing, is he actually still breathing?

'Sorry. Sorry.'

And he trips. His legs are like Jell-O. This is ridiculous. He goes down on one knee and recovers, kind of bounces back up like his knee is rubber capped or something.

'Henry Grover, if I didn't know better, I'd think you were drunk.'

I am drunk, he thinks, or this must be what being drunk is like; woozy and hyperaware and clumsy.

'Are you okay? Are you sick?'

Yes, sick, that's it. Sick and in pain and really,

294

do people *want* to feel like this? It's kind of like torture.

'Maybe this was a mistake? And we should have stayed home?'

No, no, not a mistake, he's thinking as he trips again and recovers, but just barely. Not a mistake to walk with you and dance with you and hold you and . . . Oh, boy, this is not getting better, he thinks, this is getting worse and worse.

'Henry, I think you might be hyperventilating.'

He trips again but Alice catches him, sort of, or at least manages to ease him down to the curb.

'Henry, it's okay. Just try to take one deep breath.'

'Alice,' he manages to choke out —

'What?'

'When you kissed me . . . '

She looks down at her feet. Not a good sign. He braces himself.

'When you kissed me . . . Was it . . . ?'

'Was it what?'

'A mistake?' he asks.

'No, I mean — '

' — Are you sorry?'

'No. I didn't think — '

'Because I didn't mean — '

'I know.'

'No, you don't know,' he says. 'You startled me and — '

'I'm sorry.'

'Don't be sorry. Please don't be sorry. What I mean is — '

'What?'

'I didn't have a chance — '

'A chance to what?'

'A chance to kiss you back . . . And last night, when I was holding you, just holding you — '

'Henry, don't.'

'Don't what?'

'Don't ask me.'

'I don't want to ask you, I want to kiss you.'

'Don't ask me.'

'Don't . . . ?'

And she is looking at him with her deep, newly fathomless eyes that are shining with something that is not tears and not joy, but is still urgent and unreadable, and he wants to think about what Alice is feeling but all he can think about is what he is feeling. Is this what her mother was talking about this morning, that lifetime ago? It is not careful or considerate or cautious; it is a rush that's propelling him, terrified that he could lose her forever, terrified that this could be his only chance, terrified that whatever happens in this moment cannot be taken back or erased or made right once it happens, that if he stumbles here, somehow that is who he is and who he will be forever and ever.

He looks down at his hands dangling between his knees, and suddenly it is all quiet inside of him. Too quiet, like all the air has been squeezed out of him and he is nothing but a shell. He can hear the breeze in the trees overhead; he can hear the traffic on Baird Road.

Alice kneels in front of him. She puts her hands on either side of his face.

'I don't want anything else to change, Henry.'

'It won't change.'

'It will.'

'But . . .'

'*I can't lose one more thing.*'

He can't hear her, really; he can't hear anything but this new roaring in his ears when she is so close to him, and he pulls her to him, too fiercely, they nearly collide, he pulls her to him and for a second, looks into her eyes, her unreadable eyes. He closes his own eyes and with a prayer, a wish, a pure incantation of fear and desire, he kisses her. And this time there is no mistaking it, their lips actually touch. It is equally shocking as the first time, but they do not stumble and jerk and pull away.

Instead, Alice bursts into tears. These are not girly tears pulled out and turned on for effect, not that Alice is that kind of girl; these are racking, hiccupping, blubbering sobs. Henry has one wild, terrible moment where he thinks his kiss has caused these desperate feelings, before Alice leans into him and holds on to him and sobs and sobs into his shoulder.

He manages to stand up and pull her to her feet and hand her his handkerchief, which his mother had not only thought to provide but had carefully ironed that afternoon.

'It's not you,' she chokes out, before burying her face in his handkerchief again. 'It's everything.'

Henry knows that everything is her dad and that her dad is everything, which is not exactly the way he feels about his own dad, and if anything, if it is even possible, this fills him further to the brim with Alice feelings.

And while it is true that Henry is nothing but a gangly fifteen-year-old boy, often sloppy, occasionally rude, with marginal hygiene habits, it is also true that he is still in possession of his own heart, his own inspired, musical, untouched heart, a heart capable of taking on Alice and her sadness and her loss and her love. So, on this night, when Alice pours out her grief for her father and her love for her father, and the ending of her time on earth with her father, it is Henry she chooses, Henry she pours these feelings into, Henry she blesses and burdens with her tears, Henry who has the strength of ten men as he stands up and stands steady beneath this onslaught that has knocked lesser men and boys to their knees.

May 8th

They are waiting on the airport tarmac for Angie and the military escort and the coffin to be unloaded from the plane. There is a special place at the airport for this, away from the main terminal. Alice is sitting in the front seat next to Uncle Eddie. Gram and Ellie are in the back. The hearse from Mahoney and Sons waits behind them. No one is talking. It is gray and cool, threatening rain. Good for the garden, Alice thinks, though we could use some sun.

A uniformed soldier follows Angie down the stairs as the hold of the plane is opened from the inside. She is wearing her glasses, Alice notices, even though she's dressed up. Maybe she wants to hide her eyes.

Six soldiers stand with the coffin on their shoulders. Alice had expected a flag, but the coffin is bare. Angie is directed to a place near the hold. The soldier following her stands nearby. The funeral director appears at Uncle Eddie's window.

'They're waiting for us. Just walk up and stand beside Mrs. Bliss.'

They pile out of the car and cross the gritty tarmac to stand beside Angie as Matt's coffin is carried down the stairs. The single soldier turns toward the coffin and executes a very precise, slow-motion salute. Alice steps forward. The funeral director reaches out a hand to pull her back and Alice realizes they were not supposed to stop; they were not going to wait for her to meet her father, to acknowledge his return. Their job is simply to convey the coffin across the parking lot and into the waiting hearse. But they do stop for her, each in his dress uniform, each with his eyes front.

'Are you from my father's unit?'

'No.'

'Did any of you know him?'

'No. I'm sorry.'

Gram steps forward.

'Come on, honey.'

Alice stands her ground. She turns to the single, saluting soldier.

'Did you know my father?'

He shakes his head. She turns back to the coffin.

'Can you put the coffin down, please?'

There is hesitation all around, subtle shifts in the soldier's bodies, as they cannot break rank and look at each other. Alice chooses one soldier to speak to.

'Can you just let him touch the ground, please?'

The wind picks up; sand and dust swirl around their feet. It is possible that the soldier could choose to let the wind blow Alice's words away, but she is standing firm and speaking clearly and looking him in the face even though he cannot meet her eyes.

He speaks a brief command, and then, moving as one, the soldiers lower the coffin to the ground and take a step away. She kneels beside the coffin and lays one hand on the smooth wood. She wants a moment for her father to land on the ground, for his body to arrive here, at home. She does not want her father's soul to be lost in Iraq or in a plane flying above the ocean or somewhere in an army hospital in Delaware. She wants his soul to come home, however briefly, *home*, before it goes on whatever journey a soul must take, and she doesn't believe this is possible if he never actually touches the ground. If she could she would open the coffin and put his feet on the ground, but this is the best she can do.

Angie reaches out to take her hand, pulling Alice to her feet, releasing the soldiers. They lift the coffin to their shoulders, walk the last steps to the hearse, and slide the coffin into the waiting bay.

300

They all wait where they are until the hearse starts up. The soldiers remain at attention while the family piles back into the car and slowly drives off, following the hearse. Ellie kneels on the seat and watches out the back window. Not one soldier moves a muscle while she can still see them. Uncle Eddie takes the turn onto Columbus Avenue too fast and Ellie slides into a seated position in between Alice and Gram. Angie puts her head back against the headrest and closes her eyes. She is as pale as the moon.

Gram reaches up and strokes Angie's hair. Alice notices that Gram's hand is trembling. Gram, realizing what Alice has seen, shifts to rest her hand on Angie's shoulder.

'We'll get through this,' Gram says.

Angie clasps Gram's hand, and Alice sees that she is wearing Matt's wedding ring on her second finger. When did they give that to her? In the morgue? Was it in a small plastic bag or an envelope? Did she slip it off his finger herself? Did they let her touch him? Why did Angie go alone, why didn't she take Gram or Uncle Eddie with her, why did she refuse to let Alice come along?

Why are all of these things happening so quickly? There is too much to do, there are too many steps to take, no, no, there is not enough to do, she sees now; it will all go by too fast, it is out of her hands, it will all happen whether she wants it to or not, and he will be gone, truly gone, dead and buried, and there will not even be this, this strange hollow awkwardness, this

301

unnatural quiet to fill up the emptiness he has left behind.

'Home?' Uncle Eddie asks.

'Mom, where are Dad's dog tags?' Alice asks.

'Home,' Angie answers, touching her throat and the metal chain under her shirt collar.

'Can I have them?' Ellie asks. 'Alice has his watch.'

'Not now, girls.'

* * *

They ride in silence, a terrible brittle silence. The air of the car is so full of unspoken feelings Alice is surprised the windows don't blow out. She wants to shout or jump on the seat or scream; instead she opens the window to try to release the pressure. If they weren't traveling I-90 at seventy miles an hour, she would stick her head out the window; her head, her torso, her arms, her legs, and suddenly she is fantasizing about jumping out of the car window, landing on the pavement, being hit by a car . . . Jesus! Where the hell did that come from? She can't bear to think about the autopsy. But what about his spirit, Alice wonders? Where is it? Can she touch it, reach it, capture it like a firefly in a bottle? She doesn't believe that. And even if she could believe it, even if his spirit is still alive and even if she could find it somehow, know where to look or what to say, if she could still talk to him; even then, it's not enough. She wants all of him back, his face, his body, his voice, his big feet, his laugh, his patience, his impatience. She even wants him correcting her math tests, making her mad, holding her to a higher standard, holding her to seemingly impossible standards all the time. She wants him back, that's all.

She starts to cry. She looks down at her hands, suddenly wet with tears. She tries to stop, but this silent weeping seems to be beyond her volition. As long as his body was still moving, she thinks, he was somehow still alive.

Ellie releases her seat belt and climbs into Alice's lap. She snuggles under Alice's chin as Alice's arms go around her. She insinuates her little hands right around Alice's neck as she shifts her head to Alice's shoulder.

Alice closes her eyes and breathes in Ellie, her clean hair, her compact little kid body, her clattering runaway heartbeat, her perfect shell ears. She rests her cheek on top of Ellie's head and turns to look out the window. She closes her eyes against the day; she tries to let Ellie anchor her, hold her to the earth, when all of Alice just wants to let go, stop breathing, and float away into the sky, to let go of this life and to find her father, wherever he is.

★　★　★

They have left Matt's body at the funeral parlor, dropped him off like delivering a package, and driven home, where they all scatter to their own corners: Angie to unpack and lie down, Gram to the restaurant, Ellie to visit Janna for the first time in days, Uncle Eddie to the garage. And Alice, where does Alice go?

She is furious that they have to leave Matt in yet another place that is not where he belongs; where he is being taken care of by strangers, or worse, stacked among the dead and left alone.

Alice heads out the back door and past the workshop to the garden. She does not pick up a tool. If she had a tool in her hand, she thinks, she would wipe out every plant in front of her. If she had a tool in her hand, she would knock down the workshop or smash the windows in the car. She briefly thinks of which tool would be best for smashing the car windows. The mattock, probably, or the ax.

She kneels at the first row, the beets, the hell with the mud and the nice khakis her grandmother insisted she wear to the airport, and she begins to weed the row and thin the seedlings. She always hated thinning until her father said fine, and they conducted an experiment. Two rows of carrots, one thinned, one left alone. And Alice saw for herself the result of overcrowding and lack of nutrients. Now she is an expert at this.

The earth is cool and damp and it has begun to drizzle. The sky is a dull oyster gray, almost the color of a sky threatening to snow, though it is much too mild for snow. Still she is cold, with a chill that seems to come from inside of her.

She puts both hands flat on the ground and leans on them. She wants to find her father here in his garden. She wants to believe something, anything, about an afterlife. She wants him to slam out of the backdoor, the way he always

304

does, calling out to her, telling her the plan for the day.

But the door doesn't slam. Her father does not call out to her.

★   ★   ★

She peels off her jacket, trades her khakis for running shorts, her muck boots for sneakers, and heads out for a run. It begins to rain in earnest. At first Alice listens to the rain, the hiss of the water under the tires of passing cars, and beneath that, the dead silence without her father and his voice in her head. She wants to run until her heart explodes. A funny way to die.

Soon Alice is so drenched that her sneakers and her clothes grow heavy and start to make squishing sounds. But somewhere in the road beneath her feet, or the rain on her face, somewhere in the cadence of her stride, in the rhythm of her breathing there is solace. A moment, a small sliver of light, a pause, a breath.

Sustenato, Henry would say, pressing that pedal at the piano. Sustaining.

May 9th

Angie sends Alice back upstairs to change her clothes for the 'hours' at the funeral parlor. Wearing black jeans and one of her dad's polo shirts has been deemed inappropriate, disrespectful, and annoying beyond belief.

She is frantically searching her closet for the

305

black skirt and white blouse she wears for chorus concerts. The skirt is on the highest shelf rolled into a ball. She tries to smooth out the wrinkles as she pulls it on, but she still can't find the white blouse. She tears into her parents' bedroom and grabs her mom's cream silk blouse off its hanger and pulls it on over her head. Shoes, shoes, shoes. Back to her room. Her flats from the dance. A scrunchie goes around her wrist; she'll fix her hair in the car. She doesn't really understand how her body can be moving so fast when her mind is stuck in slow motion, when her mind is still in bed, still dreaming about last year and last spring and the days and the weeks and the hours before all of this happened.

Running downstairs she can see that the front door has been left open and everyone is already in the car. Uncle Eddie, almost unrecognizable in a suit and tie, is at the wheel; Gram and Ellie are in the backseat. Alice thinks, I can't do this, I can't go through the motions, I can't stand in a room with my father in a casket and talk to everyone; I can't do this.

She sees her mom lean over Uncle Eddie in the front seat to give the horn a long blast, and on the wave of that sound, she propels herself through the door, slamming it behind her, running down to the street and the car and her family and the final ritualized steps of letting go of her father.

Another funeral director, one of Allison Mahoney's brothers, meets them at the back door. There is a line of people out the front door, down the sidewalk, and around Middle Street. He ushers them into the room with the coffin and the flowers and the folding chairs and a book to sign on its own stupid, phony stand, and all Alice can see is the coffin. There are so many flowers the smell is taking up all the air in the room. The late-afternoon sun is slanting into sunset outside, while inside the shades are drawn and the lights are on. Alice is ready to bolt, when Uncle Eddie rests his hand on the small of her back. Suddenly she sees the roof and the ladder and remembers her father with his hand on her back telling her to breathe.

The funeral director says that they will have a few moments alone in the room with Matt before they open the doors to the neighbors, to the baseball players and the teachers and the firemen and the wives and the children of the other men in his unit, and all the rest of the world. How did her father know so many people?

Angie walks in first and kneels at the coffin, Ellie beside her. Alice recoils; she turns her back on her mother and her sister and the coffin and all that it contains.

She suddenly wants Henry. Where is Henry? Why isn't he here?

Gram is at her side.

'I'll go up with you.'

'I can't.'

'Yes, you can.'

'Gram — '

'These are hard things.'

'I *can't*, Gram.'

307

'You have to think about what you can do for your father now.'

Alice begins to back away from her grandmother.

'You'll never forgive yourself if you don't do this.'

'Gram — '

'Never.'

Alice lets Gram take her hand and lead her up to the coffin. They kneel together. Alice is looking down at her clasped hands; Alice is looking at her grandmother's hands; Alice is looking anywhere but at the figure in the coffin, at the uniform that is not her father, that is something else, someone else, because it is still not possible to believe that her father could be dead and cold and lifeless and gone.

Gram stands and leans over and kisses him. She kisses Matt on the forehead and touches his crossed hands, as though this is normal, as though he will feel her touch and her warmth. When Alice stands up she can smell her mother's perfume as it is released from the cream-colored blouse. She takes hold of the edge of the coffin to keep from falling. She closes her eyes. She feels a reassuring hand again on the small of her back. Gram.

Alice lifts her head and opens her eyes and looks at her father. Now she can't get enough of looking at him. He is not the same; he is not the same at all. But what there is, what there still is, right here in front of her, close enough to touch, is this broken body, this man, this soldier. Her father. Hers.

She reaches out and covers his hands with her own. And with that touch, she knows that she will never see his eyes again, his smile again, she will never see him pick up a hammer, or stake a row of tomatoes, or drive a car, or twine his hand in the hair at the nape of her mother's neck.

She lets herself be led away by Gram. The family is receiving instructions from Allison Mahoney; she is telling them where to find the restrooms, where they can take a break from the receiving line to sit down, how they should arrange themselves in line. She will be standing right behind them, she tells them. She will do what she can to keep the line moving. It looks like it is going to be a long night. They can cut it off whenever they want, if they can't go on. People will understand.

Somehow Alice had not really paid attention to the fact that she would be standing in this room, while friends and neighbors came through to pay their respects and speak to the family. Mom, safely hidden behind her glasses, had instructed Alice and Ellie on shaking hands and saying a simple thank you, but Alice had not imagined facing all of these people.

'Mom,' she says.

'Not now, Alice.'

'What do I do if I feel sick?'

'Go to the restroom.'

'Can I go home?'

'Now?'

'If I get sick — '

'You're not going to get sick. Stop being so dramatic. Mom, can you deal with Alice, please?'

309

'Mom.'

'What?'

'I can't handle it.'

'This isn't about you, Alice. Pull yourself together.'

Gram takes Alice by the hand, which only makes Alice angry. She pulls away and stands in sullen, stubborn silence, looking at the floor, shaking hands without looking up or saying anything, until her mother reaches around behind Gram and pinches her. Then, shivering, with cold, sweaty palms, Alice shakes hand after hand, and thanks friends and neighbors and perfect strangers for their condolences. She keeps glancing at the coffin as if she could draw strength from her father, but there are always people kneeling or standing there, blocking her view.

Mrs. Piantowski comes through the line with baby Inga in her arms. She speaks for some minutes to Alice's mother and when she stands in front of Alice, she does the most unexpected thing; she pulls her into a quick embrace and says:

'Come sit down with us for a minute.'

Alice looks to her mother who nods permission. Mrs. Piantowski leads Alice to one of the waiting chairs. Alice sits facing the coffin, and Mrs. Piantowski puts baby Inga in Alice's arms. Inga is a sleepy, yielding bundle. When Alice brings her close she molds her little body against her. Mrs. Piantowski has one hand on Alice's shoulder and one hand on Inga's back. She is sheltering them, making a safe space for

310

Alice to catch her breath, to find herself again. Alice listens to Inga breathe amid the noise and the hush of this room, this odd, nowhere place where they are all suspended between life and death. How strange to have a dead man in their midst; how strange to visit a dead man to say good-bye, how strange to hold a baby in a place like this.

Mrs. Piantowski is humming right into baby Inga's ear, and Mrs. Piantowski's warmth and the baby's warmth is somehow warming Alice. She has stopped shivering finally. Alice looks up at her own mother who meets her glance and smiles at her before someone else moves down the receiving line and blocks her view.

There are people waiting in the anteroom, and there is a line out the door and down the sidewalk. Matt's baseball team is here, spilling through the doorway, nearly unable to contain their physical energy in this room of stillness. B.D. and Ginger are right behind them.

She looks at her family in the receiving line. For the first time she notices what a small group they are. Matt's parents are dead and buried ten years or more. His brother, Mark, who works for the Congo Basin Forest Partnership with U.S. AID, is on site in the rain forest. They don't know if their telegram has reached him. So there's only Angie and Gram and Uncle Eddie and Alice and Ellie to wake and bury Matt. And now she's remembering her great aunt Beryl on the phone from the nursing home, 'It's a good thing your Grammy and Grampy didn't live to see this.'

311

Ellie is standing next to Angie now. In her favorite spring green dress, her new haircut, and her new glasses, she is kind and polite and efficient; she is a miniature mom. How can she do that? Is she pretending, playing a part, so she won't feel anything?

Here is Lillian Balfour, just arrived from San Francisco, her mom's best friend. Behind her in the line are the Hoyts, her parents' close friends from the old neighborhood, and oh, God, there's Johnny Mason, Matt's oldest friend, the fancy lawyer all the way up from Virginia, with his wife and his three little kids. And Mr. and Mrs. Holscher. This is too much, Alice thinks; this is unreal.

She can't believe it. Stephie Larson and her parents are in line behind the Holschers. Stephie has her head down, and she is crying so hard her dad has to put his arm around her to steady her. He says something to her and she looks up and sees Alice. She lifts her hand in a wave. Alice tries to smile but can't tell if she actually does or not; it feels like her face is frozen.

Lillian walks right up and puts her arms around Angie, Lillian with her red hair and artsy clothes, and Angie is losing it, Alice can see it from here. Her mother's face has gone bright and blotchy and she is fighting back tears. Only with Lillian here, she can't win this fight, with Lillian here, she can no longer pretend she is just going through the motions, or it's all a bad dream, or somehow, somehow she will wake up tomorrow and find Matt peacefully asleep beside her. All of these people, these caring, lovely people, each one like a hammer blow, each one striking a gong, ringing a bell: he's gone, he's gone, he's gone.

Uncle Eddie stands in front of Angie, shielding her from the people waiting in line, giving her a moment to collect herself. He pulls a flask from his back pocket and hands it to her. Both Lillian and Angie drink from it, Lillian even manages to giggle and snort the way she usually does before Eddie takes a good long pull and they are back in business. Lillian positions herself just behind Ellie, one hand on Ellie's shoulder, one hand on Angie's shoulder. Not in the way, not obtrusive, but there, solidly there beside her friend.

Henry is in front of the coffin now, Alice notices with a start. Henry and his mother and his father. Henry is kneeling for a long time; she can see Mrs. Grover urge him to his feet, but not before Henry places something in the coffin. He can't look up as he goes through the receiving line. He shuffles and shakes hands and hangs his head. He makes his way to a chair in the back of the room with his parents. He is trying to compose himself before he speaks to Alice, and he is having a mighty hard time of it; nothing he can say to himself can change the unalterable facts of this day.

'That's my best friend,' she tells Mrs. Piantowski.

'Henry Grover, yes?'

'Can I show him baby Inga? Can I let him hold her?'

'Yes, you can.'

Alice crosses to Henry and nods to Mr. and

Mrs. Grover, who make room for her to sit across from him. Henry is looking at his hands and weeping. He hasn't cried like this in years. He feels the fool, the total fool, but he can't stop. He is undone by Alice's father lying in the coffin. All of his magical thinking, that somehow this could all come right; all of his hopes and wishes for Alice, for her family, all undone by the simple fact of the coffin and the body within it.

Alice leans in and speaks to him. He tries to tell her that he's sorry but can't find his voice. She places baby Inga in his arms. He has to unclasp his hands to take the baby; he has to pay attention to keep from jostling her or dropping her. He has never held a baby before; he must be doing this all wrong. Alice has one hand on Inga's back and one hand on Henry's arm. They are knee to knee and he is holding the baby, he is actually holding the baby, without disaster. When Henry dares to look up at Alice he is met by her bruised eyes. She is saving me, he thinks. I should be helping her and she is saving me.

'Inga likes it when you sing to her.'

Does she remember, he wonders? Did she hear him that night when he thought she was asleep?

Alice leans in close to him: 'What were you doing up there? Did you put something in the coffin?'

'A baseball. And a picture of you and me when we were six and you were wearing that bathing suit you like so much.'

'I didn't bring anything with me. No one told me.'

In a panic she tries to think what she has with her that she can put inside the coffin. But she doesn't carry a purse, or a wallet. She needs time to think about this, to plan. She has no coins in her pocket to weight his eyes, she has no picture to slip into his hands, or a stone from Small Point, or an old, handmade iron hinge, or a roofing shingle, or a drawing of the garden.

'We could go back and get something for you. If you know what you want,' Henry offers.

Baby Inga starts to cry. Mrs. Piantowski picks her up and she quiets immediately.

'See you tomorrow,' she says, and carries baby Inga away.

Alice turns to Mr. and Mrs. Grover.

'Are you sure you don't mind?'

'Not at all.' Mrs. Grover smiles at her.

⋆　⋆　⋆

Two hours later, when everyone has finally left, Angie returns to the coffin. Alice and Ellie kneel on either side of her. They are exhausted and yet it feels like they are living outside of time now, with the minutes speeding up and slowing down, with wanting it to be over, and wishing it would never end.

'Can we see him again tomorrow?' Alice asks.

'No.'

'Why not?'

'They'll seal the coffin tonight.'

'I wish — '

'I know.'

Ellie puts a book of drawings next to Matt's body.

'Why can't I see him one more time?'

'Alice — '

'Why? What difference does it make? I'll ask Ms. Mahoney. You won't have to do anything.'

Angie touches Matt's face.

'I'm not ready, Mom.'

'No one's ready.'

'I'll never be ready.'

Ms. Mahoney steps up to them. She doesn't have to say a word. It's late and everyone is waiting for Alice and her family to leave.

'We just need another minute.'

Ms. Mahoney is looking at Angie. She is not so nice now. Maybe she's tired, too. But this is just a job to her, Alice realizes; she's ready to kick off her heels and take a bath and be done with the Bliss family for the night.

An old man in a dark suit flips on the overhead lights.

'Could you please . . . ?'

He stands at the light switch, his arms crossed over his stomach. The glare of the lights is cruel. Her father looks less and less like himself and more and more like something that no longer belongs to this world.

In the harsh light Alice can see that the chintzy velvet that surrounds the coffin is attached with Velcro. A stage set, that's all it is. Why do they do it like this? It's supposed to mean something, but does it?

She has packets of marigold and zinnia seeds in one hand, and Matt's father's hammer in the other. How weird is that, she thinks. A hammer in a place like this. She places them in the coffin, the hammer by his side where he can reach it, the seeds in his breast pocket. What had seemed so important a few hours ago, now she wonders what difference it will make. Is it all superstition; is it all just piling up little moments, little stacks of memories against the devastation of the future? As though she will somehow feel better next month when she remembers, *at least I put Grampa's hammer in the coffin?* The hammer and the buttons on his uniform will last longer than his clothes or his body or the coffin itself. This is a horrible train of thought.

She jumps when she realizes that the old man is standing just behind them.

'Your father put a new roof on my house ten years ago. Good man. Good roof, too.'

They exchange a glance and then Alice and Angie and Ellie step away from the coffin. He turns to let them pass before him to the doorway.

'We'd like to stay until you close the coffin.'

He has to stand on tiptoe to reach and close the lid. The hinges are silent.

Angie takes both of her girls by the hand and walks through the building to the door, to the sidewalk, to the night air, to Gram and Uncle Eddie, heading for home.

May 10th

It's four o'clock in the morning when Alice wakes up to find that Ellie has climbed into bed

with her. She crawls over her to get up, sees
Ellie's pajamas and underpants discarded on
the floor, and realizes she must have wet the
bed.

She pads quietly down the hall and pushes the
door to her parents' room open. She is startled
to see another head on the pillow next to her
mom until she remembers that Lillian is staying
with them.

'Mom?'

Angie sits up immediately; she has not slept.
She grabs her bathrobe and follows Alice down
the stairs and into the kitchen. Alice puts the
kettle on though she's not sure she really wants
anything. Angie finds the Drambuie and pours
herself a glass.

'You want to try it?'

'Sure.'

She passes Alice her glass.

'Ellie wet the bed.'

'Poor kid.'

'She got herself into clean PJs and she's in my
bed now.'

'Is that what woke you up?'

'I guess.'

Alice tastes the Drambuie.

'Mom . . .'

She hesitates.

'We can't bury him.'

'What are you talking about?'

'It's not right for Dad. He can't . . . I
can't . . .'

'What?'

'Put him in the ground.'

318

'Where do you want to put him? The backyard?'

'No. The ocean, a boat, maybe . . . '

'And never be able to visit him?'

'I don't know.'

'Never be able to go to where he is?'

'I just can't think of Dad trapped under the ground. I can imagine scattering his ashes from a rooftop, or by the ocean, or — '

'Daddy thought about cremation,' Angie says.

'He did?'

'But I asked him for a burial. I wanted a headstone, somewhere to go.'

'Why?'

'I need to know where he is. And I want to be buried beside him.'

'But maybe — '

'Do you really want to have your father cremated?'

'I don't know. I just — '

Alice turns to look out the window.

'I don't think I can stand there and let them put him in a hole in the ground and cover him with dirt.'

'That's what's going to happen, honey. I can try to help you, but you're going to have to accept this.'

'Did you and Daddy talk about it?'

'Some. Not as much as we should have.'

'What do you believe, Mom?'

'What do you mean?'

'About heaven or an afterlife or the soul . . . '

'It's hard to say.'

Angie pulls her robe close around her.

Alice stands there looking at her, needing her mother to know things. Angie hears Matt's voice inside her head, *Try, Angie.*

'I always thought holy rollers were ridiculous, and I never put my faith in any church.'

'And . . . ' Alice waits.

There's Matt's voice again: *Keep trying.*

'But now I realize I had a lucky life. I had the luxury of not needing to believe in anything. Now that Daddy's gone I wish I believed in all of it.'

'Really?'

'Yes and no. I'm trying to figure that out.'

'And Daddy?'

'Oh, honey, you know Daddy . . . He was a pragmatist; he liked facts and figures. But this, this is a whole new ballgame.'

Alice pushes the glass away.

'When I wake up,' Alice says, 'at first I don't remember. Every day I wake up and I have to find out he's gone all over again.'

'Me, too.'

'Really?'

'That's part of why we go through all of this. It seems so strange and bizarre even, but the rituals — saying the words, touching his body, putting him in the ground, remembering him with friends — all of it starts to make it real for us.'

'I don't want it to be real, Mom.'

'I know.'

There is a pause.

'What have they told you about what happened to Dad?'

'Very little.'

'I need to know.'

'Alice . . . '

'I have nightmares. I keep seeing him.'

'Honey . . . '

'How did they find him? Was there a rescue? What happened, Mom? I need to know what happened.'

'I don't have answers to all of your questions.'

'Just tell me what you know.'

'And we don't have the results of the autopsy yet.'

'How hard is it to tell whether he died from his wounds, or further injuries, or pneumonia? That's pretty simple.'

'Nothing is simple with the U.S. Army.'

'You're stalling.'

'All that they've told me so far is that he died from his wounds.'

'When?'

'That's what the autopsy is for.'

'How did they find him?'

Angie takes a sip of her drink, looks out the kitchen window to the dark shadow of Matt's workshop. She does not want her daughter to hear these words, to be haunted, as she is haunted by this knowledge.

' . . . Mom . . . ?'

'His body was dumped on the side of the road.'

'Where?'

'Eleven miles from where he was captured.'

Alice leans against the counter.

'Was he mutilated?'

321

'No.'

'Don't lie to me.'

'I'm not.'

'Did they take his organs?'

'No.'

'Are you sure?'

'Yes.'

'Really sure?'

'Yes. Alice — '

'Did they ever give you Travis Boyd's phone number or address?'

'They say they're working on it.'

'Was anyone else with Dad?'

'I don't know.'

'How bad were his wounds? Have they told you?'

'No, they haven't.'

'I keep imagining the worst things.'

'So do I.'

'It must have been terrifying.'

'Yes.'

Angie reaches out to Alice just as Alice takes a step away.

'Mom, sometimes I think I can't stand it; I won't be able to . . . '

Alice looks down at her hands, clenching and unclenching her fists.

'Daddy would want you to . . . He would want us all to really live, honey, really live in this world and try to make a difference.'

'I know.'

'He was so proud of you.'

'I don't know why. I never did anything amazing.'

'He was proud of the person you are, the person you're becoming.'

'I want him back.'

'So do I, sweetheart. So do I.'

★ ★ ★

Alice is the last one in the shower later that morning. The hot water runs out before her hair is rinsed so by the time she gets the shampoo out she's chilled to the bone. But that's okay, that's perfect, in fact. She is dog tired and feels like she is hearing and seeing and feeling everything through thick layers of cotton wool. Everything is a little vague, a little removed; cool and distant.

Upstairs, she pulls on her dress from the dance and slips on her flats. She rakes her fingers through her hair and goes into her mom's room to grab a sweater. She tries not to look at all the pictures of her dad on the dresser, but there they are: the early morning sun is streaming into the room and lighting them up.

Ellie is sitting on the top step of the stairs, dressed in a new plaid dress Gram bought her with white socks and brand new black patent leather shoes with straps. Ellie has her stuffed polar bear in her lap and her thumb in her mouth, which she yanks out as soon as Alice sits down.

'I put my sheets in the hamper.'

'I'll help you make your bed later, okay?'

'You'll forget.'

'No, I won't.'

'I don't want to go,' Ellie announces.

'Me neither.'

'I'm scared he'll be stuck in that stupid cemetery forever,' Ellie says.

'Me, too.'

'I hate that idea.'

'Daddy would hate it, too.'

'You're lucky.'

'Why?'

'He loved you best.'

'He did *not!*'

'And you got to be with him longer than me. Seven years longer. That's almost double.'

Angie calls to them to come and get in the car.

'Do you have the passage you're supposed to read?' Alice asks.

'Why are they making us do this?'

'You scared?'

'I'm gonna want to cry and I can't cry up there . . . Alice?'

'Yeah?'

'I don't want this day to happen. Can't you tell somebody? Can't you make it stop?'

'It won't be any easier tomorrow, Ellie.'

'How about never, then. Never would be good.'

From downstairs they hear:

'Girls! Let's go!'

They stand up. Ellie takes Alice's hand.

'I wish we could absquatulate.'

'What's that?'

'Flee.'

★ ★ ★

They get through the service somehow. Little old Sacred Heart is packed to the rafters. There's crying all around them, but the Birds and the Blisses seem to be seated in a no-cry zone. That could be because they are all pretty furious every time the priest opens his mouth. Each of them is sorely tempted to shout: Stop saying those stupid things about Matt! Jesus this and blah-blah better place that. It's enough to make you sick. Matt would have hated it. Absolutely hated it. The only thing that's kind of nice is Ellie's reading of that old standby from Corinthians and Johnny Mason's little speech or eulogy or whatever it was. But really, Johnny's speech would have embarrassed Matt to death. He hated testimonials.

Even the music, which might normally be a weep fest, is so baggy and saggy, Alice wonders if there's something wrong with the organ or maybe it's the four-foot-tall crone of an old woman who is playing it. Maybe she can't reach the pedals. That would explain a lot. Henry must be grinding his teeth.

There's a big holdup on the church steps with people wanting to stop and talk. Come on, already. Chat, chat, chat, sorry, sorry, sorry, over and over; it is driving Alice crazy. Perfect strangers some of them, wanting hugs, wanting to be comforted themselves. You just want to give some of these people a good shove.

Then there's the hustle and bustle in the parking lot with the hearse and the cars and who goes where. The family is alone in Uncle Eddie's latest Mercedes. A little respite. Lillian, who has been basically joined at the hip with Angie since she arrived last night, is riding in the car with Johnny Mason and his family. The Birds and the Blisses are directly behind the hearse with Lillian and company directly behind them.

In the pause before they pull out, Eddie passes his flask around. When Alice reaches for it, Angie just rolls her eyes and takes it away.

They take the scenic route to Locust Lawn, avoiding the highway and winding along Plank Road and then out on Blossom. It's a beautiful day, which is what everyone keeps saying in order to have something to say. But it's true. It's a perfect spring day, a perfect baseball day, a perfect garden day. Uncle Eddie rolls the windows down even though Angie and Gram complain about their hair. They're only going a stately fifteen miles per hour, how wrecked can your hair get? And Eddie is right to roll the windows down; the air is soft and sweet and it buoys them all, at least for a moment.

'Would you look at that?' Uncle Eddie says.

Dozens of cars line their route all the way to the cemetery, pulled over on the side of the road, their hazard lights flashing. Some people stand by their cars, their hands on their hearts; others sit quietly, their heads bowed.

On the last hill up to the cemetery, two Boy Scout troops stand at attention, holding flags.

The honor guard is already in place when they arrive. They have arranged Matt's helmet, rifle, boots, and dog tags next to the grave.

Allison Mahoney and her father and both brothers are everywhere at once, escorting old people from their cars, seating people, signaling the priest to begin. These people should plan weddings or maybe warfare. They've got it all down.

The honor guard, just like the detail that escorted Matt's body home, lives in another dimension, a world of precision and perfectibility. It is almost soothing to watch their smooth exact unison motions. Until they present arms and start shooting off their damn guns.

Then it's the priest again. Again?! And the sign of the cross and something about silver cords and broken bowls and the spirit returning to the earth. Okay, Alice gets that part. That's okay.

The soldiers take the flag from the coffin and fold it tightly, timing each fold, each move, the number of steps toward each other, the number of steps to hand the flag to Angie, the number of steps away.

In unison, they execute a slow ceremonial salute.

Angie holds the flag and Alice and Ellie hold each other and Gram as one soldier plays taps and they lower the coffin into the earth.

Normally playing taps would undo her. Alice can hear people quietly crying all around them, followed by all the unsuccessful attempts to discreetly blow noses. But the super quiet winch lowering the coffin into the grave and the fake grass hiding the raw earth and the way everything stops at this point is so jarring that Alice can't even imagine crying. Like it's all done, it's all finished. But it's not. She doesn't get it. They are here to bury her father, not leave him alone in a gaping hole. What is going on? Do they think it's too real to see broken sod and turned earth; too real to actually fill in the grave? As if the family somehow needs to be protected from these gory details? There is no detail worse than the plain fact of Matt's death. The rest of it should be simple and honest and handmade. Not this stage set.

Some people have brought flowers, which they throw into the grave. Alice doesn't like that; she thinks it looks like litter. She manages to stay focused on her anger until Uncle Eddie's surprise makes his appearance: a bagpiper standing on the green grass rise above them. Oh, no, she thinks, there is nothing more mournful than bagpipes. But what he plays is not mournful. It is a rollicking march; it is joyful and raucous and fast and alive. You could follow this song into battle or through the gates of hell.

As Alice listens to the piper she knows that she wants real dirt and real shovels; as real as this music, as real as the coffin that contains what is left of her father.

In the silence that follows, there's a kind of rush to get out of the cemetery, with friends and relatives leading the way to the cars. Mrs. Grover and Mrs. Piantowski and Mrs. Minty are already back at the house with Sally and Ginny from The Bird Sisters, putting together the collation. The night before, Uncle Eddie and Mr. Grover and Henry supervised the gathering of all the neighborhood picnic tables and folding chairs. Food has been pouring in for days.

The promise of that food, and maybe even a

328

good stiff drink, or simply getting away from the land of the dead and back to the land of the living, has put a spring in the step of most everyone who turns away from the grave to head to their cars.

The piper has left the rise and is walking through the woods that border the graveyard. Now he is playing a dirge, now he is playing an ending, not a beginning, gathering their tears and their sorrow into song.

★ ★ ★

Alice wants to stay until they fill in the grave, but there is not a shovel in sight. Angie is preoccupied with some family friends who can't come back to the house and are saying their good-byes now. Alice scans the graveyard looking for the actual tools of the trade or even a pair of gravediggers. Instead, she finally spots a small backhoe tucked discreetly out of sight behind some trees and an older man in overalls patiently smoking a cigarette, waiting for them to leave so he can finish his job.

That's when she sees him: a young man in uniform standing too far away to have heard the service, but focused intently on her father's grave. He somehow manages to look ramrod straight and broken at the same time. Before she even has time to think, to formulate words, she is running toward him.

He backs away from her, holding his hands out in front of him to keep her from coming closer.

'Are you Travis Boyd?'

He looks at Alice for a long, uncomfortable moment. Alice is taking in the circles under his eyes, the way his dress uniform hangs too loosely on his frame, the tremor in his hands as he tries to figure out what to do with them.

'You are, aren't you?'

He looks at the ground.

'You knew my dad, didn't you? You were in his unit.'

He nods, not lifting his head.

'You were with him when — '

He begins to back away from her, still looking down.

'Wait. Don't go.'

He turns and begins to limp up the slope toward the drive where his rental car is parked. Alice runs to catch up with him. He keeps her at bay with a sharp gesture. She stops as he continues toward the car.

'Please. You were the last person to — '

He stops. She can hear that he is struggling for breath from this quick walk and realizes that he is probably in pain.

'We've been trying to reach you. My mother wanted to write to you. Or call you or — '

He straightens his shoulders and turns to face her. He is not crying. Nothing as simple as that. His eyes are hollow and his face is contracted in a grimace of suffering so intense Alice stumbles as she takes a quick step away from him.

'He was a good soldier. He looked after his men.'

330

He pauses. It is not clear he will continue. Alice waits.

'He was like a big brother . . . That was the worst day for me . . . Not being able to get Matt out . . . That was the worst day . . . '

'Was he — ?' Alice begins.

The car door opens and another soldier emerges to hold open the rear passenger door for Travis Boyd.

'I have to go.'

'Would you like to come back to the house? We have so much food. My mother would like to meet you.'

'I just wanted to pay my respects.'

'I could show you my dad's workshop.'

He tilts his head so he can look at her out of the corner of his eye.

'He talked about you.'

'And I could show you his garden.'

'I saw pictures of you. And your little sister.'

The soldier at the car calls out to him. And suddenly Alice realizes that he is a nurse or an orderly.

'Sergeant Boyd.'

He turns toward the voice and the car and his escape. And then, with a great effort, he turns to her again, pulls himself upright, stills his hands by pressing them against his thighs.

'I am so sorry for your loss.'

Alice waits while Travis Boyd is helped into the backseat of the car. He takes his hat off and leans his head back and closes his eyes. He turns his head to look at her as the car starts up and moves away. She holds his gaze for as long as she

331

can and then watches the car disappear down the grassy drive headed for the main road.

She can't begin to take this in, to process what kind of horror and trauma can destroy a young man like Travis Boyd. She suddenly knows, like a kick to the gut, that what happened to her father is even worse than she has imagined, worse than it is possible to imagine.

She turns back when she hears a new motor sound and heads down the hill in time to see the backhoe emerge from the copse of trees and approach her father's grave. The fake grass has been rolled up, the winch taken away. Now there is a hole in the ground and a coffin and dirt.

She waves at the man driving the backhoe. He stops and cuts the engine.

'Do you have a couple of shovels?'

'That's not how we do it anymore, miss. A lot of people, they have the wrong idea.'

'I'd just like to be the one to bury my father. If you don't mind.'

'You're not exactly dressed for the job.'

'I'll manage.'

'Aren't you supposed to be with the rest of them?' He indicates the cars pulling out of the cemetery.

'They'll keep.'

He reaches behind him and pulls out a pair of shovels, climbs out of the backhoe and hands one to Alice. He turns back to grab a work shirt and a pair of rubber boots.

'That dress is too pretty to mess up.'

'Thank you.'

Alice buttons the shirt over her dress and steps into the rubber boots.

'My name is Caleb,' he offers.

'Alice Bliss,' she replies.

The sound of the clods of dirt hitting the wood of the coffin may be the most upsetting sound she has ever heard. But as they continue the sounds become muffled, dirt on dirt, and she can concentrate on the bend, lift, swing of her body and the shovel; the simplicity and rhythm and relief of real work.

She looks up to see Henry and his father walking toward them, carrying the folding snow shovels they keep in the trunk in case of an emergency. They have left their suit jackets in the car. They take a moment to roll up their sleeves and then, without a word, set to work alongside them.

'This is Caleb,' she tells them. 'And this is my friend Henry and his father, Mr. Grover.'

The men nod to each other without breaking stride. Alice breathes in. It smells like the garden, but it's not.

'It doesn't take long,' Caleb offers.

'No.'

'You appreciate the machine on the other end of this job, I can tell you that.'

'I bet.'

'Or in bad weather.'

'My father worked with his hands.'

'Soldier, I thought.'

'Carpenter. Engineer.'

'Awful young.'

'Yes, he was.'

The earth is dry and fairly light and they make good progress.

'I have to rake it out now and then seed it.'

She hands Caleb her shovel. Mr. Grover takes out his handkerchief and mops his brow.

'You did the right thing, Alice Bliss,' Caleb says.

She tries to smile at him as she returns his shirt.

'Anybody tell you that you need to be extra careful these next few weeks?'

'No.'

'The body gets accident prone.'

'Really?'

'You ask people. Ask people who have lost someone whether they were in a little car crash or a little bike accident or took a fall.'

'You want to come back to the house, Caleb?'

'No, thank you, that wouldn't be right, I didn't know your father.'

'All right then. Thanks again.'

Alice heads up the rise to the dirt road leading out of the cemetery with Henry and his father. The digging has tired them all. Alice thinks it's good to be tired in her body.

The Grovers' ancient Honda is the only car still parked on the verge. It hadn't occurred to Alice to be worried about a ride home. Now she realizes that Henry and his father were patiently waiting for her after everyone else had left.

Mr. Grover tosses their shovels into the trunk. Henry and his dad don't interrogate her like her family would. Henry just opens the door to the front seat for her. But she surprises him and slips into the backseat, where she leans back and rests her head against the upholstery. Just like Travis Boyd, she thinks.

She closes her eyes for a moment before turning in her seat to look back at the road winding behind them, at the green bowl of this section of the graveyard, at the newly turned earth over her father's grave, at Caleb, raking the ground, preparing it for seed. They keep leaving Matt behind, she thinks, in each of these places; they reenact leaving him, over and over until finally they will realize that he has left them and gone where they cannot follow.

★ ★ ★

There are cars parked in their driveway and all along the street. The backyard almost looks festive and the workshop, which Uncle Eddie set up as the bar, looks like they're having a party. At least anyone old enough to drink is having a party.

One table is stacked high with Mrs. Piantowski's bread and tubs of butter. Other folding tables are nearly groaning under the weight of casseroles and fruit salads, green salads, Jell-O molds, and condiments. Cakes, cookies, pies, and brownies are on the dining room table inside along with two jumbo coffeemakers from church.

Alice walks slowly through the house, taking it all in, the groups of people talking and eating and drinking. Some of them are even laughing. Everyone is here, she thinks, everyone that's left from their life. Were they all sitting behind her in the church and riding behind their car to the cemetery? Her principal, Mr. Fisher; the school secretary, Mrs. Bradley; B.D., her coach; Mrs. Baker, Ellie's teacher; Mr. Herlihy, the high school janitor; Sally and Ginny from The Bird Sisters; the Hoyts and the Holschers; and even Stephie and her parents. Mrs. Minty is sitting at a picnic table with John Kimball and his father and his little brother, Joey. And Melissa Johnson. Janna and her mom are sitting with Ellie, and oh my gosh that's Luke Piacci, the third-grade heartthrob, Ellie must be going out of her mind.

Alice keeps walking, looking for her mom, maybe, or maybe not. She makes one more tour of the house and there, sitting on the stairs, where she did not think to look before, is her mom, a Styrofoam cup of coffee abandoned on the step beside her. She is looking down at her hands and does not notice Alice. She is twisting her wedding ring on her finger, round and around.

'Mom . . . ?' Alice ventures.

Angie looks up, wipes her face with the back of her hand.

'I can't . . . ,' she begins. 'I should be out there, talking to people . . . '

'It's okay, Mom.'

'I just . . . I was on my way upstairs, and . . . '

She looks so lost, Alice thinks.

'That's when I knew . . . ' she says. 'That's when I really knew.'

'I'll get Lillian,' Alice offers.

'Just stay for a minute,' Angie says, pulling

336

Alice down on the step beside her.

She's twisting the ring again.

'We couldn't afford an engagement ring. Did I ever tell you that? And we saved up for months to buy our wedding rings.'

She pulls the ring off her finger.

'Here. Try it on.'

'Mom, no,' Alice says, as she tries to hand it back.

'Go ahead. I could never wear any of Gram's rings. Her fingers are so tiny.'

Alice slips the ring on. It feels strange. Alice can see where the ring has made a ridge on Angie's finger. She wonders if that's permanent.

'I was wondering if I'm still married.'

'*Mom!*'

Alice tries to give the ring back.

'Keep it for me. Just for a few days. I'll ask for it when I'm ready.'

Angie stands, smoothes her hair and her skirt, and heads down the stairs.

'Wait!' Alice says, a note of panic in her voice.

'Just for a few days,' Angie says, before turning toward the kitchen and the backdoor.

'Mom! . . . *Mom!*' Alice follows Angie down the stairs, reaches out to her, the ring in her palm. 'Please put your ring back on.'

Angie hesitates. She seems a little dazed.

'Okay, okay, let's not make a federal case out of it,' Angie says, slipping the ring on her finger. 'I just thought . . . Oh, I don't know what I was thinking.'

Alice watches her mother head back out to their friends and neighbors, to the voices and the sympathy and the dozens of reminders that life goes on in its brutal and sometimes beautiful way, whether you want it to or not.

★   ★   ★

Not knowing what else to do, Alice heads outside to the workshop. Uncle Eddie has rolled up her sleeping bag and stood the pallets up against the side wall to make room for the bar. Easily done. One plank on two sawhorses and two coolers full of ice and beer underneath. All the 'good stuff' is here; whatever you might want to pour into a glass in honor of Matt Bliss, Eddie's got.

She wants to keep on going. Or find her sneaks and start running and maybe never stop.

She walks past the workshop and up the little rise to the garden, which is hoed and weeded, just the way her dad likes it. Filled with promise. Everything at the beginning, just getting started.

She continues past the end of the garden and through the new neighbors' yard. She can't remember their names. She is not worried about trespassing or upsetting anyone; she doesn't care if someone comes out and yells at her to stay off the new grass. At Baird Road she decides to go left heading out toward the old Barnes estate where maybe she can get lost for five minutes in what's left of the old apple orchard, or maybe she'll find that their old fort inside the lilacs is still there, and she can crawl inside and lie down and disappear for a little while.

The apple trees are in bloom and humming with bees. No one has pruned these trees in a long time, but here they are, still blooming and bearing. She heads past the barn where they used to have two Percheron draft horses and a pair of Chincoteague ponies. Old man Barnes hated tractors and loved horses, even after he got too old to work them. They were a kid magnet for the whole neighborhood and also contributed to the most beautiful roses in all of Belknap.

Alice walks between the curved rose beds to the circle of lilacs. The 'entrance' is on the far side. Half a dozen lilacs have grown together, forming a dense wall of foliage, with a circular open space in the center. No one can see you in there. She hesitates and then pushes sideways through two slender trunks and she is inside.

It doesn't look as though other kids have found this spot. There are no beer bottles or cigarette butts, no mangy blankets or milk crates. It was Alice and Henry's secret fort through much of grade school. Alice wonders if her parents knew about it. It would be just like her dad to let her go and explore, even if it made her mom kind of crazy.

When did they stop coming here? Was it a decision? Or did they just stop? She thinks she might remember waiting for Henry in here one day, but he never came. Did that happen to Henry, too? Waiting once more and then once more for Alice to come and play.

The branches stir and John Kimball pushes through into the interior. Alice watches him materialize out of thin air and take shape in the dim, green light of the lilac leaves. He crosses to her, it's not more than a step or two, but when he crashes into her it's as though he has been running toward her from a great distance, and without warning, he is kissing her. In the green light, he is kissing her. He grabs her in a tight embrace, his mouth on hers. There is no hesitation, no talking, no asking. His hands are startling on her skin, his lips and his teeth and his tongue and his body are pushing her and she is pushing back, she is kissing back, she is holding him, she is pushing into him, she is feeling everything and nothing.

Is it the rough cloth of his jacket, or the uneven ground beneath her feet; or is it the sun, coming out from behind a cloud and pouring through the leaves, or is it the sound of a truck, grinding its gears as it crests the hill behind them — when suddenly the truck she hears in the distance is the truck that slows but doesn't stop as a body, her father's body, is pushed from behind the wheel well, to fall, to roll, to lie in the sand and gravel at the side of the road. His uniform filthy, stained with dirt and blood, torn, both boots missing, his feet incongruously bare. His face, she can't see his face; he has landed with one arm flung out, his face turned sideways, turned away, his fingers, his short, strong fingers curled into fists.

She opens her eyes and pulls away. She looks around; she shakes her head, as if she could clear these images from her mind. When her mother told her how they'd found her father she couldn't take it in and now, here, kissing this boy, what is she doing kissing this boy, here it is, in a rush, in a flood.

'I have to go.'

'Wait . . . Alice — '

'This isn't right.'

'Are you okay?'

'I'm — ' And she struggles to find the right words. 'I don't know what I'm doing.'

'Alice?' Henry calls out . . . 'Alice? Are you in there?'

She pushes past John Kimball and slips between the lilac trunks.

'Henry, what are you doing here?'

'I saw you leave. You looked upset.'

'Of course I looked upset.'

'I was worried about you. I followed you.'

'You shouldn't have done that.'

John Kimball materializes once again. He reaches out to take Alice's hand; she jerks away from him. She can see Henry jumping to conclusions and she wants to stop him. She wants to explain, but doesn't know how she can explain trying to get away from everything and everyone, coming here, coming to this place, *their* place, looking for, hoping for . . . she doesn't know what, the surprise of John Kimball, the kiss, her father, her childhood, the pictures that are haunting her . . .

Suddenly there is that roaring inside Henry's head that makes it impossible to hear; he can't hear the birds, or the wind, or even his own thoughts. Instead, he sees the lilac leaves quivering in the aftershock of John pushing through them; he remembers the interior green-glass shimmer of that space and imagines Alice and John and without warning, he steps

341

forward and shoves John so hard he falls backward into the lilacs. It looks at first as though the branches will be supple enough to bend under this burden, but then there is a terrible ancient keening sound as branches and an entire trunk groan and then crack and fall under John's weight. As John scrambles to his feet, both Henry and Alice register the gaping hole in the circle of trees.

Henry can see that John is beginning to move toward him, but he doesn't care what John does right now, let him do his worst. Henry is looking at the lilacs and the broken trunk and branches and something shifts inside of him.

'Henry,' Alice says, and her voice breaks as she says his name.

He looks at her for a long moment, hurt and betrayal and anger loud in the space between them, before he turns to leave.

'Henry!' Alice calls out to him. And then again, more urgently, '*Henry!*'

She is about to break into a run to follow him, when John reaches out to her.

'I'll walk you back.'

'I have to go alone.'

'Alice — '

'I'm sorry.'

And without another word she heads for home.

★ ★ ★

She walks through the yard and it's eerie the way no one seems to notice her and no one says

342

anything, like she's invisible. She steps into the workshop, where she realizes she is really angry at Uncle Eddie or whoever the hell it was who messed with her stuff and changed everything around in here without even asking her.

But this could be a good place to test out the invisibility shield. There's a knot of guys from Matt's baseball team sitting on or leaning on her dad's workbench, drinking beer and laughing. She punts a 'hey, how you doin'?' right back at them as she circles the table loaded with liquor. Could she grab something? Where would she put it? No pockets in this dress, and the bottles are mostly jumbo size, too big to hide. Then she sees two possibilities: a small squarish bottle of Southern Comfort and a skinny, dark brown brandy bottle.

She lifts her dad's jacket off its peg on the wall and on her way out the door, grabs both bottles, one for each pocket.

In the house she nabs Uncle Eddie's car keys from the bowl in the foyer and before anyone can say one, two, three, she's out the front door. Uncle Eddie has thoughtfully parked his car down the street a ways, to leave room for all of the guests' cars. She slides in behind the wheel, adjusts the seat, rearview and side mirrors, just like he taught her, starts the engine, and she's off. She doesn't look back.

She pulls up in front of Henry's house and leans on the horn.

When he comes to the door she can see he's so mad he's about to brush her off, but then the fact of the car, the pure physical presence of the

343

car, with Alice behind the wheel, pulls him right out to the curb.

'Get in,' she tells him, without looking at him.

'Are you crazy?'

'I'll let you drive it.'

'Your uncle's gonna kill you.'

'Maybe that's a good thing.'

'Alice, I don't know how you think you can just come over here and . . . '

'Get in. Or I'm going without you. And you know that's not a good idea.'

Furious, he gets into the car. Puts his seat belt on. Refuses to look at her.

'Relax. We're just going down to the lake.'

'And you've driven what? Twice in your life?'

'Four lessons from the master. Think of this as practice.'

'You're in no condition to . . . '

She pulls out, the big sedan purring quietly. There's a hush inside the car as they glide along East Oak Street.

'Look in my jacket.'

He grabs the jacket; the liquor bottles clank together.

'Jesus Christ, Alice!'

'I could have taken anything I wanted. If I had pockets big enough.'

'Driving. Plus alcohol. Does this sound like a good idea to you?'

'Don't be a priss.'

'I don't want to be a statistic, if you don't mind.'

'So what, you want to go to your room or something?'

'What are you talking about? With you?'

'Yeah, with me.'

'Right now?'

She takes her eyes off the road and looks at him.

'Watch what you're doing!'

Eyes front.

She drives like a little old grandmother all the way out to the lake, speedometer hovering right around thirty-five. She can tell it's driving Henry crazy, but he's still too mad to say anything. She heads straight to the parking lot for the town beach and pulls into the last possible spot, car pointed toward the water, next to a huge willow tree, relatively secluded, nice view.

'This is where kids come to make out,' Henry ventures, and a blush instantly suffuses his face.

'So I hear.'

Alice pulls out both bottles, opens them.

'You ever had this kind before?' she asks.

'A taste. Maybe.'

She tries the brandy and nearly gags.

'That's disgusting!'

Then she tries the Southern Comfort. The cloying sweetness helps the alcohol slide down a little easier.

'This one's not so bad.'

She passes it to Henry.

'Alice, what do you think you're doing?'

She takes another taste.

'Not thinking for five minutes.'

He grabs the bottle.

'Is that what you were doing with John Kimball? Not thinking?'

'Definitely not thinking.'

'Longer than five minutes.'

'One kiss.'

'I don't believe you.'

'It's true.'

'I don't get you, Alice.'

'I don't get me, either.'

Henry stashes the bottle between his knees. When Alice reaches for it he jerks away from her.

'What, do you think I'm going to attack you?'

'No!'

She takes the bottle.

'How could you . . . with John Kimball and — '

'I didn't know he was following me.'

'Ha!'

'I didn't. I was just trying to get away.'

'Why did you go *there*, Alice?'

'I don't know . . . It's a safe place.'

'It's more than that.'

'I know.'

'Do you? Do you even care anymore?'

'I do. You know I do.'

She can't look at him. She offers him the bottle; he shakes his head. She takes another taste. There's a long, uncomfortable silence.

'You're not helping,' she tells him.

'What do you want me to do?'

'I want you to get drunk with me and . . . and — '

'And what?'

'And do whatever it is that people come here to do.'

Alice is starting to make a pretty good dent in

346

the bottle with all her little tastes.

'You're kidding, right?'

Of course she's kidding, she has to be kidding, he says to himself.

'There's a blanket in the trunk.'

'How do you know *that*?'

'My mother told me. She also told me to watch out for boys like Uncle Eddie.'

'I'm not like Uncle Eddie.'

'I know.'

Henry's brain is running on high-octane fuel as he calculates what's about to happen. Alice is going to drink herself silly, possibly drink herself right into puking. There could be kissing. Hopefully before the puking. But is that even what he wants anymore? And what is she doing? What is she out to prove and just what the hell was she doing with John Kimball? He's really furious but it's hard to be angry, or stay angry on the day your best friend buries her father. So maybe he's just supposed to stay with her and try to keep her safe and try not to worry too much about, well . . . everything. But by then, the sun will be going down and here they are all the way out at the lake and Alice won't be able to drive and Henry has driven like once in his life for maybe twenty minutes and this is a nice car, a really nice car, that Henry does not want to crack up or dent, or even mess with.

So how the hell is he supposed to get her home?

Alice exits the car, bottle in hand, and heads for the beach. Henry grabs the keys and follows her. She takes off her shoes — for a moment he thinks she's going to take off her dress, too — drops the bottle, and starts running down the beach. He picks up the bottle, thinks maybe he should pour it out, realizes she'd be purely pissed at him then, puts it back, and heads over to the car to get the blanket out of the trunk, which is a good thing, because by the time he returns, Alice has finished off the Southern Comfort, taken her dress off, and gone swimming. And is now, of course, freezing.

He wraps the blanket around her. She presses into him, he tries backing up, she follows; it might be funny if he weren't so mad at her, she keeps pushing against him until he has no choice but to hold her.

'You could have drowned.'

'Shut up. You sound like my mother.'

'Sobered you up a bit.'

'I'm really dizzy.'

She tries to kiss him. It's sloppy and none too smooth with her arms trapped inside the blanket. Henry thinks, she's had too much to drink, she's got her dress off; they've got the blanket from the trunk of Uncle Eddie's car. How is it that this turn of events, minus Alice being crazy with grief and drunk, is the stuff of fantasy, only it's all wrong, it's confusing as hell, he can't trust one single thing Alice is doing or saying.

Next thing you know Alice is spewing all over the sand. Thank God she turned her head fast enough. It's disgusting. She's on her knees now, wiping her mouth with her hand and spitting and, oh, God, there she goes again. And then she just passes out, sprawled on the sand right next to the guck. In her underwear. Which Henry has never seen before, and certainly never expected to see in quite this context.

Henry tries to pick her up to move her. Can't. Gets hold of her under the armpits and drags her several feet away. Kicks sand over the mess and the smell, covers her with the blanket, and sits down beside her. Lies back in the cool sand, sudden sorrow washing over him as he listens to Alice snuffling, almost snoring, as he listens to the waves lapping the beach.

She's sound asleep, her mouth is a little bit open and she's kind of drooling. He realizes she probably wouldn't want to be seen like that so he closes his eyes and before he knows it, he falls asleep right there, right beside her, like all this heartache and craziness and anxiety is more exhausting than running ten miles or something.

When he wakes up, Alice is lying in the crook of his arm, her head on his chest, the blanket covering both of them. He can't believe it. He is lying on the beach with Alice in her *underwear*. And the sun is going down. And she has her eyes open and she's looking right at him.

'Henry,' she says, her voice thick, her throat scratchy.

'What?'

'I'm sorry.'

How can she do this? Why does she always do this to him? Why does he let her?

'You don't believe me,' she says.

'Not right now I don't.'

She leans over and kisses him. He pulls away from her.

'You just *puked!*'

'That was hours ago.'

'So?'

She cups her hand to her mouth and tries to smell her own breath.

'I don't smell anything.'

'I think you're immune to your own smell.'

'I don't taste anything.'

'You were almost passed out when you puked. You didn't see it; you didn't smell it.'

Alice grabs the foul tasting brandy. Henry tries to grab it away from her.

'Not again.'

She takes a swig, swishes it around in her mouth like mouthwash, turns away and spits it into the sand. Does the breath test again. Henry is trying not to smile, Henry is trying not to laugh, but he is not, he notices, trying to get up.

When she leans over him again he wants to look in her eyes, but her eyes are closed, she is already far away on the Ferris wheel of this hoped-for kiss.

She moves closer to him, if that is possible, she moves closer and presses against him. She puts her hand inside his shirt, her cool hand on his warm skin. She's never done anything like this before. He doesn't know what to do with his hands; he doesn't know what to do with the confounding fact of her, the body and breath and near nakedness of her.

She takes his hand and pulls it under the blanket.

'What are you doing?' Henry can't keep the alarm out of his voice.

'Touch me . . . '

'Wait.' He can feel his heart smashing against his ribs. 'Alice . . . '

'Shhhh . . . '

'I don't know . . . '

'It's all right.'

'Is this what you really want?'

'Henry . . . '

'You've had a lot to drink — '

'I puked, I napped, I'm pretty sure I'm back to normal.'

'But how would you *know?* For sure?'

She laughs.

'I wouldn't want you to change your mind or something tomorrow,' he adds.

'I won't,' she promises.

★ ★ ★

Touching her is overwhelming; it is like trying to read a symphonic score. It is, in fact, so overwhelming it is nearly impossible, but there are glimpses of comprehension, like something inside of him understands this; the way clusters of notes combine, make melody and counter melody and he is reading something with his fingers, with his body, he has never read before.

The hollow beneath her throat; her clavicle, he thinks, and his mind flashes on an ivory key and a clavichord and he remembers why he loves that word and that fragile bone. There are the bones in her shoulders, the hard knobs of her spine and

351

then there is the elastic of her underpants. He stops. His hand stops.

'Will you take your shirt off?' she asks.

He is looking at the singular, hollow-eyed, broken beauty of her as he starts to unbutton his shirt and then pulls it over his head, and he wants to tell her he can see the broken places, he can see where she is blasted by grief. He somehow knows that what she wants is to obliterate her anguish with their bodies, with their longing, with the whole symphony of sensation that is washing over each of them right now. And he knows it might work, for a minute or two or ten, it might work long enough to gulp down a few clear, pain-free breaths. But he also knows that she will still be brokenhearted when this moment ends, and that she could even blame him for that, for coming back to earth, for not being able to truly rescue her or comfort her at all.

Still, there is no chance that he will refuse her; that he will refuse her anything.

★ ★ ★

This is what no one tells you, Henry thinks. The nearness of her, the unguarded nearness of her, the wonder and simplicity, now, of what had seemed so complicated and impossible just moments before. He will remember everything, he tells himself, every single thing. Alice lying on the blanket and wriggling away from an ant, which is funny and he has never seen her like this and he is relaxed enough and safe enough and close enough to laugh. He helps her find her shoes; he brushes the sand from between her shoulder blades, from the backs of her thighs. This kind of easy closeness, this is what he wants for the rest of his life. Here is the surprise of it, the simple surprise of intimacy, the deep secret at the center of things, as clear as a glass of water dipped from a well.

There is grace in this, a blessing, a still, quiet pool for each of them.

Alice stands there looking at him as he straightens his clothes and brushes the sand out of his hair and finds his glasses; then she looks at the sky and the sand and the lake. Standing up she takes on the weight of knowing again, the weight of the death of her father, which has been hurtling toward them like a comet falling to earth from the day he got on the bus to go to Fort Dix.

And Alice knows, suddenly, that his death can only hurt her more, not less, as time passes. It is as if the grief is growing inside of her, larger than the shell of her fifteen-year-old self. The burden of this grief makes her feel that she is not a kid anymore; that the most essential part of growing up has happened overnight. And if she must suffer adult loss she wants her own life beyond the borders of her family, beyond the borders of her own body. This is why she is reaching for something of her own, for something as large as this pain and emptiness inside of her. This is why she is reaching for Henry.

★   ★   ★

They are in so much trouble when they get home it could almost be comic. Every single person in both their lives is angry and upset with them. From Uncle Eddie and the car: Do you have any idea what that car is *worth?!* To Mom and the standard: *How could you?!*

The general themes that are touched on, or pounded on, by anyone even tangentially aware of their multiple misdemeanors are trust, responsibility, trust, danger, stupid choices, trust, et cetera, et cetera, et cetera.

No one seems to have picked up on the personal part of the story, the beach and the blanket part of the story, except for maybe Uncle Eddie who is watching them with a very quizzical expression on his face. He might actually be able to follow that train of thought if he weren't pretty drunk and pretty consumed and distracted with rage about his car.

Alice and Henry listen to the harangues as best they can, trying to remain straight-faced, trying to maintain the proper contrite demeanor, trying not to look at each other. They both feel that they are floating above this moment, deliciously immune to it. Something so much more important has happened to them today, they can't believe that people can't actually read about it right on their faces. But everyone seems oblivious to the warmth radiating off the two of them. This only makes Alice and Henry feel more closely aligned, as though they are, once again, coconspirators, just like when they were kids.

Gram, of course, wants to feed them. They are

released to the kitchen where Gram and Mrs. Grover pile food on plates and watch them carefully, each of them beginning to sense something, they don't know what, perhaps picking up on the fact that these two young bodies are vibrating in new and disturbing ways.

'Henry?'

'What, Mom?' he says without looking up from his food.

'Henry — ?'

He looks up, startled by her tone. Mrs. Grover tilts her head, looking at her son. Alice watches as Henry meets his mother's eyes and in the next instant blushes so furiously he has to take his glasses off and shade his face with one hand. Mrs. Grover's glance travels from Henry to Alice, then to Gram. Gram shakes her head. Alice is biting her lip to keep from laughing.

'You're too young! Do you hear me, Alice?' Gram says.

'Yes, Gram, I hear you,' Alice manages to say quietly, looking down at her lap.

She hopes this looks like remorse rather than an attempt to contain hysterical laughter.

'It's all about trust, Henry,' Mrs. Grover says.

'I know, Mom.'

'Trust you earn every day.'

'Yes, Mom.'

Henry's head is bending lower and lower over his plate.

'We didn't . . . ' Alice begins.

'Good!' Gram finishes for her.

'You're too young!' Mrs. Grover adds, picking up on Gram's perennial theme.

'Can we go now?' Henry asks.

'Go where?'

'Just for a walk,' Alice says in her most innocent voice, like, remember how we were in diapers together?

Miraculously, they let them go. Everyone is so distracted and overwhelmed and exhausted, eating and drinking too much, or not at all, relieved that Henry and Alice and the car are safe and sound, that they return to their conversations and refill their glasses, as Henry and Alice walk out the kitchen door and head off through the backyards.

Gram and Mrs. Grover watch them go and even though Henry and Alice are very careful not to touch each other, Gram and Mrs. Grover can see in their bodies, the way they yearn and turn toward each other, that something has happened. Mrs. Grover sits down suddenly in one of the kitchen chairs, a dishtowel in one hand, a serving platter in the other, feeling an overwhelming urge to cry. Gram sits down beside her and takes her hand.

'He's loved her all his life,' Mrs. Grover manages to say.

They ponder this a moment as Henry and Alice pass out of sight into the deepening twilight.

'Maybe that's a good thing,' Gram says.

May 31st

The Memorial Day parade passes right by their house, as it always does. Uncle Eddie is driving

356

the newest Miss Belknap in a bright yellow Corvette like he does every year. Different car, different Miss Belknap, same old Uncle Eddie. But Uncle Eddie looks a little different, too, Alice notices, a little uncomfortable, or distracted, like his heart's not really in it. Maybe this is the last year for a lot of things.

Alice and Henry have set up chairs on the sidewalk. Ellie, Angie, and Gram are marching with the local Veteran's Association. This year the Greater Belknap VA invited all the families of men and women serving in Iraq to join them in the parade.

Alice and Ellie made Angie a sign to carry:

MATT BLISS
1968–2006
New York National Guard
42nd Infantry, Iraq

Alice joins Henry, bringing lemonade, though she refuses to sit down. It is too soon to be out here, too soon to rejoin their friends and neighbors like this. Alice still feels raw, as though her emotions are constantly on the verge of being out of control. Some days she can pretend to be normal, some days she can't; so she stays on her feet, ready to clear out if necessary.

She has been drawn to the curb almost against her will, to hear the school bands and see the old soldiers and the young soldiers, to see the policemen in cruisers and on horseback, to see the teams marching, and the Boy Scouts and the Girl Scouts. She is not with her team; in fact, she

357

is off the team. She has promised B.D. that she will run all summer and rejoin them for cross country in the fall. Right now, though, Alice still can't predict what she can and can't do each day. She is only now beginning to think that she could ever go back to school.

She waves at Mrs. Minty across the street and down a ways, and Mrs. Piantowski, a bit farther down, surrounded by her children. And there's John Kimball and his father and his brother, Joey; and Stephie, with her mom and dad.

Here comes the Folding Lawn Chair Brigade. Their annual comic routine of synchronized and choreographed moves with lawn chairs and music is always a big hit. This is Ellie and Henry's favorite part of the parade. Next are the politicians in convertibles, the fire trucks, and the high school band.

The World War II vets and the Korean War vets, in their faded uniforms, their numbers dwindling each year, follow the band, walking a bit slowly, some with pinned up sleeves, some with canes. Next come the Vietnam vets wearing bits and pieces of jungle fatigues, some with ponytails, or bald, with pot bellies or green berets. And finally, bringing up the rear, the Iraq veterans' group in their desert fatigues. People fall silent as they pass. You can hear the hush rolling up the street, the same way you could hear the bands approaching. It's eerie to hear the crowds go quiet.

As they get closer Alice can see that Mrs. Grover is walking with Ellie and Gram. Ellie walks between them, holding their hands. And there's Angie with her sign. Mrs. Piantowski steps off the curb to join them, and so does Mrs. Minty, who is carrying a homemade flag over her shoulder that reads **PEACE**.

Alice surprises herself and walks into the street to join her mother. As if this is what she had planned all along, though in all of the confusion she has been feeling, this is the one thing she was sure she would not do. But here is her mother, carrying a sign with the name of her husband on it, her husband and the father of her children.

There are two other young widows carrying their husband's names, and a few other Iraq vets and their families. There's a young man in a wheelchair, missing both legs, another on crutches, another with part of his jaw gone. A smaller group of men and women march under the banner: Veterans Against the War.

At first Alice just walks beside Angie. Henry joins his mother, and he and Mrs. Grover walk right behind them. Alice links arms with her mother, and finally, Angie hands her the sign. Alice carries her father's name; she holds it high. Angie rests her hand on the small of Alice's back, and Alice thinks of Matt and the roof and his voice in her ear telling her: *You can do it, Alice.* She carries her father's name through the streets of her town, past the houses and yards and faces of her neighbors.

She can hear the band playing up ahead of them. She looks back to get a glimpse of Henry and can see that more and more people have joined them. Not a movement, exactly, but a dozen more people publicly standing with the veterans and their families.

Angie leans over to whisper in Alice's ear before she puts her arm around her waist and draws her close. They walk in unison, more together than they have been in months, possibly years, until Alice hands Angie the sign and peels off from the group and sprints the few blocks home.

★ ★ ★

She walks through the house. Past the six black boxes that arrived a week ago and that none of them can bear to unpack. Each pair of socks, each T-shirt, each letter, each photograph is inventoried on twenty sheets of paper. Everything has been washed, so when you breathe in the scent of a shirt, it doesn't smell like him. Only his pillow, Alice has found, has any trace of his scent. Maybe they don't know how to wash feather pillows.

It's strange but there is really nothing left of her father in these boxes, in these sheets and towels and uniforms. These things are not Matt, they are just things.

She heads out to the garden and sets to work picking baby green beans, peas, radishes, greens. The gourds are going crazy, the tendrils of their vines fanning out across the low fence Alice and Matt built last year. Looks like it's going to be a bumper crop come fall.

It's quiet in the garden aside from the buzz of insects and the occasional birdsong. She stops for a moment to really listen: she can hear cars on Belknap Road and poplar leaves stirring like soft coins in the breeze. She closes her eyes and listens again. The moments when she hears her father's voice in her head are less and less frequent as each day passes. Alice wonders if his voice has gone silent and if this silence will last for the rest of her life.

She heads for the workshop, leaving her basket of produce in the shade. Inside, she stands for a moment, trying to find him. She runs her hands over the workbench, feeling the nicks and dings in the old wood. She trails her fingers over the tools hung along the wall and opens his tool chest, touching everything inside.

She stands looking at the box of letters stored up in the rafters. She desperately wants to read every single one and just as desperately wants to wait as long as possible to read the first sentence. She can feel the promise of his voice in those letters and she also feels a terrible foreboding that reading them will be the end of something; that reading them now, too soon, will diminish the power she is sure they hold.

Finally, she climbs up to get them. She grabs a folding chair and sits quietly for a long time. Her father is trapped inside boxes everywhere right now, except here in his workshop and in the house, in his closet. How soon before her mother cleans out the closet and gives away his clothes? How soon until Angie wants to turn the workshop back into a garage? Maybe Alice is going to have to learn how to use all of these power tools, learn how to make things and repair things, to justify keeping this workshop just the way it is. Who can teach her, she wonders? Maybe she could work with a carpenter this summer, like an apprentice, like being on the roof with her dad. And in that thought, she thinks, there is the echo of Matt's voice.

She lifts off the top of the box, flips through the letters. The big events he wrote about haven't happened yet, graduations and a wedding and losing her mother. So she looks through the series of letters with the heading, 'the little moments that make up the big moments that might get forgotten.' The first one, 'the moment you realize you want this boy to kiss you' seems just right. She opens it and begins to read:

Dear Alice,
Okay, you're not going to need my help with this one. Lots of boys are going to want to kiss you. Trust me on this. Obviously, you'll figure out who you want to kiss and who you don't want to kiss. But when a boy is kissing you, maybe for the first time, maybe not, other things start to happen. I don't think I have to be too graphic here.
Just remember, he can't help it.
Love,
Dad

Alice laughs. Her father is writing to her about kissing and also more than kissing and he's funny; she forgot how funny he is. Maybe one of these letters includes his manual on farting and all the special names he has for different kinds of farts: frips and gribbles and spilbers.

362

He's funny, she remembers with relief. He was funny and full of life and loved to work hard and get dirty and eat ice cream and play baseball and play with his kids. She remembers his patience those spring twilights playing catch with her and with Henry, the endless pitches to Henry for batting practice, his patience with her in the garden, in the workshop, his delight in teaching her things. Did she really like to garden or did she like to elicit that delight in her father? Does it matter? He was so easy to please. Stand up straight, tell the truth, do your best.

She sees a letter she doesn't remember noticing before: 'Dad's words to live by,' and opens it right up. Just exactly what she was thinking about.

Dear Alice,
Cogitate on this list when you're in the mood, but not too much and not too often. You know all of this already; these are just little reminders. These are probably the things that my father or my mother said to me; there's nothing original here. But most if not all of these ideas have stood the test of time.

In his perfect block printing, here it is, his list:

Cultivate gratitude.
Think for yourself.
Treat all people equally.
Respect your body.
Don't be afraid to ask questions.
Ask for help when you need it.

Be your own best friend.
Don't be afraid to fail.
Do one thing at a time.
Learn how to dance.
Write thank-you notes.
Good manners never go out of style.
Treat your family and your friends like gold.
Give more than you receive.
Aim high.

If she closes her eyes, she can hear him, in each of these words and phrases, she can hear him.

June 19th

School has ended. Alice kept up with classes, more or less, from home. The readings and assignments for English were no big deal, and her English teacher, Mrs. Cole, even came by the house twice to talk to her about themes and possible essay questions for the final. Henry helped with history, and her mom hired a tutor for math and science, this incredibly shy eleventh grader named Kimmie. They stretched the rules and let her log her running miles for gym credit, and chorus is just pass/fail anyway. When it came to exam time, Gram sat with her in the kitchen every afternoon for a week as she took her finals, one by one.

The day after graduation, John Kimball drove over to say good-bye. He was leaving for basic training later that day.

Angie, who had never really met John before, or couldn't remember meeting him at the funeral, fights back sudden tears when Alice introduces them. She holds on to his hand for a long moment, just looking at him.

'Be careful, okay?' she says, before releasing his hand.

'Yes, ma'am.'

When Alice walks him to his car he surprises her and takes her hand, pulling her into a hug.

'I've had really bad timing with you. Maybe one day you'll give me another chance.'

Alice steps away, looks at him. She knows, now, that you can't send a boy into the unknown with nothing to hold on to.

'Maybe you'll visit when you're home on leave.'

'That could be a year.'

'I know. I'll still be in high school, remember?'

He laughs.

'Getting less interesting to you with each passing day, probably,' she laughs back at him.

'You could write to me.'

'About what? Trigonometry? Homeroom? Track practice?'

'That wouldn't be so bad. Everybody says letters, real letters . . . '

'That's just like my dad: *'You can't carry an e-mail in your pocket.'*'

He hands her a piece of paper with his address.

'I'm not expecting . . . ,' he says.

'I know.'

He looks at his hands.

'You know I want to kiss you.'

'Are you asking permission?'

'Well, after last time . . . '

'I don't . . . ' She hesitates, looking at him, and realizes she's memorizing him.

'What?'

'I don't think that's such a good idea,' she manages.

He reaches out and touches her face, his palm against her cheek, his thumb pressed against her lips.

'That's okay.'

Knowing that her mother is watching, and Ellie, too, for that matter, and possibly Henry down the street, she stands on tiptoe to kiss him, surprising both of them. It's a quick kiss, a child's kiss thrown into the heart of this boy, not a promise, not a pledge, maybe just hope or a prayer.

'I'll write to you,' he says, before he ducks into his car and drives away.

★ ★ ★

There are signs of life everywhere. The garden is thriving, the grass in the yard is growing like crazy; Alice has already had to cut it three times. They are eating peas and radishes and lettuce from the garden almost every night. Alice has planted the warm-weather crops: tomatoes and basil, and the marigolds and zinnias are already budded out. Matt would be proud.

Uncle Eddie has taught Alice how to rotate tires and inspect brakes and brake pads, and the two of them, with Henry's help, have installed the pair of horizontal windows in the west wall of the workshop. Alice can see the sunsets now, just like Matt always wanted.

During another driving lesson, which took a lot of wheedling on Alice's part after the incident with the Mercedes, Alice enlisted Uncle Eddie's help with her plan to go to Small Point. First she begged to be allowed to take the car on her own, with Henry along as a sort of safety guarantee, of course, but Uncle Eddie wouldn't buy it. He reminded her that she can't get her license until she turns sixteen in October, and there's no way in hell he'd authorize an out-of-state trip without a license. Then he convinced her to take her family along, that she might actually need them on this trip.

In preparation, Henry and Alice and Ellie have spent hours and hours in the workshop together, making small boats out of scraps of wood. Henry and Alice had long discussions about design, arguing back and forth about flat bottoms versus keels, et cetera. They made paper, then cardboard boats, planning to implement the best designs in wood. But they ended up just winging it and making boats with the pieces of wood that they have, with glue guns and staple guns and the occasional nail. Ellie was the inspiration. She didn't need discussions or prototypes; she just picked out pieces of wood and started to put them together. Her boat is finished and painted and it even has a sail. And a name, of course: *Bibliobibuli*, one who reads too much.

Ellie has also made a mini dictionary of long

words. She cut and stapled the pages and then copied out all of her favorites. She does not yet have a superlong word for every single letter of the alphabet, but almost.

'Guess what?' Ellie says one afternoon in the workshop.

'What?'

'I want to be a *neologist* when I grow up.'

'What's that?' Henry asks.

'Someone who makes up new words.'

'Perfect.'

June 21st

They are driving to Maine: Alice, Angie, Ellie, Uncle Eddie, and Gram. The boats are packed in a box in the trunk. Alice wanted Henry to be with them, but had to concede the point of 'family only,' and being too squashed in the car. She asked each of them to bring a memento for Matt, something small enough to fit in the palm of their hand. She suspects that Ellie may have spilled the beans to Gram about the boats, but that's okay.

Courtesy of Uncle Eddie, they are in a 1982 pale yellow Cadillac convertible. The seats are so comfy it's hard to stay awake. Gram packed lunch and dinner in a cooler. They'll spend the night in a bed and breakfast because Mom says Gram's too old to camp.

They left at noon, stopped once in Massachusetts, and shortly after sunset they make the turn down the Phippsburg peninsula heading to

Small Point. The minute they make the turn, Alice makes them roll down all the windows. She closes her eyes and breathes in the salt water, the bracken and the piney smells. She leans her forehead against the back of Uncle Eddie's seat.

★ ★ ★

And Matt is alive in front of her, he is driving and she is in the backseat with her forehead resting against him, like this, just like this. She remembers the murmur of her parents' voices in the dark car, Ellie curled up asleep on the seat beside her, Matt with one hand on the wheel and one hand lightly twined in the hair at the nape of Angie's neck. And Alice, part of it, part of that feeling, by a thread, by her forehead just touching his shoulder.

★ ★ ★

It is twilight. It is the solstice. It is a clear, calm night.

'Can I drive?' she asks.

'What?'

'I want to drive the rest of the way.'

Uncle Eddie pulls over. Alice slides into the driver's seat; Mom takes her place in the back and pulls Ellie onto her lap so Uncle Eddie can sit beside Alice.

Alice drives the curving two-lane road slowly, ticking off each landmark as they pass: the turn-offs to the state park, to Secret Beach; Sebasco, with the snack bar that makes the best

369

lobster rolls in Maine; the general store, the granite house, the house with two white barns. She makes the turn onto the causeway to Hermit Island, drives past the Kelp Shed, and carefully maneuvers the sharp turn up the single-track dirt lane leading to the beaches, the Devil's Bathtub, and the campsites beyond. It's midweek; the campground is not even half full. Alice parks next to a picnic table.

They pile out of the car, pull on sweaters, and head down to the beach with the picnic basket, a ground tarp, and some blankets. Alice, Ellie, and Uncle Eddie scrounge the beach and the dunes for wood to make a fire. They roast hot dogs, eat Gram's famous potato salad and cherry pie, and wait for full dark.

Clambering up the rocks, Alice stops at the top. The sky is thick with stars, just as she imagined it would be, there is a sliver of a moon low in the sky, and the Devil's Bathtub is nearly full as the tide reaches its peak. She finds a flat rock to use as a staging area for the boats. She has brought scraps of kindling and paper and matches. Uncle Eddie has his arm around Gram and is guiding her with a flashlight. Mom and Ellie are holding hands.

Alice sets the cardboard box down on the rocks. There are six boats, one for each of them, and one for Henry.

'Okay,' Alice begins, and finds she needs to stop for a moment to collect herself. 'Okay, so I thought we'd each launch a boat with a wish for Dad. Wherever he is, whatever you believe. If there's something you want to put on the boat, I think it'll work. Ellie has a book that she made.'

'A dictionary,' Ellie pipes up.

'We tested Ellie's boat in the bathtub to make sure it won't capsize. So the boats should all be able to carry a little something. After you make your wish, we'll light each one on fire, and set it afloat in the water.'

Alice opens the box and Alice and Ellie unwrap the boats and set them out on the flat rock. Ellie's *Bibliobibuli* with its pink hull and white sail almost glows in the dark. Henry's bright red tugboat *Fernticle* lies alongside Alice's blue skiff, *Jillick*. Ellie hands the yellow barge named *Penny* to Gram, the orange tug named *Tupelo Honey* to Uncle Eddie, and a graceful little green skiff with a pink and yellow striped sail named *Bliss* to Angie.

'Did you make these?' Gram wants to know.

'They're beautiful,' Angie says.

'What the heck does *fernticle* mean?' Uncle Eddie asks.

'Freckle!' Ellie shouts.

'*Jillick*?'

'To skip a stone across water!'

'*Bibliobibuli*?'

'One who reads too much!'

'Really beautiful,' Angie says again, picking up *Bliss* and turning the boat over and over in her hands. 'I had no idea.'

'Do you like the names, Gram?' Ellie asks.

'I love the names, sweetheart.'

Alice pulls a photograph from her pocket.

'Ellie,' Alice asks, 'should we launch them one by one or all together?'

'All together. We make our wishes and then light them all at once so no boat will be lonely.'

'Okay. I'll start with Henry. This is a photo of Henry and Dad and me having a catch in the backyard when we're about six. Henry's wish is that there's baseball in Dad's heaven.'

She puts the photo on Henry's boat.

'I made Daddy a dictionary of my favorite long words. It's illustrated. My wish . . . Do I have to say it out loud?'

'Only if you want to.'

Ellie considers, then: 'My wish is that Daddy will get to see me when I'm almost grown up like Alice and I'm wearing a beautiful dress and going to my first dance.'

Ellie ties the dictionary to *Bibliobibuli* with a piece of twine.

Uncle Eddie pulls a feather from his shirt pocket. As he starts to speak, he finds he can't trust his voice. He coughs and clears his throat and pulls out a handkerchief. He looks at the boats and the rocks and the water and the night sky, at his mother and his sister and his nieces and he feels, as he has perhaps not allowed himself to feel before now, the enormity of Matt's absence. Finally he says:

'My wish is that if you're worried about Angie and the girls up there in your baseball playing heaven, Matt Bliss, I'm gonna do my best to be there for them right here on earth. Not like I could ever fill your shoes. But I'll do whatever I can.'

He weaves the feather into the rigging of *Tupelo Honey*.

Gram has made a miniature cherry pie that she has carried carefully in its own little handmade paper box.

'I know cherry pie is your favorite, Matt. I wish you all the cherry pie you want every single day. But mostly, I wish you were right here with us. Somehow maybe you are.'

The tiny pie sits like a crown in the middle of the yellow barge.

'Mom . . . ?'

Angie had no idea that this is what Alice has been up to. The request for this trip on this day was, frankly, one big headache. Alice was secretive about almost all of the details and would not compromise on one single element, except for staying in the B&B instead of camping, and even that was a fight. And the more stubborn Alice got, point by point, the more irritated Angie got. But here they are, and Angie can see the plan, she can see the care and design and love in the plan, and now that it's her turn she finds she can't even begin to speak. She looks at her daughter and she looks at the boats, the boats made, she now realizes, in Matt's workshop, on Matt's workbench, with Matt's tools. And the choice of this day, the solstice, and Alice's stubbornness about timing, because she needed to time the boats with the tide, is so exactly like Matt it could make her cry.

Angie kneels beside her little boat. She has a letter in her hands from their college days when they thought they would live forever. She found the letter in her lingerie drawer, jumbled in with the girls' letters to Santa and handmade anniversary and birthday cards. She has read it so many times in the past few days she could recite it by heart.

She thinks, I will always love you, Matt. She closes her eyes and wishes it were last summer, before any of this had happened, she wishes and wishes and wishes that she could have him back. When she opens her eyes she realizes she doesn't want to let any single bit of him go, not this letter, not this night, not this beautiful boat. She looks at Alice, who is waiting patiently. She looks at the boat again. *Bliss*. How perfect. Matt Bliss, she thinks, you should be here for this, you should see your daughter now. She folds the letter and slips it into the boat.

Alice has a small envelope in one hand and a sand dollar the size of a dime in the other.

'This is some dirt from our garden and one of the tiniest sand dollars we ever found together right here on this beach. I hope there are tomatoes in heaven, Dad. I hope you can see our boats on the water tonight. We're lighting them up just for you.'

Alice pours the earth into the hull of *Jillick* and places the sand dollar on top.

Alice and Ellie carefully lay their tinder and their scraps of paper on each boat. One by one they light them on fire and launch them into the water. The boats wobble a bit when they enter the water, and Alice has a moment of panic before they steady themselves. They cluster together at first, floating like a small regatta, magically aflame.

Angie takes Ellie's hand and watches Alice,

still kneeling where they launched their fleet at the narrow, closed end of the Devil's Bathtub. The tide is turning now, pulling the boats out to sea, where they begin to fan out a bit, each one responding to the current and the wind and the tide. *Bibliobibuli* and *Bliss* are in the lead, it's almost as if their sails actually work, followed by *Penny*. *Tupelo Honey* wallows along bringing up the rear. *Jillick* and *Fernticle* are in the middle, their decks burning brightest of all until the sails on *Bibliobibuli* and *Bliss* catch fire in a spectacular burst of light.

Angie wants to call them all back, or she wants them to stay just as they are. Uncle Eddie is in the unaccustomed position of having a slow-motion method of transport and finds himself wishing his boat would hurry it up. Ellie is thinking that maybe she shouldn't have burned the dictionary she worked so long to make. Alice is looking at the burning boats and wondering if it is at all possible that they will make it out to open ocean before they sink; and wondering at the same time, if it is possible that any of this, the boats, the flames bright in the darkness, could reach her father? Can anything she will do or say for the rest of her life reach her father?

She looks back over her shoulder at her mother, Ellie, Uncle Eddie, Gram, and they are all caught and held in this moment. All their hopes and their wishes launched on fragile boats, lit on fire and shining like stars in an upside-down sky. Stars floating on the water. Just for a moment, a moment longer. Here. And then gone.

Acknowledgments

With thanks to:

* David and Kate, for everything, always.
* The Kleban Foundation for giving me two years to write.
* Paulette Haupt, commissioner and producer of *Alice Unwrapped*, the musical that inspired *Alice Bliss*; Jenny Giering, composer for *Alice Unwrapped* for the magic of her music and for making Alice sing.
* Rachel Kadish, Ann Ziergiebel, Angela Marvin, Jane Potter, Lillian Hsu, Kim Garcia, Liza Rutherford, and Lynn Barclay, my first readers.
* Melanie Kroupa, for seeing the potential.
* Carol Green for giving me space to write, and so much more, in Truro.
* Beth Hartley for information and insights about teens and grief.
* Molly Ziergiebel for information and insights about running.
* My agent, Stephanie Cabot, as well as Sarah Burnes and the entire staff at The Gernert Company.
* My editor, Pamela Dorman, and also her assistant editor, Julie Miesionczek.
* The team at Viking Penguin, with special thanks to Hal Fessenden.